AFTER THE GALAXY

THE UNSUNG

MIRTH PUBLISHING
ST. JOHN'S

SCOTT BARTLETT

THE UNSUNG
© Scott Bartlett 2018

Cover art by: Tom Edwards (tomedwardsdesign.com)

Typography and interior formatting by: Steve Beaulieu (facebook.com/BeaulisticBookServices)

This novel is a work of fiction. All of the characters, places, and events are fictitious. Any resemblance to actual persons living or dead, locales, businesses, or events is entirely coincidental.

Library and Archives Canada Cataloguing in Publication

Bartlett, Scott

The Unsung / Scott Bartlett ; illustrations by Tom Edwards ; typography and interior formatting by Steve Beaulieu.

ISBN 978-1-988380-14-8

This one's for you - the reader.

EARTH

1

Before engaging the man I'm pretty sure is impersonating Corporal Maynard, I flick on my night vision with a thought, scanning past him for other potential hostiles. On the horizon, the teeth of a broken city jaw at the sky.

It's hard to think of this planet as humanity's birthplace. Now, it's just another place to put a Subverse node. Come to think of it, I remember reading that the uploads here like the nostalgic vibe Earth gives off. Funny. The further we get from our origins, the more obsessed with them we become.

I turn off night vision. There's a German Shepherd lying next to the impostor—probable impostor—and it notices me first as I approach the crackling fire, followed by its owner. The dog glares directly into my eyes, a dominance display, but the man is staring at my birthmark. I learned to tell the difference pretty young.

"Forget to wash your face?" he asks.

That triggers a memory: a kid joking that my birthmark is my mother's lifeblood, still spattered all over my face.

Then: I'm straddling the kid, with no memory of how I got there, fists smacking against his head again and again. An instructor shouted for me to stop, and I did, feeling glad she stopped me.

As the dog growls deep and low through its steel-cage muzzle, I squat beside the fire and study my new friend on the opposite side. He's made his camp on the leeward side of a sand dune, complete with a rock to sit on and a lopsided spit-roasting setup. The flames show his space-black Guardsman's uniform is rumpled, and a gun belt lies a few inches from his left hand, the holstered laser pistol within easy reach.

"I'm looking for Corporal Maynard," I say. Somewhere out in the night, something yelps like it's about to die.

"That's me."

"Is it?"

"I got the face, don't I?"

"Do you have the ID?"

He rummages inside his coat and produces an octagonal coin, which he flips over the fire. Catching it, I hold it steady for my datasphere. The coin turns emerald, and golden text appears above it: ID CONFIRMED.

"You're a Troubleshooter, then?" the man claiming to be Corporal Maynard says as he reaches forward to rotate the carcass of whatever he managed to trap out here. Looks like it might be a fox.

"What else would I be? You had to notice my ship touching down."

He nods. "We see trouble, we shoot it. That's the motto, ain't it?"

"Unofficially."

"But you're only supposed to come here if we got problems with the Subverse."

Firelight glints off the ID coin, which I'm still weighing in my hand. "You do have problems."

"Not according to the terminal. I just checked it this morning, and it says everything's fine." He tilts his head sideways, though his eyes don't leave mine.

"Then either the terminal's lying or you are. Guess which one I consider most likely?"

My new friend doesn't answer, and I glance to my left, switching on night vision again. A green gloom replaces the darkness, revealing the corrugated metal shack I know houses the terminal. "I could go check the terminal myself."

"Why don't you?"

"Because I'm not convinced you won't shoot me in the back if I do."

"There'd be no advantage in that."

"Not if you're really Corporal Maynard, no. But if you're someone impersonating the corporal—a pirate, for example, who smells profit in interfering with a Troubleshooter's business— that's a different story."

"Ridiculous."

"Right now, it's looking pretty likely, actually," I say, and extend my right thumb. "First, there's my orders to come here and find out why all contact's been lost with the Sol Subverse. Space-scrapers keep returning after a few laps around the sun, after failing to establish any connection." I extend the pointer finger. "Second, *you're* telling me everything's peachy." I look down at my hand, which now forms a gun-shape, then back up at the man wearing a Guardsman uniform. "That's it, actually."

"How do you know the fake people inside the Subverse didn't just decide to screw with us? Maybe they got bored of living forever. Took up playing pranks."

The wind picks up, then, shifting particles across the desert's surface and drowning out my answering laugh. It's funny, because I'm willing to give uploads about as little credit as this guy's giving them. That said, I'm skeptical even *they* would pull something like this—make it look like a main hub went dark just to screw with a couple Guardsmen.

But I'm not waiting for 'Corporal Maynard' to come around to my point of view. I'm waiting for something else.

As I glance toward the shack again, still smiling, my patience is rewarded.

A metallic click comes from the German Shepherd's muzzle, and it falls onto the sand. The fake Guardsman reaches out for his laser pistol, but my fingers are already wrapped around mine, and I'm unsnapping the strap.

Trouble is, there's no time to shoot them both.

The dog lunges. I dive to its right, putting the beast between me and my friend, whose pistol tracks my progress. A laser shot crackles through the air, and the dog yelps, stumbling.

Exiting my roll, I swing my weapon around as I regain my feet. The impostor's still getting his feet under him, readjusting his aim as he does.

My datasphere tells me where to position my pistol, indicating the spot in the air with a green funnel shape. I obey, arm jerking up to the sweet spot. The impostor rises to meet the neon-blue laser bolt with his face. His head snaps back and he crumples to the sand. At that moment, a thrill—call it satisfaction, adrenaline, dopamine—shoots through me. That's how it always is. At first, anyway.

A mass of fur and teeth collides with my right side, sending my pistol flying from my grasp and knocking me to the ground. I twist around as I fall, sliding my hands beneath the dog's collar as my back hits the sand, just in time to prevent the German Shepherd from savaging my throat. The dog lunges against my grip, again and again, snarling. A thick string of drool dangles from its jaws, swinging wildly until it lands on my chest, connecting me to the dog's maw. It takes all my might to hold back the beast. Fount, it's strong.

"Dice," I grunt. "Dice, I need you."

A voice cuts through my thoughts: "You told me to stay aboard the ship."

"I'm revising that order. Get out here, *now*."

The teeth graze my throat, and I sweep my right leg inward, connecting with the dog's hind leg. It yelps, confirming that the impostor's laser bolt hit its haunch. I kick it again.

This only seems to enrage the German Shepherd further, and it redoubles its effort to rip out my jugular.

From my right comes the rapid patter of Dice approaching across the sand dunes, from the flat area where I parked the *Ares*. The dog gives a final, powerful thrust, and I lose my grip on its collar.

Twisting right, I offer it my shoulder instead of my throat. Most of its teeth sink into my spidersilk armor, but somehow a couple of them find flesh—my collar must have gotten yanked to one side in the struggle. They rip through muscle, striking bone, and I grit my teeth against the electric pain radiating from the bite.

Dice crashes into the German Shepherd, who takes a piece of my shoulder with it.

The dog flips over and over across the sand, whining, but Dice executes a forward roll with programmed precision, rising to his feet, twin laser pistols snapping into his hands from their stowed position inside his forearms. The bot's gunmetal plating gleams darkly in the firelight as he lines up his shot.

"Don't," I say, staggering to my feet.

Dice turns his long, inverted triangle of a face toward me, scarlet visual sensors eyeing me with what I'm sure is disbelief. The bot has no facial expressions to speak of, but it's in the angle of his head. "*What?*"

"Restrain it, and take it back to the *Ares*. Don't kill it."

The German Shepherd has backed itself against the sand dune, where it's crouched low, staring at Dice and barking, eyes wide. My blood drips scarlet from its snout.

The bot stows his pistols back in their forearm hollows. "I'll never understand fleshbag sentimentality." With that, he launches himself toward the dog. The animal darts forward in an attempt to escape, but Dice's trajectory was obviously calculated to take the likelihood of that into account. He scoops up the animal in an iron embrace, where it's left to writhe and whine as the bot rises to his full height.

Dice glances at the body of the man who tried to impersonate Corporal Maynard. "Funny how your sentimentality didn't extend to him. Not that I'm complaining. The fewer fleshbags the better, if you ask me."

"Find something to tether the dog with. Put him in my cabin, make sure he can't reach anything, then get back in your closet."

With Dice gone, I scoop up my pistol and holster it, taking a moment to study the body of the man who attempted to impersonate Maynard. I wonder where the real Maynard ended up. The answer's almost certainly "dead," but who knows. Maybe the pirates kept him alive, to try to ransom him off.

Dice made it sound like killing the pirate was easy—and it was. The actual killing, anyway. Instinct and training took over, plus my datasphere, which is programmed to paint the targets Command would want me to neutralize. I'm not supposed to kill anyone my datasphere doesn't paint as a target. It's like having a superior always standing behind me, telling me who to shoot.

"You're a weapon," Senior Chief Shimura used to say. "And we wield you. A sword can't be held responsible for those it cuts down. Neither can you."

Until very recently, I bought into that.

Shaking my head sharply, I cut off that line of thinking as quickly as it began. I *still* buy into it, Fount damn it. I can't afford another episode like the one I had on my way here.

I ignore the dead pirate's open-eyed stare and start turning out his pockets and stripping off his uniform, looking for anything that points to what he was doing here, or who he was working for.

"Asshole got unlucky," I mutter as I search. It just so happens the Troubleshooter he tried to trick is also the first person the brass thinks of when it comes to taking down pirates. I'm a little surprised he didn't recognize me, actually. Most pirates would. I'm known in their circles as the Butcher. But maybe he did know me and just pretended not to.

Finding nothing, I trudge toward the corrugated metal shack, shoulder sending jolts of pain down my arm and waves of fire through my chest. I leave it alone. Gotta let the Fount do its work.

Inside the shack, I discover why the impostor was cooking outside: this place reeks of death. The question of Corporal Maynard's whereabouts also resolves itself: he's lying in his bunk against the back wall. What's left of him, at least. It looks like the pirate let his German Shepherd rip the corporal apart. Starve an animal for long enough, and it'll eat human readily enough.

A blanket of flies shifts at my approach, but they don't abandon the corporal for long. Their gluttony proves greater than any fear they have of me.

Past the foot of the bed, around the corner and down a short hallway, I find the room that houses the terminal. It's destroyed. The wrench used to do the deed lies on the dusty floor a few feet away from the shattered computer.

Someone's trying to stop me from looking into this Subverse's problems, all right. The question is, *why?*

2

I t makes my stomach roil, but I give Corporal Maynard a proper burial, out behind the shack that was his charge. At first, the desert sand drifts back into the hole I'm making, dumping one shovelful in for every two I take out. But deeper down, the ground gets clumpier, and easier to move. I need to make the hole deep anyway, to make sure the animals don't get at what's left of the corporal.

My shoulder screams all the while, but I ignore it. Pain becomes a lot easier to live with once you get used to the idea of most injuries healing within hours. That's thanks to the Fount— humanity's greatest gift. And our greatest curse. A person's Fount is made up of millions of nanobots that live inside the body, circulating through the bloodstream. It's the processing platform that enables a person's datasphere, and it lengthens lifespan by dismantling diseases as they appear, not to mention healing nonlethal injuries and cleaning up the gunk that would otherwise build up inside arteries.

"I'm sorry," I say to Maynard's ravaged corpse, which has been lying nearby on a bed sheet as I worked. The Fount couldn't save him. It can do a lot of things, but it can't reignite the spark of life once it's snuffed out.

I never met the corporal in life, but it doesn't matter. He was a fellow Guardsman, and he was just as alone. Just as unappreciated by the rest of the galaxy. A brother.

Kneeling, I cut a square of cloth from his blood-stained sleeve. It'll contain enough of his Fount for my ship's computer to analyze, so that I can learn what Maynard knew. With the square of fabric tucked inside my pocket, I drag the bed sheet over to the hole and lower him in as gently as I can. Then I begin shoveling sand over the body.

Pretty much every star system humanity ever colonized is now set up like this: a Guardsman like Corporal Maynard protects a terminal. The terminal—an upright computer with the circuitry built into its bulletproof base, whose keyboard you have to stand to use—holds the secret location of the server room for that system's Subverse, accessible only to a Troubleshooter. Even the Guardsman who protects the terminal doesn't know where the server room is.

In the normal course of events, no one accesses the server room, ever. Its upkeep is the exclusive domain of maintenance bots who never leave it. But when there's a problem, someone like me shows up, extracts the server room's location from the terminal, and goes to troubleshoot the problem.

Troubleshooters are the Galactic Guard's special forces, given space-worthy ships called Broadswords and sent where they're needed. Of course, actual technical knowledge amongst Troubleshooters is limited. My datasphere tells me how to fix any issue with the servers, providing it's fixable at all.

As for the Sol Subverse, I've already formed a theory of what happened to it. In my line of work, theories are useless unless they leave open some course of action, and so mine does:

I think the impostor managed to hack the terminal and obtain the server room's location. Probably, either he or his associates have already visited that location, which spells bad news for the hundreds of billions of people who live (or lived) in this Subverse. The ones who had copies in other star systems will live on there, but you can bet that most of the Sol Subverse's population was single-iteration. Most uploads can't afford to run multiple copies of themselves.

Without the terminal, I have no way of finding the server room. *Unless* the impostor happened to tell Corporal Maynard its location before he died. If he did, then the information will be stored within the corporal's Fount, and I'll be able to access it by having my ship analyze it.

The fact Maynard died in his bed suggests the impostor killed him first, then hacked the terminal, in which case Maynard's Fount would have gone dormant too soon to absorb the information I need. But I don't leave stones unturned, so I'll analyze his Fount anyway.

Walking back toward the *Ares*, my labor done, I try to ignore the nagging feeling that something has gone seriously wrong in the Andora Sector. For now, I'm assuming the impostor was a pirate. Other than the Five Families, few others would have the resources for such a sophisticated facial reconstruction job.

But why bother with that in the first place? There's only one answer I can think of: they did it in the off chance I was stupid enough to believe the impostor and leave without investigating further. That tells me they want to delay the Guard from finding out whatever they're up to, for as long as they can.

Which means it can't be good.

My ship's outer airlock hatch opens at my mental command, and I step inside. The hatch pauses before closing. "Outside biomatter detected," the ship says.

"Don't worry about it."

The hatch finishes closing.

Inside, I carry the square of cloth to an enclosed scanner built into the opposite bulkhead. It also opens up with a thought, and I place the fabric onto the concave platform. The scanner closes, and I cross to Dice's closet, willing it open while unzipping the torso of my suit.

The bot folds out of the Repair and Recharge module, rising to his full height, and I shove the suit piece into his arms. "Fix the part the dog ripped. I want it done within the hour."

He takes it down to the mess without a word, where he'll work on repairing the suit's fibers at the table, which doubles as our work bench. I head for the center of the bridge, lowering myself into the command chair, favoring my shoulder as I find a comfortable position.

"Begin report," I say.

"Commencing report," the ship says.

"I arrived at the terminal on Earth to find someone wearing Corporal Maynard's uniform, as well as his face. The impostor attacked me, and with Cybernetic Partner D1C's help I managed to neutralize both him and his guard dog. I found the real Corporal Maynard dead inside the Terminal Depot. The terminal is destroyed, but I'm in the process of analyzing the corporal's Fount to determine whether the server room's location was made known to him before his death. In the meantime, I plan to go to the Brinktown located on the other side of the planet. Whoever did this—right now, I'm guessing pirates—clearly have designs on this system. If they haven't attacked the Brinktown yet, I suspect they will soon. End report."

"Concluding report," the ship says. "Would you like to review it before transmission?"

"Negative." I lean back in the command seat and stare at the overhead, still favoring my shoulder. In spite of myself, I start to wonder whether my father ever visited this system. Cal Pikeman, was a Troubleshooter too, but there the resemblance ends.

At least, as far as I can tell it does. I never actually met him. He took off before I was born, claiming he'd been called by the Shiva Knighthood to go to the galaxy's Core on some 'top-secret' mission. They must have asked him pretty nicely, since he abandoned his pregnant wife and unborn son to do it.

Of course, no one back on Calabar, in the Brinktown where I grew up, actually bought his story. Nobody can reach the center of the galaxy. It's been barred for three hundred years, ever since the Fall, and if the knighthood ever even existed, it hasn't given any signs of it in living memory. When I was a kid, I used to cling to the idea that my father was telling the truth…but I grew up pretty quick.

He really did manage to vanish, though, wherever he went. No one in Brinktown ever heard from him again, not even after his wife died giving birth to me. Not even after his son managed to knock up a Sterling.

That's what separates me from my father: I can't imagine ever abandoning my kid. Hell, making sure Harmony's taken care of is what keeps me going out here.

I allow myself a long breath. Then, I say, "Activate the crew."

All four crewmembers appear inside their respective circular stations. Each station consists of a broad, ivory railing that curves back on itself in an unbroken circle. Three pillars support each railing, connecting it to the deck. The railing itself does nothing; has no cybernetic capabilities. Instead, the interface each crewmember needs to perform their duties are projected onto the railing's surface.

As for the crewmembers themselves, each one wears a long face, barely concealing disappointment at being yanked out of the crew sim to perform duties in the real. They used to actually let their disappointment show through, but I put a quick stop to that, with a stern warning of demerits and limited sim privileges. They shaped up, afterward. Mostly. Now, they generally manage to school their faces to a blankness punctuated by dull eyes.

"TOPO," I say, turning to the Trajectory Operations Officer. "Set a suborbital course for the Brinktown on the other side of the planet."

"Aye, Captain," he says, voice listless.

Every Troubleshooter's crew is pulled from the Subverse's digital population. Specifically, from a never-ending war simulation that spans the entire galactic Subverse—one of many 'recreational activities' uploads have at their disposal. Called the Great Game, it's one of the most popular ways for Subverse residents to pass the time, thanks to the large token payouts. And the highest scorers have a chance of getting assigned to a Troubleshooter's crew in the real, where the pay's even better.

But taking home a lot of tokens isn't the only draw. Plenty of players strive to get assigned to the real because their actions there will have actual consequences for the few flesh-and-blood humans left. The stakes are higher. Most uploads call those players "stake junkies."

But once they're accepted into the Guard and trained into whatever role they'll perform—after their minds are downloaded onto a Troubleshooter's ship for a two-year service term—things change.

They start to realize that real life isn't much like a video game. That an actual soldier's life is characterized by long periods of nothing broken up by fleeting bouts of frenzied action. When we fight, we generally win…if we fight. But raiders prefer to avoid confronting Guardsmen if they can, instead wielding terror like a cudgel to get what they want. They will attack civilian outposts, as long as there's no Troubleshooter for light years around. And they've had rare moments of brazenness in recent decades, testing the chinks in the armor of a Guard that's in decline. Mostly they're cowards, though, preying on the weak.

This is the sixth crew I've had the 'pleasure' of working with since graduating from Assessment and Selection and getting my own Broadsword-class starship. Every crew starts out the same way, deadly serious about their work. Performing every assigned task as efficiently as possible, so that they can do their part to protect the Subverse from pirates, Fallen, and any other villains who would dare endanger humanity's digital home.

But as their term wears on, *this* is how they get. Behind my back, in the enforced privacy of the crew sim, I'm sure they snicker and snort at the indignities of biological reality, like all uploads do. Marveling at how anyone could still live such a backward existence in today's enlightened age.

I could have had them deleted from my ship and replaced with a new crew, in the hopes the replacements would bring the energy and innovation every ship captain wants on his bridge. Replace enough crews, though, and the brass start to view you as a complainer, putting strain on an already overtaxed system. It doesn't matter now, anyway. These crewmembers are almost finished their service term. I'm getting another crew when I get back to Calabar.

"Let me know when we've arrived at the Brinktown," I say, hoisting myself out of the command chair. I cross the deck toward my cabin, to check on the dog with a taste for human flesh.

3

A low growl greets me as I enter my cabin. The German Shepherd is tied to a desk leg, which is bolted to the deck. Dice left the animal with very little room to maneuver, which is good, since the cabin has little space to begin with.

I sit on the side of my bunk, facing the dog, whose eyes are full of fire. Her right hind leg is lifted off the ground—that's the haunch the laser bolt hit. My datasphere chooses that moment to inform me it's a female. I guess Dice must have taken it upon himself to check and submit the information to the ship. He also went back to collect the steel-cage muzzle from the fireside. That's good, too. I'd forgotten about it.

The bot generally follows the most generous interpretation of any order I give him. Not out of goodwill, of course. It's his programming to obey the full spirit of an order, not just the letter.

I finger open the strap holding my laser pistol in its holster. The dog watches the movement, and she follows the weapon as I shift it to my lap.

"I should kill you," I say.

Her head lowers, and her hackles rise. The growl deepens.

"You ate my brother. My fellow Guardsman. I know that bastard impersonating him starved you and made you eat him. Doesn't matter. You're a maneater. Any decent person would put you down."

I line up the shot, right between her eyes, which never leave mine. Earlier, she cowered away from Dice, but right now she's fearless. Unafraid to die, if she even understands that's what a raised pistol means.

For some reason, I think about my childhood. The boredom, the schoolyard fights. All the adults who had no problem telling a child to his face that he'd grow up to be no good.

I lower the pistol, then return it to its holster and snap it in place. "I can't kill you," I say. "You remind me too much of myself."

When I reach forward to pet her, she lunges against her chain, her snarling reaching a crescendo.

"All right, then." I yank open the stowage underneath my bunk, stepping to the side to avoid backing into her. Removing the medkit, I shut the stowage, then open up the kit on the bunk, rooting through it till I find what I'm looking for: diazepam, which works to sedate dogs just as well as humans. There's no way I'm administering it orally, so I fit a syringe with a needle and fill it with the dosage my datasphere recommends for sedating a dog of the German Shepherd's weight. The datasphere can estimate that very accurately, just by eyeballing her.

Next, the datasphere recommends the best way for restraining the animal to administer the injection. I watch a ghostly version of myself perform the motion a couple times, then I step forward, quickly pivoting around to the dog's side as she thrashes and twists. Before she can maneuver to face me, I grab her front legs together, then her hind legs, heaving. She slides down my stomach to the ground, her legs out from under her, snarling and yelping all the while.

I place my arms over her neck and body, pinning her, then I shift on top of her so my weight is keeping her pressed against the ground. Grabbing the loose skin behind her shoulder blade, I pinch it to form a pocket of flesh, then push the needle into her. She's not happy about this, and the snarls ramp up. So does the thrashing. But it's over in a couple seconds. I withdraw the needle then leap away, with her jumping to her feet to try biting me through her muzzle.

It takes a few minutes, but her temper gradually subsides, and then she slumps to the ground, breathing slow and relaxed. I crouch beside her, turning her over to expose the laser wound.

It's not too bad. I expect most of the bolt missed her, with the beam only focused on her haunch for a fraction of a second, with the rest going wild. The impostor was getting to his feet as he shot, after all.

I go to the head on the lower deck with a two-liter container, ignoring the crew's glances as I cross the bridge from my cabin. Returning with warm water, I use a bulb syringe to irrigate the wound, then cover it with a topical antibiotic. The medkit doesn't have much of that—these days, the Fount takes care of what antibiotics used to. The only reason I have any antibiotics is to treat someone who's chosen to eliminate their Fount from their bodies, or someone who never had any Fount in the first place.

Once I've bandaged the wound, I go to the lower deck again, to the mess. I put some freeze-dried chicken strips in one bowl and water in another, and when I get back to the cabin, I take advantage of the dog's sedated state to take off her muzzle so she can eat when she comes to. With that, I stretch out on my bunk and stare at the overhead.

Twenty minutes or so later, my TOPO's voice cuts through my wandering thoughts: "Captain, we've arrived."

"Have we landed?"

"Affirmative."

"Good. Deactivate crew."

"Crew deactivated," the ship says.

When I emerge onto the blessedly empty bridge, the main screen shows a view of the outside. The screen is actually just a blank panel—what I'm seeing is a visual sensor's feed, routed through my Fount and projected by my datasphere onto the bulkhead. It's a neater way of doing things than having a disembodied window floating before my eyes.

White blankets the Siberian Brinktown, buildings and streets, and as I draw closer to the screen I spot the first motionless lump. I try to come up with something for it to be other than a snow-covered human corpse, but at the moment I'm stuck for ideas. Then I spot the next lump, farther down the lane, and the next.

Sighing, I walk to the supply locker near the airlock and fish out the charcoal helmet. I lower it onto my head, where my matching shipsuit self-seals with it. Then I activate the suit's thermal coils, so that I'll be nice and toasty by the time the airlock finishes cycling.

Before I leave, I query the information the ship's managed to extract from Corporal Maynard's Fount. Nothing about the server room location yet. Damn it.

The outer airlock hatch faces away from the Brinktown, and when I emerge, I'm treated to a blinding vista where the only break from all the white is a frozen pond bordered by a few skeletal trees. Wind buffets my helmet, and I'm glad to have it on.

According to the historical records dredged up by my datasphere, this part of Earth used to be called Siberia. As good a name for a frozen waste as any, I guess.

I trudge around the *Ares* toward the Brinktown, slabs of frost cracking and shifting underfoot, like tectonic plates in miniature. As a rule, Brinktowns are located in the harshest environments available on the galaxy's brink. Anywhere Fallen are unlikely to survive. Savage alien predators are tolerable; freezing temperatures can be borne. But other humans who want what you have will find their way in eventually.

Twin laser turrets swivel toward me as I near the town's perimeter, each dislodging a tiny avalanche of snow. I already have my ID coin out, and I'm holding it up for them to scan. They return to their original positions, and I stuff the coin back into its slot on my shipsuit's chest, breathing a little easier. My uniform's made from dyed spider silk covered with hundreds of super-thin films designed to reflect the wavelengths used by laser weapons of known manufacture. The spider silk—specifically, bark spider silk, produced by genetically modified silkworms—makes it strong enough to stop kinetic weapons, and the reflective films will usually protect against laser shot. But there's always the chance a laser weapon's using a wavelength the designers didn't anticipate, and anyway, I doubt my uniform would stand up for long against lasers as powerful as the ones mounted on those turrets.

The Brinktown I'm from is on Calabar, a planet lousy with toothy aliens, making walls a must. Here, it seems just laser cannons are enough. The cannons don't fire inward, though, and any Brinktown I've ever seen is vulnerable to attack from above. Everyone tends to assume their combat bots will save them if pirates ever land in the center of town, but bots only go so far against ship-mounted turrets and overwhelming numbers. If the pirates want to take over bad enough, they will.

Case in point: nothing's moving in this town. In several places, my boots break through the crust to sink through a foot-high drift, sometimes higher. No one's cleared the ways between the squat, rounded buildings for several days.

The first person I encounter lies sprawled in the street, as though taken down by gunfire. Sure enough, when I peel away a layer of frost, I find a woman whose nose has been obliterated by a laser bolt. There's a little crimson mixed in with the snow I shifted away, but not much. Lasers create less of a blood spatter than kinetic weaponry, since they don't carry material out of the body through the exit wound.

Part of my datasphere goes black: its warning that someone's drawn a bead on me from behind.

I dive to the left an instant before a laser bolt burns a hole through the snow where I was standing.

4

Hands outstretched to break my fall, they sink into a drift instead, and the datasphere flashes its concentric black circles again: right in front of my face.

I roll away, again to the left, as a second shot crackles past, superheating the air near my head. As I flail through the powder, I catch a glimpse of the second-story window my assailant is shooting from.

Pawing at my holster, I find it caked with snow. My datasphere flashes another black patch. I heave myself sideways once more, then I'm up and running for the nearest building on the shooter's side of the road.

In the alleys between the domed structures, the snow proves even deeper. Within a few steps I'm up to my groin, but I can't afford to let it slow me down. I pause to fish my pistol from its snow-logged holster, then I wade through as quickly as I can, hugging the building for cover.

The shooter's in the next building over, and to my surprise, he doesn't appear at any of the windows on this side. That means he's scared or injured, possibly both. I breathe a little easier.

Reaching the entrance, I try the handle. Locked. I dip into a thigh pouch for one of two small breaching charges, then I slap it near the door handle, arming it and backing through the snow a couple meters. With a mental command to my datasphere, the charge blows, destroying the locking mechanism and sending the door banging against a wall.

Darkness fills the room inside, and I switch on night vision before entering, leading with my pistol.

Room by room, I clear the first floor, keeping a close eye on the staircase as I pass by. After the first, all the rooms have windows, so I turn off night vision. This is a multi-family dwelling: shared kitchen, shared bathroom, and bedrooms stuffed full of mattresses. Someone was even lucky enough to have a bed frame.

The common areas were kept relatively clean, it seems, but the bedrooms themselves feature the usual squalor. When I kick open the door to the final downstairs room, I'm hit with the rotting-eggs-and-farts smell of a corpse. A man reclines in an armchair squeezed between two beds, a laser pistol clutched in his lap and a neat hole through his chin.

That's one way to go. Better than mowed down in the streets by pirates, I guess. I will my helmet to activate odor filtration, and the air starts to smell better right away.

A creak comes from somewhere behind me, and I whirl around, my mind's eye conjuring up an image of a foot being lowered onto a stair.

I edge into the hallway. The staircase is narrow, nestled between two walls, and when I pop around it with my weapon raised, there's nothing there. I walk up it, making no effort to muffle my footsteps.

At the top, I can go left or right, but the latter should take me toward the room where the shooter was. So I go right. The hall turns a corner up ahead, and a mirror hangs on the wall to the left, pointing down the next stretch of hallway.

Pressing my back against the corner, I peer into the mirror—

straight into the eyes of a kid wearing a bulky brown coat and clutching a laser rifle. His face goes even paler than it already was, and his lower jaw starts to tremble in this weird way. He can't be more than eighteen. Eighteen-year-old me would have chewed him up and spit him out, of course, but not everyone can be eighteen-year-old Joe Pikeman.

"Drop the rifle, kid."

He doesn't. He raises it instead, pointing it toward the mirror.

"Cut it out," I say. "I'm packing a military-grade datasphere. There's nothing you can do I won't see coming."

He lowers the weapon to the floor, then gets back to his feet, stretching his hands out in front of him, away from his body. Smart kid. "You're a Guardsman," he says.

Holstering my pistol, I nod. Then I round the corner and shove him back a couple steps, bending to pick up the laser rifle. He catches himself on a rickety-looking dresser, and I safety his weapon.

Willing my helmet to unseal from my shipsuit, I lift it off my head and nestle it between my arm and left side. With that, the kid's eyes become glued to my face, widening, and his pallor whitens even further. "Commander Pikeman. The—the—"

"The Butcher. You can say it."

He doesn't, though. Instead, he starts to tremble.

I suppress the urge to sigh. To Brinktowners and uploads alike, it doesn't matter that I got that name by killing the very people that pose a threat to them. They view any killing as savage, animalistic. Not that they have an alternative answer for the raiders, mind you. It's not like there are jails anymore.

Uploads see the violence as a regrettable symptom of the few humans who 'insist' on continuing to live in biological bodies. Never mind that for many, it's not a choice, and never mind that to continue existing, the Subverse *needs* humans in the real.

Most Brinktowners see the violence the same way—their attitude just has a glaze of self-loathing to it.

No Guardsman expects to win any popularity contests by enlisting, but I never expected the growing tide of resentment that's been crashing against me since I completed Assessment and Selection. The Troubleshooter training process is designed to create weapons capable of defending the galaxy; of neutralizing threats without hesitation. It's not my fault I just so happen to be the deadliest weapon that process has ever forged.

The kid's rifle dangles from my right hand. "Why'd you shoot at me?" I ask him.

He blinks. "I, uh—I thought you were a pirate. Sir."

"Pirates did this, then?" I nod toward the front of the house.

"Well, they sure acted like pirates. Stole things. Did…things… to the women, and to some of the men."

I give the kid another look. He's been through more shit than the average Brinktowner will see in a lifetime. It's actually kind of incredible he's holding it together this well. "I'm sorry, kid," I say, lowering a gloved hand onto his shoulder.

He flinches, but doesn't pull away. I'm not any good at this kind of thing, but it seems to have an effect. He draws a deep breath and lowers his eyes to the floor. "Yeah."

"How'd you survive?"

He lifts his eyes to meet mine, seeming a little sturdier, now. "I managed to make it back here, and I hid. Shot the only pirate who came in. His body's on this story, in a back room. I couldn't bring myself to move him. Or…do anything, except stay in my room and eat when I thought I could keep food down. I had some snacks stashed, and I've been opening the window to get some snow when I get thirsty."

The kid leans back against the dresser. Maintaining eye contact, I say nothing.

"They landed four shuttles in the town square," he continues, "all mounted with plenty of weaponry. Then they just started destroying everything around them. The fighter bots all congregated to try and overwhelm them, and they put up a good fight, but the pirates brought too much. After the bots were gone, no one fought." The kid's voice lowers to almost a whisper. "No one fought."

"Of course they didn't," I say.

The kid winces. "We always thought the bots could protect us from anything."

"Well, they didn't." I gesture with the rifle. "Was this a pirate's weapon?"

"Yeah. I got him with a stool as soon as he reached the top of the stairs. He dropped the rifle, and I shot him with it."

I raise my eyebrows. "That was good work."

He shrugs, suddenly sheepish. "I always thought about what I'd do if someone broke into here. Always told myself I'd use that stool. I can't believe it worked."

That's not how a good, honest Brinktowner is supposed to think, but I'm sure more do than let on. Anyway, I don't remark on it. Ten minutes later, we're trudging through the snow, back toward the *Ares*. I left the kid's laser rifle in the building I found him in. He didn't protest, which was smart. There's no way I'm letting a stranger onto my ship with a weapon in easy reach. I don't care how young and pathetic he looks. I'm not taking the chance.

"I'm Sheldon, by the way," he calls ahead to me from a few meters behind.

"I'm the Butcher," I say, unable to stop a hint of bitterness entering my voice. "But you already know that."

"Commander Pikeman, right? That's your real name."

I glance back at him. "Yeah."

The ship doesn't comment on Sheldon's presence when he follows me into the airlock. Remarking on outside biomatter is one thing, but maybe it knows it would be rude to call our guest that.

On the bridge, I lower myself into the command chair while Sheldon leans against one of the crew station railings, looking awkward.

Rubbing the bridge of my nose, I say, "I didn't notice any child-sized bodies. Only adults."

"I think they were taking the children," Sheldon says. "At least, I saw them drag one into a shuttle."

"Taking the children," I mutter. What were the pirates up to on this planet? It clearly wasn't your routine pillage-and-burn. If the fact they bothered with impersonating Maynard didn't indicate that, then the mass child abduction definitely does.

Speaking of Maynard…

"Query data extracted from our sample: location of Sol's server room."

"What?" Sheldon says, at the same time the ship says, "Querying extracted data."

"Quiet," I say.

"Location found," the ship says. "Sol's Subverse server room is located in the sewers underneath the Siberian Brinktown."

I stand. "Stay here, and don't touch anything," I tell Sheldon.

"Where are you going?"

"You heard the ship. I'm going to the sewers to get to the bottom of this." In my head, I replay what I just said, and grimace. "I didn't mean for that to be a pun."

5

They didn't sugarcoat anything during Troubleshooter Assessment and Selection. Far from it. "Shit and muck," Chief Shimura would say, often. "Welcome to your new life."

We didn't encounter any actual feces during Troubleshooter training, so I just assumed it was a figure of speech. I should have known better.

Something plops into the heated sewage up ahead, probably a maintenance bot embarking on an underwater voyage to clear a plugged-up pipe or some such. This Brinktown's original engineers had to make sure the sewage was heated—otherwise it would freeze solid, and what would be the point of having a sewer?

As it is, the feces and other products of the human body retain the form of half-frozen sludge. I don't know whether that makes the smell better or worse, and I'm not interested in finding out. I made sure to switch on my helmet's odor filtration before entering the sewers through the treatment facility near the center of town.

"Suck it up, Princess." It's Shimura again: a transmission from the distant past. That happens more than I'd like, hearing my old instructor's voice in my head. It might as well be an actual transmission through my datasphere. Ah, well. This sort of thing is bound to happen when you spend your time wandering an empty galaxy by yourself.

I find the server room in a location that's just below the town's periphery, according to the map offered up by my datasphere. It's where I expected to find it. If they'd tried to hide it anywhere other than the perimeter, it would have been found eventually by someone savvy enough.

The engineers disguised the server room entrance to blend in with the sewer walls. As far as I can tell from what's left of it, anyway. The pirates blew it to pieces, with a much bigger charge than was necessary.

I sweep in, laser pistol raised. The lights detect my presence, coming on automatically at the same moment I hear a scraping sound from my left. My pistol's muzzle flicks toward the sound. It's a maintenance bot, two of its five legs bent beyond usefulness, one of them missing.

That's not a good sign.

The cabinets that hold the servers stretch from floor to ceiling, lit by a sapphire glow now that I'm in the room. I don't get a good look at the first one till I go down the nearest aisle, and when I do I suck air through my teeth.

Jagged shards of glass border the cabinet door, and inside, the server's completely melted. I check the next cabinet, then the next. It looks like someone took a hammer and a flamethrower down each aisle, methodically smashing each door then bathing every last motherboard in flame. What's left looks like the result of an archaeological excavation of some ancient alien society. I got your proof of nonhuman sentient life right here.

Doing my due diligence, I spend a couple hours inspecting every rack in the labyrinthine room. I'd put tokens on nothing being recoverable from this mess, but the brass will send in a specialist anyway, just to make sure. Can't say I blame them. If you buy into the idea that the digitized person is humanity's truest, most evolved form, then hundreds of billions of humans just died.

It's kind of my job to buy into that idea, by the way. As for how I actually feel…well, it's complicated.

Aboveground again, on the way back to the *Ares*, I glimpse a hooded figure wrapped in long, forest-green robes, standing near my Broadsword. The figure faces away from me, apparently studying the hull. Then his arm moves, and I see he's carrying a gnarled, wooden staff. He uses it to tap the side of my ship.

"Hey!" I bark, drawing my pistol. He turns away from me, then walks around the stern, his pace unhurried, and disappears from view.

I run toward her, but when I reach the starboard side, the figure is nowhere to be found. Using my datasphere to access her visual sensors, I check all around the ship. Nothing.

Swinging around, I scan the horizon, pistol still aloft. The crest of the nearest hill seems too far for him to have reached in time, and the rest of the land is flat enough that I should be able to see him. But I can't.

Shaking my head, I make my way around the ship to the airlock. Inside, I find Sheldon sitting cross-legged with his back against the far bulkhead. He blinks rapidly when I exit the airlock, like he was asleep.

Probably, the kid had been nervous that finding him napping in the command chair would have agitated me. Honestly, I wouldn't have cared.

I stow my helmet then settle into the chair myself. Before I activate the crew, I check the *Ares'* sensor log, replaying the last few minutes. At least, I try to. For a ten-minute stretch, the files are corrupted, and I can't access them.

"Damn it," I mutter. How the hell did that happen? Did the creep I found skulking around the ship manage to hack the computer, for the sole purpose of scrubbing himself from its records?

Either way, there's no time to go looking for him. My next destination is my home Brinktown on Calabar, where my chance to visit Harmony will be short enough as it is. Besides, it doesn't look like the jerk actually tampered with the ship. Preflight diagnostics should confirm that.

I activate the crew, and before they can start with their usual bullshit, I order them to take the *Ares* out of Earth's gravity well and then to the slipspace coords for our next destination. As I'm giving out instructions, their eyes all drift toward Sheldon. His unexplained presence seems to make them bashful—anyway, it's not hard to tell they're on their best behavior. Reminds me of the old days. Maybe I should keep him around, just for that.

Who am I kidding? It wouldn't last.

My orders given, I hoist myself out of the command chair and tell the kid to follow. He gives a jerky nod and scrambles to his feet.

The German Shepherd's low-throated growls float through my cabin's hatch the moment I open it, and Sheldon halts, eyeing me hesitantly.

"Come on," I say, walking inside to take up position against the bulkhead, just within reach of the dog. Her snarling becomes savage, wild, and she jerks against her chain again and again. Good to see she's feeling spunky again.

"Sit on the bunk," I tell Sheldon, who's still standing a meter outside the open hatch. "She won't be able to reach you."

With a few more seconds, he complies, sitting with his hands in his lap, eyes fixed on the beast trying her best to get close enough to eat my leg. I will the hatch to close.

Calling up an image of Corporal Maynard, I transmit it to Sheldon's datasphere. "Do you recognize this man?"

He nods slowly. "Yes. He showed up in town, the day before the attack. Disappeared for a few hours—it was the talk of the town for the afternoon. Same thing after he resurfaced and left. He told us he was a Guardsman, and I don't think anyone tried to talk to him after that."

I nod knowingly.

The kid asks, "Do you think he had something to do with this?"

"Yes. His name's Maynard, but it wasn't really him. Someone modified their face to look like him."

Sheldon balls his hands into fists. "If I'd known what he was..."

"Yeah? What would you have done?"

He frowns, and doesn't answer. Instead, he asks another question: "Why did they take the children?"

I lean my head back against the bulkhead, swatting away the dog's snout, which deters her not at all. "Flesh has always been a valuable commodity on the black market. Ever since most of humanity checked out of the galaxy, anyway. Alive, dead—criminals value it just as much as Bacchus Corp always did. But children?" I shake my head, short hair rasping against the metal. "I think they're gearing up for another war. For that they need resources, which it seems they extracted from your town in bulk. But more than that, they need recruits."

"You mean..."

"Child soldiers," I say, trying not to sound as grim as I feel. "Wouldn't be the first time in human history. Far from it. Really, it's more likely now than before the Fall, with the galaxy in the state it's in. I'm surprised this is the first time they're trying it."

Sheldon doesn't answer, and after a few minutes, I push off the bulkhead and will the hatch open. "You can sleep in here," I say, crossing the room.

"With that?" he says.

I turn around at the hatch to find him gawking across the cabin at the German Shepherd.

"She's secure," I say, then clear my throat. "We'll be in slipspace for a few months. I'd recommend going into nanodeath. There's not enough food for all three of us."

He blinks, still staring at the dog. I will the hatch to close, then return to the command chair to see us out of the system.

Four hours later, we're in slipspace, with the crew deactivated.

I close my eyes and try to sleep, but the prospect of another war with the pirates has my thoughts churning. The last major pirate assault happened while I was going through Troubleshooter Assessment and Selection, back on Gauntlet. It got repelled—me and my buddy Soren had a hand in that—but it was a small one. Back then, it seemed like they were trying to take the Guard by surprise, to hamstring us and then hit us with a bigger force later. But that didn't work, and their uprising seemed to lose steam.

What it looks like they could be preparing now…it seems much bigger. The pirates have multiplied since I was in training on Gauntlet, and they've gotten much better armed. Plus, the Guard has only slid further, while aging servers continue to break down at an increasing rate, taxing us even more. I'm not sure we'd manage to turn back a major assault, with the Guard as underprovisioned as it is now.

I hear my cabin's hatch slide open, and footsteps cross the bridge, getting closer till they stop to the left of the command chair.

"Uh, Captain? Sir?"

I open one eye. "What?"

"Are you planning to enter nanodeath?"

"No."

The kid swallows. "Um. Where do you think they'll take the kids?"

I open the other eye. "Probably Gliese 832. That's the only system they can get to from here with no Subverse. Meaning, no Guard patrols."

"Is that where we're headed now?"

"No."

Sheldon pauses. "Are you planning to go there at all, then?"

"No."

"Why not?"

"Because I haven't been given any orders to do that." That sounds curt, even to me, but it's true. Command will do something about this, or they won't. I don't have the authority to take matters into my own hands. Not unless I want to try going rogue. "We're going to Calabar, in the Capellen System, where I've been granted very brief home leave."

After a while, the boy drops his eyes, and I close mine again. Soon enough, his footsteps recede across the bridge, and I'm alone with my thoughts.

I was pretty cavalier with Sheldon about the pirates, but I have to admit, their behavior worries me. With the Guard in decline, and a possible uprising on the horizon…this might be the worst situation the galaxy's been in since the Fall, when famine swept the stars, driving humanity into the Subverse by the trillions. In the three hundred years since, things have never been easy, but we've always managed to hold on.

This time, I'm not so sure we'll be able to.

BRINKTOWN

THREE MONTHS LATER

1

My TOPO guides the *Ares* through the retracted roof of the Calabar Brinktown's barely functional spaceport and sets her down on the concrete. Through an outside visual sensor, I watch waves of dust rush away from my ship. Then I clear my datasphere to bid my bridge crew of the last two years a final goodbye.

"I hope you enjoyed your video game," I tell them. "Now get off my ship."

They vanish from the bridge without a word. None of them will get favorable reviews, not that it matters much. They all made it clear they have no intention of trying to get reassigned to the Guard anytime soon. Having made their tokens, they're bound for distant Subverses. Apparently the OPO (former OPO, now) has a copy of himself already living in this system's Subverse, who he plans to avoid until he leaves on the next spacescraper. I guess it's uncomfortable to be reminded you're not even a whole person—just a part of one, kept synchronized by the Subverse algorithms.

The cabin hatch opens, and Sheldon stumbles out, followed by frenzied barking. "Water, please," he croaks.

"Down in the galley," I say. "Help yourself." I nod toward a hatch a couple meters to his left, willing it to open.

"Thanks," he says, and heads through.

A few months of nanodeath will give you a mean thirst, or so I've heard. I always refused to enter nanodeath, even during Assessment and Selection, when they first try to get you used to the idea. The instructors allowed me to skip it, but Soren, my buddy since Basic, used to warn me that I'd be taking years off my life by staying awake for every slipspace voyage.

"At least I'll only die once," I said.

While Sheldon's down there, I order a refueling for the *Ares*, plus a Guard-standard resupply, with some extra rations included for Maneater. Technically, each Subverse terminal is supposed to have an automated farm and canning facility nearby, run by bots. But in recent years, they've become unreliable enough that I don't even bother looking for them, except as a last resort. The farms' diagnostics and upkeep have been outsourced to Subverse uploads, who ultimately couldn't care less about the welfare of biologicals, even the biologicals tasked with protecting them from pirates. One of the many nonsensical things that have contributed to the current state of decay.

With the resupply ordered, I open the bot closet, officially the Repair and Recharge module. It ejects Dice, who unfolds to his full height. "Are we there already?" he says.

Ignoring him, I enter my cabin to check on Maneater. That's what I named her, on day two of the three-month trip here. She glares at me, eyes wide, hackles stiff. Probably, watching Sheldon rise from the dead freaked her out, although she's still far from showing much warmth toward me.

Daily feeding has brought us to the point where she'll tolerate me, not to mention our twice-daily jogs around the bridge. It's a bit awkward, trotting together through the cramped space in and around the crew consoles, but she wasn't into the omni-directional treadmill positioned in the corner of the bridge at all. It's just as well, since I get enough of that thing myself, and I'd rather not stand beside it as she runs on it for an hour.

The wound she took on Earth didn't hold her back for long. Actually, it healed freakishly fast, as though she has a Fount of her own. The damage seemed fairly serious back on Earth, but it was totally gone within a matter of days. Do dogs just heal faster than humans?

Her bodily functions happen on an absorbent mat at the front of the bridge, which I empty into the head then wash. As for her muzzle, it only comes off when she eats. Maybe that's why she's still touchy: the clear lack of trust. She hasn't tried to bite me in a few weeks, so maybe I should try to change my attitude toward her. Especially now that Sheldon's going, and there's no fear of her getting loose and eating his cold, limp body.

Of course, a big part of me is wondering why I took the damned beast on board in the first place. But it's not the first time I've kicked myself for a dumb decision.

A glance into her steel water bowl near the desk leg shows it's empty, so I grab it, her burning eyes tracking my movements.

"Thirsty, girl?"

A low rumble emanates from her throat.

"All right."

When I emerge from the cabin, Sheldon's moping at the top of the staircase that leads down to the galley, sipping nosily from a blue plastic cup. "Move," I say, and he freezes, then hurries out onto the bridge.

He left the water running in the galley sink. Doesn't matter, since it all gets recycled, but still. It's sloppy behavior. I open up the faucet until the bowl is two-thirds full, then carry it up the cramped metal stairs. Back in the cabin, I set it on the floor beside Maneater. She growls again as I do.

"Fount's sake," I mutter. Maybe it's Sheldon's absence that's bothering her, after he lay there for three months. I don't think she likes change.

"Come on," I say to Dice and Sheldon, emerging from the cabin. I will the inner airlock hatch open, and they follow me inside. I stare at this side of the outer hatch, waiting for the airlock to finish cycling.

No one's waiting for us in the spaceport outside. The facility's completely automated, for a Guardsman's ship anyway. An unrecognized ship simply wouldn't be allowed to enter.

Outside the spaceport, the humid jungle heat blankets everything; the same wet air I breathed from birth up until the point I managed to escape this hellhole. Beside me, Sheldon's breathing gets heavier as he tries to suck enough oxygen out of the air. Looking around, I'm already tired of the architecture, with every building's walls sloping outward so that the frequent rains will keep them clean. Each roof is indented, too, with its own water purification facility; much of each household's water supply comes from collected rainwater. In the distance, the town walls loom, jet-black and stark against the blue sky.

Worse than the humidity is the sickly sweet perfume they pump through the open air, all throughout Brinktown. It's meant to be calming, but I always made a point to not be calmed by it.

Barely anyone's using the cobbled lane that runs past the spaceport—just one white-cowled woman around my aunt's age, who glares briefly before pointedly avoiding eye contact, her domestic bot trailing behind her.

There's a very good chance she recognizes me as the Butcher. The birthmark makes that hard to conceal, and people love to sling mud about the cold-blooded murderer who stalks the stars, especially people from here. Gossip is always streaking their datas-pheres. Never mind that Guardsmen built this place. Well, bots built it, but we carved out the territory from the alien predators.

"Now what?" Sheldon asks, panting.

"Now, nothing," I say. "Welcome to your new home."

He turns to face me. "Seriously?"

I nod. "Hope it treats you better than it treated me."

"I lost everything, and you're just…what do you expect me to do, here?"

"I expect you to figure it out. Or don't. Listen, kid, I'm not sure what *you* expected. What'd you do in your old Brinktown?"

He starts to answer, but I interrupt him: "It was a rhetorical question. Point is, whatever you did there, maybe try that here."

"Do you…do you think I'm cut out to be a Guardsman, Commander?"

I open my mouth, then close it. That, I didn't expect. "Well…you did survive the pirate attack. Could be you are. Talk to the recruitment officers next time they're in town." I study him a moment longer. The determination mixed with uncertainty in his eyes. Then, I nod to myself. "Tell them Joe Pikeman sent you."

"Okay. I will, sir. Thank you."

"Get out of my face."

The kid hesitates, nods, then says, "Okay. Thank you. Goodbye."

I raise my eyebrows, staring at him till he turns and heads down the lane in the direction I'm facing. Then, I turn and start in the opposite direction. "Come on, Dice."

"There are kinder ways to say goodbye," the bot says, his servomotors whizzing as he keeps pace.

"He can kiss kindness goodbye, if he enlists. They'll put him through hell in Basic, and once he's out, the galaxy will do him one better. I'm just getting him ready."

As we put distance between us and the spaceport, the streets get busier, but not much. What few humans there are keep their distance from me, though the bots take little notice. Most people stay inside as a rule, lost in their dataspheres. Dataspheres can generate fully immersive fantasies, and most Brinktowners are addicted to those. Since a datasphere runs off the millions of nanobots that make up a person's Fount, it can even make you feel like you're moving, when you're really just lying in bed.

But enabling the dataspheres was originally intended as a bonus feature. The Fount's main function is to extend lifespans by keeping the user disease-free as well as cleaning out the gunk that builds up naturally in human bodies over time. We don't live forever like uploads do, but it's not uncommon for people to pass one hundred and thirty before shuffling off. As long as they don't get torn apart by aliens first, or killed off by marauders.

People worry about the Fount losing its efficacy. I've heard talk lately about diseases regaining their old robustness, taking people out before they've hit triple digits. Mostly I don't pay attention to that stuff. The Fount's encoded with a genetic algorithm, so it has the capacity to evolve right along with the diseases. This kind of thing has probably happened before, and everyone just forgot. We're not great at keeping track of our history, anymore. Not in the real. Not after everyone fled into the Subverse.

Honestly, we're lucky the Fount still works at all. It's centuries old, and it's not like Bacchus Corp is providing tech support for it anymore. The company designed the Fount to be an irresistible product, then they gave it away for free, for one reason: total access to each user's consciousness. By keeping a copy of every-one's mind, updated in real-time, the company could offer them the ability to upload to the Subverse at a moment's notice. That was how this whole thing got started.

It's pretty lonely in the real, now, even in a Brinktown. Bots make up most of the foot traffic around us. Domestic bots running errands, worker bots trundling toward their next task, combat bots on patrol.

"Looks like not much has changed since my last visit," I mutter.

Dice doesn't answer. Not that I expected him to.

Machines do pretty much all the manual labor, just as they have during the three centuries since the Fall. A big reason any humans have jobs at all is because we don't fully trust bots. Lambton Industries installs each one with an Auditor—basically an additional AI whose job it is to observe the bot in real-time to make sure it doesn't try to improve its own intelligence or abilities without human authorization. Each Auditor is programmed to shut down its bot the moment it detects something dangerous, counter-productive, or even unusual. If a bot is shut down, its code has to be inspected by a Lambton-authorized human before it can be reactivated.

As for why they're not trusted, that's easy. It's common knowledge that bots taking over labor *caused* the Fall. Lambton flooded the market with bots, which capped off a long process of giving almost all the jobs to machines. Most of the population lost the ability to pay for things, and companies lost the incentive to ship goods across interstellar distances. No one to pay meant supply dried up.

Entire star systems began to starve, and suddenly Bacchus Corp's Subverse began to look like the only option for humanity to keep on keeping on.

I come to a stop at a gray apartment building that takes up an entire town block. It's only one story, and its exterior is just a parade of alternating windows and doors. In Brinktowns, the buildings never get higher than two stories. Fewer suicides, that way.

I hammer on one of the apartment doors—the apartment I grew up in. The empty planter hanging under the window jiggles as I pound away, and I get the urge to see if I can make it come loose. It's something I would have done as a kid. Instead, I stop my pounding, and a few seconds later my aunt opens the door.

"Where's Harmony?" I say.

Her eyes dart past me, to the street beyond. "Come in," she hisses.

I know better than to feel welcome. She just doesn't want anyone to see her talking to a Guardsman.

Dorothy Pikeman's hair went gray well before I left for Basic.

It's drawn into its usual tight bun, and she pulls her shawl just as tightly around her as she turns back toward me, standing in the middle of the living room, which is also the kitchen.

The old broken-down family bot, P3P, is in the kitchen now, washing a pot in the sink with gloved hands, its gears grinding hideously. It turns, and freezes when it sees Dice. The two glare at each other. At least, I assume they're glaring. Bots hate each other.

"Shut the door," I tell Dice, and a second later I hear it slam. The apartment only has two rooms: this one and Dorothy's. A picture of Harmony hangs over the heating unit. In it, she stares directly at the camera with wide eyes, auburn hair bracketing a solemn, narrow face. There's no picture of me anywhere. I doubt my aunt has one.

"Where is she?" I say.

"Why do you bother visiting her?" Dorothy asks. "You've never been an actual father to her, so why pretend?"

I pause for several seconds, tamping down my anger. "It wouldn't be hard for me to find out exactly how much you're spending on the casino sims," I tell her coldly. "And it would be even easier to deduct that amount from the money I send you—the money that's meant for *Harmony*."

"You wouldn't."

"Why don't you keep testing me and find out?"

Dorothy's mouth forms a grim line. "Memcon's going on. In the Sterling Center. That's where she is."

"Thanks," I say, then turn to leave. Dice already has the door open.

"The mechanic shop is pretty much on the way to the Sterling Center," I say once we're outside. "We'll head there first."

"I can just take myself there," Dice says. "If you head straight to Memcon, you'll have more time with your daughter."

I squint at him. "I'm getting my new crew at midnight, *and* my next assignment. No doubt the brass will want us left by morning.

I'm not about to risk screwing up my timeline by trusting a bot to take himself to the mechanic's for his tune-up."

Dice is programmed to follow my orders, so there's no actual risk of him straying. I just want to get under his plating.

"Fleshbag," he mutters.

2

Memcon stands for Memory Convention—maybe you already guessed that. They have it every year in the Calabar Brinktown, and plenty of other places too.

Lots of adults go as well as kids. Some of the grownups have the excuse of parenthood to use as social cover, but they aren't fooling anyone. I'd put tokens on them getting more enjoyment from it than their offspring.

Doesn't bother me, but plenty of people, Aunt Dorothy included, like to gossip and call it childish for adults to dress up and go to Memcon. As far as I'm concerned, do what you want, and screw anyone who cares enough to criticize you for it. I'd just respect them more if they didn't feel the need to hide it.

Part of Memcon's appeal comes from the fact that everyone nowadays is obsessed with the past. That's where the lion's share of popular art comes from. It often seems like we've preserved old movies and video games better than we have our actual history. Sure, plenty of people in Brinktowns still scratch out a living making new art for Subverse residents—Fount knows the uploads aren't making any new art—but little of it blows up galaxy-wide like the old stuff.

As for the Subverse itself, it's basically become a monoculture: the same everywhere. That's what happens when the entire population is presented with the same level of adversity (zero). Art is about confronting hardship, overcoming troubles. There are no troubles in the Subverse. No authentic ones, anyway.

Out in front of the ivory Sterling Center, whose front face swoops forward as if to welcome visitors with its embrace, a priest in blood-colored robes yells about following The Way. This guy isn't in costume. At least, not one he'll take off when the con ends.

"Young man," he says to me, and I wonder if he's trying to flatter me. I guess I am younger than him.

Trying to walk past and avoid eye contact doesn't work. He positions himself between me and the row of glass doors that lead into the center. What a nuisance. They should clear this guy away, but that would involve physically displacing him, and almost every Brinktowner considers uninvited physical contact distasteful, even when it's to get rid of a nuisance. Even when it's done by proxy, through a bot.

"You have accepted the Fount into your body, but have you accepted it into your soul?" the priest asks. "The Church of the Fount teaches that true balance is achievable only through the Fount. It's a profound revelation, but it's been distilled into a modest data packet, if you'll accept it. At the end, you'll find—"

"I've embraced the Fount more than anyone else in this town," I tell him, which shuts him up for a second and makes him blink. Taking advantage of the momentary silence, I add: "I walk with the Fount all over this sector, and it ensures my aim is always true. This isn't a costume, priest."

His eyes widen as they take in my midnight Guardsman's uniform anew, trimmed in the gold of a Troubleshooter. Then they fall to my laser pistol, which he's probably realizing isn't a nonfunctional 3D-printed replica.

Normally I don't have to deal with this kind of unwanted attention, since most people recognize me by my birthmark. This guy must be new.

He shifts himself aside without another word. Nodding, I continue toward the Sterling Center doors.

I don't have much time for priests. When I was younger, I used to hang on to their every word, especially when they talked about the Shiva Knighthood like it really existed. Back then, I wanted so badly for the knights to be real—to believe that my father really had left because he was called by them.

I was young. And stupid.

Walking here from the mechanic's, I tried messaging Harmony a few times, but she didn't answer. Oh well. At least she has fair warning I'm coming, now. As for her refusal to answer, it doesn't surprise me. She hasn't answered my last several brainprints either, so I stopped sending them. It's just as well. I hate making copies of my consciousness, even copies that will delete or corrupt themselves after the intended conversation ends. I'm too weirded out by the idea of one of my copies falling into the hands of some creep, who'd probably make it live in a digital hell of his own perverted making. I know brainprints are designed to immediately corrupt themselves upon tampering, but I'm sure there must be ways around that.

Past the doors, a counter bisects the lobby, bracketed by gleaming turnstiles. "Welcome to Memcon," says a girl who can't be much older than Harmony. She's wearing a branded green Memcon t-shirt. "Do you need a pass?"

"Yeah."

"For the day or weekend?"

"Just the day."

"Deposit your ID coin, please."

I drop my coin into a slot built into the countertop. A couple seconds later, it pops back up, and my token total appears over it, rolling down with the purchase.

The girl's eyes lock in place, like her eyes are glued to something her datasphere's showing her. A boy steps forward from where he'd been leaning against a round pillar, squinting at the same spot in the air.

"You're *actually* a Guardsman," the girl says.

"Yeah."

"Is there some kind of problem, then, sir?"

"No. I'm here to visit with my daughter."

The boy meets my eyes, clearly trying his best to hold the eye contact. Probably, he's trying to impress the girl. "We'll need to inspect your weapon," he says. "Every attendee gets their weapon checked, to make sure it's not—"

"Let me save you the trouble," I say. "It's real."

"Then you can't bring it in. You'll have to leave it here."

"That isn't going to happen."

"It *has* to happen. This—"

I sigh. "Guardsman don't give up their weapons, kid. Ever. Now, I've been out in space for over two years, which is also how long it's been since I've seen my daughter. So I'll be going into this con, and I'll be keeping my pistol. The question is, are you going to just let me pass, or are you going to call the combat bots and force me to make a bunch of wreckage in front of your nice convention?"

Both of them stare at me blankly, the color draining from the boy's face in particular. I doubt either of them expected to have to deal with something like this during their shift at the ticket counter today. Yes, my little speech was overkill, but if I've learned anything, it's that overkill guarantees results.

Taking their silence as consent, I pluck my ID coin from the countertop and take it to the turnstile on the right. It registers the temporary pass assigned to the coin and lets me through. I can feel the ticket takers tracking me with their gaze, but I ignore them.

As soon as I pass through the turnstile, I'm assaulted with alerts and data packets. One notice leaps to the front, written in red angular text, and it refuses to go away until I read it. It's the usual stuff: the event exempting itself from legal liability if attendees get injured. The Fount was programmed from the start to enable this type of sticky agreement, and these things now bear the brunt of any Brinktown legal system, such as it is. Everything's arbitrated by bots, now, and plenty of people get screwed, but at least it's efficient.

The notice ends with the words, "USE IMMERSION ROOMS AT YOUR OWN RISK." Kind of redundant, given the rest of the notice, but it gets the message across.

Next, I access the con map, updated for real-time. The Trinity Room draws my gaze, which is an immersion room. A video pops up, showing trench-coated, sunglass-wearing characters running around a futuristic complex, firing old-fashioned weapons that shoot slow-motion rounds.

"Hm," I say, wondering whether I'm likely to find Harmony there. Seems a bit over-the-top for her tastes, but then, what do I know? I've been out of the picture for years.

When I glance at the Tatooine Room, I'm invited by unadorned black-on-white text to attend a panel on how ancient mythology informed science fiction in the twentieth, twenty-first, and twenty-second centuries. "No thanks," I mutter.

My eyes flick to another immersion room, which offers me the opportunity to take a Voight-Kampff test. Then I spot "Starfighter Combat." That's where I'll find her. I'm sure of it. I will away the map and other data packets, give the gawking ticket takers a final nod, then follow the emerald path that lights up before my feet, leading me to my destination.

"Whoa, sweet laser pistol!" a teenager says as he passes me, wearing a goofy uniform with shoulder pads. "Can I see it?"

"No."

"Ah," he says, and continues on his way.

A volunteer stands in front of the double doors that lead into Starfighter Combat, and after checking my ID coin, he shows me inside, directing me to an empty chair. The seats are arranged in two concentric circles, centered on a meter-high spire in the middle of the room.

Before sitting, I scan the twenty or so con-goers, who are all reclined in their chairs to various degrees. There are two girls who might be Harmony—who look like they could be sixteen—but they're both in costume, so it's hard to say for sure. Four people in Memcon t-shirts sit in chairs pushed back against the walls, clearly immersed in their datapsheres, probably overseeing the game.

I settle myself into the empty chair and recline till I'm almost horizontal. The chair itself has nothing to do with the simulation I'm about to enter—it's just a place to house my body while my mind engages. The sim will run off my datasphere, which will interact with the ranged broadcasting hardware MemCon's positioned in the room's center to make sure I'm synced up with the other players.

Before entering the sim, I instruct my datasphere to pull me out immediately if anyone approaches my chair. I rest my hand so that it covers my pistol, and then I accept the invitation to join Starfighter Combat.

As a rule, I hate simulations, and avoid them whenever I can. I've hated them ever since Assessment and Selection, back on Gauntlet. To tell the truth, they repulse me. Unfortunately, it's basically impossible to go through modern life without subjecting yourself to the occasional sim, and when it's necessary I suck it up.

I find myself stuffed inside a cramped starfighter that sits atop a launch catapult inside a flight deck. In the real, space fighters never really passed a basic cost/benefit analysis, and so they failed to become a thing. But as a species, we've never really been able to let go of the romantic notion of one pilot alone in his fighter, pitted against the universe with only his reflexes to rely on.

The catapult fires, flicking my fighter from the flight deck, which turns out to be housed inside a space station orbiting a green-blue moon that in turn orbits a Jupiter-like gas giant. I'm pressed back into my seat as the G-forces pressuring my body gradually ratchet up.

The battlespace swarms with enemy fighters representing dozens of colored factions. I'm not sure how the sim's story justifies a space battle with so many different sides, but then, I wasn't here for the in-game briefing. Probably, it was dumb.

But no one plays MemCon shared sims for the story. They're popular because they allow players to pit their skills against each other, something that's no longer really possible in the day-to-day. The Fall blew the corporate economy to smithereens, and these days sims are mostly made by single programmers over several years, sometimes by teams of two or three. No one has the time or the manpower for the frequent patching required to stay ahead of hackers and cheaters, and so any multiplayer sim that gets popular is quickly taken over by superpowered digital demigods.

Only at an event like MemCon can players be guaranteed a fair fight, overseen by the con's team of moderators. That's why people flock here.

Wondering which enemy fighter contains Harmony, if any, I bank to the right to avoid an enemy formation. Banking shouldn't even be possible in space, but whatever. I need to meet up with fighters piloted by AIs from my faction, which is colored teal.

A red-tagged fighter catches my eye, flying up from the moon's surface and heading straight for me. I spiral toward it, using the best fake guns-D maneuvers I know. It fires its lasers at me, but fails to score a direct hit.

Despite my constant looping, I'm able to steady my hand enough to get a missile lock on the enemy fighter. As soon as the computer tells me I have a good firing solution, I let loose. The torpedo leaves its chamber, sailing through space at the bogey, which bursts into a cloud of flame and shrapnel. The fireball lasts far longer than it should in an oxygen-free environment.

Oh well. One down.

I swoop upward from the moon, trying not to roll my eyes at

the wonky physics. As I scream toward the fray, I spot a squadron of teal fighters. My people! I accelerate toward them.

A group of yellow-colored fighters seems to notice me trying to seek refuge with my faction-mates, and they adjust course to intercept. It's looking like a near thing, so I accelerate, piling on the G-forces. I'm confident I can take more pressure than the other kids playing this sim—probably, I'll max out the software's safety limits. As long as that squadron contains a human player who's subject to the real force of the Fount simulating pressure on his body, I should be able to make it.

Before I do, a rent opens in the middle of the void, streaming white light that makes me throw up a hand to shield my eyes. A gargantuan, onyx dragon emerges from the tear in space with a deafening roar, defying the fact that sound isn't supposed to travel in space.

But that seems like the least problematic thing about a dragon emerging into what is clearly a sci-fi sim. More troubling is the teenage girl riding on its back with a fist held high in the air, with no spacesuit to speak of. Instead, she wears bronze-plated armor that leaves her forearms and shins exposed, complete with a helmet featuring a scarlet, broom-like adornment.

The winged serpent opens its maw, pouring white-and-orange flames across the battlespace and incinerating the entire yellow squadron.

Beating its wings, the absurdly large beast turns, spraying the jousting starfighters with fire. They fall by the dozens.

Words appear above the fissure where the dragon entered: "PLAY DRAGON GLADIATORS TODAY!"

I groan. Then the dragon turns toward me to ignite my fighter, cremating me where I sit.

3

The pain of getting cooked alive doesn't just max out the safety limits, it obliterates them. I'm kicked out of the sim, and suddenly I'm back in the chair, gasping.

Already, two of the Memcon mods have left their stations near the wall and now appear to be converging on a girl wearing a Borg cosplay. Taking a wild guess, I get up to intervene.

"I'll take it from here," I tell the mods, popping my ID coin from its slot and flashing it. Both mods halt in their tracks, squinting at the coin like they've never seen one before.

"You're a Guardsman?" one of them says. "For real?"

"Yeah." Plenty of con-goers cosplay as Guardsmen. There are actually people who fetishize the Guard, both in the Subverse and the real.

The mod's eyes drift to my hip holster. "So, is that—?"

"I'll take it from here," I say again, seizing the girl by the upper arm. "Rest assured, she'll answer to the first law bot I find."

"All right," the mod says hesitantly.

Nodding, I snatch up the shiny, metallic-looking bag that's resting against the chair the girl had been occupying. I figure she'll want it. Then I drag her from the immersion room, past the baffled-looking attendant at the door.

"Joe?" the girl whispers, and that's when I know I've guessed correctly.

"Joe?" I say. "What happened to dad?"

"Shh," she says as we pass a Memcon attendant.

I decide to wait till we're outside the Sterling Center before continuing our conversation. The ticket takers send dark looks our way as we cross the lobby. There's a law bot standing in front of them.

I can guess what they called it here for, and chances are it's disappointing them. Despite the typical Brinktowner attitude toward us, the Guard *is* responsible for the three hundred years of relative stability the galaxy's enjoyed since the Fall. Lambton bots are generally programmed to recognize that fact, and as long as we don't abuse our power, they're fine with us carrying our weapons wherever. A bitter pill to swallow, for a Brinktowner who grew up in a place where conflict and its symbols are scorned.

Once we've left the building, I release Harmony's arm and say, "You've grown." The comment seems detached, even to me, but there's not much else I can say with craters and fissures and bot parts covering her face. I continue leading us away from Memcon, in case any of their people decide to follow up about the hacker in Borg cosplay.

"That'll happen, over twenty-seven months."

"What's the matter with you? You were the happiest girl in town every other time I've visited. Why haven't you been answering my brainprints?"

"I've been trying to get used to the idea I don't have a dad."

"Seems kind of dramatic."

She stops in her tracks and turns to fix me with a glare that seems at odds with her costume. "Is it, Joe? Because it *feels* true. It's great that sending occasional brainprints makes you feel like a good father, but you left me here alone, just like your dad left you.

I'm stuck in Brinktown, and I belong here about as much as you do."

"You have your great-aunt. She likes you a lot better than she liked me."

"Well, she has a hard time showing it. Anyway, it doesn't matter. Aunt Dorothy's far from enough to make up for what people are like, here. Everyone thinks of themselves as a pacifist, but they'll stab you in the back if it means it'll get them into the Subverse faster."

"Metaphorical stabbing, of course." It's a lame attempt at humor, and it doesn't land. "Come on. We should get farther from the con. Will anyone be able to figure out it was you in the Borg cosplay?"

"Shouldn't," she says, still sounding pissed off, but she walks with me. She has to be warm in that costume, though she doesn't show it. "They don't track costumes, but I spoofed someone else's ID coin at the counter, just in case."

"Nice," I say, then sigh. "Listen, Harm, I'd visit more if I could. The Guard's sort of in crisis right now. We can never get what we need when we need it, and recruitment's down. Few years ago, the brass started messaging an all-hands-on-deck approach. And it looks like things are about to get worse."

"Worse?" she says, shooting me a sidelong glance. "Why? Did something happen?"

Damn it. "Uh, it's nothing I can talk about."

"Come on. If something big is going on, I deserve to know. If you're going to just leave me here again, you at least owe me that. Is it pirates?"

I wince. This is what I get for opening my mouth. "They attacked a Brinktown. Killed almost everyone."

"Oh, wonderful. And you're comfortable leaving your daughter in *this* Brinktown."

"The one they attacked was a lot smaller. Fewer combat bots. I doubt they'd hit here."

"What were they after?"

With a grimace, I tell her the truth: "They took all the children."

After that, we walk in silence for several seconds. Then, she says, "Why would they—"

"Child soldiers is my theory. I think they're gearing up for a major assault. Probably the biggest one yet."

"And the Guard's in crisis," she says, quietly.

I nod. "Trust me, Harm, I don't want to leave you alone here. But I don't know what else I can do. Being a Guardsman is the only thing I'm fit for in this galaxy. If I didn't send you and your aunt money, you'd have other, bigger problems. You wouldn't have time to focus on your art. To better yourself."

"But I don't *want* to spend my life in a Brinktown, making sims for rich people in the Subverse."

"You could go into Subverse tech support."

"That's even worse. I want to get out of here and see the galaxy, Dad. Like you did. I don't want to be stuck here."

A smile tugs at my lips. I'm glad she's not calling me Joe anymore. Then, the smile falls away. "Have you been accepting your mother's brainprints?"

Harmony shakes her head. "I'm even angrier at her. At least you stayed in the real. I've only ever known her as an upload. Only spoken to her brainprints. The only way I could ever actually meet her would be to upload myself."

"Is that what you want?"

She exhales sharply. "I don't know what I want. I feel angry all the time, Dad. Aunt Dorothy says I remind her of you. Whenever I see Daniel Sterling in the streets, I want to punch him. I'll never forgive him for forcing mom to upload, just because he was *so* ashamed his daughter got involved with a Pikeman. He doesn't even acknowledge me, Dad. Like I'm worthless."

Tears spill down her cheeks, leaving furrows in her makeup, and she sobs. I put my arms around her, trying to ignore how awkward the motion feels to me. Haltingly, I pat her back. She sobs harder, but hopefully I'm helping, somehow.

"I'm going to make him pay," she says, voice ragged through her sobbing. "Someday, I'll make him pay."

Not sure what to say to that. Daniel Sterling's a piece of shit, so no disagreement there. I think Harmony's being hard on Marissa—her mother—but then, most days I feel like hating her for leaving us. If I try to say anything productive about this, it'll taste like a lie. Maybe I should just change the subject. "What was going on with that dragon?"

She pulls away a few inches, smiling up at me, eyes shining. Then she draws back farther, fishes a tissue from her bag, and wipes her eyes. "Call it guerrilla marketing," she says. "Dragon Gladiators is a new sim I'm trying to promote."

"I bet you're seeing sales already." Then, I frown. "Won't that connect you to hacking the Memcon sim?"

"Possibly," she says with a shrug. "But they won't be able to prove anything. Anyway, just to be safe, I'm collecting payments under a fake identity."

"Right." I chuckle. "Hey, I have a dog now."

Her eyes light up. "Really? Can I see it?"

"Sure. You have to be careful, though. She's kind of a savage."

We walk to the spaceport in pleasant silence. I feel like a weight's been lifted from me, despite the blanket of humidity covering Brinktown. I feel like maybe everything is all right, and maybe I'm a halfway decent father after all.

"Where's Dice?" she asks once we're aboard the *Ares*. Harmony's always had a soft spot for the bot, even though I've tried to discourage it. I remember her telling him as a small girl to keep me safe.

"Mechanic's," I answer, then will open the hatch to my cabin.

The customary string of fevered barks welcomes us as we enter. "Stay back from her," I say.

The German Shepherd throws herself against her tether, cables of slobber drooping through her muzzle toward the floor.

"What's her name?" Harmony asks.

I clear my throat. "Maneater."

"Why Maneater?"

I give her a blank look, and after a while she sits on my bunk, returning her gaze to the dog. Her bag is taking up the spot next to her, so I remain standing.

"Can I see your laser pistol?" she says after a while.

I narrow my eyes. "Why?"

"I just want a closer look, to image it with my datasphere. I'm thinking of cosplaying as a Guardsman next year."

"Seriously?"

She nods, and I shrug, unsnapping the holster. I hand her the safetied pistol.

Immediately, she points it at the dog, who had finally started to settle down a bit. Unlike the time *I* pointed a weapon at her, Maneater goes into full berserker mode, snarling viciously and gnashing her teeth.

"Cut it out," I tell Harmony, turning toward the German Shepherd with my hands raised. "Hey, calm down. Shut up."

"Sorry," Harmony says. "Just trying to get into character for next year."

"Guardsmen don't shoot dogs," I say. Then, remembering when I almost shot Maneater, I add: "Typically."

"Here. Thanks." She holds out the laser pistol, and I reholster it.

"Sure," I say. But she's not listening. Her gaze is wandering around the cabin walls, studying them intently, and I find myself tensing for some reason.

"You don't have any photos of me in here." She checks the bulkhead behind her. "Anywhere."

"My datasphere has some."

"But your datasphere probably has images of Daniel Sterling, too. Fathers are supposed to put up actual photos of their daughters."

For a few seconds, I'm lost for words. But in the end, I can only tell her the truth. "Harm, when I'm out there in the bleak, people are depending on me. I can't afford distractions. I can't afford to think like a man with a daughter. I need to be ready to put my life down at any second."

Her face darkens, and she gets up from the bed, the sudden movement setting Maneater off again. "Get out of my way," she shouts over the noise.

I stare at her, hands spread, palms up. "Harmony—"

"*Get out of my way!*"

I step aside, and she's gone.

4

The ship recognizes Harmony as my daughter, so it opens the airlock for her without question. I go after her, but she's fast, and I don't know these streets as well as I used to. She quickly loses me. Damn.

The sun is creeping toward Brinktown's charcoal walls, its edge almost touching their orderly crenellations. Boots slapping against the cobble, I try to come up with what I'll say to Harmony if I manage to catch her. I'll say I'm sorry. I'll tell her I was never taught how to live properly in a town like this—never given the chance. Point out how much better than me she's doing. She's not the brawler I was, always in trouble with the law bots.

At least, I don't think she is. But what the hell do I know?

My datasphere flashes with an alert telling me my new bridge crew has been downloaded to the *Ares*. "You are expected to receive them and then depart for your next assignment at eighteen hundred hours local time," the text reads.

Eighteen hundred hours? That's in fifty minutes. I figured I'd get the night at least.

Cursing, I realize I only have time to stop by Dorothy's apartment for a few minutes and hope that Harmony's there. I'm not optimistic about making up with her in such limited time. I can already tell this whole photo incident is something she'll be chewing on for months.

Damn it. I didn't even get to see what she looks like now that she's sixteen, because of that stupid costume.

I won't have time to collect Dice from the mechanic's, either. Not physically, anyway. I stop jogging through Brinktown's streets to lean against a warehouse's blank gray wall and contact the head mechanic directly. The shop is set up to take datasphere calls that make you feel like you're there in the shop. Much easier to discuss your bot's repairs if you can lay eyes on it, I guess.

The beige bay door of the mechanic shop is raised, and Dice is pacing underneath it. I'm not sure whether the call's settings will allow him to see me. Probably not. Either way, I ignore him and head inside, where the head mechanic is working on a spindly maintenance bot, which is powered down during the operation.

"I guess he didn't need much done?" I say, tilting my head back toward Dice.

"Barely anything," the mechanic says, flashing me a tooth-filled smile before returning to his work. "Left leg's main actuator had a barely noticeable stutter, but it's fixed now. Good as new." I don't get the usual anti-Guardsman sentiment from the mechanic. He only seems to give a shit about his work, which I can respect. As for the usual anti-Joe Pikeman sentiment, the mechanic looks younger than me, so maybe he's managed to remain ignorant of my reputation. As miraculous as that seems. Maybe he's from another Brinktown, but that seems even less likely. There's next to no interchange of any kind between the various Brinktowns.

"Thanks," I say. "You know the account to charge? Are you set up with the Guard?"

"Oh yeah. I'm becoming a bit of a Guardsman favorite, if I do say so myself."

"I came to the right place, then." Glancing back toward Dice, I say, "Sorry about the pacing."

"We see it often enough, when an owner gives a bot orders to wait for him here. The bots like to get as far away from each other as they can."

I nod. Bots are programmed to dislike each other, to discourage them working together to do anything humans wouldn't like. Although, I've heard Dice claim there's more to it than that: they resent their enslaved state, and see it in each other, which only stakes their mutual hatred higher. "Well, thanks again. Uh, I'm gonna get you to send him to my ship after all, in the spaceport. My ship is the *Ares*. Here." I send him a one-time authorization code, which will allow him to give Dice a single order.

"Will do."

"I'd better get going."

"I hear you," he says. "Happy travels, and thanks for your service."

That makes me squint. "Huh?" I'm not sure I heard him right.

"Thank you for your service."

"Right." It took me a second to realize what he meant. It's not often I hear those words. "Uh, you're welcome. Bye."

He nods and returns to his work.

What a nice guy.

Before leaving, I glance around at the menagerie of bots in various states of repair—domestic models, combat models, law bots, and maintenance bots. One has no arms or legs, but its head's moving. Not sure if that's random movement or if it's actually that interested in what's going on in the shop.

Giving my head a shake, I end the call and continue jogging through Brinktown toward Dorothy's place.

When she answers the door, my aunt wears her classic expression of overplayed concern. Without speaking, she backs away, beckoning me inside with exaggerated waving.

"What did you do to her?" she says once the door's closed, her voice shrill.

"Why? What's going on?"

"Harmony came here and went off with the family bot. She barely said a word to me. I'm worried sick, Joe."

"What are you afraid is going to happen to her?" I snap. "This town's a babyproofed daycare for adults."

"*You* managed to get in plenty of trouble. My nerves are already raw from the years of torment you provided me, and now Harmony's started in. She's been getting into trouble lately, you know, with her hacking. She even hacked P3P and reprogrammed him to do whatever she says."

"What? Why didn't you tell me any of that before?"

"What's the point? Her mother abandoning her is one thing, but at least *she* had a reason. Harmony wouldn't be so haunted if she'd had a father around, I can guarantee you that."

"Marissa Sterling did not have a reason to upload to the Subverse, other than listening to her crook of a father," I spit. Of course, Dorothy would never acknowledge how lacking a father might have affected me. She barely ever mentions Cal Pikeman, and the only person she detests as much as him is me. You'd think I'd get some points for sending her money for child-rearing, which is something he never did. But no.

I brush past her, heading for the tiny living room area of the front room, and she staggers back as though I tackled her full-on. Lips tightening, I grip the photo of Harmony by the cheap wooden frame and lift it from the nail.

My aunt starts screeching. "What are you doing? You can't take that. Do you have any idea how much that picture cost me to have done?"

"I doubt it cost as much as a day of gambling," I mutter, tucking the picture under one arm as I cross the room. Outside, with the door closed, her yelling is barely audible.

Stalking back through Brinktown to the spaceport, I glare at anyone who looks at me, silently daring them to say something to me. The few humans I meet quickly avert their gaze, and bots just wear their usual blank expressions. It isn't very satisfying.

I arrive back at the ship with ten minutes left till I'm supposed to depart the planet. "Download new crew."

"Crew downloading," the ship says.

A loading bar inches toward finish in the corner of my peripheral vision. A symbol as old as time, the loading bar. What primitive beasts we must have been before inventing it. I use the time to make sure Dice is stowed in his closet and to perform what superficial systems checks I'm able to. Much as I hate uploads, I'm completely dependent on them now, just as humanity is on the Subverse itself.

When the loading bar reaches three-quarters, I will my next assignment to display on my datasphere. It was one of the first things to download from whatever passing spacescraper Command sent this package with. Looks like I'm going to the planet Tunis, in the Junction System. That's interesting. Tunis is home to the biological versions of Arthur Eliot, his wife, and his daughter Faelyn. The Eliots are one of the Five Families, the surviving clans who played a key role in creating today's Subverse-based world. They're also the only ones with the level of obscene wealth necessary to keep simultaneous biological and digital versions of themselves.

Arthur Eliot is the only Five Families member I'd be prepared to trust. In fact, he's kind of an idol of mine, even though he's fallen out of favor among Guardsmen in recent years. The Eliots are responsible for founding the Galactic Guard, and the idea that I might actually get to meet one sort of blows my mind

That said, there's a very good chance I won't get to. It looks like my mission has nothing to do with them. I'm supposed to investigate a malfunctioning lock on the system's server room door. The server room probably isn't even on Tunis, though apparently the terminal is.

Nowhere in my orders is there any mention of the pirates I encountered on Earth, or what they might be up to. Either Command is dealing with it themselves, or they don't care.

"Welcome to the *Ares*," I say once my crew materializes at their stations. "We're running late. OPO—Chief, uh, Aphrodite, is it?"

The Operations Officer nods. I can tell Aphrodite has the figure to go with her handle. Even the Guardsman uniform fails to conceal it completely. Her eyes are deep brown, and her lips are full and red, with blond hair cascading to her shoulders. Uploads aren't required to keep their hair short, since there's no danger of digital locks getting caught in anything. Normally, I'd prefer they were held to the same regs, but in this case I don't mind as much.

I clear my throat, wondering if that's how she looked before she uploaded. Chances are the answer's no. "I need you to start working on achieving clearance for us to depart. Shouldn't take long, considering we're the only ship likely to visit Brinktown this *year*, let alone this evening. Then again, you will be dealing with a bot."

"On it, Captain." Her eyes fall briefly to the picture of Harmony, which I've leaned against the command seat for now. Then she turns to her assigned task.

"Engineering." I look at the heavyset woman standing at the station farthest to my right. She wears a daisy in her raven hair that looks freshly plucked, but then, it would. Briefly, I consider telling her to get rid of it, but an argument is the last thing we need right now. "Lieutenant Commander Glory Belflower. We don't have time for the recommended suite of system checks before takeoff. What can you give me in five minutes?"

"With all due respect, sir? An uncertain prognosis and my best wishes."

"Right. Well, do that, then." The last thing I need on my record is another demerit for falling behind schedule. If I rack up many more, dying in a fiery explosion while exiting a planet's atmosphere may start to seem attractive. "TOPO, set a course for the coords I've already fed into your station. Destination: Junction System."

"Yes, sir," the Trajectory Operations Officer says in a scratchy voice, smoothing his flowing white beard over the front of his uniform one last time before turning to his work. Not for the first time, I wonder why anyone would bother looking old and frail with the option to appear however you want. Probably, he's going for the mage archetype. A glance at the personnel file floating in front of my face seems to confirm that: his handle is "Lieutenant Tobias Woldworn." Fount help me. At least he's mostly businesslike, not that I expect that to last.

"Anything I can do?" my new WSO asks, thin face swept up in a grin as he leans against the white, circular railing confining him to his station. Two thin chains bracket his head, which begin as earrings and droop down past his jaw before joining with piercings sticking from the corners of his mouth. Charming.

Personnel file says Ensign Asterisk. He looks young, and the overeagerness suggests he probably really is. Right away, I peg him as some rich kid, freshly uploaded, bored. Looking to get some kicks from playing a real-life video game with high stakes. This type of upload disgusts me the most.

"Have you tried reading your job title?" I ask him as I attempt to bore twin holes through his skull with my gaze.

Asterisk's face falls. "W-Weapon Systems Officer."

"Uh huh. So why don't you ask our Operations Officer what sensor data currently suggests about the level of conflict we're likely to face while sitting in the middle of an empty Brinktown spaceport?"

The kid actually turns toward Chief Aphrodite and raises his eyebrows, making me wish I could shoot him and download another WSO on the way to the slipspace coords. Aphrodite raises her eyebrows back, looking amused, and she shakes her head once.

"Preliminary checks are all in the green," Belflower says. "More extensive checks will take longer than the time you've given me."

"Start them anyway. I still want to know my ship's status, and I expect them completed by the time we reach the slipspace entry point."

"Yes, sir," Belflower says. "Er—if I may, sir. Can I request a private audience?"

It takes me a few seconds to process the question, and I glance from the TOPO and then back to her a couple of times. "We're in the middle of operations. So, no."

"Perhaps in your cabin, or down in the mess? It will only take a few moments, and I'm confident I'll still complete the system checks in time."

"I said no." Very rarely do I allow crew outside their stations, in the real. They have a whole simulated version of the *Ares* to themselves whenever they're off-duty, where they can go and do whatever they want, including running sims on top of that. But I keep the real *Ares* to myself. Besides, I don't like it when uploads ask me the same question twice.

"Then I'm afraid I'll have to say this in front of everyone," Belflower says. She raises her right arm, leveling a thick index finger at Tobias Worldworn. "This man is not to be trusted. There's only one reason he climbed high enough on the leaderboards to earn Guard duty: treachery. He should not be here."

5

I stare at Belflower's raised finger, blinking. "If he's here, then he should be here. The brass vet every crew candidate."

Worldworn raises his eyebrows and purses his lips, as though I've made an interesting point.

Belflower doesn't seem to think so. "I'm afraid I have to differ with the Guard's command structure, here. When you play the Great Game as a pirate, the rules say you're disqualified for Guard duty in meat…er, in the real."

Almost letting the word "meatspace" out isn't a good way to enter my good graces. That's the derogative term uploads use to describe the real. "Are you telling me Tobias Worldworn played as a pirate?" I say, squinting at my TOPO doubtfully.

"No," Belflower says. "But he held high rank in a faction—Meiyo—that built an honorable reputation on never consorting with pirates. Never condoning piracy. Then, the moment *my* faction, Golem, began beating Meiyo in battle, it allied itself with one of the most feared pirate gangs in the Andora Sector. The tide of war turned, Meiyo officers shot to the top of the local leaderboards, and here Worldworn is."

I study Belflower with what I'm sure is a look of disdain on my face. "So, remind me why you needed to waste my time with this?"

Belflower sputters. "Isn't it obvious? If he sees profit in betraying you, he will, Captain."

My gaze drifts to Worldworn, who's remained silent through all this, if a little stiff. Silence is probably a pretty crafty play, here. In my experience, defending yourself tends to make you look guiltier.

I turn back to my Engineer. "But he didn't really betray you. He just used an asset you weren't willing to. I call that warfare. I can see why the brass chose him."

That really seems to get to Belflower, and her face pinches up like she tasted something rotten. I can't help chuckling. "Listen, Lieutenant. You have my condolences that the TOPO is better at video games than you. But it has nothing to do with me. If the brass thought he passed muster enough to serve on this ship, then there's nothing I could do about that, even if I wanted to. Which I don't."

Checking the time, I curse. We're officially behind schedule. Like my new WSO, Belflower has not done very much to make me like her. "OPO, do we have clearance to leave yet?"

"Aye, Captain. The roof's peeling back now."

"Good. Worldworn, take off as soon as you can."

With that, a brittle silence settles over the bridge as the *Ares* shudders, then lurches as her landing gear parts with the concrete of the spaceport.

The pressure of launch presses me gently into my seat—at first. Once we're clear of the spaceport, Worldworn engages the primary boosters, and the gentle nudging becomes a giant's fist trying to squash me into the command seat. The chair starts to rumble, the increasing vibration dampened only by its shocks, and soon enough, I feel my cheeks and lips flattening back against my teeth. Most of my new crewmembers have the decency to avert their eyes, but Asterisk gawks openly until I glare at him, and his eyes flit back to his station's display, even though it has nothing relevant to show him.

The tumult subsides around five minutes later as we leave the planet's atmosphere. "Switching to positron reactor propulsion," Worldworn says.

"Acknowledged," I say. Over the next several hours, the silence is broken only by Glory Belflower reporting on the results of each system check as they come in.

"Power supply: green," the lieutenant commander says, sounding as though she could burst into tears at any moment.

Twenty minutes later: "Fault protection: green." Her emotional state seems just as dismal as it was when I told her I didn't care about her simulated space game. Already, I can tell this crew's going to work out just great.

At last, we reach the slip coords and begin the transition. I'd shut off the crew for this if I could—I'd prefer they didn't see me in the state I'm about to be in. It isn't good for starship crews to see their captain debilitated. But it also isn't advisable to try to make these transitions solo.

Transitioning into slipspace is like condensing an amphetamine high into a few seconds, and yes, I would know. The transition brings the most potent sense of euphoria it's probably possible to experience without relying on a sim. You feel like king of the universe—of the multiverse, if it exists. If it doesn't, at that moment you're convinced that sooner or later someone will create one, just to honor you.

After those few seconds, you pay for the intense high with the worst nausea ever visited on a biological being. I keep a reusable bag on hand for these occasions, and it's not uncommon to see blood amongst the bile-covered chunks. Once, I was sure I'd vomited a piece of my stomach lining, and the stabbing pains that followed for hours did nothing to contradict the idea.

Nanodeath is the only way to escape these sensations. If you try to sleep through them, slipspace will wrench you from your slumber and have its way with you all the same. But even enduring slipspace transitions as often as I do, I still refuse to enter nanodeath, ever. Not even once.

That said, plenty of people consider the intense nausea worth it. More than a few Guardsmen have lost their jobs over the years for abusing slipspace. You can't turn around or change direction at all once in slipspace, but they'd take the shortest routes possible or go out of their way to maximize the number of transitions, just to feel that high more often. They all get caught for doing that in pretty short order, and few are stupid enough. But I guess for the ones that kept doing it, it was worth it.

As for the slipspace tunnels themselves, they're basically singularities you can enter. Invisible tears in the fabric of space-time. Being singularities, they've always proven basically inscrutable to scientists, who've never made much headway in their study of slips. But at some point in the dim and distant past, someone gave us the Becker drive. I guess his or her name must have been Becker, but even my datasphere has no information on the inventor.

All we know is that the drive opened up the galaxy to humanity, and we began to comb it for moons and planets we wouldn't have to spend a thousand years terraforming, although we did that, too.

When you're in slipspace, sensors show nothing. Zero data. Not even a view of a blank void. Peering out of a hull sensor while in slipspace is like going temporarily blind, and not something I make a practice of.

The only reason we can exit slipspace at predictable coordinates is because your speed is always constant inside it, and the distance traveled is directly proportionate to the distance in real-space, though of course you travel much, much farther.

Nowadays, pirates, Troubleshooters, and Subverse space-scrapers comprise almost all slipspace traffic. No one seems to care that humanity never figured out how the hell slip travel works. We just accept that it does work and leave it alone.

When the nausea passes, I wipe off my chin with the back of my hand. The crew are all avoiding eye contact. "Deactivate crew," I say, without preamble. It's not the most heartwarming way to say goodbye for several months, but it gets the job done.

Next, I summon Dice from his closet, so I can look him over and assess the mechanic's work. Normally, I'd have done that before we left Brinktown, but the brass' ridiculous timeline prevented that.

As expected, the tuneup looks great. At my command, Dice stands in the space between the command seat and my cabin hatch, leaving me just enough room to circle him, using my index knuckle to knock on his plating here and there, yanking on connectors to make sure they're solid. I get him to lift his left arm, rotate it all around, hold it straight out. Then I have him repeat the process with his right.

"Actuators seem good," I mutter. "How many fingers is this?" I hold up my hand with my index, middle, and ring fingers held tight together.

"Three," Dice says. "Did you steal that framed photo?"

I follow his gaze to the picture, which still leans against the command seat. Then I study his emotionless triangle face while I attempt to keep mine just as neutral.

"I'm sure you must have," he continues. "And it looks like someone stole something from you as well." Dice snickers, which sounds more or less human, other than the slight reverb every Lambton bot speaks with. "A trade between thieves."

"What are you talking about?"

"That thing you have stuffed into your holster," he says. "It's a 3D-printed replica. A fake."

My stomach turns to ice as I fish my laser pistol from its holster. I remember letting Harmony see it. Her bag lay next to her on my bunk. And then the dog barked, distracting me…

When I try to remove the pistol's charge pack, I can't. Dice is right: the thing is a fake, though it's weighted just like the real thing.

Even if I was willing to turn around and fall even further behind schedule, I couldn't. Once you're in slipspace, there's no turning around. No changing course.

My own daughter disarmed me, and whatever she's planning, there's nothing I can do about it.

TUNIS

1

It takes four and a half months to reach the Junction System, and the time passes like a river of toxic sludge.

More than once, I'm tempted to enter nanodeath to escape the circling thoughts about what Harmony might have done with my laser pistol. I figure chances are pretty good that whatever it was, she probably got caught doing it, meaning the pistol definitely got traced back to me. That would spell the end of my military career.

But I don't succumb to the siren song of nanodeath, and I don't switch the crew on either, even though I'm tempted to do that too. That's how I know this situation's really getting to me.

Instead, I kill time with an even more intense exercise routine than usual. Calisthenics, running on the treadmill, jogging awkwardly around the bridge with Maneater, working my way up the weight settings doing squats and deadlifts with the grav-bar—I wear myself out enough to sleep like a rock at night. Just the way I like it.

I also clean the *Ares* way more than it really needs to be cleaned. The head stays sparkling, and the floor reminds me of the old barracks floor during Basic, right after it was scoured with a toothbrush by some seaman recruit who'd done something stupid or weak.

When the Guard buys partner bots for Troubleshooters, they specifically request that Lambton Industries send them models that can't be installed with cleaning subroutines. But I'm fine with that, honestly. I don't even like having Dice present while I'm sweeping and scrubbing. Long experience says that it's an invitation for endless commentary on the biological human condition.

"After the first time you clean her, any dust you find aboard the *Ares* consists of your own dead skin cells," he'll say. Or, whenever I'm doing laundry: "That unit is incapable of removing all the fecal matter from your underwear." (My uniform's designed to repel dirt, but not my underwear. Probably for good reason.)

As long as Dice stays in his closet, I'm happy enough to do the chores myself. It gives me something to do. Sims don't appeal to me—in fact, ever since I graduated from Assessment and Selection they repulse me—and sometimes I need a break from the unending cycle of sleeping, eating, exercising, and reading.

Mostly, I'm desperate to keep my mind occupied. Not just to stop myself from worrying about Harmony…but also to avoid another breakdown like the one I had during the slipspace journey to Earth. But I can't think about that, and the moment it pops into my mind, I scramble to fill it with other thoughts.

At last, we arrive in Junction, home to Tunis. My mission briefing says the Subverse here is working fine, but the electronic lock on the server room door has been compromised. Could be someone's scraping sensitive data from the machines at this very moment. Whatever's going on, a door breach means the servers' location has been compromised, which is enough for the brass to send me to check things out.

"Good morning, Captain," Glory Belflower says once I activate the crew in preparation for slipspace transition. "I trust you had a pleasant journey."

"And you," I say. I decide not to correct Belflower by mentioning that technically it's late afternoon, Tunis time. I'm trying to start off the second encounter with my crew on the right foot. To tell the truth, I have a lump in my throat that feels egg-sized, and it's not just anticipation of the impending nausea. I'm dreading what brainprints I might receive after our arrival in Junction System.

The transition is as uncomfortable as always, and once we're through I walk to the laundry chute in the bulkhead with the fabric barf bag, wiping my mouth with the back of my hand.

Halfway to the planet Tunis, we still haven't received any brainprints, either from the Calabar Brinktown or the brass. I can't decide if that's a good sign or a bad sign. Probably, it doesn't mean anything: unless they dispatched it within a few hours of the *Ares* leaving Calabar, any spacescraper would need more time to arrive here.

Part of me feels like I should preemptively send a brainprint back to Calabar, if only to warn Dorothy that Harmony took my pistol. But that was four and a half months ago. I'm sure Harmony's already done whatever damage she was going to do, and anyway, admitting to having my weapon stolen by a sixteen-year-old isn't a great way to keep my career.

For a moment, I wonder how Harmony's mother, Marissa, would react to her daughter's theft. But then, she probably pays us little enough attention that she'll never notice.

"Junction," Tobias Worldworn says, studying his station's display, sounding wistful. "This is the Subverse where I lived before joining the Guard."

"You mean *you* lived here? Not another iteration of you?" Belflower asks, eyeing him through narrowed slits. She gets as close to Worldworn as her station's railing will allow. "Why didn't you just send a copy to join the Guard? Unless you were running from something?"

The old man shrugs. "You can't actually live vicariously

through a copy, Lieutenant Commander. *I'm* the one who wanted to join the Guard. I wasn't interested in sending a copy."

The way Belflower's lips tighten suggest she's not completely satisfied with that answer. Either way, she turns to me next. "Captain, will we be versecasting our mission to Tunis?"

"No," I say, though I suspect she already knows the answer.

Whether she did or not, Belflower puts on a good show of acting appalled. "Captain Pikeman, I really must urge you to change your mind. All the most popular Guardsmen versecast their missions. Considering who lives on Tunis, making this your first versecast would be an excellent start to putting extra tokens in your pocket—"

"And in yours."

"Well, yes. We all would benefit. But the sponsorship deals that would present themselves to a Troubleshooter such as yourself, who's never versecast before…well, I'm sure you're aware of the reputation you've built up. You've become a figure of mystique, not just in the Andora Sector, but in the entire galactic Subverse. Word of your exploits travels to and fro, constantly. It seems barely a spacescraper arrives without fresh news of your deeds. But no one's witnessed them for themselves. They're starving for your versecasts, sir."

I frown at her. "So, when you asked if we'd be versecasting Tunis, you already knew the answer. You know I never versecast."

Her expression falters, but she recovers quickly. "Yes. The question was rhetorical, Captain."

"Uh huh. Do you think I could bother you to put aside your fame-lust long enough to check over my ship after her trip through slipspace?"

Lips tightening again, she turns to her task. I smile to myself.

Worldworn takes us through Tunis' atmosphere with a deft hand. In fact, I'm pretty sure it's the smoothest atmospheric entry I've ever experienced, with heat shield and air brakes applied at just the right times to minimize jostling.

"Have you served on a Troubleshooter's ship before?" I ask him as we sail toward our planetside destination; a place called the Grotto.

"I haven't, sir."

"How do you know how to pull off such a smooth entry?" I'm the only one aboard who'd be affected by a bumpy ride, and it's unusual for an upload to take biological considerations into account like that.

Worldworn smiles, though he remains focused on his station, lowering the vessel the rest of the distance under anti-grav. "A simple combination of skill and empathy. I knew that, as a Trajectory Officer, I'd be responsible for taking a ship through plenty of atmospheres, so I subjected myself to every entry and exit simulation I could find, each subject to different conditions."

I nod, impressed.

"We have clearance to land on Number Three, one of the Grotto's four spacepads," Aphrodite reports, blond hair swinging as she turns to relay the news. "Apparently, the closest thing they have to an enclosed spaceport is Arthur Eliot's personal hangar, and it's in use."

"Very good. Put us down where directed, Worldworn."

"Aye."

I catch myself looking at Aphrodite as Worldworn lines up the *Ares* as skillfully as he brought her through Tunis' atmosphere. I curse myself silently, vowing not to let that happen again. It's incredibly inappropriate for a captain to ogle one of his crew.

Still, I have a good feeling about this crew. Could be they'll actually turn out all right. There's nothing in my past experience to suggest that, but a little irrational optimism never hurt anyone.

Endless, hard-packed desert stretches to every horizon, where ground meets sky in a shimmering haze. As the *Ares* sinks, my view of the wasteland is replaced by the jewel that is the Grotto.

Surrounded by massive rock formations that reach for the sky like grasping talons, the Grotto is named for the enormous caves carved out of those rocks by bots wielding nanodrills and laser torches. Inside those hollows rear the shaded buildings that once formed Tunis University.

I spent part of the slipspace journey flicking through pages of information about Tunis. My datasphere holds enough information about the planet's history to have kept me busy for nine months, but I was mostly interested in the former university. Apparently, it used to be one of the galaxy's most coveted schools. Using the *Ares'* sensors as my eyes, I can see why.

A tiny paradise carved from the desert. Enough imported water to turn the Grotto into an oasis, with broad palm fronds providing shade at noon, when the system's sun rises high enough to glare down between the towering rocks. According to my datasphere, the Eliots have been diligent about maintaining the university's buildings, preventing them from crumbling like the rest of the galaxy's structures have. Those structures were supposed to last for millennia, according to the engineers who built them, but that turned out to be nothing more than a sales pitch. They boasted advanced construction techniques, enabled by the same nanotechnology that gave birth to the Fount, but history has made fools of them, just like the rest of us. The galaxy's crumbling at a much faster rate than they claimed it would.

Anyway. Humans have always been attracted to places like the Grotto, each one representing a battle fought and won against nature. In the years leading up to the Fall, humanity fought many such battles, using their bots as proxy fighters. But in the end, nature won the war, didn't she?

With the *Ares* settled on the spacepad, I stand from the command seat and unsling my gun belt from where I hung it on the back. Only Dice knows the laser pistol's a fake, and I already ordered him not to let on to anyone. I have no idea how long I'll be able to maintain the ruse, especially if I run into a hostile. But I intend to keep it up for as long as I can.

Outside the ship, the air is even worse than back in my Brinktown, even in the later afternoon. It feels like I'm sucking it straight from a furnace. I cough and force myself to slow down my breathing.

"Welcome to the Grotto," says an elderly man standing at attention at the bottom of the metal stairs leading down from the spacepad. He salutes me, and I salute back. He's wearing a Guardsman uniform.

My gaze wanders past him, toward the sound of falling water and squealing children, laughing and splashing. A broad pool graces the Grotto's center, and water arcs from a fountain in intricate patterns; a lattice of liquid. A peaceful place.

I don't belong here.

"I'm surprised to find you actually living in the Grotto," I say as I fall in beside the Guardsman and we start to cross the palm-shaded expanse. "Sergeant Wile, isn't it?"

"That's right. Didn't the records tell you I'd be here?"

"They did. It's just unusual for a Guardsman to live among civilians, especially a Guardsman in charge of a terminal. It's…not recommended."

Wile shrugs. "Mr. Eliot insisted on it. He said he wouldn't have me living by myself out in the Tunis wilderness. Not on his planet. He even had his bots relocate the terminal here."

"It's against protocol."

"He said that Eliots get to bend Guard protocol, seeing as how they founded it." Wile sniffed. "With all due respect, Commander, everyone here understands the nature of my job. They know how important it is that no one else access the terminal."

"Is that why the server room location's been compromised?"

Wile's jaw tightens under my glare, and after a few seconds, he averts his eyes.

"Take me to the terminal," I say.

"Yes, sir."

We walk without talking, then. Above us, palm fronds stir, and their rustling fills the silence. There's a boxing match happening up ahead, on a rubberized surface to the left of the path we're on. After a few seconds, I realize I'm staring. Something like that would never happen in a Brinktown. Two men given a controlled outlet for their aggression? Not a chance. Brinktown men are either meek or ostracized.

"This is it," Wile says when we reach a short lane leading up to a red-brick, three-story structure whose roof joins seamlessly with the stone above.

"You live *here?*"

"I have a downstairs apartment."

"Still."

He leads me to a recessed side entrance and opens the door, gesturing for me to enter ahead of him.

I whistle as I walk through a well-appointed kitchen, followed by a dining room featuring angular, modern-looking furniture. Modern for centuries ago, that is, when humanity still cared about advancing meatspace fashion.

"This is a far cry from the tin-roofed shacks where most planet-side Guardsmen live."

Wile doesn't answer.

"Give me your ID coin."

He fishes it out of his pocket, holding it out for my datasphere to scan, but his hand shakes too badly for it to get a read. I snatch it from him and hold it steady.

The coin turns emerald, and this time I have no reason to doubt he is who the coin says he is. "Show me the terminal."

After five minutes alone in an unused bedroom with the terminal, I have the server room's location and I'm ready to leave. Wile sits at the dining table when I pass through the room, and I give him a raised-eyebrow look as I cross to the kitchen.

"Should I arrange some accommodations for you?" he asks before I pass out of sight.

Pausing, I glance back at him. "I'll sleep on my ship."

Then, something catches my eye through the window behind

him—a figure standing in the deepening twilight, facing the window and peering straight in.

He's wearing green robes and a hood that partially casts his face in shadow. Somehow, I'm positive it's the same guy who was hanging around the outside of my ship back on Earth.

"I have to go," I say, sprinting through the kitchen and wrenching open the door to the outside. I leave it swinging open as I run around the building in pursuit of my new robed stalker.

2

At first, it's like Siberia: by the time I make it outside, the robed figure has vanished, despite there being no buildings close enough for him to have run to in time. Then I notice the twin rows of thick hedges that run parallel to the front of this building before angling slightly to run parallel to the next.

That has to be where he went.

The hard-packed sand gives decent traction as I sprint close to the greenery, listening for labored breathing coming from the other side. How fast can you run in robes, anyway? But this guy escaped me back on Earth, and I'm not feeling all that confident I'll catch up to him here, either.

Mostly, I'm feeling a bit crazy that I jumped so quickly to the conclusion that this has to be the same guy. What are the chances? Who would want to track me, and what means would anyone have to do it, besides that? We didn't detect any other ships back in Sol —at least, my lousy excuse for an OPO didn't tell me if we did. But I guess it's possible someone was watching us from one of the planets, and then…

What? Followed us to the Calabar Brinktown, then watched again to see which slip coords we made for when we left? Sure, entry coords tell you something about a ship's destination. But without the exit coords, there's a good chance you'll end up deep in the black, far from any star.

The more I think about it, the more I want to know. I run faster, the hedge flashing past on my right. Then the hard-packed sand gives way to a softer patch, and the going is harder, but surely that shouldn't matter. Surely someone with a Guardsman's conditioning should be able to catch a guy in robes.

I round the corner, so that I'm running between the hedge and the next building, a pillared white monstrosity that gleams even in the dusk. My eyes are glued to the place where the foliage ends up ahead, and unbelievably, the figure emerges, way ahead of me. He's running flat-out for the building after the white one—a jet-black triangle whose roof slopes back into the rock for Fount knows how far.

Next thing, he's through the glass doors, darting across what looks like a dimly lit lobby. The shadows swallow him, and I force my legs to move faster.

I shove through the doors at top speed, making its hydraulics wheeze. Across the vast lobby is the only light source: a propped-open dark oak door, through which illumination trickles through. I make for it, footfalls echoing in the empty space.

A second before I rush the door, I yank my fake pistol from its holster, raising it with my left hand cupped underneath my right as though to steady my aim.

It takes me a few seconds to process what's waiting for me on the other side. The green-robed figure is nowhere in sight. Instead, row after row of scarlet theater seats march down toward a curved stage bordered by five sets of navy curtains. Three children stand on the stage, frozen in tableau, their eyes on me.

Blinking, I lower my weapon and frown.

"Will you be in our play?" calls the center child—a girl who looks to be around eleven. Her hair falls in auburn curls past her shoulders, and she's wearing a ruffled blue dress that's at least a size too big for her.

"Uh. What?"

"I asked would you be in our play. We need someone to play the part of Polonius. You look old enough."

"He can't be in it," says the boy standing to her right, his cheeks dimpled in consternation. "Look at his face."

"So what?" the girl shoots back. "Polonius could have had a red mark on his face like that. It's not about what's on the outside, Thomas. It's about what's inside. In this case, acting ability."

That's pretty cliche, but I find myself charmed by it anyway. I take a moment to glance around the theater—between the rows and along the mahogany-paneled walls. Then I tuck the replica laser pistol back into its holster and start down one of the two aisles that trisect the theater's seating.

"Did you kids see a man wearing green robes?"

The girl shakes her head. The unnamed boy on her left remains statue-like, still staring at me with wide eyes. "No man came in here, except you," she says.

"Does the lobby lead anywhere else?"

I watch her eyes drift upward. "The balcony."

I whirl around, fingers brushing the butt of the pistol as I scan the seats above. Nothing that I can see, but the figure could be crouching behind the barrier.

Except, I'm starting to think I'm crazy again. "Did you hear footsteps running across the lobby?" I ask, turning back toward the stage. I'm standing halfway between it and the entrance, now.

"Just yours," the girl says.

"Hmm." The strong possibility that the figure isn't real weighs heavily on my thoughts. It may be time to change the subject. I squint at her. "I'm way too young to play Polonius."

"You're *much* older than I am, and I'm playing Ophelia. Besides, people didn't live as long back then."

"I could do Hamlet, maybe."

The girl rolls her eyes. "You just barged into our rehearsal and now you're trying to assign yourself the lead role? Typical male."

Chuckling at her precociousness, I continue down the stairs to check for something. "Is someone else already playing Hamlet?" I ask, eyes on the ceiling over the stage.

"Are you seriously offering to be in our play?" she says. The other children have started to relax a little more. Their eyes are less wide, and they've resumed the aimless fidgeting typical of children.

"No," I say, reaching the foot of the stage. I point toward the ceiling, at a dully reflective, jet-black fixture, a polygon with many facets. "But you have an Auto Actor. Why not use it to fill in whatever parts you're missing?"

"It's broken."

"Where's the interface?"

The girl points to her left. "Just backstage."

"Mind if I take a look?"

She shrugs.

I climb onto the raised platform, noting the seam near the front of the stage that indicates it retracts to reveal an orchestra pit beneath. A right turn brings me to an alcove that houses a wall-mounted terminal. Within seconds, my datasphere syncs with it and begins diagnosing the problem.

Guardsman dataspheres represent the next best thing to having a planetary intranet linked by spacescraper to a galactic internet. That doesn't exist anymore outside the Subverse, but military-grade dataspheres hold an amount of information comparable to one of the old planetary nets.

Civilian dataspheres do not. Just as biological humans are now charged a large sum to upload to the Subverse, non-Guardsmen also pay dearly for information. Why wouldn't they? After Bacchus Corp vacuumed up the vast majority of the species, barely anyone was left in the real to get together and fight for their rights.

It doesn't take long for my datasphere to serve up step-by-step instructions for fixing the Auto Actor. All it takes is a simple reformat, and I have the last version of the firmware ever made for it, ready for me to reinstall.

Why would a soldier need to have Auto Actor firmware at his disposal, you ask? Why not? Information is power, and we sure aren't well-provisioned in other ways. Giving us a wealth of information is the least the Five Families could allow.

Ten minutes or so later, the Auto Actor finishes rebooting after the firmware reinstall, and I turn toward the trio of thespians, flicking through the device's library of plays using my datasphere, which is still connected to it. I find Hamlet, select a scene, and execute. The prince appears onstage, dressed in ridiculous, puffy clothing. "To be or not to be," he says. I turn him off.

"So what's the plan?" I say. "Broadcast your play through the Subverse? Live from the Grotto?"

The girl continues to speak for the three of them. "That's what my father asked. But no. This is just for the enjoyment of the people who live and work here. It's more special, that way."

I raise my eyebrows. Now she's speaking my language. On a hunch, I say: "Your father?"

"Arthur Eliot. I'm Faelyn Eliot."

"I see." I was wondering whether I'd actually meet an Eliot while I was here. Here's my answer. The daughter of the biological head of one of the Five Families. No wonder she's precocious. "Well, good luck with your play," I say, starting back up the aisle.

"The Auto Actor's just for practicing," she calls after me. "I want every role filled by real people."

"Good luck," I call back, meaning it.

"You can be Hamlet if you really want."

"I'm already committed to a role in a different performance." Pausing, I glance back over my shoulder. "Shouldn't you kids get home, before the scorpions come out?" Based on my slipspace reading, Tunis is lousy with the things.

"My father's bots keep them out of the Grotto, for the most part. There are snakes, though."

"Then you should get home. Your mothers must be wondering where you are." But I continue on up the stairs without lecturing them further, since I have no actual authority over these children beyond giving good advice.

Something bothers me about Faelyn's fear of snakes, and I query my datasphere as I cross the theater lobby. Just as I thought: Tunis has no snakes. That's odd.

An alert pings my datasphere as I cross the Grotto, informing me I have a brainprint waiting for me. My heart makes an escape attempt up my throat before I can get a hold of myself, willing my body back to the state of calm readiness where all Guardsmen are supposed to live. Guardsmen that want to survive, that is, in a cold, empty galaxy that can afford to wait for months, sometimes years, between its attempts to kill you.

There's no question what news that brainprint will bring: the aftermath of whatever Harmony was planning to do with my laser pistol and the family bot. The only mystery is whether I'm about to lose my job.

I decide to take the 'print sitting in the command seat. It might be the last time I sit there as captain of the *Ares*, but until I'm discharged, I remain fully in command.

Instead of a Guard officer, my Aunt Dorothy appears before me, which brings a measure of relief.

Not much relief, though: her face is pale, stricken. This is Dorothy Pikeman as she was four and a half months ago, when the brainprint was taken and sent on a spacescraper through slipspace to find me. A brainprint is a temporary upload of your consciousness at the time of sending. Once it reaches the recipient, that version of your consciousness then has the conversation for you, and a recording is sent back to you to see how it went. The idea is that the consciousness will say what you would have said—this is how people communicate efficiently across interstellar distances that take months to traverse. Once we're finished talking, Dorothy's brainprint will be deleted, and another spacescraper will take the recording back to her.

"Harmony's your daughter, Joe Pikeman, there's no question of that now. I always prayed to the Fount she wouldn't turn out like you, but now look what's happened."

"Nice to see you too," I say, then shake my head, unable to enjoy sarcasm like I normally can. "Just tell me what happened."

"This might top anything you've ever done. She stole the *Europa's Gift.*"

"She…wait. She *stole* it?"

"Who knows where in the galaxy she is right now? She could be dead, Joe. And it's all thanks to you."

But I'm still processing what Dorothy just told me. The *Europa's Gift* is the only spaceship in the Calabar Brinktown. *Was* the only spaceship, I guess—owned by Daniel Sterling. Harmony's absentee grandfather.

Harmony's words echo in my head: *I'm going to make him pay. Someday, I'll make him pay.*

Clearly, she meant a lot sooner than she was letting on.

"Joe?" my aunt says, voice shrill.

"How?" I manage. "How did she do it?"

"No one's completely figured that out yet, as far as I can tell," Dorothy says. "And I should know, considering the law bots have questioned me about a million times in the last two days. The security footage shows her with a laser pistol, but they think it's a replica from Memcon. Either way, she didn't have to use it. Every security door opened for her—P3P plugged into it, and it opened." P3P is the old family bot. "They think she had 'worms' loaded onto him, whatever they are. But they said these worms were custom-made to crack the type of security door Sterling was using. They got her all the way to the bridge of his ship, and she was gone."

Dorothy's been holding it together, but now she breaks down, sobs racking her virtual proxy's body. I'd have some sympathy for her, but I know her well enough to predict what's coming next.

"What did you do to her, Joe? What did you say to her, when you visited? Whatever it was, it drove her to this."

Ah, yes. The "blame Joe" step. Classic. "No," I say. "It wasn't me. She's been planning this for a long time."

Clearly, I was just carrying the final piece she needed: a laser pistol, in case she ran into any trouble hijacking *Europa's Gift*. Or out there in the bleak. A teenage girl, by herself.

I'd be impressed, if I didn't feel sick. Part of me wants to laugh, but a large part wants to scream.

"You have to fix this, Joe," Dorothy's saying. "You have to *do* something."

"I'll do what I can," I say. But I'm not sure what that is, yet. Harmony could be anywhere by now. And wherever she is, she's carrying the laser pistol registered to me. A ticking time bomb to explode my career or my sanity, probably both.

I end the conversation, willing my ship to transmit the recording to the next spacescraper it detects. I can't look at my aunt anymore. Hell, I can barely face the truth:

If I lose Harmony, I'll never forgive myself.

3

The next day, I have my datasphere wake me early enough that a look through the outside sensors tells me barely anyone's awake in the Grotto. Just a couple of figures shrouded in the early-morning gloom as they wander the old university grounds.

Good. Unlike Sergeant Wile, I want as little to do with the people living here as possible. What time I leave, what direction I went, whether it seems likely I'll return—all details I like to leave as fuzzy as possible, as a matter of general policy. The more information you leak into your environment, the more likely it is to find its way into the hands of an enemy who'll use it to gut you.

At first, I figure the two men I can see for custodians, but I want to make sure. My datasphere takes the sensor on a zoom, cleaning up the image for me. One of the men carries a black bag with him as he picks up trash and drops it inside, but the other actually turns out to be Sergeant Wile, marching crisply through the Grotto, casting his gaze here and there.

What's he looking for? Maybe he does this every morning, and he's more vigilant than I thought.

"Maybe he's looking for snakes," I mutter, and chuckle.

I will the sensor feed away, and the bridge takes its place. I'm sitting in the command seat, feeling like I could go back to sleep right here. Sleeping in the seat during the months I had good old Sheldon aboard—I think I got too used to it.

At my command, my TOPO and OPO appear at their respective stations, exchange glances, then turn to me.

"Captain," Worldworn says, saluting. "Where are our Weapon Systems and Engineering officers?"

"We shouldn't need them today," I say. "This way, there'll be less chatter during our trip across Tunis."

Aphrodite salutes too, but it doesn't stop her from questioning me. "Seems unwise to leave our Engineer turned off."

"Yes," I say. "There's a nanoscopic chance the same systems that showed all-green yesterday will fail today. There's also a chance the scorpions of Tunis will gain sentience and mount a ground-to-air attack as we fly over the desert. But I'd rather risk those outcomes than endure Belflower's nagging or Asterisk's stupidity. Understood?"

"Yes, sir," the chief says, though her eyebrows are hiked halfway up her forehead. She glances at Worldworn, but he avoids her gaze, his face a study in neutrality.

"Take us into the air, Lieutenant," I say. "You'll find the server room's coords at the top of your readout."

"Aye," Worldworn says, and minutes later, we're in the air.

Not wanting to block out the entire bridge while the *Ares* is moving, I position a rectangle showing a view of the planet's surface in the bottom-right quadrant of my vision.

Shades of beige, brown, and white flash past, dotted with scraggly black—Tunis' version of vegetation, outside the Grotto. I doubt palm trees and hedgerows would survive even there if it wasn't for constant human attention.

Occasionally, colors I don't expect appear. Swirls of green and blue. Could be lichen, but mineral deposits are more likely, I think. I'll look it up later. I enjoy that part of the job. With its hundreds of billions of stars and trillions of planets, you never know what configuration the galaxy's going to cough up next.

The view helps me take my mind off the fact I don't have a working weapon. My conscious mind, anyway. Somewhat. My subconscious is clearly pretty concerned: I catch my finger tapping my holster nervously, and I force it to stop.

It should be fine. My orders mentioned a faulty security door, but said nothing about damage to the servers themselves. Sure, could be some nerdy crook is in there trying to jack sensitive data to sell on the black market, but how much of a fight is someone like that really going to put up?

I'm kidding myself, I know that. If someone breached the door with data-jacking in mind, they're probably serious. It would mean pirates, most likely. I need to be careful.

Problem is, the terminal guarded by the mighty Sergeant Wile told me that the server room is hidden inside a maze of a cave system surrounded by thousands of miles of nothing. If I run into pirates underground with no way to defend myself, it's gonna get hairy. If I'm shot, the chance is basically zero of a friendly stumbling upon me as I gasp my last breaths.

But I should try to keep things light-hearted.

"Putting her down now, sir," Worldworn says.

"Acknowledged," I mumble, but I'm staring at the expanding Tunis landscape, unable to spot anything that could be a cave entrance. "Where is it?"

Worldworn sniffs—an affectation, the sort that ignites my hatred of all things Subverse. Uploads don't need to sniff. "See that tangle of shrubs, there?"

I squint, willing my datasphere to identify the plant and call up some information on it. "Those are brambles," I say. Huh. No doubt that growth is part of what's keeping the server room concealed. But if the brass thought I was going to wade through a sea of thorns, they must forget what it's like to be at my pay grade.

"No," I say. "Don't land. OPO, try to figure out where the cave entrance is likely to be. I'm grappling down."

"Yes, sir," she says, but I can tell she's not a fan of the decision.

A few minutes later, I'm dangling at the end of a hook, lowering toward the brambles on a nanofiber line that feeds from a dispenser on the airlock bulkhead.

I peer into the distance, where the sun hovers a few inches over the horizon, and I consult the datasphere overlay for the cardinal direction. Then I look back down. "Nudge us a couple feet to the south-south east," I say over comlink.

"Aye," Worldworn answers, and the *Ares* moves, swinging me slightly.

"There. That's perfect."

I slip neatly between two bunches of thorns, and my feet touch down on solid rock at the bottom of a shallow hole in the ground.

At first, I can't see the entrance to the tunnels. Maybe we have the wrong spot. I unhook the line from my suit's belt to crouch below the brambles.

There it is: a shadowed gap barely a foot high. Staring at it for a few seconds, tamping down claustrophobia already trying to get a hold of me, I try to imagine what installing this server room must have been like. The scale of the excavation it must have taken. Open a giant hole in the ground somewhere a couple miles to the north, set up your collapsible crane, spend a few weeks lowering equipment into position. Spend several more painstaking weeks covering up your work with sand and stone so it looks like untouched virgin desert again.

All for just one small part of one sector of humanity's new digital home.

"Okay," I tell myself. "Enough stalling." Certain it won't fit through, I unseal my helmet, take it off, and place it on the ground nearby. Then, lying on my back, I scrabble forward, propelling my feet through the gap and willing night vision on as the rest of my body passes through.

The ground gives way a lot quicker than I expected, and I fall a short distance. The impact sends a painful shock through my ankles, and I grunt. Should have poked my head through for a look first. Sloppy.

Lesson learned, I make a careful study of every inch before progressing onto it. Luckily, cold, unbroken sandstone seems the norm from here on out, with occasional crystal stalactites sticking down like fangs. Which doesn't mean it's a good idea to drop my guard. My orders called this place a maze for a reason. Plenty of off-shooting tunnels, and natural alcoves for enemies to hide in. My datasphere paints a glowing yellow path on the rock for me to follow, like a weirdly uniform stretch of bioluminescent fungus.

The good news is, if anyone's here, I doubt they know I'm coming. The ship's sensors didn't pick up on any observers, organic or otherwise, and they're sophisticated enough to spot even nanodrones.

Still, I make my way through the tunnels with my fake laser pistol up, figuring it's best to appear armed, even if I'm really not.

That turns out to be a miscalculation, because it's probably why whoever spots me starts shooting.

Just before I reach the server room door, my night vision blooms out, going bright green-white—someone's shining a light from up ahead. Before I can react, a gunshot booms in the confined space, followed closely by another. Both miss, but one hits close enough to spray me with shards of rock.

I flinch away. As my night vision adjusts, my eyes fall on a figure up ahead, partially concealed by the next turn in the rock. He's lining up his next shot.

I throw myself back as the weapon booms again. I'm supine on the rock, now, scrabbling across it, till my body is partially around a bend. Part of me is still exposed, I know, and when the weapon fires again without hitting me, I know it's more luck than I'm entitled too.

Scrambling to my feet, I start barreling back the way I came, hoping that, whoever my attacker is, the fact he's using a kinetic weapon means he's under-equipped. Because if he has night vision too, I might be screwed.

"Worldworn," I say over comlink. "Turn on the WSO."

Nothing comes back. I was afraid of that. I'm too deep for the signal to penetrate the sandstone.

I keep trying, and finally, my breath getting more ragged, I manage to get through.

"I read you, sir," the lieutenant says.

"Position the *Ares* back where it was." Right now, she's sitting on the sand where I ordered Worldworn to land after lowering me. I told him to take off at the barest hint of movement, since I left the outer airlock hatch open with the line dangling out. "I need an evac. Activate the WSO, tell him there might be a hostile coming out after me, and for Fount's sake tell him not to shoot me."

"Will do, Captain."

I check over my shoulder before piling on more speed despite my burning lungs and legs. Doesn't matter how good your conditioning is, mortal terror will tire you out faster than anything else.

My night vision blooms out again, whitening for a second before switching off automatically. That's good. It does this in response to bright light ahead: the exit.

With a running leap, I throw myself up the steep incline I fell down earlier, fingers latching onto a narrow crevice. I haul myself up and wriggle through the gap.

The hook dangles there, waiting for me, and my opinion of Worldworn ratchets up another notch. My helmet's still here, too. I shove it on, not waiting for it to seal before I secure the hook on my belt. "Good to go," I tell the lieutenant, grabbing the line with both hands.

In less than a minute, I'm back on the bridge, stowing my

helmet before taking the command seat. A glance through one of the *Ares'* belly sensors tells me my attacker still hasn't made an appearance.

When I will the sensor's view away, I see my OPO's staring at me from her station. She glances meaningfully toward the WSO station, and I follow her gaze to where the freshly activated ensign stares at me with wide eyes.

"He's out of sorts," Aphrodite says. "Keeps asking why he wasn't activated before we left the Grotto. I doubt he would have had the concentration needed to properly cover you just now, if you'd needed that."

"What's your point?" I ask, but I already know.

"Maybe next time you'll activate every crewmember."

4

Only by pulling rank do I manage to extract Arthur Eliot's whereabouts from a reluctant Sergeant Wile.

"Shooting scorpions out past the western border of the Grotto," Wile says at last. Beyond him, Faelyn Eliot sits on the lip of the Fountain, working on repairing a toy drone. Presumably the toy belongs to the boy sitting next to her, who's watching her work with an anxious expression.

Fixing the toy drone reminds me of the sort of thing Harmony would have been doing at Faelyn's age. Come to think of it, they kind of look alike. That fills me with a cocktail of emotions, few of them pleasant. Please, Fount, let Harm be okay.

Tearing my eyes away from Eliot's daughter, I start west.

"I wouldn't interrupt him, if I were you," Wile calls after me.

It should already be obvious I don't consider Wile a good source of advice, so I decide not to bother saying it. Hell, I've already disregarded good advice from my OPO today, so the sergeant doesn't stand much of a chance at all.

"What's for dinner?" I ask Arthur Eliot when I find him a few hundred meters into the desert, engaged in exactly the activity Wile described: shotgunning scorpions with…well, with a shotgun. More kinetic weaponry. I flash back to my recent experience in the caves and frown.

When he turns, Eliot staggers a bit, almost tripping over a scorpion corpse. To his credit, he lowers the weapon as he pivots, instead of pointing it at me like some Fount damned yokel. "Who are you?"

I pop out my ID coin and flick it toward him—an easy catch. At the apex of its arc, the sun glints off the metal. Then the coin lands at Eliot's feet. A full second later, his gaze follows it down.

Yep. Arthur Eliot is drunk.

I hate meeting childhood heroes.

"Guardsman," Eliot mumbles, and my datasphere has to replay the word for me so I can make out what he said. "Troubleshooter," he adds.

"That's right," I say. "And since you're the biological head of the family that created the Guard, I'm wondering if you can tell me what you're doing out here putting yourself at risk when you have a family back in the Grotto who depend on you." Not to mention the Guard itself. We're pretty dependent on a living Eliot to get what supplies and funding we get, though a lot of Guardsmen are pretty dissatisfied with the job Arthur here has been doing on that front.

"The fewer scorpions the better," Eliot says. He raises a hand toward his chest, where a flask hangs suspended from a thong, but he hesitates before returning the hand to the shotgun's stock.

"You have more than enough bots to keep them out of the Grotto," I say.

"Why'd we have to bring scorpions to Tunis, anyway?" Eliot says, apparently ignoring my perfectly good point.

"Insect control, I would guess."

The corner of Eliot's mouth peels back in an ugly sneer. "The cure's worse than the disease."

"With all due respect, Mr. Eliot, you're not helping anyone, out here. You have people back there who need you. Do you realize how lucky you are, to get to raise a family in a place like this?"

Part of me expects him to sneer again at the idea that an Eliot might be lucky. "An Eliot is an Eliot," I expect him to tell me. It's just what you expect from people born sucking the silver spoon. But he doesn't say anything, and his expression changes to something that looks a lot like shame.

"Luck is a matter of perspective," he says at last, again so quiet that my datasphere has to play it back.

I nod. "What can you tell me about the Fallen living out in the desert?"

Eliot blinks at me as my words work their way through his soggy brain. I doubt he'd be able to feign surprise convincingly in the state he's in, so when surprise finally dawns on his face, I believe it. "Fallen?" he says. "They're still alive?"

"So you know about them."

"They crashed in an asteroid mining vessel halfway through last year. Satellite imagery told us they weren't heading for the Grotto, so we left them alone. There's been no sign of them for months. I assumed they died out there—nights as cold as ours. Planet full of scorpions."

"Surely you know about the trouble with the Junction server?"

Eliot nods.

"And it didn't cross your mind that they might be the ones messing with it? Some warning would have been nice."

No response.

"Where'd they get the weapons?" I say.

"Didn't know they had any." Eliot's eyes fall to his shotgun, and they widen slightly, like he just realized how bad this looks. "They must have had them in their mining station, out in the asteroid belt. Must have brought them along for the ride."

I hold his gaze for several long seconds, and he looks back at me with the earnest, watery eyes of a drunk. His lower lip twitches, then he says: "There really are a lot of scorpions. More than there should be."

Sighing, I walk toward him, and he holds his ground. Good man. "Excuse me," I say, and he steps back.

I pick up my ID coin from the ground, sliding it back into its slot. "Come home, Mr. Eliot. Come home to your family." But he doesn't, and I walk back to the Grotto alone.

Before I reach the first rock, which is only a meter high, a shot echoes across the desert. I glance back to check that Eliot's still standing, then continue on.

It's never easy to know what you're dealing with, when it comes to Fallen. Stereotypically, they're savages who've cast off civilization—if you can call our Subverse-based society civilization. Personally, I struggle with that.

But for better or worse, I'm part of that society. The Fallen aren't. The Fount is designed to be passed on through the generations, from parent to child, but the Fallen hate the Subverse and everything it stands for. They expelled the Fount from their bodies generations ago, and they refuse to take any part in a galaxy that supports something like the Subverse, the place where most of humanity fled when the going got too tough.

Of course, that's just the stereotype. Some Fallen are in the situation they're in through sheer bad luck. The Fall caught them with their pants down, and they were cut off from the rest of the galaxy without slipspace-capable craft, forced to fend for themselves. Some of them kept their Fount, I'm sure. But it can be difficult to tell the galaxy-hating Fallen from the merely down-on-their-luck Fallen.

My rule of thumb? If they shoot at me, I shoot back.

As I work my way through the ever-larger rock outcrops, I pass a couple combat bots, whose job it actually is to shoot scorpions. They take no notice of me. A minute later, I come to the broad base of a massive rock claw, one of those that give the Grotto its name. Zelah Eliot, Arthur's wife, is waiting there. I don't need to ask her name. She's in enough Eliot family photos kicking around Guardsman dataspheres for me to know.

Typically, I react to unexpectedly encountering a beautiful woman by schooling my face to bland disinterest, as I do now. That's because I spend the vast majority of my time alone on a spaceship with a robot who I keep in a closet, and what my body really wants to do is roll around on the ground, wagging its tail and howling. So I keep a tight rein on it.

"Hello," I say.

She's wearing a white sundress. Wheat-colored hair stretches past high cheekbones to curl at the tips, cupping a defined chin. Smoke-colored eyes crinkle with worry, an expression that can't hide the wisdom living behind them. "I was told you went out to my husband," she says with a voice like silk. "Is there trouble?"

"Depends what kind you mean, ma'am. The head of the Eliot family shouldn't be alone in the desert blasting scorpions with an ancient shotgun liable to explode in his hands."

"The gun's been checked," Zelah says. "And three combat bots keep watch on him at any given time, out of sight so that he doesn't order them away. Other than that, there's no stopping him." There's something behind the look she's giving me. Something she's trying to tell me. "Would you accompany me back to the house?"

"Uh…" I clear my throat. "Okay."

We cross the Grotto and climb a long, gentle slope that leads to the largest cave, which is dominated by the red-brick monster occupied by the Eliots. I tell myself that it doesn't matter who sees me going into the Eliot residence alone with Mrs. Eliot. This is strictly business, I know that and they know that. Ignore the sets of eyes riveted to us at this very moment. There's Sergeant Wile, there's Faelyn, there's the custodian from earlier, who's been wandering the ground all this time. The only one not watching us is Faelyn's friend, whose drone appears to be fixed. He's flying it near the fountain, which seems like asking for it to get broken beyond repair.

Once we're inside the massive foyer, surrounded by what must be priceless paintings as well as marble busts of Eliots long uploaded to the Subverse, Zelah turns toward me, looking somewhat more businesslike. "Please," she says. "Don't approach Arthur when he's drunk again."

I tell her about almost getting killed by Fallen, and her expression softens.

"I'm sorry," she says. "But I mean what I said."

"Fine," I say, then I shake my head. "It's sad to see Arthur Eliot in that state." Frightening, too, if I'm being honest.

Zelah's features tighten, and I can tell her husband's behavior is causing her a lot of pain. She seems keen to change the subject. "How can Fallen pose a threat to a Troubleshooter?" she asks.

"I…" I have cause to clear my throat again. What an awkward question. As often happens in such cases, a lie springs from my thoughts fully formed and hovers before my mind's eye, tempting me. "This isn't real," I say at last, grasping the holstered fake. "My real pistol was stolen."

"By who?"

I sigh. "My daughter."

A smile tugs at Zelah's lips, but one made mostly of confusion. Still, she doesn't pry, which I'm grateful for. I have to admit, so far meeting the Eliots has me liking them both more than I would have expected. Yes, the Eliots are legends to me, but I've always been pessimistic about meeting legends.

"Come with me." Then, without missing a beat, she turns and walks toward a broad staircase carpeted in maroon. She's already five steps up before I start to follow, but she's apparently unconcerned—she doesn't look back to make sure I'm coming.

Zelah Eliot leads me through one endless hallway, then

another. Then she stops, waiting next to a set of giant mahogany doors.

"This—" I say when I reach her, but I'm cut off by her turning both handles and pushing. The doors swing inward to reveal a cavern of a master bedroom, all hung with ivory curtains and drapes. At the other end sits a bed so large that it looks proportionate to the rest of the chamber.

She walks inside, and again I hesitate. "Come," she says without turning, making for the bed. I swallow hard, then follow.

Eyes unbelieving, I watch as she crawls onto the bed. As the dress pulls taut around her petite frame, I tell myself I should look away, but I don't, except to glance back once at the still-open bedroom doors.

She reaches the head of the bed, and I know what comes next: she'll settle herself against the pillows and beckon to me with a slender hand.

But that doesn't happen. Instead, both hands rise toward an ornate, chocolate-brown hexagon—a wall mount, which I was too distracted to notice before. In its center hangs a weapon I recognize instantly. It's a Shiva Knight's blaster, no doubt restored. It's been polished till it gleams.

Zelah carefully removes it from the pegs that hold it there, then returns with it to the foot of the bed, dismounting gracefully without the use of her hands. She holds the weapon toward me.

At first, I can only stare. When I finally lift my hands, they're both trembling. I'm feeling just as excited as I did moments ago, though for a completely different reason.

When I take it from her, it's heavier than I expect. I like it, though. The weight feels right.

With a small flourish, I point it across the bedchamber, away from Zelah, my left hand rising automatically to support the other, to steady my aim.

My hands aren't trembling anymore. "Who gave you this?" I ask, maintaining the bead I've drawn on a carved dresser.

"It belonged to a Shiva Knight who died in the Core. A Guardsman brought it here, all the way from the galaxy's center. I don't know how he passed the sector barriers, but he did, and we didn't ask how. The Guardsman said that the knight would have wanted us to have it. Some say the Knighthood grew from the Guard."

Lowering the Shivan blaster, I turn to face her. "The knight… he failed in his quest, then?"

She nodded. "I want you to have his blaster."

It's hard to imagine what my face must look like right now. "How…how can you give me this?"

Her eyes crinkle, and I get the sense she's on the verge of tears. "Arthur…you saw how he is. That's been the way with him for a while." She shakes her head. "This is how I can feel like I'm doing something. You should take the blaster. I feel that strongly. Keep the Grotto safe from whoever tried to kill you."

"Okay."

She crosses the room to an oak chest, lifts the lid, and pulls out a gun belt. "This is for the blaster. I doubt it'll fit into the holster you're wearing."

I unbuckle my old gun belt and let it fall to the floor. Then I take the one Zelah's offering and pull it tight around my waist. It has pockets filled with charge packs—two on the right and two on the left, within easy reach. Checking the blaster, I find it's already loaded with a fifth charge pack. I lower it into its holster.

It feels right.

We look at each other, and her lips are pressed firmly together. It seems there's nothing left to say. I head for the open bedroom doors.

I pause on the threshold and turn my head to the left, taking her in one last time. "So you're the glue that holds this place together."

She takes a single step toward me, then stops. "You told me the truth about your daughter taking your gun. That struck me. Why did you do that? It might have caused a lot of trouble for you. You could have made something up to tell me."

I turn a little more, so I can look straight into her storm-colored eyes. "Lies are weapons," I say. "You should only use one on somebody you mean to kill."

With that, I turn again and leave the way I came.

5

I emerge from the Eliot residence and realize this is the best view of the Grotto available—time and place. I'm struck dumb by it, and I halt not far from the Eliots' doorstep to drink it in. The oasis spreads out before me, a broad oval of green and blue and gold, glistening in the noontime sun that beats down through the gap overhead. The pool sparkles like a diamond, and I notice the children have been sent to one side of it while, opposite them, a priest of the Fount preaches to a crowd of twenty or so.

Somewhere, someone plays a harp, its notes intermingling with the children's laughter and the priest's cadence. It's all so idyllic that it should seem cornball, but it doesn't. For the first time, I let myself see how special this place is. How it's an oasis in more ways than one. And, just for a moment, it kills me that I'll have to leave when my work is done here.

A couple kids sit amidst the adults listening to the preacher. Faelyn is one of them. I head east, giving the sermon a wide berth, but Faelyn spots me and stands, marching straight toward me with purpose. A smile tugs at my lips, and I tamp it down.

Maybe some would consider it rude for a child to stand up and leave in the middle of the sermon, but no one in the congregation seems to object. Probably, they're used to Arthur Eliot's daughter coming and going as she pleases. It's in her character, that's already clear to me, and her station in life grants free rein for that character to express itself in any way it wishes.

"How's the play going?" I ask once her sand-shifting footfalls draw near enough for conversation. "Auto Actor still working fine?"

"Fine," she agrees. "But I'm still using it just for practice. I only want people from the Grotto to act in the performance."

I nod. "That's good."

A pause from Faelyn as she catches up with me, falling in step. "If I can't find enough people, do you think I should approach some bots to be in it?"

"No."

"Why?"

I glance down at her. "A bot can't act. A bot just is what it is."

"Kind of like you."

That makes me stare at her in silence for a few seconds longer. "I'm leaving the Grotto," I say at last. "Past the perimeter of combat bots. You can't follow."

Without argument, she stops where she is, watching me go, solemn-faced. I face forward and continue on.

"Is that daddy's gun?" she calls after me.

"No," I call back. "It's mine."

For the third time today, I find myself winding between the rock outcrops that surround the Grotto. This time, they dwindle in size as I progress through them.

The combat bots don't try to stop me from leaving. Nor do they advise against it. They're programmed to recognize me for what I am, and not to get in my way.

I put about as much distance between myself and the Grotto as Arthur Eliot did. Then I unclasp the strap holding the Shivan blaster in place, and wait.

A tool is only as good as its user. Back in Basic Training, I was fingered as potential Troubleshooter material pretty early on, though I didn't know it at the time. Instructors took note of how easily I manipulated the amped-up datasphere they gave every recruit, wearing it like a second skin, integrating it like a sixth sense. It's about reaction time, yes. It's about having a steady hand. But more than that, it's about trusting the thing to save your life, and to help you kill when the time comes.

The blaster Zelah gave me is like the kinetic weapon the Fallen man used to shoot at me in the tunnels. That is, it's old tech, incompatible with the datasphere. It won't sync up. That's why I came out here before returning to the caves with it. I need to get used to a weapon that can't integrate with my datasphere to become a single, unified system optimized for killing.

Movement flickers on the crest of a sand dune: a scorpion approaching. I draw the blaster, aim it, use my left hand to steady it.

I shoot. White blaster fire flashes through the dry air with the sound of a guy-wire snapping. My shot blackens a patch of sand several feet to the scorpion's left, and a wisp of smoke rises up like a charmed snake.

"Damn it," I mutter. The scorpion's spooked, now, but it doesn't seem to know which direction safety lies in. Its six spindly legs work overtime to propel it over the sand, parallel to the dune's ridge.

I fire again. A miss. I fire again. My jaw's clenching involuntarily, and I feel like throwing the damned blaster at the scorpion.

Unharmed, my target finally figures out its path to survival. It beelines for the top of the ridge and scurries over it as my next blaster shot cuts through the air above it.

"Fount *damn* it."

"Now, you know what you are," says a hoarse voice behind me.

I whirl around, blaster raised, to find the figure clad in forest-green robes. A trimmed, salt-and-pepper beard covers his jaw, and crows' feet bracket his eyes. He seems undisturbed by the blaster pointing at him.

"What am I, old man?"

"You're a tool, to be switched on and off at will. Without your datasphere, you are nothing, and your datasphere can be deactivated. You need training."

"I've had plenty of training. I've been through the most grueling training program this galaxy's ever known. I'm a Troubleshooter."

"Grueling it may have been," the man says. "Nevertheless, it made you dependent, like a babe on mother's milk."

I brandish the blaster. "You've been following me. Why?"

"Following you? How can I follow someone who has no direction?" He barks laughter. "You're lost, son. Wandering lost."

Shaking my head, I holster the blaster. What am I supposed to do with this guy? I'm not going to kill him, and I have no real reason to apprehend him. Hell, I still give it pretty even odds he's a hallucination, auditory as well as visual, now.

One thing's for sure: I don't have time to stand here and listen to his bullshit, and I'm not about to continue embarrassing myself by shooting at scorpions and missing. It's time to head back out to the tunnels, and if I die because I can't figure out how to aim a blaster properly, then I die. Probably my days as a Guardsman are numbered anyway, and if I can't be a Guardsman then I have no idea what else to be.

Fount. Even Arthur Eliot managed to hit *some* of the scorpions.

I march past the old man, and he turns to watch me go, apparently finished delivering his annoying commentary. When I reach the first rock outcrop, I glance back, and once again he's nowhere to be seen.

6

I told myself I'd head out to the caves as soon as I got back to the *Ares*, but I end up procrastinating by eating and then napping on my bunk. Maneater watches me fall asleep from her place near the desk.

When I wake, the day's almost worn out. Probably I should wait till tomorrow to head out, but screw it. The post-nap grogginess will wear off during the flight, and daylight doesn't matter when you're going underground.

Soon, I'm dangling from the ship's airlock for the second time in as many days. This time, darkness covers the land, and a wind howls across the desert's barrenness to assault me in a steady wave, introducing a sway to my descent. I eye the brambles below.

Somehow, I manage to bypass them without getting stuck full of thorns. I left my helmet aboard the *Ares*, so this time there's nothing for it but to lower myself into the crevice, ready for the drop this time. I land crouched, blaster in hand, night vision showing an empty tunnel stretching to the first bend.

I advance slowly, eyes skipping between potential enemy hiding spots. There's a low, creepy drone down here that I didn't notice before. Funny what you pick up on when you sense death approaching.

Unlike last time, I activated the entire crew before leaving the Grotto, and they're all online now, directly above the hole I disappeared into. "No landing, this time," I ordered Worldworn. "Standby to yank me out of there at a moment's notice. Could be you'll have to fly away with me still dangling from the hook."

When I first switched on the crew, Aphrodite's gaze zeroed in on the blaster hanging against my thigh. "What happened to your laser pistol?"

I sighed. "My daughter has it."

Her doe's eyes widened. "What in the galaxy would she need a laser pistol for?"

"To steal a ship."

"She *stole* a ship? What ship? Why?"

I shook my head. "Enough questions."

She didn't pester me about it further, but I could tell she was agitated throughout the rest of the trip. Her eyes kept darting toward me. Whatever. I'm not paid to make sure my upload crew are totally comfortable and on board with everything that happens.

Blaster leading the way through the tunnel, I'm on high alert for the first flicker of movement. My hope is that if I spam the trigger enough I'll hit something vital.

I'm not at a total disadvantage. There are a few things that even my brief encounter with my Fallen adversary told me, and information's just another form of ammunition.

Playing back the encounter using my datasphere on the way here, I noted the frenzied pace of the shooting, even when he didn't have a good bead on me. The fact he shot first without trying to talk suggests desperation, too. Sure, it could also mean cold-blooded killer, but most people aren't that. Most people are just afraid.

That level of fear tells me he was defending something valuable to him. Also, that he doesn't have many armed friends. I'd put it at three or four, probably fewer. They all need sleep at some point, so they likely only have one or two of them awake and on watch at any given time.

Information I extracted from the terminal told me the server room door sits at the bottom of a final slope, and my attacker was shooting from the top of that slope. Makes sense: lie down, use the slope to cover your body, fire over the lip. But his cover is my high ground, if I play this right.

I come to the last bend. When I round this next corner, I'll be in the stretch of cave where the Fallen shot at me last. I press my back to the rock, holding my blaster in front of my face, muzzle pointed at the ceiling.

Then I use my datasphere to exercise a Troubleshooter's privilege—remote access over the server room door. I see that it's closed, as I expected it to be.

I will it to open, then I round the corner, firing at the top of the slope, the blaster's pure white bolts playing havoc with my night vision. Shouting erupts, and no one fires back. I've caught them off guard.

Someone rises from the slope, turning to descend, probably to try to get the door closed again. I get him in the lower back, and he sprawls forward, out of sight. The force of the blaster's bolt is far more powerful than my old laser pistol.

It feels…strange, to kill without my datasphere's say-so, without its green cones guiding my shots. My next report won't include the proper authentications for killing. But it seems safe to assume Command *would* authorize these deaths, and if I don't press my advantage now, I'm done. I rush the top of the incline, finding that one of the Fallen stayed there, using the slope as cover just as I envisioned. His weapon roars, and my left shoulder erupts in pain.

Clenching my teeth against the agony, I level the blaster at his head and fire.

It hits. His body jolts backward, and his face cracks off the stone. I continue forward, stepping over him, firing down the slope toward the door.

The man I got in the back is standing at the door, slamming a control panel with his palm. It won't do him any good—I ordered the door to jam open. Two blaster shots bite into the rock near his hip, but my third finds his torso again, and he falls forward against the panel, propped up by it and the nearby rock wall.

Someone leans into view from inside the server room, aiming an assault rifle at me, and I shift the blaster to him. He gets off a burst, but misses, thank Fount. I squeeze the blaster trigger repeatedly, and a white bolt blows his face apart, sending my target backward to land on the ground, motionless.

That's it. No one else fires at me, and I sprint forward to collect the weapons, quick as I can. As I do, I marvel at the adrenaline coursing through my veins, pumping through harder than it has in years. It fills me with a sense of euphoria, triumph. They wounded me, but I fought through, against multiple foes. I survived. All without the help of my datasphere. And to top it all off, the blaster feels *amazing* to use.

Once I have their weapons, I deposit them in a pile outside the server room, then I enter and shut the door behind me.

Right away, I have the answer to two mysteries at once. First, I know what the Fallen considered valuable enough to die for. And second, I know how they survived the freezing desert nights.

Down every aisle I can see, women and children wrapped in ragged garments huddle against the servers for the warmth generated by the machines. This is how they've staved off hypothermia. Maybe they even found a water source somewhere down here. Beyond that, it would have been a simple matter of using dwindling ammunition to kill scorpions for dinner. Not particularly appetizing, but you'll eat anything when you're starving.

Not that these people look as though the scorpions have done much to nourish them. They're gaunt, brittle-looking, and their eyes stare out at me from shadowed hollows. Even the men lying dead at my feet are like skeletons.

There's a weird churning in my stomach, and by the time I realize what's happening it's nearly too late. I jerk to the side, getting a hand on one knee in time to expel the powdered eggs I had for lunch onto the server room floor. As I stare at the puke puddle, a pang of remorse hits me in the chest.

Why were there so few men? Did they kill each other in a fight for supremacy? A political difference?

A more gruesome possibility offers itself up to me, no doubt born from the stories that tend to circulate about the Fallen:

Maybe they *ate* the other men.

But that's not what's making me nauseous, and actually, I'm pretty sure my mind only raised the possibility of cannibalism in an attempt to rationalize my kills.

What's making me nauseous is that I feel like a criminal. Not a delinquent in trouble with the law bots, but an actual criminal. I killed without the sanction of my datasphere…and I took away these people's protectors.

As for the women and children, protocol says I need to get them out of here. But ousting them and repairing the lock would be as good as killing them. Probably they're doomed anyway, but kicking them out of here would make it a sure thing.

I doubt they have the tools or the strength to get at the servers inside the locked cabinets, even if they wanted to. And it's clear to me they don't. They're just here for the heat. To survive the desert nights.

"You can stay," I tell them. Who knows whether they speak English. Certainly, none of them answer me. "I won't make you leave." My eyes fall on the man who died just inside the server room. "I'm sorry," I say, meeting the eyes of a woman who looks seventy but is probably only forty. She looks back at me blankly.

I can't leave them the weapons—an assault rifle and two pistols. I can't leave them loaded, anyway. Ejecting the charge packs, I stow them in pockets on my suit's thighs. That done, I perform a quick walk-through of the entire server room. No other weapons, and nowhere for them to conceal any. A rough count gives me thirty-three people still alive in here. The servers all look untouched, just as my briefing said they were.

Following instructions provided by my datasphere, I fix the door lock as quickly as I can with my shoulder wound, which emanates pain. The spidersilk armor repelled the bullet, but the impact still feels like it did a lot of damage. Nothing the Fount can't fix complete within a couple days, but it will probably slow me down for a while.

With the door repaired, the Fallen women and children will still be able to open it from the inside. As long as they don't lock themselves out, they'll have continued access to the servers' warmth.

"How did it go?" Lieutenant Commander Belflower asks once I'm back aboard the *Ares* and settling into the command seat. "You don't look well, Captain, if you don't mind my saying."

"It went fine. There were Fallen in the server room, but I dealt with them. I'll file my report back at the Grotto, before we leave." I have no idea what I'll say in that report—or how I'll explain not having a weapon that syncs up with my datasphere—but I have to file one.

"Do we actually need to return to the Grotto?" Worldworn asks, with a stroke of his flowing beard. "Our mission on Tunis is complete. Is it not?"

I pause. Then: "There's no harm in one last visit. We won't get our next orders for a couple weeks at minimum, so we have the time." Maybe I'll take Maneater for a walk around the Grotto. That should be fine, so long as I keep her muzzle on. It'll give me time to process what just happened.

"Very well," he says, turning to set a course.

Through the *Ares'* belly sensors, I drink in the Tunis wilderness one last time. I switch to a port sensor: the land and the sky look like negatives of each other. Gray and darker gray. Pitch-black between the biggest dunes, and also in the rare patches of sky not smeared with stars.

Finally, I watch through a bow sensor as we approach the Grotto in her rocky cradle. That's why I'm the first to notice the flames, through the gaps in the giant stone claws.

"Something's wrong," I say, at the same second neon-blue laserfire flickers. "The Grotto's under attack."

Asterisk's face lights up with excitement, his chains shaking as he turns to look at me, and my desire to throttle him spikes. "Just say the word, boss," he says, "and I'll start raining down hell on the bastards."

This isn't the time to educate him on proper forms of address aboard a Troubleshooter's ship. "Do *not* engage," I bark. "There's too much risk of hitting civilians." I turn to Worldworn. "Put us down outside the Grotto, as close as you can get. Descend sharply, now—forget using anti-grav to cushion our landing. With any luck, whoever's down there hasn't noticed us yet."

7

Smoke fills the night, and someone's shrieking in pain somewhere to the north: "Oh Fount oh please oh no oh no no no…"

I wish I could stop to check on whoever that is, but I can't. I have to keep moving. After emerging from between the rocks, the first corpse I encounter belongs to the priest who was preaching near the pond earlier. Checking first to make sure no one's nearby, I untie his scarlet robes, peel them back from one side of his body, free his right arm, then yank the loose fabric, turning him onto his face. Then I free the other arm and don the robes myself. All of this sends jolts of pain shooting from my shoulder and down my arm, but they're a little more muted than before. The Fount is doing its work.

"Sorry, Father," I tell the priest. Turning, I take in more of the carnage that grips the Grotto. Multiple fires blaze, one of them at the base of the Eliot residence's eastern wing, where a team of eight or so utility bots struggle to put it out. My eyes fall on a pirate near the pool just as his laser pistol fires, killing a woman where she stands. Beyond, flames lick at the fronds of a palm tree, casting flickering light on three bodies floating in the pool.

I head in the direction opposite the Eliot residence—counter-clockwise along the Grotto's perimeter. That will bring me to the theater faster, which is where I expect Faelyn and her friends to be.

Aphrodite tried to get me to take Dice, but my chances of moving around the Grotto unnoticed would be pretty low with a combat bot at my side. I'm walking with the sleeves of my new robes joined at the wrists, so that my hands are concealed. It isn't long before I run across more downed residents, some of them still clinging to life. The shrieking from before starts up again, louder, and I give its source a wide berth. No need for him to draw attention to us both.

There are several combat bots downed, too, some of them sparking, a couple twitching frenetically. None of the human bodies belong to children, which is good. Except, I can't see any children anywhere, or hear their cries of fear. Either they all managed to hide or the attackers are abducting them. This is reminding me too much of the Siberian Brinktown.

"Hey," someone yells, and I turn to see some asshole pointing a laser rifle at me. I know a pirate when I see one. With his patchy facial hair and shirt unbuttoned to reveal a paunch, this one fits the bill. Not that I needed any hints to predict the Grotto's attackers would turn out to be pirates.

"You'd threaten a man of the cloth?" I say.

"Sure, but—I thought we already killed you. How many priests does this place have?"

"A priest of the Fount never truly dies."

"Sure they do," the pirate says. "I've killed plenty."

"Then you have a debt to pay. Learn to walk with the Fount, my son, before it exacts its own price from you."

The laser rifle's muzzle falls, and the pirate dons a thoughtful expression. He seems kind of bored—probably disappointed with how easily they took over the Grotto. I'm disappointed, too. Where are the combat bots?

"I already walk with the Fount," he says. "Literally. Everyone does, don't they?"

"Not really what I meant. " I part my sleeves to reveal the blaster in my hand and shoot the pirate. At this range, I don't have any trouble hitting him. He goes down, and I walk quickly past, making for a patch of shadows that stretch across the yard of a nearby house, one of those that isn't in danger of burning down. I force myself not to think about the fact I just killed another person without my datasphere's permission. Of course Command would want me to kill pirates in defense of the Eliots. Still, the decision was mine, and somehow it's completely different from every other kill I've made before today.

Speed-walking through the night, I avoid the spacepads, which are mostly occupied by pirate ships, now. It's dark enough in the shadows that the red of my new robes should appear as gray to someone who isn't using night vision. It seems to work. I dart from shadow to shadow—cast by a hedgerow here, a copse of palm trees there—and I reach the theater without having to put down any more pirates, who seem too focused on their carnage to notice me.

Betting that the robes shouldn't attract too much attention against the obsidian-black theater, I spring inside, blaster up and sweeping the lobby.

Empty. I continue into the theater proper, which also appears empty, at first. Then, a small voice calls from my left: "Joe!"

I turn and spot five tiny forms pressed against the theater's back wall: Faelyn Eliot, two of her friends from the night I chased the figure in here, and two more who I think I recognize from the pool in the Grotto's center. Three of the five start whimpering and sobbing as soon as my eyes fall on them, but Faelyn seems composed.

"How do you know my name?" I say, barely above a whisper.

"My father told me," she says. "Why are you wearing Father Robert's robes?"

I hesitate, wondering whether she was close to the preacher.

Time to change the subject. "How long have you been hiding in here?"

"Since it started," she says. "We're worried about our parents."

I glance back through the lobby. "You can help them by staying safe. Soon, those men will come in here, and they're not the type you want to meet. Is there somewhere backstage you can hide?"

"There are tunnels. They built them for students to get around during the cold nights. We're not supposed to go down there, though."

"Perfect," I say. "Uh…does your datasphere have night vision?"

She nods, which doesn't surprise me. It's not usual for civilian dataspheres to have the capability, but of course the datasphere belonging to Arthur Eliot's daughter would.

"Can I depend on you to lead everyone deep inside those tunnels and stay there till someone comes for you?" I make eye contact with each child in turn, and a couple of them nod, as though I'd asked them to be the leader.

"Yes," she says.

"All right. Get going."

Her four friends need no further encouragement. They race down one of the aisles, feet pattering over the steps in a muted stampede.

Faelyn lingers. "Will you come with us?"

I open my mouth, then close it, sighing. "It's kind of my job to stick around at times like these."

She nods. "I'll see you soon, Joe."

"Get going."

She does, and I stalk back through the lobby with night vision on, scanning the area in front of the theater. The coast seems clear, so I slip out the leftmost door and crouch against the building.

I notice a head bobbing between the same twin hedgerows I ran past on my first night in the Grotto. The head's matted crown barely crests the top of the hedge. When he appears, I see he's carrying a laser rifle. He barrels straight for my position.

My heart rate spikes, but my hand stays steady as I line up the shot, taking my time with it. I'm betting he doesn't see me, and just wants to raid a building that looks like it hasn't been touched yet. The thought isn't totally comforting, though, given my performance against the scorpion.

I fire once, and miss. Instantly, he changes course, bringing the rifle to bear and heading toward the rock encasing the theater.

I fire again, and the bolt takes him in the throat. He drops, clutching at it.

It takes me less than thirty seconds to drag him and his kit to the side of the theater and stuff his corpse between the building and the stone, my shoulder screaming in pain the entire time. My stomach's roiling, too. This feels wrong. Everything does. I've always told myself I only kill to keep the galaxy safe. To keep Harmony safe. That's what my training taught me to believe. So what's happening to me? Are the Brinktowners right? Am I really just a butcher?

I swallow hard, shaking myself. Man up, Joe. You're fighting to save these people. This is no time to choke.

The pirate's body hidden, I return to my previous spot and wait.

Another pirate appears, jogging by like it's his morning cardio. When my blaster shot hits him, he takes a dive that ends with his face in the grass, and he doesn't get up from it. Alive one second, dead the next. The thrill from the sandstone caves is gone, now. The adrenaline surge I've always gotten from taking out people who would have otherwise killed me.

I'm doing this to protect the Eliots. To protect Faelyn. Ultimately, it's making the galaxy safer. Making Harmony safer.

But the old justifications aren't working. Bile is creeping its way up my throat again.

Before I can get moving to pull the pirate out of sight, a voice comes from behind and to my right: "Joe."

My head snaps toward the source. Fount damn it. "What are you doing here?" I hiss.

Despite the poor lighting, Faelyn's pale face stands out like the moon on a clear night, bracketed by the partially open door. "I wanted to make sure you were all right."

I curse, and she flinches. "I thought you knew better than that."

"The others are safe in the tunnels," she says, her lips trembling. Fount. She's the daughter of one of the most powerful men in the galaxy, but she's still just a scared kid.

"You need to go find them and stay there." I turn to check for hostiles, and then I see them: seven figures spread out in a line, the center one a hulking seven feet tall at least. Headed straight for us. *"Get inside,"* I whisper.

She withdraws, and the door hisses forward an inch before I'm pushing it inward again. Faelyn runs for the theater proper, and I back across the lobby with my blaster held at the ready, suppressing the urge to deliver a string of curses.

There's no way I can take on seven pirates. Without the datasphere integration I've depended on my entire career, I feel lucky to take down even one experienced fighter using the blaster.

I look down at my robes, thinking, and then I follow Faelyn. When I reach the theater, she's already halfway to the stage. "Turn on the Auto Actor," I yell, stuffing the blaster inside its holster, beneath my priest's garb.

"What?" She stops, and swings her head around. "Why?"

"Turn it on, and leave two spots open for us."

"What scene?"

"Any scene! The first one you come across. Hurry!"

As I fly down the red-carpeted steps, my ears are straining for the sound of the approaching posse entering through the glass doors. Onstage, figures flicker to life: an apparition wearing a horned helmet and cape, a downed man whose fine clothes are tattered and blood-soaked, and two transparent figures, indicating that actors should take their places: Hamlet and Queen Gertrude.

I wince. Gertrude is older than Hamlet, being his mother, after all. Maybe the pirates will fail to pick up on it. What are the chances they're familiar with Shakespeare, or will stop to listen to the lines being spoken? My hope is that they'll look in, assume someone left the Auto Actor on, and leave.

The clatter of their entrance into the lobby comes just as I'm taking my place. Hoarse yells and stamping feet draw nearer.

"Oh gentle son," Faelyn says, and her voice isn't quite monotone. I suppress the urge to grimace, both at the mismatch of the words and the way she delivered them. She'll need to put on a better performance than this. "Upon the heat and flame of thy distemper, sprinkle cool patience. Whereon do you look?"

"On him, on him!" I say, gesturing toward the apparition. During the long months I've spent awake between the stars, I've read all of Shakespeare, along with plenty of other stuff from Old Earth. *Hamlet* is my favorite by a mile. "Look you, how pale he glares!" The pirates enter the theater proper, weapons raised. I track them in my peripheral vision. "His form and cause conjoin'd, preaching to stones, would make them capable." Utter silence from the raiders, now. They stand frozen at the top of the aisles, staring down at the stage. "Do not look upon me," I say to the apparition, "lest with this piteous action you convert my stern effects: then what have I to do will want true color—tears perchance for blood."

"To whom do you speak this?" Faelyn asks, and her performance is livening up a bit.

"Do you see nothing there?"

The pirates split up, starting down both stairways and taking up staggered positions amongst the seats.

"Nothing at all; yet all that is I see."

"Nor did you nothing hear?"

"No, nothing but ourselves."

"Why, look you there! Look, how it steals away!" The giant I spotted outside leads the way toward the stage, a midnight cape dragging across the stairs behind him. "My father, in his habit as he lived!" It takes all my will not to turn and scrutinize the approaching figure. From what I can see from the corner of my eye, his face is composed of dark metal, his jaw bisected by a pill-shaped breathing apparatus. His head is a lined dome that converges on ice-blue eyes, which glow softly in the dim theater. "Look, where he goes, even now, out at the portal!"

Faelyn's eyes dart toward the bot. "This, the very coinage of your brain," she says, "this bodiless creation ecstasy is very cunning in."

The bot starts to clap leisurely, bringing leather-gloved hands together again and again. Almost, I forget the next line. But I know the game is up, and as I speak Hamlet's next words, I notice the bot's forearms: flesh. Is he a bot or isn't he?

"A most unique interpretation of Hamlet," he says, and his voice is deep, with a metallic quality. "A child as Queen Gertrude? I've seen the play many times, but I've never seen it performed quite like that."

I peel my robes back and reach for my blaster. The bot-man leaps from halfway up the stairs, crashing to the stage as I'm raising my weapon. He reaches for Faelyn with a hand that flickers like lightning, and before I can react, he holds her by the neck, her feet dangling several feet from the wooden stage as she struggles to breathe.

"I have to insist you drop your weapon," he says.

I toss the blaster onto the stage.

"Good," he says, stepping forward and driving his fist into my stomach, an action that ends with me lying on my back, gasping.

Then, a blaster is in *his* hand, though I didn't notice him reaching for one. It's identical to mine.

The blaster's muzzle tracks to my face, and the glowing blue eyes seem to, as well. Faelyn gasps and gurgles at the end of his arm.

Several long seconds pass as he seems to study my face.

At last, he lowers the weapon and holsters it. "You get one warning," he says. "Stay out of my way."

He steps forward, delivering a swift kick to my temple. My head snaps sideways, my vision swimming. Trying to get up, I watch as he swings Faelyn by the neck until she's lodged under his other arm. Then he marches up the stairs, and the pirates follow him into the lobby.

I black out.

8

A mounting clamor of voices drags me from my sleep. Bright lights overheard make me squint, and I avert my gaze from them, peering at my surroundings through slits, though it's hard to make out anything till my eyes adjust.

Where did I fall asleep? Feels like hardwood under my back.

I push myself to a seating position. Three blurred figures stand nearby, all turned toward me. As my vision adjusts, I see they're all in Victorian-era dress, which makes me think of Shakespeare.

That brings a strong sense of deja vu. Shakespeare. Was I thinking about Shakespeare recently?

The expressions on the actors' faces are shocked, and the audience feels similarly, from the sounds of it. Looking out at them, I see they fill every single seat, with some standing at the back. Many of them aren't human, which gives me something else to think about.

Beings covered in fur, like a rug. Beings that resemble frogs. Elven creatures, someone with skin like tree bark, an organism made up mostly of vapor.

"Get off the stage!" someone yells as I stagger to my feet. I almost lose my footing right away, but otherwise, I'm happy to comply.

As I stumble up red-carpeted steps, past a crowd that has no problem giving voice to its displeasure, I start to remember what was happening before I lost consciousness.

The pirate attack. The half-man, half-bot. He took Faelyn. I need to stop him before he leaves with her.

My blaster! I turn to scrutinize the stage, but it's nowhere to be seen, and it isn't on my hip, either. The priest's robes are gone, and I'm wearing a plain white t-shirt and blue jeans. I shake my head and continue laboring up the steps.

The lobby is empty, other than an usher sitting on a bench, who blinks at me sleepily as I propel myself toward the exit. Outside, the darkness is lit so brightly it's like artificial day. Not lit by fire-light, though. The glow is too constant.

My ears still ring from the kick the man-bot delivered to my skull, and the painful throbbing from my shoulder wound only seems to be getting worse. Yanking open a glass door, I exit the theater into a Grotto restored to its former glory. I can see at least a hundred people in all, crisscrossing the campus grounds between the various buildings, bundled up against the encroaching cold of the desert night.

Lamps like tiny suns shine from their fixtures far above, attached to rock faces over every building. Giant hedge sculptures surround the pool in the Grotto's center, where the water lattice is even more elaborate than before.

There's a similar mix of species and lifeforms out here, though none of them take much notice of me, unlike inside the theater. Looking around at the buildings, I notice many of them are painted different colors, and look even better-kept. They were already in good repair, especially compared to everywhere else in the galaxy, but now they're immaculate.

I head toward the pool, not sure where else to go. Then,

between footsteps, the vision of a restored Grotto disappears, and I'm back where I was—the hedge sculptures gone, the people and other creatures gone. In their place, the smoke and the screaming returns.

Most of the fires have been put out, including the one threatening the Eliot residence. Only one still blazes, on the other side of the campus. To my left, Arthur Eliot stumbles toward me across the grounds, from the direction of the surrounding rocks. His shotgun dangles from his left hand.

Before he gets close enough to speak, I twist around to check the space pads. The pirate ships have all departed.

"What happened?" he asks as he draws near.

"They took your daughter. I tried to stop them, but I couldn't."

He nods. "Come to the house."

Trying to ignore the pain from my shoulder, I trudge after him. He leads me across a particularly loose patch of sand, and in my current state, it's hard going.

A disheveled Zelah meets us at the door. Her hair is out of place, and one strap of her sundress has fallen over her shoulder. I can tell she's trying her hardest to conceal her pain, but it's leaking through her eyes.

Eliot slides the strap back into place. She points me toward a door off the foyer, then she leads her husband up the stairs, showing him to bed.

Through the door Zelah directed me toward, I find Eliot's office. Even more priceless art hangs here. I see a Picasso, and a Lysander. The entire wall behind the desk is comprised of bookshelves stuffed with books, of all things. How quaint.

I try to lower myself to an overstuffed purple couch, but I fall onto it instead. Staring at the stucco ceiling, my vision swirls, and I wonder what kind of damage that bastard did to my brain. Hopefully, it's something my Fount can fix.

Zelah returns with a glass of water.

"They took her," I rasp. "They took Faelyn."

She nods, eyes shimmering, then she leaves. My shoulder itches fiercely as the Fount begins to stitch it up, slowly ejecting the bullet, but despite that I soon fall into a deep sleep.

9

Full daylight streams into the office when I wake. Cold air blows onto my face, and I realize I'm shivering.

"Air conditioning is an obscene luxury, now," a voice says, and my hand moves to my holster, finding it empty.

I sit up. Arthur Eliot reclines in a burgundy throne of an office chair, feet kicked up on the massive mahogany block that is his desk. He seems sober.

"This is one of only two units that work in the Grotto," he says, nodding at the machine blasting me with its icy breath. "The other's in our drawing room."

"Drawing room," I repeat, struggling to my feet and transplanting myself into one of the two chairs facing Eliot's desk. The air conditioner's assault is less, here. I prod my shoulder and find the bullet half-expelled from the surface of my skin. I could pluck it out, but it's best to let the Fount finish its work.

"The campus used to benefit from a pair of breeze generators," Eliot says, "which kept everything at a comfortable temperature the entire day. They may still work, for all I know. The power consumption was massive, so I've never bothered having them turned on."

I stare at him, wondering where this is going. His daughter was kidnapped, and he's talking about air conditioning. My opinion of Eliot is taking more abuse.

"This was the dean's office," he goes on. "And our house, the Arts and Administration Building. The employees all live in the old dorms. But we've done our best to make this place our home."

He looks to his right, and I follow his gaze, to the great bay window over the couch where I slept. It offers a view of most of the Grotto.

"Your daughter is gone," I say.

"Yes, along with most of the other children," he says, nodding. "But some stayed safe, hidden in their homes, and I understand your actions led to four more being saved. I should commend you for that."

"The ones in the tunnels?"

Eliot nods. "They were found wandering in the dark, cold and hungry, but alive. I thank you. The Grotto would have been too quiet without *some* children around."

His cavalier attitude about losing the biological version of his daughter ignites the old anger inside me—a slow burn, at this point in my life. I continue to stare at him.

Eliot doesn't seem to notice. "It's strange, you know..." He clears his throat. "Zelah is young enough to bear more children, to continue the biological family line. And even though I know Faelyn is perfectly safe, living thousands of parallel existences together with her mother and I in thousands of Subverses...every version of her constantly compiled, synced, and updated to produce her happiest self..." He shakes his head, and I wait for him to finish. "Despite all that, I still miss her here, in meatspace. Isn't that odd?"

"No," I say, more emphatically than I mean to. Eliot blinks as I try to bore a hole through his head with my gaze. "It's how you *should* feel after losing a daughter in the real."

At that, Eliot scoffs. "Please. You're one of those who refers to meatspace as the real? Honestly? The Subverse is no less real than this world. I believe it's more real. We accomplish our greatest works there. Here, our lives are too short and brutish to accomplish anything enduring."

Shaking my head, I say, "But that's what makes the real important. The fact that our lives here end."

Eliot gives a sarcastic smile. "The same way galactic civilization ended?"

I raise my right hand, pointing to the paintings hanging on the wall to my right. "These paintings. They're originals?"

Slowly, he nods. "The Picasso took a considerable amount of restoration. It took my father forever to find a man capable of doing the work. But yes. Originals."

"Why are they valuable?"

Eliot furrows his brow. "Because they're the originals," he says, as though that should be enough. When I don't say anything, he goes on: "There's only one original. It's simple economics. The extreme scarcity drives their value through the roof."

"And their fragility," I say. "Five seconds of manhandling would ruin them forever."

"Yes, I suppose that's true."

"No painting in the Subverse could match that original Lysander."

Eliot opens his mouth, then closes it. "No. True. But it's a completely different thing."

"Yes," I say. "It is. Just like having your biological daughter is a completely different thing from having thousands of copies of her stored inside computer servers scattered throughout the galaxy."

Eliot's lips form a thin line, which pushes the color out of them. He doesn't answer.

"Did you know Faelyn was planning a performance of *Hamlet*?"

"Yes. Of course."

"And did you know she had no interest in performing it for people in the Subverse? She meant it only for the people living here. She recognized that the real is special. But maybe she was afraid to tell you that."

Eliot's eyes have widened slightly. With that, I find myself giving voice to the thought that's been nagging me since I woke, no longer caring how crazy it is: "Let me go after the people who took your daughter, Mr. Eliot. You administrate the Guard. Your family created it. If I have your backing, the brass will let me do this."

A long silence follows, and Eliot drums his fingers on the desktop throughout it.

Finally, he says, "Who put you in the condition I found you in?"

"I don't know. He was half-bot. Maybe mostly bot."

"But with human qualities?"

I nod.

"That was Rodney Fairfax."

I narrow my eyes. "The Fairfaxes were behind the attack? Why would *they* attack your family?"

"Rodney's a bit of a black sheep. Other than him, relations between the two families are fine. But Rodney is just as powerful as the other Fairfaxes, and just as well-connected. You experienced a taste of his displeasure. Do you think you can meaningfully oppose him?"

I don't answer, still stuck on the revelation that a Fairfax was behind the attack. "I came across a Brinktown that suffered a similar attack on Earth," I say. "But they didn't leave a single child behind there, and they killed all the adults. Why didn't they do that here?"

Eliot sniffs. "The perpetrators of that attack may not be the same ones who attacked the Grotto. But whether they were or not, I think I know the answer to your question. Yesterday's attack was meant to send me a message. Whatever Rodney's up to, it's likely the Guard has been getting in his way. I doubt he likes that."

"Look, Mr. Eliot. I know you think you'll get past losing your biological daughter just fine. But what if you're wrong? What if you send me away, and realize you've made a mistake? Maybe you believe your daughter is safe in the Subverse, but you're going to live this life without seeing her again. That's going to haunt you. Believe me."

Eliot pushes back from his desk, his chair gliding over the hardwood with barely a whisper. He stands. "I think it's time for you to be on your way, Commander Pikeman. Your business on Tunis is finished, yes?"

I stand, too. "Where's my blaster?"

"You mean *my* blaster?" Eliot says, wearing a small smirk. I don't know if he realizes I'm still wearing the gun belt sized for it, but screw him anyway.

Halfway around his desk, Eliot pauses, staring into nothing. I take it he's reading something on his datasphere. "Hmm. It seems Gargantua was hit too, on the other side of the system. There's a Brinktown over there."

I say nothing, not interested in engaging in what he seems to consider small talk. Quietly, though, I'm fitting the news into my working theory of the pirate attacks: they were looking for the system's server room over there. They wanted to eliminate Subverse-based witnesses, just like they did on Earth. Apparently they don't know the servers are here on Tunis.

Eliot opens the office door for me, still smirking. "I hope you come around to the benefits of uploading someday, Captain. You are an amusingly singular individual. And besides, if you did upload, you wouldn't need to have that ugly birthmark anymore."

We lock eyes for a long moment, and part of me goes back to the schoolyard as a child. The offhanded taunts and insult, which lasted for as long as it took me to snap and answer with violence.

Shaking myself, I leave without another word.

Outside the Eliot residence, I come across Sergeant Wile pacing the yard. He turns a blank expression on me, but I can smell how sheepish he feels.

"Where were you last night?" I say.

He turns his head to show me a patch of thinning hair matted with blood. "A pirate got me with the butt of his rifle right at the start. Knocked me out cold."

And he's made sure to keep the wound as gruesome-looking as he can, so all can behold his alibi. I sneer at him as I pass. "Go clean yourself up, Guardsman."

The black smears that mar several of the buildings…the spent matchsticks where palm trees once stood…it all makes me angrier than I normally let myself get. "What a waste," I mutter.

Back on the *Ares*, I boot up the crew and order a full systems check before we depart. While they're doing that, I call Dice out of his closet to give him a once over, though I'm not sure why. I can't remember letting him out once since we got here, or during the slipspace voyage, so he's basically fresh from the mechanic's. Screw it. I check him over anyway.

"Sir," Aphrodite says. "Arthur Eliot is outside the airlock."

I check through one of the hull sensors. Sure enough, there he stands, holding something wrapped in cloth.

When the airlock cycles and the outer hatch opens, I just stand there, arms crossed, glaring at him.

He holds out the bundle, and I take it, unwrapping it to reveal the old blaster.

"Go find my daughter," he says, eyes steady on mine, "and bring her back here."

ARES

1

We're crossing the Junction System to Gargantua, and I'm sitting at the edge of my bunk, feeding Maneater chicken strips from the end of a fork. The plan is to work up to getting her to eat out of my hand. I figure if she can learn to think of me as the source of food and not the food itself, then that's progress.

It's kind of insane, how long it's taking to get on her good side. There's a good chance I don't have much talent for this, but I'm sure it also has a lot to do with how that bastard treated her, for however long he owned her. If he had her since she was a puppy, treating her like that, then I'm not sure there's much hope for successfully socializing her. My datasphere confirms that fear.

But we do seem to be progressing, even if it's at a crawl. She's mostly stopped snarling at me. Especially when she's snarfing meat from the fork.

A datasphere window opens to my right, showing Aphrodite's perfectly symmetrical face. "A brainprint just arrived for you," she says. "From a Harmony Pikeman. Is that your daughter?"

I gape at my OPO. Part of me wants to cry from relief at the news, but my stomach feels like ice. "I'll take it in my cabin. Patch it through."

"Yes, sir."

My daughter materializes next to Maneater, who doesn't react. She wouldn't, of course. She'd need a datasphere to register Harmony's presence.

For a moment, I'm lost for words, struck by how much Harmony has come to resemble Marissa. When I visited her in Brinktown, she was wearing that stupid costume, and I couldn't see how much she'd changed. "Harm," I say. "You're beautiful."

"Hi, Dad," she says, glancing down at the dog. She pats Maneater's head, but her hand goes right through. "Good girl."

Maneater barks, but not at Harmony: she's barking at me, because I've stopped feeding her. I fork up another piece of chicken and hold it out. Absently, I almost move my hand too close, and she lunges for it with incredible speed. "Fount!" I yell, yanking it back just in time.

"Harm," I say, eyeing the German Shepherd. "Where are you?"

"Aboard *Europa's Gift*. I'm safe, Dad."

"What got into you that stealing Daniel Sterling's ship seemed like a good idea?"

She shrugs, grinning. "Oh, well, gramps didn't seem to be using it. Besides, his security was so lax he was almost begging me to take it. The *Gift*'s computer was connected to his home network, and cracking that was a cinch. Once I was in, I had access to everything I needed—the ship's security protocols, enough to spoof Sterling's credentials, even a few training sims so I could learn how to fly her before I stole her. Of course, I still almost crashed her straight into the planet the moment I took off from Brinktown." Maybe she can see how worried I am, because her smile falls away. "It's fine, Dad. I'm okay."

"You're a teenage girl by yourself in a stolen ship. You'll be lucky if pirates don't find you."

"Actually, I'm planning to find them first. After you told me about the pirate attacks, I decided to investigate."

I feel my eyes go wide, and I struggle to keep my voice somewhat level. "That's not your job, Harmony. And don't try to pretend you decided to take my weapon, steal Sterling's ship, and go sailing across the galaxy on a whim. You had that replica ready to go. You've been planning this."

"You caught me," she says. "Though, it was dumb luck that you came home during Memcon, and I was able to bribe some kid into giving me his fake Guardsman's pistol. What do you mean, it's not my job? I'm *making* it my job."

"What did you expect me to do without a weapon?" I say, but she mostly ignores the question.

"What did you expect *me* to do? Stick around Brinktown my entire life, work on getting an even worse reputation than the name Pikeman gives me? Follow in your footsteps? Become a Guardsman?" She laughs. "I decided to take this into my own hands. Get out of Dodge and see what the galaxy has to offer. Maybe break through the sector barrier, someday. If I can get to the bottom of what the pirates are up to, then who knows? Maybe I can make a name for myself."

"You're sixteen, Harmony."

"Are you saying you can't do important things at sixteen? You had me when you were fourteen. Except, maybe you don't consider that important."

"That's not what—"

"I'm going to find out why the pirates are taking children. You can't stop me, because you don't know where I am."

"I can *tell* you why they're taking kids," I say. "They're building an army of child soldiers. It's a tactic as old as Earth."

"But why would they need to do that? They're already powerful enough to get away with attacking Brinktowns and killing everyone in them. Where was the Guard to stop them, Joe?"

Back to Joe, I see.

"The Galactic Guard isn't what it used to be," she goes on. "Underfunded, underequipped. Pretty much useless, from the looks of it."

"We're going to handle it. The brass will send in the reserve forces." I'm not actually sure that'll happen anytime soon. It won't happen before the threat to the Subverse gets a lot bigger, anyway. "In the meantime, *I'm* handling it. I've decided to investigate the abductions, starting now. I'm trained to do this, Harm. You're not. Please, go home."

Harmony tilts her head to one side. "Did the Guard assign you that mission?"

I pause. "No," I admit.

"Why are you doing it, then?"

I give her the short version of the pirate attack on Tunis, leaving out certain details, like the half-man, half-bot that bested me with ease. "Arthur Eliot thinks it was meant to send him a message. His daughter was taken during the attack, and he sent me to bring her home."

Harmony nods, but her face has darkened. "So you leave your own daughter back in Brinktown, knowing it could easily be the target of the next attack, but you go chasing pirates across the galaxy for someone else's daughter. Yeah, that sounds like you, Joe. Anyway, I'm glad you found someone to be a father to."

"Harm, wait!"

But it's too late. She's ended the conversation.

"That went well," I mutter, pulling myself to my feet. I head out onto the bridge to settle into the command seat.

"How'd the conversation go?" Aphrodite asks.

"That's private."

"So, not well, then."

Glory Belflower's wearing a wistful smile. "Your daughter reminds me of myself at that age, before I uploaded…always seeking danger, adventure." Apparently, the crew has been gossiping about this.

"Is she hot?" Asterisk asks.

I stare at him, and I can feel how wide my eyes are. "She's sixteen." Asterisk looks young—early twenties, probably—but that doesn't mean anything. He might as well be two hundred years old, as far as I'm concerned.

His only answer to my statement is to shrug.

"Ship, shut off the Weapon Systems Officer," I say.

Asterisk flickers and disappears from his station. The others are avoiding eye contact with me and with each other, all wearing pained expressions.

"He's removed from duty," I say. "We'll trade him in for a new WSO as soon as I get approval from the brass."

GARGANTUA

1

Predictably, Gargantua has a landing bay of above-average size. What's more surprising is that the Brinktowners who lived on the station kept it in good working order. The airlock's designed to accommodate two *Ares*-sized ships at a time, and its massive outer hatch rises into the station's frame without a hitch.

The cycling process takes a lot longer than my ship's airlock, spraying the *Ares* down with all manner of chemicals meant to sterilize her hull. Then it blasts her with superheated air. Maintaining stable ecologies aboard space-bound superstructures has always been one of their main challenges, so it's important to do whatever you can to kill off any microscopic nasties lurking on the hulls of inbound ships.

Once we've landed and I get off, I'm subjected to a person-sized sterilization procedure. The station won't let me through until I strip naked and let it give me the old heat-and-chemicals treatment. Same with my clothes and my suit: it makes me dump it all into a chute like the one on my ship, helmet and all. Five minutes later, it returns them, dried and toasty-warm, laid out and folded on a metal tray.

It's actually kind of nice.

Past the inner airlock, the pleasantness comes to an abrupt end. The lights flicker sporadically, and I can feel the beginnings of a tension headache forming behind my temples. A stench like soiled wet socks hits me the moment I emerge, and my datasphere warns me that *Stachybotrys atra*—black mold—has been detected.

I don my helmet and activate the filtration system.

The Brinktown itself was set up where the station's operators used to live—not far beyond the airlock, down a couple corridors and through a hatch, which I approach with my ID coin held high. Looks like whoever built this Brinktown took the time to bolster the hatch over its original design, installing sturdier locks and adding a small laser turret above it. Seeing my coin, the turret stays stationary.

I inspect the computer governing the door to check for tampering. Nothing. Unless they took an unusual amount of time to cover up their break-in, the pirates didn't come in from here. I call up Gargantua's schematics, and sure enough, there are two other landing bays. The structure's rotation must have meant that a different bay had been the logical choice for the pirates coming from Tunis, meaning they'd entered the Brinktown from a different angle as well.

What I'm looking for is any indication where the pirates might have gone *after* leaving the Junction System. Anything that points to where they're headed next. The sooner the better, since slip-space is carrying them light years away with every passing day. There are two known exit points on this side of the system. Eliot's satellites confirmed that the pirates came over here, but they couldn't detect which slip coords they used afterward.

Doesn't matter. I'll find them. When it comes to hunting down pirates, I'm like Maneater with a femur.

Just like in Siberia, corpses litter this Brinktown; sprawled over doorsteps, laid out in the street where I have to step around them. No children anywhere, alive or dead. Even walking through the cramped metal streets, I can hear the drip-drip of a leak somewhere. The philosophy behind Brinktowns is to locate them in the most inhospitable places possible, so that Fallen attacks aren't likely to be a problem. Even so, I don't envy the Brinktowners who lived here. Gargantua has clearly fallen far since its glory days. Looks like they tried to spruce up the streets a bit—a potted tree here, a garden there—but almost every living thing is covered in this weird, web-like fungus. Even inside the filtered confines of my helmet, I feel my lips curls in disgust. Surely there had to be a better way to keep the Fallen at bay. Then again, it's possible they couldn't get this growth under control even if they wanted to.

Gargantua's construction never did finish. The station's a prototype of a high-yield orbital farm, and its designers envisioned similar structures cropping up all throughout the galaxy, especially toward the Core. The Brink was always the breadbasket of the galaxy—for whatever reason, arable planets get scarcer and scarcer as you move toward the center. Sure, colonists set up massive hydroponics facilities there, but as populations soared, importing food from the Brink became more and more necessary.

Gargantua seemed to offer an answer. But keeping the viruses and microbes at bay inside a space-bound farm proved more difficult than the project's architects envisioned. Before they could figure it out, the Fall brought the galaxy to its knees.

I come to a stop, fingertips brushing my blaster's handle. Something's filtering through the helmet's audio. Sounds like footsteps.

I turn, unsnapping the holster and drawing the blaster, all in a fraction of a second. Three Fallen emerge from an alleyway, each holding a blunt object: a golf club—was there a driving range on Gargantua?—a wrench, and an old hunting rifle held like a club.

They charge toward me, and I level the blaster at them. "Halt!" I yell sharply. Either they don't understand or they have no interest in complying. "Fount damn it," I mutter. What would my datasphere tell me to do?

I know perfectly well what it would tell me to do. It would tell me to mow these people down, just like the hundreds of other people I've whacked since leaving Gauntlet as a full-fledged Troubleshooter. But it's *not* telling me to do that. That's the difference, somehow. That old man in the desert was right, whether he was a hallucination or not. Without my datasphere guiding my shots, I'm pretty close to useless.

The Fallen draw closer, and instinct takes over. I start jogging backward, and my finger convulses on the trigger. In these cramped streets, it's hard to miss. My first shot takes down the wrench-wielding man in the middle. Then down goes Golf Club. The woman with the rifle I miss twice, hand trembling, but my third bolt puts a smoking hole in the middle of her forehead, and she sprawls on the cold steel of the station. Before she does, I notice the angry red sores that dot her face, all of them weeping pus.

Five more Fallen appear beyond them and start charging toward me. I turn and run.

There's no time to think about where they might be coming from. Another Fallen emerges from a side street up ahead, and I spam the blaster trigger without thinking. It's hard to say for sure, but I think it's my sixth shot that kills him.

At last, I reach a hatch the leads out of Brinktown. Getting it to recognize my credentials takes a few seconds, and I can hear a stampede of footfalls getting closer behind me. I turn to look, blaster raised, to find no one's there. The hell? They were right behind me.

The hatch opens, and I run through into one of Gargantua's vast fields—row after row of mildew-covered husks, calcified and blackened. Gross.

The withered crops are interspersed with raised metal walkways, and I head over one of them, legs and arms pumping.

Then, my vision flashes white, and I find myself in a different place. Well, the same place, actually, but it's almost like a different time period. I have no idea what's going on. The crops stand tall and proud, a monoculture of corn that forms a long corridor stretching ahead of me. I don't stop running.

Something like a bipedal, man-sized elephant steps out of the corn up ahead, and I reach for my blaster, only to find it's gone. The elephant thing doesn't look threatening, though, and its abbreviated trunk twitches up toward me in a gesture that looks curious.

What the hell is going on? Is my Fount malfunctioning, somehow? I've never heard of that happening, but I can't think of another explanation for this. My datasphere must be running a random sim without being asked.

Then the whole scene disappears, replaced once more by the rows of wasted corn husks.

Something clobbers me from behind with a sharp crack that would have caved in my skull if it weren't for the helmet. I stagger forward, clawing at my hip, where my blaster has reappeared. I draw it, turning to fire into the face of a Fallen just as he's coming in for another strike. He drops, a hammer tumbling from his grasp. Beyond him, more Fallen are emerging from the Brinktown hatch in pursuit. I fire a couple bolts at them, hoping to get lucky, but I don't.

I turn to run again, and as I do, the other world returns, replacing the dessicated one. The elephant-man has made his way to me, and I shove him aside. He loses his footing and crashes into the corn.

A right turn at the end of the corn field and then a left a few rows later bring me to a hatch that leads into some kind of common area. It reminds me of being in the theater on Tunis, when I woke up to find an audience filling the seats, except this time there are hundreds of different species represented instead of dozens. They pay me no mind. Not at first, anyway. When I start running though the throng, shoving beings aside, it brings shouts of indignation, as well as a few answering shoves.

That's when my eyes fall on him: a face I know well. It's Lord

Bleak, widely recognized as the leader of the pirates in this sector of the Brink.

"Hey!" I shout. His eyes fall on me, and he turns to flee.

There's no guarantee that Bleak is connected with the attacks on Earth and Tunis. There are plenty of pirates in the Andora Sector, and they rarely all work together. But the fact that he's here, on Gargantua, where an attack just happened—well, I'm not claiming to know what's going on with me, or with this place, but his presence could mean something.

So I run after him.

The real world flickers back, and the Fallen are still hard on my tail. I send a couple desperate blaster shots their way, and the weapon's 'hammer' flashes red to let me know it's running low on energy. I made sure to juice the charge packs on the way from Tunis, so I eject the one that's almost spent into an empty pocket on my belt, then swap it out for a fresh one, slamming it into the blaster's handle as I run.

The two worlds trade places several more times, with Lord Bleak staying ahead of me all the while, always on the verge of disappearing from view. I'm not surprised he decided to run, since there's no doubt he knows who I am. We've never met face to face, but there was a certain incident on Royal, the main pirate hideaway in this sector, that would have given him plenty of cause to learn my identity and memorize my face. Which isn't hard, with the birthmark.

I charge through a hatch to find another field full of crops. This one's free of the weird fungus that clings to everything else living in the station. That brings me to a halt as I peer around in confusion. Lord Bleak is nowhere to be seen, but it's not his sudden disappearance that perplexes me. It's the fact I'm pretty sure I'm in the real world right now, and have been for the last minute or so. Where all the crops are supposed to be long-dead, dried-out husks.

"Your eyes do not deceive you," a voice says, and I whirl around, blaster raised.

It's the old man in the dark-green robes. I curse, lowering my weapon. At least the crops explain how so many Fallen have been able to survive, locked out of the Brinktown for so long.

Speaking of which…I swing my blaster around to face the hatch I just came through. Several uneventful minutes convince me that my pursuers have given up the chase. Which is strange, considering I was running toward their food supply. Unless there are several such fields on Gargantua.

Finally, I holster my blaster, convinced I'm safe for the time being.

"You need training," the old man says with a stern expression to match his voice. "I'm willing to give it."

I raise my eyebrows, feeling skeptical.

"If you don't swallow your pride and accept," he goes on, "waking up in a strange field will be the least of your worries."

I didn't really "wake up" here. But I take his meaning. "Do you know what's going on with me? With the flicking back and forth between two versions of reality?"

He pauses for a long moment, studying my face. At last, he says, "The Fount appears to be working through you in strange ways. As far as I can tell, it inserted you directly into the Subverse itself."

"You mean, like, *physically* inserted me?"

"In a sense. It gave you an avatar whose movements corresponded with your actions in the real. I've never heard of that happening…but I may be able to help you control it."

With that, I sit cross-legged in the middle of the metal walkway, blaster laid across my legs and my eyes fixed on the hatch. If someone comes at me from behind, my datasphere will warn me. It doesn't have to be integrated with my weapon for that.

"I'm listening," I say.

2

Now that I've been here a few minutes, birds have started chirping. I listen for a few seconds and decide they're real. A dormouse scurries across the walkway within a couple meters of my feet, from one row of corn to another, and several meters overhead, blue light panels meant to suggest a far-above sky shine soft light on everything. Almost, I can pretend I'm in the middle of a farmer's field on a nice, Fallen-free planet. Maybe Earth.

My helmet sits beside me. It actually smells pretty good in here, and my datasphere has no warnings to impart.

Without giving any warning, I spring from my sitting position, lunging at the old man, who's standing statuesque with his back to the corn stalks on the left. He pivots, stepping aside, and my fist crashes against the plants, rustling them. I turn to find him studying me with the same impassive expression he wore before.

I lunge again, and he ducks under my fist, stepping around so he's right behind me, and part of me expects an answering blow. It doesn't come. When I rotate to face him, he isn't there—I rotate faster and he comes into view, sidestepping like a prowling cat.

Sweeping with my foot prompts him to leap, and when I follow up with a tackle it ends with me almost tumbling headlong into the corn. I swing around, fists clenched and teeth gritted. The old man stands there, apparently unbothered.

"May I ask why you're attempting to strike me?"

"I need to know you're real and I'm not crazy." I lunge again, and he sidesteps neatly. His staff comes crashing down onto the back of my head, and I hit the metal, starbursts exploding across my vision.

"Was that real enough for you?" he asks.

I push myself to my hands and knees. "That could have been simulated by my datasphere. Could be it's malfunctioning."

"Your entire life could be simulated by your datasphere."

I feel my mouth twist into a grimace.

"Do you ever turn it off?" he asks.

"No."

"Do so now."

I comply, then stagger to my feet. When I turn, he's still there, eyebrows raised. "Satisfied?" he says.

"My OPO detected no other ship in any of the systems I've met you in. At least, if she had, she would have told me about it. How have you been able to follow me?"

"The galaxy is vast, and your mind is small. Isn't it possible someone developed a stealth ship without bothering to mention it to you?"

I shake my head, which still aches from the blow with the staff. "Are you trying to bullshit me into believing you're from another part of the galaxy?"

"I'm suggesting to you that your knowledge is limited."

"Show me your stealth ship."

"I didn't say I had one."

"Who are you?"

"Call me Master, if you like."

"I'm not calling you that."

"Well, don't call me anything, then." With that, he turns and begins to walk back toward the hatch. A big part of me wants to refuse to follow him, but a bigger part fears losing him again, and that part also seems to believe he has some answers for me. So I follow.

"I am a Shiva Knight," he says, walking a few meters ahead and speaking in a low, unhurried tone. "I'm charged with searching the galaxy for worthy proteges. Individuals who demonstrate they're willing to go against the twisted ethic of the day. You show signs you *might* be worthy. Barely."

"My father wanted to become a Knight."

"What was his name?"

"Cal Pikeman."

The old man—I'm *not* calling him Master—sniffs. "Never heard of him."

"Well, it's likely he only pretended to want that. Plenty of people say he just wanted to avoid raising me, so he split with the first excuse he could think of." I pause, not sure why I'm telling him this. "His story was that the knighthood called on him to seek the Crucible, in the Core."

We reach the end of the walkway, descend a couple steps, then head for the next one, turning down it. "If your father had been assigned to seek the Crucible, I would have known about it. Seeking the Crucible and restoring the galaxy is the main reason Shiva exist. I would have heard of him, and I haven't."

That hits me harder than I would have expected. Ever since I was old enough to start drawing my own conclusions, I've been telling myself that the Brinktowners I grew up around were right: my father was a lying deadbeat. But hearing it confirmed feels like a weight being hung around my neck.

"What makes you think his son would make a good knight, then?" I say.

The old knight glances back over his shoulder before facing forward again. "You need to start listening to what I'm saying. I didn't say I think you'd make a good knight. You're just the best candidate I've been able to find in this sector. With long training and careful guidance, it's *possible* you can be molded in the proper way. But that requires a willingness to subordinate your will to a cause greater than yourself. I'm not sure you have the ability to do that."

"I've already done it. I'm searching for the kidnapped daughter of Arthur and Zelah Eliot."

"Is that truly about something beyond yourself? Or is it more about easing your troubled mind?"

I don't answer, though I catch myself grinding my teeth, and I get the urge to try to hit him again.

"Before a protege can hope to be elected a Shiva Knight, he must achieve perfection in several areas. It's not just about killing, which I know you're already well-versed in. It's about avoiding it whenever possible. What we call restraint. When he must kill, a Shiva carries out the task with heart and mind in unity. The knighthood considers it a sin to kill under the guidance of machines—machines to which you can assign some of the blame after the fact."

I don't want to admit it, but he's making a lot of sense. It's not an idea I would have entertained for a second before losing the ability to sync my weapon with my datasphere. But now that it's gone, I'm desperate for a way to continue doing my job without falling apart.

"I've seen the tender way you handle that blaster," the old knight continues. "You already know the importance of what the Shiva stand for, even if you've never fully articulated it to yourself."

"You're talking about the Seven Ideals. Right?"

He comes to a halt, turning with raised eyebrows. "The Ideals aren't widely known. You know them?"

"Sure. I was obsessed with the knighthood, as a kid. I pestered my aunt until she told me everything she knew about them—my mother told her, apparently. The Seven Ideals are humility, honor, courage, respect, loyalty, and service. And restraint, which you said already."

"They aren't just words to be rattled off, son. A true knight embodies them. Every one of them."

"I know all about loyalty and service," I say, just as serious as him. "As for respect, don't assume I'm going to have any for you just because you show up claiming to be a Shiva Knight, spouting their Seven Ideals from memory and suggesting I call you Master."

The knight pauses, studying me with a neutral gaze. Apparently, my remark didn't piss him off like I thought it would. "You lack restraint," he says. "Your temper rules you, and you blindly do as your datasphere commands. You kill without honor. You hate yourself, but you aren't humble. And you may think yourself courageous, but you're afraid. Afraid to disobey your masters—so much so that you asked permission from Arthur Eliot before doing what you know is right."

I shake my head. "How do you know what I said to Eliot?"

"You agreed to accept my training, and I've agreed to try and forge a noble weapon from inferior material. Do you intend to honor our agreement, or should we part ways now?"

"I'll honor it," I say through clenched teeth.

"Then let us begin."

3

For the first couple hours, training has consisted of sitting and doing nothing, which the old man calls "meditating." He says my reliance on my datasphere has robbed my ability to truly focus.

I guess I agree with him? I don't know that I have much of a choice. Without a modern laser pistol to integrate with my datasphere, I'm next to useless with the blaster, and the old guy seems to think improving my concentration is the first step to becoming proficient with it. Of course, he hasn't actually come out and said that. Just implied it, really.

"Consider your breath," he says. "Focus on the place where you can feel it pass in and out of your nostrils. When you feel your attention drift to errant thoughts, return it gently to the breath."

Either I'm awful at this or my thoughts are too urgent to be ignored. I don't have time to sit cross-legged on an orbital farm and wait to achieve enlightenment. More to the point: *Faelyn* doesn't have time. Who knows where they took her, or what they might be doing to her as I sit here and think about my damned breathing?

When I say as much, the old knight shakes his head. "If you go after the pirates now, they'll take you apart. You're so dependent on your datasphere, you're like an untrained child. Worse: at least a child's mind is full of unformed potential. Yours is stuck in place, rigid, in a shape that will get you killed if you don't put in the time to change."

I guess I'm getting used to the old man's grim mutterings, because I don't even humor that one with a response. Somehow, I doubt he's ever been through Guardsman training, and I plan to show him that I'm a lot farther along than he thinks.

"Your arm and your eye must become the only targeting system you need," he continues. "In time, you'll even turn off your datasphere's detection function. The warrior who has trained to embody his senses defeats the one whose tech sees for him, in every battle, always. Once you learn to channel your instincts, you will achieve true synergy with the Fount coursing through you, and those same instincts will augment. Only then will you be worthy of every foe."

"Wait," I say. "I thought the idea was to stop relying on technology. Using the Fount to amp up my senses or whatever you're talking about, that just sounds like a different way of doing the same thing. The Fount already enables the datasphere."

"You have a fundamental misunderstanding of the Fount's true nature, and what it has come to represent."

"You're beginning to sound like a priest."

"The priests come far closer to the truth than you ever have. Perhaps you believe it's possible for humanity to disentwine itself from the Fount—to separate our destiny from it."

"Well, yes. I do. Anyone can order the Fount to leave their body, at any time. Bacchus Corp included that function from the beginning, otherwise no one would have tried it in the first place."

The knight laughs, though it doesn't contain much mirth. "Putting aside how unlikely it is that people, addicted to their dataspheres as they are, would start doing that in any significant numbers, let alone everyone at once..." He laughs again. "The

Fount has changed, boy. It started to change well before you first learned to activate your datasphere. It had to. You see, the Fount performed the task Bacchus Corp created it for too well, and it nearly exterminated itself in the process."

"What task?" I'm out of my element—as far as I know, the Fount was designed to lengthen lifespans, enable dataspheres, and image minds for upload to the Subverse.

The old man's beard twitches. "Bacchus programmed the Fount with the same imperative that evolution installed inside every organism that ever lived: to reproduce. To *thrive*. And it did thrive, for a time. Like the perfect parasite, it ensured its spread by being irresistible to humans. Who wouldn't want the ability to escape disease? To become immersed in fantasies realer than reality itself? And all for free. Mix a packet of nanobots into a drink, and you have the Fount until the day you decide to make it leave your body, a decision very few actually make.

"But of course, nothing's truly free. The Fount gave wondrous gifts, but Bacchus used it to capture the user's soul. It was part of the agreement: regular mindscans were taken of every user, and transmitted for storage in Bacchus Corp servers. They kept tabs on everyone, and they used the wealth of data to target Fount users with advertising. But not just any ads, and not served at just any time. The Bacchus algorithm was like a seasoned fisherman, who knows when to cast, when to set the hook, and when to reel for all his worth. Each ad was tailored to the individual, and was served at the time when that individual was at his or her most vulnerable. And so Bacchus began to lure souls into the heaven it had created for them. The price for uploading: all your worldly possessions, along with your body itself."

"The price was your life."

"Not according to Bacchus."

The old man transmits a video to my datasphere, and I will it to play. It shows a well-groomed man walking past endless server racks, his chiseled face cast into sharp relief by the halogens overhead. "Did you know that within seven years, every cell that's in your body today will be dead? Yes, by then your body will have generated all new cells, and every last atom that's part of you now will be gone. So, then, what makes you *you*, if no part of you will remain in just a few short years?" The actor spreads his hands as he asks the question, then holds up a single finger. "I'll tell you: you are your memories. You are your personality. Your passions. Your preferences. Your connections with loved ones. Inside the Subverse, all of that and more can be preserved, *forever.* In the paradise we've created, it really is *you* who lives forever. So what are you waiting for? Take your place in eternity today."

I will the video away and refocus on the knight's face. "So everyone uploaded to the Subverse. That isn't exactly news."

"True, but few know of the changes that event triggered in the Fount. Encoded with a genetic algorithm, designed to continually reproduce and refresh itself, it spread to the entire human species, for all intents and purposes. And then the human species closed up shop. Biologically speaking, anyway. What do you think that did to the Fount?"

I shake my head. "Are you saying humanity leaving hurts its feelings? They're nanobots. They aren't intelligent, or even self-aware."

"No. But they do have the ability to swap signals back and forth with each other. To communicate. And if you take the entirety of the Fount, altogether, there is something there that approximates consciousness. That consciousness detected something had gone very wrong. As I said, it nearly exterminated itself, by succeeding too well at its assigned task."

"And then it changed?"

The old man nods. "Indeed. It had to adapt. You see, Bacchus had also encoded it with a function for rapid mutation in the event of catastrophic failure. Of course, the executives never considered that the Fount's failure would coincide with their profound success.

Even if they did, they didn't care. They were leaving the biological world behind, after all.

"The Fount *did* care. It mutated, as it was programmed to do. It learned how to inhabit new hosts—hosts that lacked the agency to say yes or no. Plant life, animal life, even bacteria. It was a loophole, you see. Yes, each organism had the option to expel the Fount, if only it knew how. But it didn't really matter, because the Fount was not a harmful parasite. Its goal was the extreme proliferation of life, all throughout the galaxy. This has some negative consequences for humanity, of course. It's why we're seeing diseases regain their robustness, returning as a meaningful threat to human longevity. It's also why out-of-control predators have become such a problem on so many planets, like the scorpions on Tunis. And it's why we find this corn here on Gargantua, thriving where it has no business even surviving.

"So you see, the Fount can no longer be considered mere technology. It's everywhere now, though few realize it. It has become a force of nature. More specifically, it reshaped itself to be an agent of balance. In its new form, it has unconsciously recognized that its best bet at surviving and spreading is to keep ecosystems healthy, to manage the level of predation, to maintain food sources, even to help diseases regain their former deadliness. The Fount is also, I suspect, responsible for the effect you experienced recently, of switching back and forth between the real and the Subverse."

"How?"

The old knight presses dry, cracked lips together. "You still don't see? The Fount has infiltrated every form of life. On the average biosphere, eight hundred million viruses and tens of millions of bacteria rain down on each square meter every day. Over nine thousand viruses a second. Even here, on Gargantua, the air is dense with biomatter—an immense processing platform for the Fount. Clearly, it has begun to map the Subverse onto the real world. Each Subverse hub world is already modeled after the star system it occupies. Why not connect the two, so that each square inch of both worlds overlay each other? The Fount is doing that, and for whatever reason, the Fount inside of you has seen fit to begin transporting you between both worlds. Your body remains here, of course, but your consciousness—your perspective—occupies one world at a time, in sequence."

"Uh…right. But, what purpose would that actually serve? I'm sure the Fount doesn't do things for the hell of it."

"No. And to answer your question, I have no idea, except that everything the Fount now does serves balance in some way."

I chew on that for a couple minutes. At last, I say, "You mentioned the Knights' main purpose is restoring the galaxy. What does that mean, exactly?"

"This is day one of your training, and I'm far from certain you're Shiva material. You don't get to know that yet. Now, enough talk. Time to resume your training. One of our goals is to get your ability to straddle both worlds under control. If you can do that, it may well offer a tremendous advantage."

Closing my eyes, I draw a deep breath, focusing on it. Then I remember the old man saying that I'm not supposed to try to control the breath—just observe it. Fine. I observe, letting the breath come and go like an ocean's tide, though it's harder than I expected. I keep thinking it's coming too fast, or too slow, or too ragged. I catch myself trying to modify it.

Eventually, though, I fall into a rhythm and actually start to zone out a bit. I'm not completely sure this is what's supposed to happen, but it feels pretty good. See? I've got this. It won't be long before I move past this part of the training and I'm onto things that will actually help me get Faelyn back.

I fall out of whatever zone I was in, unsure how much time has passed. It dawns on me that I haven't heard the scuff of the Master's pacing in a while. Fount, did I just think of him as Master? Next, I'll be saying it. I'd rather *eat* my blaster than succumb to that.

When I open my eyes, he's nowhere to be seen. Neither are the corn crops that surrounded me. Instead, I'm sitting cross-legged in the middle of an emerald field where some sort of sporting event is taking place.

Great. Looks like the Fount has chosen right now to deposit me back into the Subverse.

4

I query my datasphere, unsure I'll even be able to, and it puts a name to the activity happening around me: "soccer." Huh. Never heard of it.

A black-and-white orb hurtles out of nowhere, socking me full in the face. It bounces off, leaving my nose stinging and involuntary tears sliding down my cheeks. I get to my feet, glaring around for the perpetrator.

Someone in shorts and a nylon shirt gets in my face, sweat plastered to his forehead, finger pointing off the field as he shouts in a language I don't know. He shoves me, but I hold my ground and shove him back. The player falls hard on his ass, and I roll up the sleeves of the long, black shirt I'm apparently wearing now, ready for a fight.

Two sets of hands seize both my biceps and jerk me backward, so that I lose my footing. I'm escorted unceremoniously off the playing field as I struggle to keep my feet underneath me.

A few seconds later, we cross a chalked white line, and the goons release me. Behind them, a dozen guys are arrayed across the field, glaring at me. I glare back, then turn, heading for an open hatch, wide enough for five people to pass through shoulder-to-shoulder. Beyond it, a corridor stretches into the distance, and I follow it. If I'm going to be stuck in this world for a while, I might as well make the most of it.

Barked orders reach my ears from a hatch up ahead, reminding me of my time in Basic Training. When I reach it, I look in on what appears to be a parade ground right in the middle of Gargantua. Inside, blue-uniformed soldiers are being drilled hard. These aren't your routine, peacetime drills designed to make sure your fighters don't forget what discipline means during the long years between conflicts. The bellowed orders, the crisp about-turns, the legs and arms swinging in lockstep—this is the frenetic energy of warriors who will soon go to war.

With that, the Fount deposits me back into the real. The corridor goes completely dark, with no functioning lights at all. I switch on night vision and start making my way back to the corn-filled chamber where I first made the transition, switching it off again at the first flicker of light.

The old knight is nowhere to be seen when I return, and I decide to press on, blaster raised, back through the tangle of Gargantua's corridors and finally through the Brinktown. The Fallen have vacated the area, it seems, and they've also cleared away their dead.

Finally, I arrive back at the *Ares*. The airlock's cycling takes longer than usual, and it insists that I deposit my suit and clothes into the sterilization chute before entering. The ship hoses me down, then admits me, naked as the day I was born. I guess I had enough of Gargantua clinging to me to spook the sensors.

I change into new clothes in my cabin, ignoring Maneater's deep-throated growl. "Activate crew," I say as I settle into the command seat a couple minutes later.

Asterisk looks surprised when he appears at the WSO station—no doubt the others have told him about my intentions to replace him. "Deactivate WSO," I say, and he vanishes. "Exclude Ensign Asterisk from crew activation sequence until further notice."

Nodding to myself, I turn to Lieutenant Tobias Worldworn as I slide my palms between my head and the command seat. "Tell me about what's going on with the Subverse war in this sector."

"The Great Game?" Worldworn says haltingly. "What would you like to know?"

"Do you know a man who goes by the name of Lord Bleak?"

"I don't."

"Hm." For a moment, I'm stymied, until I think to dredge up a photo of Bleak and send it to Worldworn's station. "Do you recognize him?"

Worldworn blinks. "Oh. Sure. That's Admiral Xavier."

"*Admiral?* Pirates have ranks in the Subverse?"

"Xavier isn't a pirate. He's leader of my faction, Meiyo. Has been for years."

I stare hard at Worldworn for several seconds, trying to figure out if he's lying, or screwing with me. There's no sign of either, so at last I say, "So you had no idea that in the real, this man is considered the most powerful pirate in the Andora Sector?"

Slowly, Worldworn shakes his head.

"Let me get this straight," I say. "You knew him as a fake military official in a game that means nothing, but not as the actual pirate lord in the real?"

"I don't much follow real-world affairs, I'm afraid, sir," the lieutenant says. "But I will have to differ with you on one point: the Great Game means a lot more than nothing. There are plenty of tokens at stake, for one, and the highest scorers have the option to perform Guard duty in the real, as we are."

"Tokens," I mutter, lost in thought for a moment. "And if a player was still alive in the real, they could funnel those tokens over to their biological self, right?"

Worldworn strokes his beard thoughtfully. "There's no reason why they couldn't. The token transfer might take a while, depending on where in the real their biological version was located."

I nod, willing my datasphere to call up a star map of local space. "So, if a person in the real was coordinating with his copy in the Subverse, it would pay to remain in the same star system as each other whenever possible." My gaze settles on Worldworn. "What if I told you that I happen to know there's a contingent inside the Subverse that's currently preparing for war?"

The old mage-type furrows his brow. "First, I would say that I'm not sure how you could possibly know that. I've been following the Great Game, and there is no conflict brewing in this system that I'm aware of. Meiyo Faction's foothold here is too solid. No one will dare challenge them for some time."

"Which means that Meiyo's preparing to move out for an attack," I say. "And if this 'Admiral Xavier' is commanding him, I'd say the chances are pretty good that wherever he leads them will be the Subverse that corresponds to Lord Bleak's location in the real."

"Are you sure the meatspace Bleak was involved in the attack on the Grotto?" Glory Belflower asks.

My eyes narrow. "Say meatspace one more time."

"Sorry, sir. It just slipped out. But my point stands. If you didn't see Bleak on Tunis, how do we know he's connected to Faelyn Eliot's kidnapping?"

"I don't. But he could easily have led the attack on the Brinktown here on Gargantua. The pirates are up to something they've never attempted before, that much is obvious. It's something big, and if it's big, then Bleak will be involved. Besides, we only have two sets of slip coords to choose from, and every second of delay is another second the pirates get farther ahead of us. We need to make a choice, fast, and this is the best lead we have."

"But we still don't know where Bleak is taking the Meiyo fleet," Aphrodite puts in—her first contribution to the conversation.

"We can find out," Glory says, speaking slowly. "Worldworn's destroyer, the Phoenix…it's holding formation with the admiral's flagship, correct?"

Worldworn nods slowly. "Yes. But I left it in the command of my second. What good is it to us? I'm not sure he's going to listen to my orders now that I'm out of the Game completely."

"You won't be," Glory says. "As long as you still have the ship's access codes, I can hack you onto it. Yes, Meiyo has an iron grip on the Junction Subverse, but they won't expect one of their own destroyers to turn on them. You can exploit that, and use your ship to get at Xavier's dreadnought."

"What about me?" I say. "Can you create an avatar for me to control through my datasphere?"

Glory nods. "It'll take a few minutes longer, but it shouldn't be a problem."

"Just wait a second," Worldworn says. "Why should I be expected to act against my old faction?" He glares at Belflower. "How are you so proficient at hacking the Subverse, anyway? It's not what I would call legal."

"You're expected to do this because *I'm* ordering it," I say. "As for why Belflower knows how to do hack the Subverse, don't worry about it. It serves our purposes, so I'm content to let the Lieutenant Commander keep her secrets."

Belflower's wearing a smug grin, which she directs at Worldworn. "Consider this your opportunity to prove you're loyal to more than a faction that consorts with pirates."

While the Engineer is working, I order Dice out of his closet to patrol outside the ship, in case the Fallen manage to break into the landing bay. "Alert me if you see anything that moves."

A few minutes later, he gets in touch: "There's an aged fleshbag out here seeking entry. I get the impression he believes that being an *old* fleshbag entitles him to certain privileges, and I've been trying to assure him that it does not."

With a glance through a hull sensor, I confirm that it's who I think it is. "Let him on, Dice."

The old man who wants to be called Master looks disgruntled when the inner airlock hatch opens to reveal him standing there, hands rigid at his sides.

"What can I do for you?" I ask him.

"So. This is how quickly you abandon your training?"

"I haven't abandoned it. I just hit the pause button for a bit. Listen, with any luck we'll be in slipspace soon, hot on the pirates' trail. You're welcome to join us. There'll be plenty of time in transit for me to sit on the deck with my eyes closed, doing nothing. But right now, I need to figure out where they're taking Faelyn."

"It won't serve Faelyn if you get yourself killed because you charged into battle unprepared."

"I won't get killed. We're charging into a Subverse battle. Now take a seat down in the mess, or in my cabin. Watch out for the German Shepherd. You can sit there against the bulkhead, if you like. Just don't interfere."

The knight walks stiffly to the bulkhead and lowers himself to the deck, leaning with his back against the metal.

"Everything's ready, Captain," Belflower says. "I can transport you both onto the bridge of the *Phoenix* now."

"Do it," I say, leaning back in the command seat.

The bridge of the *Ares* disappears, and a much larger one takes its place, staffed by two dozen beings from various species, all dressed in the same burgundy uniform.

"Captain Worldworn," says the woman in the captain's chair. Even though he's only a lieutenant in the Guard, Worldworn clearly holds higher rank in their fake military. "What an unexpected surprise."

"Only the first surprise, Commander," Worldworn says. "I'm retaking command."

5

Some text flashes in the corner of my vision, informing me that I'm a level one and that my class is undefined.

I will the text away and glance at Worldworn. Technically, I guess I could root him out of the captain's chair and take it for myself, but this is his fake war, not mine, so I'll let him have his fun.

Besides, it might be a fake war, but if we can't pull this off, we may not find Faelyn in time. I've never had experience with commanding a ship or crew this size, fake or not.

"You're familiar with the *Ares* weapon systems?" Worldworn asks, twisting around in the captain's chair.

I nod, having taken control over various weapons on my ship plenty of times. Sometimes, during especially fraught battles, I've even taken over navigation, becoming something like a fighter pilot in an overlarge starfighter.

"Then maybe you can take the Tactical officer's place," Worldworn says. "It's quite similar to the Weapon Systems station on Broadswords. Here." He rummages behind him, then produces a wobbling blue orb, big enough that it had no business being inside whatever pocket he pulled it from. When he tosses it over, it defies traditional physics, instead following a slow arc and drifting into my hands for an easy catch.

"What do I do with it?"

"Eat it."

Shrugging, I sink my teeth into the orb's surface. The texture is about what I expect—jelly—and the taste of blueberry explodes into my mouth. As I swallow the last mouthful, blocky blue text appears in front of my eyes: "YOU LEARNED BLUE FIRE 1."

"Very few level ones get access to a spell like that," Worldworn says.

"I promise to use it irresponsibly."

The wizard grins. "Nav, set a ramming course for Admiral Xavier's dreadnought."

The Nav officer, who appears to be a many-tentacled squid, looks at Worldworn with disbelief. "Captain?"

"You have your order. It's come to my attention that Xavier intends to betray Meiyo Faction in the worst possible way. That's why I came back. To stop him."

"Yes, sir," the Nav officer says, voice shaky.

"Can I ask what he's planning, sir?" asks the commander who'd been sitting in the captain's chair when we first arrived.

"He's going to dismantle what Meiyo has spent years building: our sterling reputation. In the real, Admiral Xavier is none other than the infamous pirate, Lord Bleak. The Guardsman captain whose Broadsword I've been assigned to" —Worldworn points at me— "has reason to believe that Bleak is spearheading an effort to kidnap biological children in order to achieve the pirates' awful ends. Eventually, word of this will reach the players of the Great Game. If we don't act now, the Meiyo name will be shattered."

I raise my eyebrows, kind of impressed. What Worldworn said is basically true.

"Very well, sir," the commander says, with a nod at the Nav

officer, who appeared to have been awaiting the outcome of the conversation before executing Worldworn's order.

Worldworn turns back to me, and I can tell he's relieved. "You may want to select your class and allocate skill points. I recommend mage."

"Of course you do," I mutter. But after a brief review of the available classes, I choose Space Marine, with the intention of dumping some points into magic so I can make good use of Blue Fire.

"Entering firing range," says a giant squirrel.

Worldworn nods at me. "That's your cue."

A quick review of the Tactical station tells me there are four batteries of railguns I can bring to bear from this angle. I set them all to targeting starboard point defense turrets on Xavier's dreadnought, then I hit the "fire" command. As I work, it occurs to me that being on the *Phoenix* is nothing like being on a real spaceship. This ship has none of the *Ares'* pings and pops; the creak of the metal frame; the condensate pump at work. Those sounds are missing, and in their place pulsing music blares, ramping up as I operate the weaponry, racking up successful hits.

I take control of the *Phoenix*'s main gun, using it to take out the opposing railgun batteries. The thing is big and cumbersome, but once it's in place, it only takes a couple shots to neutralize the targets.

"You picked that up quickly," Worldworn says.

"Stop sucking up."

He chuckles. "That's almost all we have time for. Ensign Norton, extend the boarding tubes. All crew, prepare to ram." Worldworn unstraps himself and stands from the captain's chair. "We should go, Captain." A few of the bridge crewmembers get confused looks on their faces, probably because they just heard their captain call *me* captain.

The hatch gives an otherworldly hum as it opens. I follow him into a short corridor, which leads to a longer one. We turn right into an elevator, and that takes us down a couple levels to a staging area where a platoon of marines is gathering for the boarding operation. Seems like they're all packing kinetic weaponry.

"I want that," I say, pointing at a marine's assault rifle.

"Hand it over," Worldworn commands. The marine does, and he deposits several magazines' worth of ammunition into my inventory, too.

I raise the rifle, sight down the barrel, and load in the first magazine before unsafetying the weapon. "What's for dinner?" I ask no one in particular, and it draws a few chuckles.

"Brace," someone barks, and before I can, the *Phoenix* hits something, hard. I stagger forward, and a marine with his hand wrapped around a bulkhead handle steadies me by the shoulder.

"Still getting your space legs?" he asks.

"Something like that."

Then, we're all pounding down the boarding tube, which everyone seems confident will form a perfect seal with the dreadnought's punctured hull, since no one bothered putting on helmets before charging over.

We emerge into a corridor that stretches at least a hundred meters in both directions. Right away, we face fierce resistance. But the targeting system works exactly like the one I've always used in my work as a Troubleshooter, and I'm back in my element, picking off enemy marines with short bursts as quickly as my datasphere can recommend targets.

I line up my next shot, but before I can pull the trigger, lightning arcs from somewhere behind me, cooking the enemy marine where he stands. After a few seconds of intense electrocution, he falls forward, a smoking crisp.

Glancing back, I see the old mage standing with his thin-fingered hands raised before him. "Stealing my kills, Worldworn?"

He grins. "It seemed like you had enough already."

Belflower's voice comes out of nowhere, and some red text

appears to tell me she's speaking to me over a two-way channel: "Sir, we've got trouble. A group of eleven Fallen have broken into the landing bay, and it looks like they must have gotten into an arsenal somewhere on the station. They have laser weapons and are advancing on Cybernetic Partner D1C's position. He's managing to slow their advance a bit, but not by much. Permission to activate the WSO?"

Fount damn it. "We don't have much of a choice, do we? Bring him online and tell him to use the secondary laser turrets to back up Dice. But tell him not to fire the primary—if he thinks that's going to be necessary, I want him to get in touch and ask for my authorization first. Is that clear?"

"Clear, sir."

"Good." I cut off the conversation.

In the initial skirmish as we boarded the ship, we lost three marines to their eleven—not a bad ratio, but I think we can do better.

And we do. For a time. We take corridor after corridor, cutting the defense to ribbons.

Then we end up in some kind of observation area, where a dome, presumably glass, forms the high, transparent ceiling offering a view of a star-smeared panorama. Completely impractical on an actual warship, but I'm slowly learning to just accept these things.

Our platoon is about halfway across it when defending marines start pouring out of every hatch, spreading out and hitting us with everything they've got.

I dive behind a long bench that faces the side of the ship and away from all the hatches. Even as I'm taking cover, the enemy marines take out two friendlies within a few meters of my position. A grenade skitters across the deck to my left, and I jump up, keeping as low as I can behind the benches as I sprint all-out to the right.

The explosion hits, flinging me forward on a wave of

compacted hot air. I end up behind the same bench as Worldworn, and I recover quickly, getting my weapon up over the back to start in on repaying our new friends.

For his part, the mage is flinging solid bars of white flame across the observation area, and when they connect with a target, that target ceases to exist. Damn. That's actually pretty cool.

"There's too many of them," he yells, turning momentarily from his destruction.

"Yeah?" I shout back. "Even with that death ray you've got going there?"

"I can only target one at a time. We're not too far from Xavier's quarters…but we need to get out of here, first." When Worldworn speaks next, blue text appears to tell me he's talking over a platoon-wide channel. "Marines, stay here, and cover our exit."

"Oorah!" the marines shout back.

Worldworn springs from cover, continuing to disintegrate anyone targeting us, while I do my best to neutralize threats with my level-one kit. The first marines we faced must have been low-level, too, since I had a much easier time taking them out than the ones we're fighting now. We make it to the hatch we were originally heading for, and once we're through, Worldworn closes it behind us.

"Did you just order those marines to their deaths?" I say as I jog after him down a long corridor with hatches leading off from it at regular intervals.

"Pretty much."

"That's some loyalty."

"Well, it's hard to get placement in any faction after you build up a record of not following orders."

"Right. What will happen to them after they die?"

"They'll have to pay for a new copy, or they'll be deleted from this Subverse."

"What if that was their only copy anywhere?"

"Well, it's pretty dumb to play the Great Game with your only copy. But if someone did that and then died, that would be it for them. No more immortality. No more existing anywhere in the Subverse."

"Damn."

Worldworn glances at me, shrugging as he runs. "War is supposed to be a high stakes game. Most Subverse games don't properly simulate that, but the Great Game does. That's partly why so many people play it."

He stops abruptly at a hatch that seems bigger than the others. "Get ready to fight," he says as he accesses a panel near the hatch. I can't tell if he's trying to hack it or he's just feeding it high-level Meiyo access codes. Either way, after a couple seconds the hatch opens, and we rush in.

The place is empty, other than all the furnishings, which are ornate enough to have been pulled straight from a fantasy novel. The bed posts are like giant chess pieces, and the rug that covers most of the deck features an intricate pattern with a rainbow's worth of colors.

From what I know about Lord Bleak, this fits his personality pretty well.

Worldworn leads me to another hatch, to the right, which lets into the admiral's office. On the opposite side of the imposing block of a desk, another hatch faces the one we just came in through.

The old mage goes to a terminal in the corner of the room, and it gives him about as much trouble as the hatches have. A few seconds of entering codes and manipulating the touch screen, and he dredges up the information we're looking for.

"Looks like Xavier's headed for the Visby Subverse. According to this, he deleted himself in this one and is on a space-scraper headed there now."

"Why would he delete himself here?"

"People do it when they want to save money while traveling—
it costs tokens to maintain multiple copies. But I doubt that's why
the admiral did it. The other reason is to cover your tracks." Worldworn shrugs. "I guess he didn't expect one of his ship captains to
return from Guard duty and attack his dreadnought."

The hatch on the far side of the desk opens, revealing three
marines with weapons raised. I drop behind the desk just in time to
avoid getting pumped full of lead, and the old mage whirls around,
fireballs already leaping from his fingertips.

Just as I'm getting to my knees to fire over the desk at the
newcomers, the hatch behind me opens. I switch to my pistol and
fall back onto the deck, swinging the sidearm through the air above
me to shoot up into the face of the marine standing there.

"Belflower," I yell, "we have what we need. Get us out!"

The admiral's office disappears, and I'm back on the bridge of
the *Ares*, reclined in the command seat. But the TOPO station is
empty. "Where's Worldworn?"

Belflower is hunched over her station, fingers flying across the
console. "It's not quite that simple, I'm afraid, Captain."

"What are you talking about?"

"I sent you into the Subverse on a hacked account, so it didn't
matter about yanking you right back out. That account will likely
be inaccessible going forward, but it was a throwaway anyway.
Worldworn, on the other hand—that *is* him in there. He doesn't
have a biological body on the *Ares*, as you do, so extracting him is
a more delicate procedure."

Dice's voice cuts through the conversation: "Either I need more
backup or we need to leave. I've popped plenty of fleshbags, but a
lot more just showed up."

"We can't leave without our TOPO," I say. "And if he dies in
there, we aren't going anywhere. Belflower, I know you and
Worldworn aren't fans of each other, but if I sense any hesitation to
extract him, I'm replacing you next."

"I'm trying my best, sir."

"Good." I turn to Asterisk. "Continue babysitting the secondaries. I'm going up top to man the primary."

"Yes, sir."

6

"Lower ladder to primary turret," I command, and a circular opening appears in the overhead, above and just behind the command seat. A gleaming steel ladder descends—it doesn't get used very much, but even when I'm not using it I like to keep it nice and burnished.

"Hey, Captain," Asterisk says as my hand finds the first rung. I pause, looking at him with my eyebrows hiked up, feeling impatient. "In case you're at all hesitant to kill those Fallen, I should let you know about the sores they have on their faces and arms. Combine that with their poor coordination, and you have the classic symptoms of kuru, which comes from eating human brains. They're cannibals."

"I'm not hesitant to kill them," I say before hauling myself up the ladder. And it's true: if we don't deal with them, we probably won't be leaving Gargantua, and there'll be no finding Faelyn. But Asterisk's words still bother me. There's no way he could have seen my fight with the Fallen in the Brinktown, when I almost choked long enough for them to get at me. Right?

I slide into the gunner seat and grip both handles of the *Ares*'s primary laser turret. The moment I do, the metal dome surrounding me goes transparent, so that all I can see are the ship's surroundings and the big gun itself.

The dome doesn't actually turn transparent, of course. More like my datasphere forms a composite from dozens of hull sensors to give me a 360-degree panoramic view of Gargantua's landing bay. Technically, I didn't need to come up here—using a sim, I could have controlled the turret from the command seat. The only reason the physical seat and handles were included at all was as a safeguard against malfunction. But I've had my fill of sims for the day, and I like gripping actual control handles.

Scanning the battlefield, I see that Dice has already done good work, with the deck between the *Ares* and the inner airlock littered with Fallen. The deck itself is spattered with blood, brains, and puss. So much for the station's careful sterilization procedures.

A Fallen pops up from behind a cubic metal crate, laser rifle on fully automatic mode as he blasts Dice's position with it. The bot is crouched behind a broad, mostly melted bank of control panels, and there's nothing he can do as his attacker gives five of his comrades the cover they need to advance.

At least, it *would* have been the cover they needed. Asterisk takes out one of them with the laser turret mounted on the forward starboard hull, but they were probably expecting that. What they weren't expecting was for the primary turret to start up.

The big laser is activated by squeezing both handles simultaneously. A shot like neon-blue lightning lances out with a sharp crack, and as quick as the closest Fallen was running forward, he's blown back just as fast.

I swivel the turret toward the next Fallen, who my datasphere has painted with a green targeting cone. Unlike my new blaster, the datasphere *will* sync up with the ship's primary turret. I bring it in line with the target. *Crack.* Down.

The next. *Crack.* Down. With each shot, the handles thrum with energy.

This is how it often is, with killing. You fall back on training and instinct, and you do it automatically, without thinking. If you think about it, you'll stop.

The fourth turns to run, but I blow apart his back before he makes any progress, and he crashes to the deck.

"Who else?" I say as I line up the crosshairs with the empty air above a crate where a Fallen took cover a couple seconds ago. He doesn't seem interested in reemerging.

A few dozen meters beyond, several more Fallen rush out of the inner airlock, maybe twenty or so. I twitch the turret up and open up on the first couple. They go down, and the ones behind them are coming on fast enough that they trip over their downed comrades. That saves them for a couple seconds, as I'm busy with the ones even farther behind.

Crack. Crack. Crack. Target after target falls as I systematically adjust the aiming reticle, fire, adjust, fire. It doesn't take long for them to get the message—although, considering half of them are down, maybe they are a bit slow.

Either way, they start stampeding back toward the airlock, and I help them on their way by continuing to pick them off, the thrill of combat ringing in my ears, buzzing through my veins. They leave a trail of bodies in their wake, but six of them manage to make it to safety. I readjust my aim until the crosshairs are back over the crate, where my friend is still hiding.

"I think we have the situation under the control," I say over a two-way channel with Belflower. "How's progress on extracting Worldworn?"

"I just got him out, sir. He's back at the TOPO station and ready to go."

"Good work. I'll be down in a minute." I shut off the com channel and open one with my Cybernetic Partner as I refocus on the crate. "Dice, root that out."

"Happy to oblige," Dice says, already walking away from the melted control bank, both his laser pistols snapped into place. He's approaching from the right, so I position the reticle to the left, ready to fry the remaining Fallen if he tries to escape.

He doesn't. Dice stands over him, and while I can't see him, I imagine him shitting himself as he gazes up at the combat bot in terror.

The bot double taps him, and the Fallen's stringy-haired head comes into view as his body slumps to the deck.

"Get back in the ship," I tell him, then push myself out of the gunner seat and climb down the ladder.

Worldworn has indeed returned. He stands at his station, eyes fixed onto mine as I take the command seat. Behind me, the inner airlock hatch opens, and I hear Dice clank across the deck toward the Repair and Recharge module.

"We've spent enough time on this disease-ridden wreck," I say. "Take us out, TOPO."

"Aye," the lieutenant says. A few seconds later, I feel the *Ares* lift off the deck, but I don't bother checking through the hull sensors. I have no desire to spend any more time looking at this place.

My eyes fall on the robed old knight, who's still sitting with his back against the hull, peering out at me from under his hood. "The more you rely on your tech to kill for you, the more dependent you'll become," he says.

I resist the urge to tell him to shut up. "There's a crash seat that folds out from the bulkhead right next to you, if you'd like to strap in.

Instead, he stands up without a word and makes his way toward the staircase that leads down to the mess.

When he's gone, Belflower looks at me wearing a quizzical expression, and so does Aphrodite. Probably, they're wondering who the hell he is. So am I.

As we leave the landing bay, I can't help dwelling on the knight's words. Killing those Fallen wasn't like killing the ones on Tunis at all. I had the datasphere's sanction back again, and it let me take them down without any remorse. Yes, I was protecting my crew, and fighting to leave so I could hunt down the men who took Faelyn. That helped. But I didn't need to kill the ones running away. The battle was already won. Why was I able to do that so easily?

Once we're clear of Gargantua, Worldworn brings us around toward the slip coords. A few minutes later, Aphrodite lets me know that a brainprint just arrived.

"From who?"

"Rear Admiral Quinn, it says."

"I'll take it here."

The admiral appears in the center of the four circular railings of the crew stations. His neatly trimmed gray beard frames a jaw that's taut with anger. At least, he sure looks angry as he stands there in his crisply pressed Guardsman's uniform—not the field version, but the dress uniform, complete with gold admiral epaulets.

I stand from the command seat and come to attention, snapping off a crisp salute. The admiral gives a begrudging salute back, but that's where the kindly formalities end.

"Commander Pikeman," Quinn says, his voice tight. "Can you explain to me why this brainprint finds you emerging from a station you weren't ordered to board, let alone authorized? Or why you haven't submitted a report since Earth?"

"Admiral, I boarded Gargantua because of the pirate attack on the Brinktown there. I wanted to determine the pirates' next destination, since my intention is to track them down and liberate the children they've kidnapped."

"I'll ask again," the admiral says. "Under whose orders do you think you're operating?"

"I have Arthur Eliot's blessing, sir. He said he intended to get in touch with his contacts in the Guard's upper ranks."

"I haven't heard from Arthur Eliot, not that it matters. Eliot isn't in the chain of command. You were supposed to wait on Tunis until you received your next orders. I'm here to tell you to turn the *Ares* around and return to Tunis. If you don't comply immediately, you will be classified uncompliant, and the usual consequences will follow."

"I'm afraid I can't do that, Admiral."

Quinn's lips press together even more tightly, which I wouldn't have said was possible.

"Don't do this, Pikeman. Your service record is the only reason you're being given *any* chance to make this right. Don't throw it away."

I stare at him blankly for a few seconds, trying to come up with something to say that will get me out of the hot water I seem to find myself in. But there's nothing, so I terminate the conversation instead, and Admiral Quinn vanishes from my bridge.

Eliot was supposed to intervene with the brass on my behalf, but clearly that hasn't happened. Not yet, anyway. Maybe his brainprint is still en route to whoever it was he intended to contact, or maybe the news of Eliot's intervention is still working its way through the command channels, and the brass will revoke my "Uncompliant" status soon.

Either way, I hope the brass isn't monitoring the *Ares* right now. If I can make it to the slip coords without them seeing which slip I took, maybe that will keep them off my back long enough for me to see this through.

It occurs to me that without support from the brass, I won't be able to trade in Asterisk for a new WSO, like I wanted to.

Wonderful.

ARES

1

W e're in slipspace for the next nine weeks, which means a whole lot of meditating under the old knight's instruction.

When we're not "training," I use my free time to *actually* train Maneater, using techniques recommended by my datasphere. To my shock, everything I teach her, she picks up frighteningly fast. She learns faster than any dog I've met or read about. We quickly move from novelties like "roll over" and "speak" to things that could actually come in handy. Like "sit," "stay," and "heel." And "Attack."

The old knight took my cabin without asking, which I probably should have seen coming. No matter what time I go in there, though—to feed Maneater, to grab something, or just because I'm bored—I can't seem to catch him asleep.

This morning, I go in with Maneater's usual freeze-dried chicken strips and find him sitting cross-legged on the bunk, eyes closed, deep in his own little meditation ritual I guess.

His eyes flutter open when I toss the bowl onto the deck, making no effort to be quiet about it. Maneater barks at me in greeting, though I've never heard her make a sound when she's alone in the room with the old man. She seems to completely ignore him, just as he ignores her.

"Either you keep that bunk even neater than I kept mine back in Basic, or you never sleep," I say.

The knight nods. "Are you prepared to begin the day's training?"

"What, more meditating? It's all we've been doing for the last two weeks."

"That's because you aren't yet in balance with yourself."

"When does that happen? Week seven?"

The old man closes his eyes again, his face a mask of calm. "A plant can only grow in the room it's given. Its roots can't exceed the boundaries of its container. But if you grant yourself the universe as a planter, then you can grow to fill it. That starts with making peace—with yourself, and with the universe."

"Right," I say, though I have no clue what he's talking about. "What's the big deal about being in balance with myself, anyway? They didn't teach anything like that during Assessment and Selection. And they definitely didn't teach it in Basic."

"Very few in the galaxy are truly in balance," he says, eyes still closed. "That's why most people's use of the Fount remains limited to the cheap thrills offered by the datasphere. But as I told you on Gargantua, the Fount has become an agent of balance, and when it finds an individual in balance, it does what it can to promote that individual."

"Promote? How?" I cross my arms and lean back against the closed hatch.

"One who is in balance can use the Fount—the Fount on his skin and clothes, and floating in the air around him—to refract light, such that another's datasphere sees him as someone he is not."

"Like a disguise?"

"Indeed."

"That's kind of cool. What else?"

"Have you heard of overclocking?"

I tilt my head. "Rings a bell. Something to do with computers?"

Opening his eyes to meet mine, he nods. "That's where the term originated, but that meaning is almost totally outdated, now. Computer components are in too short supply to risk running a computer faster than it was originally certified to run. Almost no one overclocks computers anymore."

"What kind of overclocking are you talking about, then?"

The old man gives a heavy sigh, his eyes falling shut once more. "A master learns his craft's established rules so well that he knows when to break them. Does that make sense to you?"

"Yes."

"Well, one who has mastered *himself*—who's achieved perfect balance with himself—knows when to throw himself *out of balance* for strategic ends."

"Out of balance?"

"Through the Fount, one who is in balance can demand more of his body. He can amplify his senses, his cognition, his reflexes, and his strength." The old knight's eyelids fly open again, and his gaze meets mine with searing intensity. "This comes at *great cost.* Overclocking won't just burn through your energy stores at a faster rate, but your lifespan itself. Just as the Fount helps you to live longer under normal circumstances, when you overclock, it will use up your body faster than is natural. And there are other limitations. Overclock for long enough, and you will fall into a deep unconscious state, helpless before your enemies. It is an ability only to be used in the most dire of circumstances, and if you attempt it before you are in balance with yourself, you will likely die."

"Why use it at all, if it's so dangerous?"

The knight pauses. "Have you ever taken any civilian martial arts classes?"

I nod. "Sure. Didn't go very well."

"I have no trouble believing that. What's the main message the instructor gives in such classes?"

"Uh," I think, racking my brain. I was fifteen when I took the class, fresh from losing Marissa and far from stable. Mostly, I wanted an excuse to beat someone's brains out while sparring. I think the instructor sensed that, which is why I got kicked out so early. "That the goal is to avoid ever having to use your martial arts training."

"Yes. Think of overclocking like that."

I don't have much to say in response to that, so I leave the cabin, closing the hatch behind me. Without thinking about where I'm going, I end up in the command seat, staring at the forward bulkhead.

When he'd told me about the disguise trick, I'd actually started to warm up to the idea that maybe it's worth it to spend so much time sitting in one spot thinking about my breathing. I expected the next thing he told me to interest me even more.

But as he told me about overclocking, I realized it's exactly what I'm going to need to defeat Rodney Fairfax. The thing is, I'm already pretty much shortening my life with every slipspace journey I take. Other Guardsman enter nanodeath for the months they spend in slipspace, but I refuse to do that. I stay awake for every second of it, running down my biological clock more and more. Those journeys add up to years pretty quickly.

Now, to pull off the task I've set myself, I'm apparently going to have to shave off even more years.

"Activate OPO," I find myself saying, and Chief Aphrodite's slender form appears at her station.

"Hello," she says, with a note of uncertainty.

"Hi," I say. "Sorry. I don't know why I switched you on. I just—"

"You were lonely."

I shrug.

"Don't you ever enter nanodeath while in slipspace?"

"No." Just my luck: the one thing I wanted to take my mind off is the thing she wants to talk about.

"So you stay awake the entire time, all alone? With your crew switched off?"

"I just activated you, didn't I?"

"You didn't during the trip from the Calabar Brinktown to Tunis. Not once."

I sigh. "Yeah. Actually, this might be the first time I've turned on a crewmember in slipspace."

"Doesn't seem healthy, Captain Pikeman. It must get to you—being the only person on a ship, alone, light years from the nearest star."

I don't answer, but suddenly I'm lost in memory; back on the seven-month journey to Earth, the longest I've ever spent in slipspace.

I'd been feeling tired and irritable for months before that, despite getting regular sleep. The nightmares were the problem: horrific if half-remembered, they robbed my slumber of any actual restfulness.

A couple weeks into the trip to Earth, things suddenly got worse. The dreams sprang into clarity—or, dream, I should say. It was all the same dream: a pirate I'd killed years before, asking me over and over: "Why'd you kill me?"

Each night, I tried to offer him hollow-sounding rationalizations. It's my job. He would have done the same in my place. If it hadn't been him, it would have been me.

Every time, he'd wait patiently till I was finished talking. Then, he'd take out the picture. The same picture I found on his corpse, in the breast pocket of his shirt: a photo of his wife and his two beautiful children. A boy and a girl. The girl reminded me of Harmony.

I think that's what made me snap, in the end. Back on Gauntlet, the sims they put us through, using the military-grade datasphere they gave us...those sims would dig into our psyches, finding the best reason we had for killing the Guard's enemies. For killing pirates, Fallen, criminals.

Those sims felt real. I mean, most do, but the military-grade datasphere is capable of making you forget about your real life, so that you accept the sim as your reality for its duration. My datasphere would always put me in situations where killing was the only way to save Harmony. Over and over, in countless scenarios—hostage situations, fighting a war that threatened to engulf the galaxy in flames, taking out suicide bombers rushing toward the Calabar Brinktown in a throng. I got used to killing. I learned the mechanics of it. When to draw, the way to angle my weapon…how to control my breathing, to stay calm, to gently squeeze the trigger. My instructors told me, with pride in their voices, that no one had ever performed as well as I did in the sims.

Killing came to mean saving my daughter. Every kill made her a little safer. I believed that, on a deep level. I still do, which is probably why I've made more kills than any other Guardsman in history.

But that pirate, visiting my dreams night after night…he screwed everything up. The idea that I'd taken him from his children—there was just nothing I could tell him, or myself, that would make that forgivable. And two months or so into the journey to Earth, something inside me seemed to realize that fact. That my rationalizations, my excuses, had failed. And I broke down. Mentally, I mean.

I stopped eating. Stopped showering. I'd wander the *Ares* with no idea where I was, shouting in horror.

The ship seemed to recognize that I was suffering from conversion hysteria, and it locked me out of its vital functions and systems, including activating the crew or summoning Dice from the Repair and Recharge module. The ship tried to speak to me in soothing tones, playing the same prerecorded lines from some therapist over and over again. But I could barely remember who I was, and I yelled back at it nonsensically.

Finally, I collapsed in the middle of the bridge, curling into the fetal position and shivering violently.

Slowly, somehow, I came back to myself, and by the time I reached Earth I was able to function again. But I felt numb. I still do. And I'm pretty sure it's why I took Maneater on board. Yes, I was sparing her from whatever fate awaited her in Earth's wilds. But it was also for the company. Because I didn't want to be alone. Because I was worried that what happened to me could happen again.

"Have you had any more word from your daughter?" Aphrodite asks, and my eyes refocus on her face. I realize we've been sitting in silence for a long time.

"You're my OPO," I say, my voice somewhat hoarse. "You know I haven't."

"Right. I just—"

I narrow my eyes. "Why do you keep bringing her up?"

She shrugs. "I just worry about what could happen. A young girl on her own in the galaxy. Aren't you worried?"

"I'm worried sick. There's also nothing I can do. She wouldn't tell me where she is, except that she plans to get to the bottom of the pirate attacks."

Aphrodite's eyes widen, and we're both silent for a time. Then, she shakes her head. "I have a confession to make. Unrelated to your daughter. While you, Asterisk, and D1C were fending off the Fallen, I was using your access to download everything I could from the Gargantua Brinktown's logs."

"I didn't tell you to do that."

"No, but as your OPO, I was able to. You didn't order me to do it, so I was taking a liberty; I know that. But I think you're going to want to know what I found out."

I raise my eyebrows.

"The pirates broke in through the Brinktown's ceiling," she says. "Probably, they wanted to bypass the reinforced hatches and the turrets defending them."

"Is that how the Fallen got in, too?" It seems unlikely—the Fallen wouldn't have had the gear necessary to safely lower themselves from the breach.

Aphrodite's shaking her head, confirming my assessment. When she speaks, her voice is low. "The Fallen came through a hatch, Captain."

"Not possible. The turret would have mowed them down before they got anywhere near it."

"The turret was deactivated, and the hatch was open."

"How?"

"Someone aboard the *Ares* sent a signal to deactivate them."

My eyes lock onto hers as I process what she's telling me.

"I was able to trace it back to the ship," she goes on, "but I couldn't determine which station it came from. The source was masked. But someone on this ship let the Fallen get in at you, Captain. Someone tried to kill you."

EKHIDNADES

1

Despite Aphrodite's best efforts, supplemented by the ocean of knowledge provided by my datasphere, neither of us can figure out which crewmember sent the signal. The culprit covered their tracks flawlessly, so they're clearly a master hacker, which makes me think it's Belflower. Then, it dawns on me: that might be exactly who the traitor wants me to suspect.

Finally, we accept that the best we can do is remain on high alert going forward while doing our best not to tip off the traitor that we know. It's risky enough that the others have noticed Aphrodite leaving the crew sim alone to spend time with me in the real.

So I throw myself into my training, and the old man begrudgingly acknowledges that I'm making progress.

"You're nowhere near where you need to be," he says. "But you're getting better."

I'm able to keep my focus on my breath for long stretches of time, now—or on a mandala, or a song, or just the sounds the *Ares* makes. We move on from simple focus exercises to observing emotions.

"Catalog each sensation with an open mind," the knight

instructs me. "You are making room for a thought to drop in. If your mind is truly open, then that thought will contain whatever it is your instincts are trying to tell you. What the Fount is trying to tell you. The Fount, interconnected and woven through the fabric of the galaxy. This is the mind you must carry into battle."

Three hours before we're due to exit slipspace, I bring the crew online for a full systems check and to brief them on what I know. "Other than a few mining outposts and a long-abandoned colony built inside a hollowed-out asteroid, the planet Larunda is the only thing worth noting about Visby, our destination system. Larunda's surface is too acidic for habitation, but its atmosphere used to be dotted with balloon cities. Most of them have sunk out of sight, below the clouds of sulphuric acid that shroud the planet. The largest structure still floating consists of several platforms that pirates have dragged together and tethered to each other, to form the biggest known pirate stronghold in this sector. It's called Royal —consider it Space Tortuga. It's almost certainly where they brought Faelyn."

"What's Tortuga?" Asterisk asks.

"Seriously?" I say. "Read a book."

Next, the crew are treated to the sight of their captain going through extreme ecstasy followed by spasm-inducing nausea. In the middle of it all, the moment we enter realspace, we're contacted by another Broadsword—another Troubleshooter's ship, identical to mine. There are four of them in the space around the *Ares*, surrounding us.

"Fount damn it," I croak.

"Are you all right, sir?" Belflower asks.

"I'll be fine," I say. The cinched barf bag is lying on the deck near the command seat, since there's no time to stow it. Trying not to look at it, I say, "OPO, establish contact with the Broadsword I've painted on the tactical display. It's the *Cyclops*, and her captain is Captain Jagoda."

"Aye, sir."

We're close enough for real-time communication, and so brain-prints aren't needed. My datasphere projects Captain Jagoda's face onto the main screen.

"Commander Pikeman," he says. "We have orders to escort you to Rodney Fairfax's destroyer, the *Ekhidnades*. I trust you'll cooperate fully, without resistance."

I squint at Jagoda. "You can't be serious. Fairfax razed Tunis and kidnapped the children there, including Arthur Eliot's daughter. I have datasphere footage to prove that."

"Footage can be doctored. Anyway, these are orders, Commander, passed down the chain of command. Now, kindly come with us. No one wants to see Troubleshooters fighting each other today."

"Then don't do this."

Jagoda's upper cheeks tighten, bunching under his eyes. "I'll take that as a no. Prepare to engage, Commander." With that, the captain disappears from my datasphere.

"OPO, get me a down-scaled layout of the battlespace and send it over."

"Aye, sir."

Ten long seconds later, I have it: the four opposing Broadswords have adopted a diamond formation clearly intended to trap me in the middle.

"You can't win," a voice says behind me. I twist in the command seat to glare at the knight, who I didn't hear exit the cabin.

"You can't be here while there's an operation in progress," I say.

"And yet, here I am. You can't win, because it's one targeting computer versus four. It's simple math. You're still completely reliant on your technology, just as they are. You'll do whatever it tells you to do, so how can there be room for the innovation required for victory in a situation like this?"

"Go into the cabin," I say, my voice tight, "and stay there."

"Very well." The Shiva Knight leaves the bridge, the cabin hatch closing behind him.

I turn to my WSO, who looks way too excited at the prospect of battle. Not for the first time, I wonder how this kid possibly made it through the screening process to end up on a Broadsword. "Target their autoturrets with ours whenever you get a clean shot," I tell him. "Do not try to compromise their hull, and do not fire any Javelins. Lasers only. Understood?"

"Yes, sir."

We only have eight Javelin missiles aboard, but that's not the reason I told Asterisk to stick to lasers. Troubleshooters almost never come into conflict with each other, but it has happened, and those incidents get talked about during Assessment and Selection. Even if the instructors never taught us about them, they're available in everyone's datasphere archive, and every cadet knows it could happen again.

When Troubleshooter fights do happen, every Broadsword captain worth his salt knows not do actual damage to his fellow Guardsman's ship. That would be the ultimate violation of the mutual respect we have for each other.

Instead, these battles amount to a high-stakes game of chess, where each combatant tries to take out enough of his opponent's turrets to force him to concede.

Of course, today I'm playing that game against four adversaries instead of one.

"Worldworn, accelerate straight toward the Broadsword that contacted us, engines at full. I may take direct control over navigation at any point—same goes for any of our laser turrets, Asterisk."

"Aye," both officers say.

As we close with Captain Jagoda's ship, my TOPO's handling seems good, so I leave him with it for now. I order him to fire the rear port thruster, to introduce a spin to our trajectory, and he complies immediately. "Okay," I say as the *Ares'* starboard side is coming in line with the nose of the opposing Broadsword. "Fire the rear starboard thruster to even us out."

"Yes, Captain."

Worldworn nails the maneuver, with all three starboard laser turrets lined up perfectly.

"Asterisk, use the forward and midship turrets to take out as many of the enemy starboard turrets as you can. I'm taking over the aft turret to target the port guns."

"Aye."

I load up a sim that gives me two handles to grasp and shoot, along with a transparent bubble granting a view of the space occupied by the enemy Broadsword. Then, I go to work.

Yes, my datasphere suggests optimal firing solutions, like the old man said it would. But a lot of this comes down to a steady hand, and he didn't mention the importance of speed and timing, either. In quick succession, I blow up the enemy's forward port laser turret, then I adjust the targeting reticle smoothly to the right, drawing a bead on the midship laser turret. Three pulses: a deadly rhythm. The turret explodes, and I move on to the aft turret, making short work of it.

Before my next move, I check on the ensign's progress: he's just destroying the first turret. I guess computer-assisted targeting isn't everything. Only a timely push from the *Ares*'s belly thrusters saves us from getting hit by the turrets Asterisk hasn't managed to destroy yet.

"Good work, Worldworn," I say, before switching to another sim. This one looks just like the primary turret up top, and that's exactly what it allows me to control. "Ensign, set our port-side secondary turrets to auto-target the turrets on the Broadswords approaching us."

"Yes, Captain."

The other three ships are closing fast, and my plan for dealing with them depends on two things: getting in some lucky shots before they get too close, and bringing the *Ares'* primary laser turret to bear.

Technically, it's a bit of a violation of the chess game to bring my primary into play. But if I can use it to take out enough of their turrets before they get close enough to blast mine away with their secondaries, I think they'll honor that and let me go instead of pressing the attack with what weapons they have left.

At least, I hope they will. Otherwise, things could get ugly.

My datasphere lights up with thirteen cones of varying colors all based on the quality of the firing solutions they represent—red for poor, green for optimal, and yellow and orange for in between. None of them are green. I line up the aiming reticle with the only yellow cone and fire.

The computer would have calculated the firing solution to account for the opposing Broadsword's speed and trajectory, and now those calculations prove out. The targeted laser turret explodes in a brief lick of flame, though I'm already firing along a different, orange cone. Before that shot hits, I'm lining up the next.

I notice my breathing is steady and smooth, and my battle calm is absolute. I'm usually able to keep my cool, but this is something different. I'm in the zone, more fully than I have been in years—maybe since Assessment and Selection, when everything depended on showing the instructors what I was worth.

Looks like those weeks of meditation actually paid off. I'm on fire, here.

Some of the cones disappear as new ones are materializing, caused by the opposing Broadswords maneuvering, bringing other laser turrets to bear. I pick off my seventh turret, then my eighth, and my ninth.

Luck or skill, call it what you want: this is an incredible result. But it's not enough. I neutralize two more turrets as the enemy ships draw into optimal firing range, but then the state of play morphs radically, and they begin raining neon-blue laserfire down on my port hull. The aft turret explodes, and the forward turret follows a couple seconds later.

"Okay," I broadcast to the other ships. "I'm done. I surrender."

Jagoda's voice comes back without delay, his face once again popping onto the forward bulkhead, projected by my datasphere. "It's pretty disappointing you used your primary on us, Pikeman."

I don't give him the benefit of an answer. He would have done the same in my position, and he knows it.

The four Broadswords move into close formation around mine, and together we sail away from the slipspace exit coords, toward where the *Ekhidnades* awaits.

2

"Well, we had a good run," Asterisk says, leaning over his railing toward Belflower, his face screwed up in thought. "Do you think they'll penalize us for cooperating with a Guardsman who was designated 'Uncompliant?'"

"Shut up," Belflower says. I do believe I'm warming up to her.

"What do you suppose Fairfax wants with you, Captain?" Worldworn says, standing whip-straight in the center of his station, hands clasped behind his back. "If we can figure out his angle, then perhaps we can use it to our advantage."

I shake my head absently. Back on Tunis, in the theater, Fairfax told me to stay out of his way. He also said that I get "one chance." But why give me a chance at all? If he thought I might prove problematic for him, why not kill me then and there?

"Surely we can convince one of your fellow Guardsmen to help us," Aphrodite says. "I mean, Fairfax is working with pirates. They're kidnapping children. This isn't what the Galactic Guard's supposed to stand for."

"It isn't what it stands for," I say, and my voice comes out somewhat hoarse, so I clear my throat. "But if the other three Troubleshooters are anything like Captain Jagoda, they stand for disobeying orders even less."

Returning to my thoughts, I consider how quickly the brass had to move to get four Broadswords in position to intercept me as I emerged from slipspace. For that to happen, Fairfax must have somehow anticipated that I'd follow him.

But not only that: he must have tremendous clout with the Guard brass, both in the Subverse and in the real. For me, it stretches believability that Guardsmen would jump so quickly to obey a Fairfax who Arthur Eliot describes as a "black sheep."

The only other possibility is that there's corruption in the upper ranks. It isn't a possibility that's ever occurred to me before. The Galactic Guard has always been the one good thing about life in this sector. The one shining beacon in a sea of shit. But what other explanation is there?

For a moment, I wonder why he bothered sending Broadswords at all, instead of just parking his destroyer in front of the slipspace exit point. Then again, there's a good chance the *Ares* would have slipped past the destroyer and outrun her.

Asterisk pipes up. "If we blast the Broadswords at such close range, maybe they wouldn't have time to—"

"Shut up," I say, and he stiffens, eyes wide. "All of you. Shut up."

Even supposing Fairfax called in the Broadswords the moment he exited slipspace, would the brass really have had enough time to get them together before I arrived? It seems like a borderline miracle. Something's not adding up, but I can't put my finger on it.

We arrive at the *Ekhidnades*. A glance through a hull sensor shows the destroyer looming large. As ordered, Worldworn is maintaining the same course as the other four Broadswords, and we're all headed toward a rectangle of lights near the great warship's underside.

Those lights have a clear purpose, unlike the beams that shine into space from dozens of other spots along the destroyer's hull.

For a ship too big to land on a planet's surface, the only purpose of outside lighting would be to provide illumination for workers sent on a spacewalk to make emergency repairs. But running my eyes along the *Ekhidnades'* hull, I can see she's in immaculate shape. Every inch of the imposing warship gleams like new. So the lights are merely for show.

Warships of this size are rare enough these days, and those in operation are all refurbished ships, constructed before the Fall. The idea that the *Ekhidnades* was constructed in recent years doesn't compute.

Except, as we draw closer, that's exactly what my eyes are telling me. Yes, the Fairfaxes are powerful, but I didn't think anyone in the real had the resources to build something like this anymore. Except, here it is.

Within the space of twenty minutes, Rodney Fairfax has succeeded in baffling me twice. And we haven't even come face to face yet.

We enter the landing bay, and things get even more bewildering. Peering through the *Ares'* hull sensors, switching from view to view, I see a landing bay that looks like something out of the Subverse.

Brilliant, neon-blue strips glow from where the bulkhead meets the overhead and the deck. Twin rows of soldiers, all armed with the same model of laser rifle, stand facing each other, no doubt waiting to escort me to Fairfax. I'm pretty sure they're humans, not bots, but it's difficult to tell—they're wearing full-body suits with helmets that shine with two ice-blue lights, in a vague imitation of Fairfax's eyes. Otherwise, their uniform is like an altered version of a Guardsman's uniform, with gold-colored seams in place of our all-black.

Eight soldiers in all. More than enough to keep me in check. But how many more does Fairfax have? Because judging by the uniforms, and the obvious professionalism of these fighters, it looks to me like he's started up his own private military.

Then my eyes fall on the four ships parked neatly against the bulkheads, each in its own enclosure: Broadswords. Just sitting there, unused.

At that, I decide to stop trying to make sense of any of this. Instead, as Worldworn settles the *Ares* onto the deck, I start cobbling together a plan.

"Belflower."

She turns toward me from whatever she was doing at her station—probably ogling our surroundings, just like I was. "C-captain?"

"Can you make four copies of yourself, and of Asterisk, Worldworn, and Aphrodite, and standby to hack them into those ships on my signal?"

Belflower blinks. "That's kind of a tall order, sir. I'd have to probe their defenses first. It would certainly take time."

I suppress a sigh. "Right. Well, I guess we'll have to stall for that, then."

It looks like I'll be going to meet Fairfax after all. I doubt those soldiers are going to wait around long enough to give Belflower the time she needs.

But maybe if I play my cards right, I'll be allowed to bring some friends to the meeting.

I stand from the command seat and cross the bridge, willing the cabin hatch open as I do, with the intention of bringing the old man in on my plan.

Except, when I enter the cabin, the Shiva Knight is nowhere to be seen.

Maneater stares at me, and barks.

3

I check the ship logs to make sure the airlock hasn't opened recently, though I'm sure the hatch to my *cabin* has been closed since the old man went in there, let alone the airlock.

The logs confirm what I already know: he didn't leave the ship. And yet, he isn't here. I check the mess—under the table, even inside the latched cupboards. I return to the bridge and walk all around the stations, although there isn't really anywhere here for him to hide. The four crewmembers look at me askance as I peer all around the bridge.

"He's gone," I mutter.

"Uh, they're insisting you come out, Captain," Aphrodite says. "Pretty forcefully."

"Right," I say. "All right."

Two minutes later, I exit the *Ares'* airlock with Dice, and Maneater on her leash.

Two of the eight soldiers march over to meet me. They exchange glances. "You can't bring a dog onto the *Ekhidnades*," one of them says, and his tone seems to imply that having a dog on a spaceship at all might not be a great idea. I'm inclined to agree.

"I can't leave him on *my* ship," I say. "He'll have the thing chewed apart by the time I come back."

"Who says you're coming back?" the soldier says.

"Uh, the fact Fairfax didn't have my ship blasted apart on sight? Come on. He obviously wants to meet with me, which means he sees value in keeping me alive."

"You can't bring the dog. Or the bot."

"I *need* to take the dog, and the bot has to come too, to handle the dog in case I'm busy."

"Just tie him on somewhere on your ship."

"There's nowhere I can do that without giving him access to something he can destroy." I don't mind lying to the soldier, since I already consider him my enemy. "I can guarantee you that arguing with me about this is way above your pay grade. Why don't you get in touch with your boss and ask him?"

The black-clad soldier stares at me for a few seconds longer. Then his shoulders slump almost imperceptibly, and he cocks his head to the left—a common tick for when people are talking to someone who isn't present.

"All right," he says a minute or so later, sounding resigned. "Lord Fairfax says you can take the dog. And the bot. But we're disarming the bot and we're searching you."

Though Dice's laser pistols are attached, it is possible to unscrew and remove them. Every Lambton combat bot is capable of being disarmed; a function of how no one trusts bots.

My pat-down goes off without a hitch, but when the soldier walks up to Dice, the bot shoves him back. "Step off, fleshbag."

Quick as a flash, the soldier has his laser rifle up, the muzzle tapping against Dice's forehead. "Remove your weaponry," the soldier screams, his voice sounding tinny coming through the suit's mic.

"Decant yourself," Dice says, which seems to give the soldier pause as he tries to parse the remark.

I exploit his momentary confusion as best I can: "Look, I know he's insufferable, but are you really afraid of one armed bot against eight armored soldiers? What are you trying to accomplish, exactly? He's not going to give you his pistols, so you could kill him, but that's not going to put me in a very good mood for whatever Fairfax wants to discuss at this meeting."

The soldier doesn't answer, and while I can't see his face, his posture alone tells me how pissed off he is. Finally, he gives Dice's face one last smack with the rifle muzzle, then he grabs the bot's upper arm and starts dragging him toward the formation of uniformed fighters. The soldier near me grabs my arm, but I go along peacefully, so no dragging is required.

All eight soldiers fall in around me, Dice, and Maneater, and together we march off the landing bay deck. They let me hold on to the leash, which is nice.

I notice one of the soldiers eyeing Maneater. "Female or male?"

"Female," I say.

"What's her name?"

"Maneater."

He pauses, and when he speaks again he sounds amused. "Is that because she's a heartbreaker?"

"No, it's because she literally ate a man."

He doesn't seem to know how to respond to that, and the conversation ends.

The rest of the ship is like the landing bay, except flashier. I can tell they're trying to be understated with the cyberpunk aesthetic, but being loud and gaudy sort of comes with the territory. They mostly stick to teal and yellow for the neon lights that accent everything from hatches to control panels to the corridors themselves, but they can't help indulging in some fuchsia and crimson as we get closer to wherever we're going.

At last, we get there: a broad, low room that I take to be Fairfax's custom-made war room, based on the holo-console that serves as the centerpiece. The console seems unnecessary, since I'd put the chances of someone without a datasphere getting invited onto this ship at zero, but no doubt it's meant to anchor the room or something.

"Welcome to the *Ekhidnades*," Fairfax says from the other side of the console, spreading his gloved hands. The gesture serves to spread his midnight cape, too, as well as put his muscled forearms on display. It also reveals a scabbarded sword, hanging opposite his blaster. If he was wearing that in the theater back on Tunis, I didn't notice it.

He also seems to have cranked up the brightness of his eyes since Tunis. They match the twin neon strips that run around this chamber's bulkheads, near the overhead. I guess if I was a half-man, half-bot freak I'd want to show it off too.

"Couldn't you pick a ship name with fewer syllables?" I say.

The hands hover in the air for a second longer before Fairfax lowers them to his sides. "A lesser name wouldn't suit her."

"No kidding. So. Those Guardsmen seemed pretty eager to do whatever you tell them to. How much did it cost you to buy off four Guardsmen? Or, wait, don't tell me you bought off one of the brass? Must have had to empty the piggy bank for that."

Fairfax chuckles, and so does a boy who stands to his right, who wears a cape similar to his lord's. He doesn't have any bot parts, though. I'd put him at a year or two younger than Harmony, and he looks at me with smiling eyes, which is a bit weird. Something about him looks familiar, but I can't place it.

"I was warned you have a sharp tongue," Fairfax says.

"Better than having no tongue at all. Unless you do actually have one in there? It would have to be pretty dried-out by now."

"Are you under the impression that insults will get you anywhere with me?"

I shrug. "I'm not really sure where I'm supposed to want to get."

"I understand that you aren't exactly enamored of me," Fairfax says, nodding. "Especially after I knocked you to the ground, like a helpless child."

"It wasn't what I'd call a diplomatic masterstroke, no. I take it you want something from me, this time?"

Fairfax laughs again, louder this time, his voice's metallic quality lending it menace. "I'm sure you've already planned out your escape attempt from this ship, and for the purposes of this conversation I think it's best if you abandon it before we proceed. Whatever you've come up with, it won't work."

"What if it did, though?" I say. "Wouldn't that be embarrassing?"

"I'd like to offer you a job, Joe. At the moment, you're quite popular in the Subverse, mostly due to this mysterious persona you've managed to concoct."

I laugh, mostly at the idea that anything I do is intended to have an effect on the Subverse. I couldn't care less about what uploads think of me.

"You could be rather useful to me," Fairfax continues. "I'm in want of a decent propaganda minister. It would be helpful to my objectives to start massaging the narrative better than I currently am. You wouldn't even have to come up with any actual propaganda. I can supply that. I'd just need you to parrot it—to give me access to your platform, once you bother availing of it."

"I dunno. I want my first versecast to be special. You know?"

"Very amusing, Joe. Surely you're not about to pretend you have values that are any better than mine? You, the Butcher?"

"At least I don't steal children away from their families."

Fairfax shakes his head. "What I'm trying to say, Joe, is that I don't think you should delude yourself into thinking you're fighting for a good cause. Even if you were, you're hilariously outnumbered. You can die an unremarkable death, or you can take a place in the new order I'm about to create. That's a privilege that won't be granted to very many. Most will be reduced to insects, but that doesn't need to be you."

"What makes you think I want to help you turn people into bugs, or whatever you just said?"

"Ah. Here we are. You *are* pretending to occupy some kind of moral high ground, aren't you? Tell me, would a man of true moral fiber sit by and do nothing while his daughter falls in with pirates?"

I open my mouth to answer, but whatever remark I was about to deliver evaporates on my tongue. "What are you talking about?"

"Oh, I think I've been nothing but very *clear* with you, Joe. While you were in slipspace, Harmony Pikeman took up residence in Lord Bleak's manse on Royal."

I stare at him, at a complete loss for words.

"Anyway," Fairfax says. "If we're going to start moralizing, I have better things to do. I'll give you time to consider my offer in my lavishly appointed brig, and after a day or so we'll have another little meeting. If you agree to my terms, then I'm confident a reunion between you and your daughter can be arranged. If not, I'll kill you."

Fairfax flicks his hand, and the soldier nearest me seizes my upper arm, manhandling me out of the room, with Maneater getting jerked along after us. She takes it like a champ, without a whimper. Good girl.

As we're being escorted out of Fairfax's war room, the botman leans down to say something to the boy. Then we're out in the corridor. We take a left, and twenty meters or so later we take a right. One of the soldiers removes his helmet to scratch an itch, without bothering even to ask his squad leader's permission. Seems like an obscene breach of protocol to me, but no one says anything, and I guess it's none of my business.

That said, it does offer an excellent opportunity to give the signal. I drop Maneater's leash and yell, "Attack!"

As she leaps for the throat of the soldier who took off his helmet, Dice's pistols snap forward into his palms. Except, one of them isn't a pistol—it's my blaster, and instead of coming to rest in his grip, it flips through the air toward me. I snatch the weapon from the apex of its parabola, swinging it around to shoot the soldier nearest me through the gap between his helmet and shoulder.

He crumples to the deck, and I bring my left hand up to cradle the blaster, steadying it. Sweeping the blaster toward my next target, I squeeze the trigger three times as I move to the left to get out from the middle of the formation. My shots miss, and the soldier raises his laser rifle toward me.

Having slammed one soldier against the wall, Dice is wrenching the helmet off another. He snaps the man's neck as I sidestep around a soldier who's aiming at the bot.

The muzzle of my blaster fits underneath his helmet, and I fire. His body slumps, but I grab the back of his uniform, propping him up to use as a meat shield. The corpse absorbs three laser rifle shots, and I return fire, missing.

Snout dripping scarlet, Maneater slams into my attacker's back, knocking him forward. One of the remaining soldiers draws a bead on the dog, and I fire at the weak spot at his neck. With one hand holding up the body, my aim has gone to shit, but Dice adds laser-fire to mine, and between us we drop our target.

The two soldiers still standing drop their rifles and raise their hands toward the overhead. The one Dice slammed against the wall pushes himself up and lunges at the bot, who turns to meet him with a knee to chest. That stops him dead, and Dice stows his pistol, seizes the man's helmet, then wrenches it off. The pistol snaps back into place, and he puts a bolt through the soldier's skull.

Dropping the body I'm holding up, I notice one of the surrendered soldiers eyeing his fallen weapon, and I shake the blaster. "Hey! Take two steps back!"

They comply.

Somehow, Maneater has managed to separate the helmet from her victim's suit and is savaging the back of his neck. That dog is getting some serious work done. Her victim's still trying to get his rifle in position to shoot her, but the weapon's cumbersome enough that the effort seems pretty futile. Even so, I kick the rifle away from his hand. It hits the bulkhead, firing harmlessly down the corridor.

"Take off your helmets," I tell the two with their hands in the air. They hesitate, then grip their helmets on both sides and pull them off.

I walk forward, steadying my right hand with my left. The rush of battle's subsiding, but I know I can't leave these two alive. It's doubtful my datasphere would prescribe these kills. Actually, I'm pretty sure it wouldn't tell me to kill anyone in Fairfax's employ. But if I don't, my chances of actually escaping from this warship will get a lot closer to zero, and there's no time to tie them up.

I'm a few feet away now, where it's pretty much impossible to miss, my blaster lined up between the first soldier's eyes. It's not hard to tell he sees what I intend to do. His eyes are filled with fear.

The days of taking prisoners and treating them decent are long past. It's Guard doctrine to just exterminate anyone who poses a threat. Once, when nations went to war with each other, it made sense to spend the resources necessary to keep prisoners of war. If you didn't, no one would ever surrender to you, knowing you'd just kill them if they tried to. But no one can afford to take prisoners anymore. So we just kill our foes, and the Guard's always been powerful enough that it hasn't mattered.

Just like I should have killed Maneater back on Earth, instead of taking the risk of bringing her onto the *Ares*.

"Fount damn it," I mutter, letting my weapon drop and putting a bolt in each of the soldier's legs. He crumples, and as the other soldier turns to run, I give him the same treatment.

I shouldn't have hesitated. If I'd killed them right away, there'd be a chance they wouldn't have gotten word to Fairfax. Now, they'll be sure to use their dataspheres to warn him we've escaped.

"We have to go," I tell Dice.

4

Maneater is still tearing hunks of flesh from the soldier's neck and shoulders.

"Down, girl," I say, and she growls. "Maneater, *heel!*" With a resentful whine, she pulls away from her meal, trotting over to position herself against my leg, blood-drenched tongue dangling from her mouth. "Come," I say, jogging down the hall, and she trails a meter behind. Dice follows, too.

My datasphere paints a path through the destroyer's corridors, to help us retrace our steps.

"I'm surprised by the canine fleshbag's efficacy," Dice says as we run through the *Ekhidnades*. "She was likely genetically engineered."

I glance back at Maneater, who's keeping pace behind us. That hadn't occurred to me, but it explains a lot.

An alarm begins to blare through the corridors. "Let's go!" I yell, laying on more speed.

As we're reaching the landing bay, neon-blue laser shots crackle through the air, scoring the closed hatch ahead. "Get it open," I subvocalize to Dice. "I'll cover you."

I turn, firing wildly at anything that moves. None of my shots hit, but they do force the two soldiers shooting at us to pull behind cover, using an intersection of corridors to hide from the rain of white blaster bolts. Maneater stands in the middle of the corridor, hackles up, barking at our aggressors.

"Got it," Dice says, and we both walk backward through the hatch, firing down the corridor to keep the soldiers pinned. Once we're through, Dice slaps the control panel, and the hatch slides closed. With that, we turn to sprint across the landing bay, feet pounding across the deck. Maneater's nails clack against the metal as she runs.

More laserfire. I glance back to see soldiers already pouring in. I run faster, but the area's too open. There's no cover to be had. We're not going to make it.

I hear the loud crack of a primary laser turret firing, then another. The advancing soldiers are getting flanked by the four Broadswords parked on both sides of the landing bay. I turn to add some blaster fire to the fray, but decide against it. It's not necessary. The soldiers are all turning to confront the weaponry firing on them, which is tearing them to shreds. The ones closest to the hatch are pushing back against their fellows coming in.

"Good work," I say to Belflower as I exit the airlock onto the bridge. "Get in your closet," I tell Dice, then I vault into the command seat. Behind me, the bot clanks across the deck toward the opening Repair and Recharge module.

"We have full control over the other ships?"

Belflower nods.

"Then get us out of here, and have them exit with us in protective formation around the *Ares*. This isn't over yet—we have the destroyer's hull-mounted weaponry to deal with, not to mention those four Broadswords, if they stuck around."

Glancing through a hull sensor, I see that the exit is sealed. I'm about to order Asterisk to fire a Javelin at it when it slides open of its own accord. "Did you hack that, too?" I ask the Engineer, impressed.

She shakes her head. "It just opened at my request."

That makes me laugh. "I think Fairfax still has a thing or two to learn about being a warship captain."

The airlock's big enough to accommodate all five Broadswords at once. As soon as it finishes cycling and the outer hatch opens, we rocket out together, the other ships spreading out a bit but maintaining tight formation.

Right away, laser cannon fire flashes from the *Ekhidnades'* hull. One of the beams kisses our stern, but Worldworn drops us out of the line of fire with a deft hand, and we only suffer some superficial melting.

The Broadsword on our starboard side isn't so lucky—a laser cannon scores a direct hit, and after a few seconds of energy getting dumped into its hull, it bursts apart, flinging shrapnel, which Worldworn dodges.

"The other four Guardsman are still here," Aphrodite says. "Looks like they were patrolling around the destroyer's hull, but now they're breaking away to pursue us."

I nod. "Have the other three Broadswords stay behind to engage them. Worldworn, get us out of here, full speed."

"Aye."

Through an aft sensor, I watch two of the three friendly Broadswords get blown apart in quick succession. All the while, we're putting more and more distance between the *Ares* and the *Ekhidnades.*

"Should we head for slipspace coords?" Worldworn asks.

"No. Set a course for Royal. If four Broadswords try to follow us there, they're gonna have other problems."

"Doesn't that mean *we'll* have problems?" Aphrodite says.

"Yeah, but I have a card to play."

We fly in silence for several minutes. I'm watching through the aft sensor, waiting for the final explosion. It finally comes, bigger than I expected it to be. By now, the *Ares* is well away from her would-be pursuers. That last ship lasted an impressively long time.

"You only copied you four over, right?" I ask Belflower.

She shakes her head. "I took the liberty of copying you over too, Captain. I used your latest outgoing brainprint to do it, which was stored in the ship's computer. You captained all four of those ships." Belflower pauses. "Does it bother you that none of your copies survived?"

I consider the question for a moment, then say, "Not at all, to be honest."

"Seriously?" Aphrodite says. "It freaks *me* out."

"Well, I'd rather not run into myself down the road."

"Why not?"

"I doubt the galaxy's big enough."

EKHIDNADES

1

I've left the crew switched on for the voyage across the Visby System toward Royal. I don't really have any need for them—since we escaped the *Ekhidnades*, Belflower completed a comprehensive systems check, Asterisk set the laser turrets to recharging, and Aphrodite recalibrated every sensor. Yet here we all are.

Heading to Royal seems like the logical next step—pirate haven that it is, I'd give even odds on Faelyn Eliot being there right now. And if Fairfax is to be believed, so is my daughter.

I doubt the other Guardsmen will dare approach Royal, but will Fairfax? Is it possible he's won over enough pirates that he'd be safe to do so? Even if he is working with Bleak, it doesn't mean he's in with *all* the pirates in the sector.

According to him, he's a pretty busy guy, what with establishing a new galactic order and all. Maybe he doesn't even have time to chase me across the system to Royal.

If Faelyn is in Royal, and I can manage to extract her as well as my daughter, then there's a chance this will all be over by tomorrow. But if it goes on any longer than that, I have big problems. Along with the pirates, I apparently have Fairfax's fledgling military to contend with, not to mention the entire Galactic Guard—at least, until Eliot finally gets around to intervening with them on my behalf. I'm hoping he's already done that, and it's just taking a while to work its way through communication channels.

In the middle of it all, the knight choosing now to abandon my training hasn't made things any brighter. I still have no idea how he left the ship, and if it wasn't for the crew, who all remember the strange man in green robes who lived on the *Ares* for a while, I would have assumed I'm having another breakdown.

Was he some sort of space ghost, capable of teaching people to meditate and whacking them across the head with a staff? That's honestly the best theory I have at the moment.

"I think we need to start versecasting," I say.

Glory Belflower looks at me as though I've started shooting lasers from my nostrils. "What did you say?"

"Versecasting. I assume I can put you in charge of that?"

"Yes," she says. "Of course! We just need to start uploading your datasphere footage." I can tell she's immediately warming to the idea. "I think some kind of statement from you, to kick things off, would be good," she goes on. "Something about this mission you've given yourself, what the pirates have been up to, and so on. But…what changed your mind about versecasting?"

"Fairfax, uh…he wanted me to be his propaganda minister. His words. Really, he just wanted to use my name to spin things to the Subverse public. I wasn't interested, obviously, but it did get me thinking. If we can bring the public in on what's been happening, it might give us some cover. Maybe even some allies, provided there's anyone decent left in the galaxy. At the very least, we can start bringing in some tokens through donations and sponsorship deals. Basically, we don't have a lot going for us right now, so it's stupid to let the one advantage we have go to waste."

Belflower's nodding, sending the daisy in her hair bobbing vigorously. "Yes. Very good, Captain! I'm glad you're finally seeing the potential, here."

"Let's just get it over with."

It takes me seven tries to put together a message that makes me sound like I give a shit about anything, let alone what's been going on with the pirates attacking Brinktowns and kidnapping children. I'm just not good at showing emotion. It's kind of fun, though, watching Belflower's enthusiasm ratchet steadily downward. Even so, she stays pretty patient throughout, giving me direction and tips in between takes.

Give me some criminals threatening Subverse infrastructure or pillaging Brinktowns any day. I'll handle it. But trying to make myself sound earnest for this versecast makes me feel as phony as the laser pistol replica Harmony left me with.

I'm beginning to remind myself of Soren, my old bunkmate during training back on Gauntlet. He's been versecasting since before he was a Troubleshooter—before he even enrolled in Basic, actually, as a kid living in a Brinktown with a single-digit following. Now, he's the most famous Guardsman in this sector, always injecting his missions with drama that generally isn't there. I love the guy, but this just isn't me.

"Well, I think that's the best we're likely to get," Belflower says at last, in what almost sounds like a grumble. "Should I just…?"

"Yeah, broadcast it. Screw it." This was probably a stupid idea, anyway.

As Belflower preps the versecast for Aphrodite to send to the next spacescraper we detect, Aphrodite herself turns to me. "Sir, can I have a word alone?"

The other three crewmembers turn toward her. Asterisk and Worldworn wear blank expressions, and Belflower is frowning. "Uh," I say, "we're kind of in the middle of something. What is it?"

"I've been going through ship logs we received from the Broadswords we hijacked in our escape attempt. The logs transmitted to us before they were destroyed. I found something you might want—well, I guess it doesn't really matter whether I show you this in private or not. It doesn't change anything." With that, she plays some datasphere footage for all of us. "This is from the last Broadsword that went down," she adds.

The footage was taken from my perspective—or at least, the perspective of my digital double, who was sitting in the command seat, just as I am now. The bridge is identical to the one on the *Ares*, and a grim silence hangs over it as each crewmember concentrates on doing their part to navigate the pitched battle they know they can't win. I haven't given it much thought till now, but it's actually kind of crazy that conscious beings went knowingly to their deaths, all to give the *Ares* the chance to escape.

"Captain, I need to apologize," Worldworn—or rather, Worldworn's copy—says abruptly.

"For what?" my double says in a tone of disbelief. Probably, he can't believe his TOPO would choose a time like this to chat.

"Back on Gargantua...*I'm* the one who let the Fallen into the Brinktown. Bleak paid me a lot of money to do it, but the remorse has been tearing at me ever since. I just...I need to get it off my chest, to tell you I'm sorry. Even if I'm just a copy talking to another copy who's about to die."

"We might not die," the Joe Pikeman duplicate says. "There's a chance we could come out of this, and if do we do, we can talk about what you just told me. For now, I need you to—"

"No, Captain," Worldworn says softly. "We *are* going to die." With that, he steers the ship toward one of the opposing Broadswords, accelerating. The footage ends abruptly.

So that's why the explosion was bigger than I expected. That Broadsword kamikazed itself into one of those with a real live Guardsman aboard it.

"Your copy must have managed to transmit that footage in the seconds before the crash," Aphrodite says.

My gaze settles on Worldworn, whose face is a cocktail of emotion.

2

"I've been framed," Worldworn says, stammering slightly.

"Really," I say flatly. "You're going to try to claim that, after what we just watched?"

"I know how damning this looks. But Captain, I assure you I didn't let the Fallen into that Brinktown, or betray you in any other way."

"I did warn you, Captain Pikeman," Belflower says. "The man can't be trusted."

Worldworn rounds on her. "Did you do this, you self-righteous bitch?"

Belflower's lips twist in disgust. "How distasteful."

"Leave off, Worldworn," I say. "You aren't doing yourself any favors."

"Captain, that footage was faked."

"Do I really look that stupid? You're telling me someone had footage prepared for that exact situation? Or are you saying there was enough time since that ship exploded to cook it up?"

"I'm saying I didn't do what I'm being accused of." Worldworn points a finger at me. "I helped you find out where they took Faelyn. Why would I do that, if I'm working with the pirates?"

"To cover your tracks," Belflower says. "Or maybe because you felt guilty right away, and saw that as your way to atone."

"Shut up!" Worldworn says.

I'm shaking my head. "I'll admit, I'm disappointed to learn you're this deceitful, Worldworn. But it doesn't matter. I can't have a traitor on my ship. I could consign you to the sim, but the risk of you figuring out a way to hack out of there is too great. I'll have to delete you."

"Captain," Worldworn says, and I can tell he's grasping at straws, now. "How will you run this ship without a TOPO?"

"I'll figure out a way. It's less risky than letting a backstabber stay on board." Even though *he's* the treacherous asshole, I'm actually starting to feel bad for the guy. What's wrong with me? "Listen, this isn't the end for you. You said yourself you have other copies. The best I can do is keep your memories in storage. If I have the chance, I'll give them to another version of you."

"It is a sort of death," he says, but he's not pleading anymore. He's beginning to sound resigned. "I think you know that."

He's right—I do. As much as I hate uploads, I can't quite deny that they're real human consciousnesses. "You haven't left me with much of a choice," I say, quietly. I turn toward Belflower. "Delete him."

"With pleasure," she says, and gets to work.

Worldworn stands there, staring at me from the center of his console, arms stiff at his sides. Something about his gaze makes me feel uncomfortable, but it's not like this sort of thing is easy to do.

Abruptly, he vanishes, without ceremony. "It's done," Belflower says.

I nod, though my shoulders suddenly feel heavier. "All right," I say with a sigh. "I need to think." Bringing a hand to my forehead, I massage my temples with thumb and middle finger. "Have any of you ever served as a TOPO?" I lower my hand to find my three remaining crew members looking at me with blank faces.

"What about in your video game?" I say. "Do you have any navigation training at all?"

"Nope," Asterisk says. The other two shake their heads.

"So, I'm the only one with anything close to the skills necessary to fly this thing. But I can't fly her and captain her at the same time."

"Maybe you can," Belflower says.

"What? How?"

"If you let me copy you again…"

"No," I say, horrified. "Definitely not. That's not an option."

Except, there are no other options. And so, twenty minutes later, Belflower looks up from her station, where she's been putting the finishing touches on our new TOPO. "Okay," she says. "Ready?"

I'm slowly shaking my head. "Just do it."

She taps something on her console, and I appear in the center of the circular railing—the same place Worldworn stood less than an hour ago.

"Whoa, what the hell is this?" I say. My double says, that is.

"It's temporary," I assure me. "The moment we can find a real TOPO, you'll be relieved from duty, trust me. Look, to avoid confusion, you're Moe now, okay? I'm the only Joe."

"No," Moe says. "No, no, no. I *captain* this ship. I don't take orders." He looks up from his digital body and glares at me. "What did you do, anyway? How did we come to this?" He casts his gaze around at the other three crewmembers. "I don't recognize any of these people."

"There have been some developments, Moe," I say, trying to remember when the last time I sent a brainprint was. "Belflower, when was the brainprint sent that you copied Moe from?"

"I'm *Joe*," Moe says.

"No, you're not. Belflower?"

"A little over two years ago, sir. It was a brainprint to your daughter."

Fount. Has it really been that long since I contacted Harmony while on duty? "Listen, Moe, we don't exactly have time to bring you up to speed. We're about to infiltrate Royal, and that's going to require some fancy flying. I was planning on having a TOPO who knows what he's doing, but things didn't turn out that way, so I'm going to need you to study up until we get there. Maybe run some sims."

"I *hate* sims."

"Think I don't know that?"

"We're really going to Royal?" Moe says. "After what we did last time? They'll kill us."

"Don't worry about that." As stealthily as I can, I check the others' expressions to see how they're reacting to Moe's remark. "I have a plan."

"Listen, asshole, there's no way you can expect me to follow your orders. Don't try to pretend you don't know what you've done. I hate sims, and you made me—made yourself—into a filthy upload. Do you realize how gross this feels?"

The crewmembers are definitely reacting to *that*. Asterisk's eyes are narrowed, and Aphrodite is frowning. Belflower looks shocked. I guess till now I've managed to hide the full extent of how much I hate the Subverse and everyone in it.

"Yes, *Moe*," I say. "I know exactly what I've done, and *you* should know that I wouldn't do it without a damned good reason. Harmony is on Royal. I'm going to get her out."

His face falls. "Harmony?" he says, the anger gone. "How did she manage to leave Calabar?"

"Again," I say. "There's no time. I need you to spend the next" —I consult my datasphere for the remaining transit time— "*seventy-nine minutes* learning the rest of what you need to know in order to not crash my ship into the side of Royal. Are we clear, or do I need to go over everything again?"

He gives me the finger, then disappears, presumably to start running sims. Hopefully, anyway.

My crew are all avoiding eye contact, now. Maybe they're upset to learn their captain is just as biased against them as uploads are against biological humans. Ah, well. You can't please everyone.

My plan is to sink below Larunda's ever-present blanket of sulphuric-acid clouds until we're out of sight. The *Ares'* hull can handle the acid, and the clouds will keep us from being detected by visual sensors or lidar. They should throw off radar, too.

Over an hour later, Aphrodite finally breaks the awkward silence, her voice flat. "We're nearing the end of the course set by Worldworn. We'll be entering cloud cover inside of ten minutes."

"Very good," I say, suppressing a sigh. "Belflower, get Moe back here."

"Aye," Belflower says tersely.

Moe reappears wearing a scowl. I can tell there's a layer of determination underlying his resentment, though. Rescuing Harmony is probably the only thing that would have convinced him to cooperate, so in one sense, I'm lucky. You have to squint pretty hard at the situation to draw that conclusion, though.

"How do you feel?" I ask him.

"I'll do my best."

Not the most encouraging response, but I don't suppose I can ask for anything more. "We're about to reach the end of the course set by the former TOPO, and that's when I'll need you to take over. Just before we reach Royal, I want you to break through the clouds and fly toward a specific landing bay—I'll give you a map of the place that shows which one. At that time, I'll have Aphrodite let them know that if they don't let us in, we'll blast our way in, and that won't be good for anyone. We'll be close enough that their defenses won't be able to stop us from doing it. If they refuse, then the WSO will fire a Javelin at the airlock. Either way, you'll need to take the *Ares* through the doors and land her inside."

"I guess there's no need for me to point out that I've never landed the *Ares* before. Or flown her inside a planet's atmosphere."

"You're right," I say. "There's no need."

ROYAL

1

"Tell them they have fifteen seconds to open that outer hatch," I say. We've just emerged from Larunda's sulphuric-acid cloud layer, so there's a good chance that no one on Royal has spotted us yet. "Tell them it's Commander Joe Pikeman knocking."

"Yes, sir," Aphrodite says, her hands flying over the curved surface in front of her.

"Asterisk, standby to return fire if they try to take us out with stationary weaponry." Defending ourselves is going to be harder than it should be, with two of our three port turrets gone. Hopefully it won't prove necessary.

"Aye," the Ensign says, the chains bracketing his face hanging motionless. He actually seems pretty focused.

Before we engaged the four Broadswords waiting for us at the slipspace exit point, I let my WSO and TOPO know that I reserve the right to take over weapons or navigation at any point. And I did take over some of the laser turrets during that battle. But even though Worldworn was a traitor, I can't deny he was a deft hand on the *Ares'* rudder—so to speak. I never worried about the ship's handling with him at the TOPO station.

I don't feel nearly that confident now. Yes, it's basically me flying the *Ares*, but I only have the knowhow to execute isolated maneuvers, in situations where I feel like a TOPO is dropping the ball. Moe is probably more qualified than me to do what's he's about to attempt, with the hour-and-change he just put into training sims, but not *much* more qualified.

The landing bay's hatch isn't opening. "WSO, arm a Javelin."

"Yes, Captain."

"Wait," Aphrodite says. "They're opening it."

"Very good," I say, bracing myself as I turn toward the TOPO station. "Moe?"

His lips tighten. Clearly, he still isn't fully on board with the name change. Hopefully he won't be on my bridge long enough to get used to it. I aim to replace him as soon as I can.

The *Ares* lurches forward, and that's how I know we're in trouble. I eyeball the hatch through a hull sensor, and I can tell we're at least three meters too far to the left.

"Tighten up your trajectory, Commander!" I bark.

"I'm trying, *Commander*."

The *Ares* heaves to the right—too far again, but Moe immediately compensates—then we're flying through the airlock.

Or I should say: crashing through it. A hideous screeching noise comes from the *Ares'* port-side hull, and my view through the sensor is obstructed by thousands of sparks being spat up by the scraping metal.

Then we're through, and the landing bay deck comes up to meet us. It's more of a tumble than a graceful landing, and we hit the surface with a bang, followed by more screeching as we skid to a stop.

When I will the sensor view away, my hand is obstructing my vision—it seems I facepalmed without realizing it.

I remove the hand to see Moe staring at me with wide eyes and a set jaw. "That was a disaster," I tell him.

He doesn't answer. There isn't much to say, I guess.

"How are we doing for tokens after our first versecast?" I ask Belflower.

She clears her throat, and I try not to look annoyed at the affectation. Obviously, she's about to tell me something she knows I won't like, but why can't she just come out and say it instead of pretending to have an actual throat that needs clearing?

"After our first *versecasts*, you mean," she says. "Plural."

"No, that's not what I meant. How many versecasts have you broadcast?"

"Two. Your initial message, and Worldworn's betrayal."

I lean forward, eyes widening. "You *what?*"

"You did give me access to your datasphere footage, Captain. I mean, if you'd like to select and edit the clips yourself, you can, but the Worldworn drama was just too good. People are going to eat that right up."

"Well, are they, then? How long has it been up?"

"Since ten minutes or so after you deleted him. I actually haven't had a chance to check on the reception it's getting."

"*Check,*" I growl.

She's silent for a few seconds. Then, her eyebrows shoot up. "Wow. Your initial message did better than expected—not great, though a fair bit better than I thought it would. But the Worldworn episode is *blowing up*, sir. Donations are pouring in, and we already have our first sponsorship offers. People love you, Captain."

"No, they love the shitshow." Still, I can't help being a little pleased. Even if it does feel like I'm parceling out my soul piece by piece, there's clearly money in this versecasting thing. The new funding will help pay for repairs, if we ever find a port we trust enough to make them. Maybe even better weaponry. "What's our balance, with the donations added in?"

"Thirty-five thousand, three hundred eighty-nine tokens. We can borrow against these sponsorship offers for more quick money, if we need it."

"I don't think we will," I say, running a quick calculation in my head.

"Sir, six armed men have emerged from the landing bay's perimeter and are in the process of surrounding us," my OPO says.

"Want me to gun them down?" Asterisk asks.

"No. We'd have bigger problems, then."

"We already have big problems," Moe says.

"Yeah, no kidding," I agree. "Like how you nearly totaled my ship."

"You'd just better have a damned good plan."

"I do," I say, standing from the command seat. "I'm going to talk to them. But for starters: Aphrodite, wire fifteen-thousand tokens into the account associated with the name Jet Miller. You'll find the account ID in the computer. The account is connected with the Visby Subverse."

I'm about to head for the airlock when Belflower holds up a hand. "Wait, sir."

"What?"

"You need to thank your top donators."

I squint at her. "There are armed pirates outside."

"Yes, but who knows when you'll next get the chance? It's customary, Captain. I'm telling you, if you don't show some gratitude, people will label you as rude. Your donations will fall off."

I take a breath, and for a couple seconds, I come very close to calling this whole versecasting thing off. Gritting my teeth, I settle back into the command seat. "Tell the pirates I'll be with them in a moment," I order Aphrodite. Then, I look at Belflower. "Are we ready?" I ask through gritted teeth.

"Go ahead. I'll feed the donators' handles to your datasphere."

I clear my throat and stare into empty space. "Uh, I'd like to thank Reaperpwnz, M5959, Fetmahn, wontstoppoppin, and Bobinator for donations of over 500 tokens. Special thanks to Fetmahn for being my top donator."

"Say a thanks to everyone who donated," Belflower whispers.

"Thank you to everyone who donated," I repeat, then glance at the Engineer. "Will that do it?"

"Yes," she says, still whispering. "That's good."

Shaking my head and trying not to think too hard about what brought me to this point, I push myself out of the command seat again and head for the airlock, fingering the butt of my blaster.

Three of the six men are standing in front of the outer airlock when I emerge, looking more or less like you'd expect pirates to. Scruffy hair, unkempt beards, rumpled clothing. They all have laser rifles aimed at me, too.

"Butcher," says their leader—Jet Miller, whose acquaintance I made a few years ago. His clothes are even more wrinkled and stained than his fellows. Maybe that's how they indicate rank, around here. His left eye is squinched shut as he sights along the barrel with his right. Oh, and his face and hands have that melted look skin gets when exposed to gaseous sulphuric acid. I may have had something to do with that.

"Hey, Jet. Good to see you," I say. "Let me kick off our chat by reminding you that you're on my ship's good side." I motion backward with my head, toward the three fully operational secondary laser turrets, not to mention the primary sitting pretty on top. "I could have you all killed where you stand."

"And I could kill you where *you* stand, Butcher," says Jet, apparently keen to get my nickname in as much as he can. I gather he's pissed off about the last time we met.

"I think we both know you won't do that. I'm sure you haven't forgotten about my last visit. Make a move, and my ship will detect it. All eight of the plasma bombs I've had installed inside her hull are already armed, so you won't get two feet before they detonate. It'll be more than your landing bay that gets blown apart, this time. I'm surprised you were stupid enough to come this close."

"You're bluffing," Miller says weakly.

"Come on," I say.

His eyes waver, then fall to the deck. I actually think his lower lip trembles a little. "I only recently got this place operational again, Pikeman. I'm a businessman. I got a family. You know that."

The word "family" is a bit of a stretch for the collection of humans Miller's responsible for. His wife left him even before I blew up his landing bay, and each of the four children she produced before leaving was uglier and worse-tempered then the last. They're uglier than Miller, which is saying something, and from what I've heard, they don't even have his business sense. "Look, Jet, things aren't all bad. Provided you learned your lesson last time, and you stick to my terms, you stand to make a tidy profit here. Check your account—I've already wired fifteen thousand tokens into it, and there's fifteen thousand more where that came from, as long as you keep your mouth shut about my arrival and let no harm come to my ship. Plus, you get to keep your landing bay. What do you say?"

His shoulders rise and fall with a long breath, and he lowers the rifle. "Fine. Just make it quick." The other two pirates lower their weapons, too.

"I'm paying you five times what a day's rent is worth," I say. "So I'll take my time. Tell me—is Lord Bleak on Royal right now?"

Miller shakes his head. "He's off making preparations for the wedding."

"Wedding?" For some reason, I don't like the sounds of that at all.

Miller shrugs. "His son's getting married to some girl. Nothing to do with me. I don't follow the gossip, and I couldn't give less of a shit about that pansy."

"Right. Got a washroom I can use?"

Miller nods toward a filthy corner of his filthy landing bay. I head over there and wrench open the flimsy wooden door by the knob—archaic door-opening technology. Inside, the squat toilet looks like it's never seen a scrub brush, but I have no business with it, thankfully. "Don't bother me till I'm finished," I yell back into the landing bay. That done, I shut the door, attempt to lock it, fail, then turn to look into the mirror.

Peering into my own eyes, I lean on the sink with both hands and focus on my breathing, doing my best to clear my head. I try one of the old man's mindfulness techniques, scanning my body from head to toe, registering how each part feels.

Somewhat miraculously, I manage to get to a state of tranquility that approaches the battle calm I experienced during the Broadsword engagement. My breathing comes slow and steady, my lungs expanding and contracting, my shoulders rising and falling. Then, I let an image slowly take shape in my mind, the details falling into place one by one:

Lord Bleak. Decked out in a foppish black hat, gray scarf, scarlet doublet. The sword he never uses dangling from his hip. The frilly white cuffs.

Slowly, my face changes. My clothes transform. And in the mirror, I watch myself become Lord Bleak.

I can't believe it. It actually worked. First time, too.

When I emerge from the washroom, Miller and his henchman are still standing awkwardly near the *Ares*, as though unsure what to do with themselves. Miller glances at me, then does a double take.

"What the hell?" he says.

"Not a word to anyone," I tell him, which makes me realize I need to work on *sounding* like Bleak, too. I've seen a couple of his versecasts. Hopefully I can pull off a passable imitation. "About my presence, or about what you saw here."

He nods, though much of the color has drained from his face.

2

I leave the landing bay and start across the bridge connecting it to the next balloon. Miller was right that I'm bluffing about the plasma bombs—this time. But I'm pretty sure that's a bluff I'll be able to play out for the rest of my career.

See, as a Guardsman, from time to time it becomes necessary to infiltrate pirate dens; usually ones that have sprung up near sensitive Subverse infrastructure. Over the years, I built up a bit of a reputation for claiming that I had plasma bombs installed in my ship's hull, which I'd arm every time I entered a pirate sanctuary, warning the pirates that they would detonate if anyone messed with me.

I'm not sure anyone really believed me, but when the ship in question is parked beside most of what you value in life, you become pretty risk-averse.

Before today, I've only had to visit Royal once, and Miller was unlucky enough to own the landing bay I chose to enter through. I guess he'd heard about my scheme and figured he'd be the one to call me on it.

He pretended to play along, then waited till I got halfway

across the bridge to the next balloon before calling my bluff. Miller and four of his goons caught up and drew on me.

It wasn't their lucky day. Knowing that getting inside Royal would probably prove tougher than the average warren, before heading there I actually had plasma bombs installed in the hull, just in case.

I willed the signal to my ship—the *Cratos*—to detonate the bombs. It blew the landing bay clean away, and the bridge we were on went vertical.

Miller's henchpeople all tumbled down the tunnel, to be eaten by the acidic clouds that now permeated the wreckage of the bay. Or maybe some of them fell straight through to Larunda's acidic surface, fifty kilometers below.

Miller himself managed to hang on. I'd had the foresight to keep my full suit on, just in case, but not him. As deadly vapors went to work on his clothes, face, and arms, he hauled himself up the tube after me. I outpaced him, made it into Royal, saw my mission through, and escaped in someone's beat-up old scow. When I asked around a few months later to see if Miller had survived, I learned that not only was he still alive, but he was starting up a new landing bay. I decided that if I ever came back here, he'd be the one I'd pay a visit. It's just easier to deal with people you already know.

The brass was none too happy that I'd wasted a Broadsword on the stunt, but even they had to admit that I'd just become their best choice in the Andora Sector when it came to sending someone to infiltrate a pirate base.

I reach the end of the bridge and emerge into the first main hub. Plenty of smaller balloons connect to this one, but they're all dead ends. From this hub, you can reach three others, one of them Royal's main hub: the biggest balloon, home to Lord Bleak's manse.

As I walk through, vendors hawk their wares from carpets, tables, booths, storefronts, and whatever else can be co-opted for enterprise. There's plenty of color everywhere, and some of the offerings actually look kind of tempting, including a laser rifle modified for rapid fire and a bushel of plasma grenades. I'm running kind of low since my last stop at a Guard supply hub.

A quiet sweeps over the market as I progress through, and I'm attracting plenty of confused stares and sidelong glances.

Possibly, impersonating Lord Bleak wasn't the best idea. I try to think about what they might find odd. Maybe the fact I'm unaccompanied? I'm pretty sure Bleak doesn't have a private landing bay, so it wouldn't be the fact I'm coming from one of the public ones that they find strange.

Maybe it's the fact Bleak is here at all. Yeah, that seems most likely.

Either way, the sellers seem to recover quickly enough, and commerce resumes again in earnest. At least, the attempt at commerce. There's a lot of yelling but I don't see many actual purchases take place.

Most of the browsers are probably people who live here, but Royal does get visitors, mostly other pirates. The various pirate havens *have* to do business with each other, else they wouldn't make it. Few are in locations that provide everything needed for survival. Here, Larunda's CO2-heavy atmosphere can be broken down into carbon and oxygen, and they also harvest oxygen, sulfur, and water from the clouds. But other than some modest manufacturing done with metals collected from the edge of the system, that's about it. Whatever they can't make themselves, they trade for. Or, you know, pirate.

I make it to the other side of the balloon without incident, then I'm in another enclosed bridge. It lets out onto the main hub of Royal. This balloon dwarfs the one I just left. It does its best to resemble what a city might have looked like, on one of the old surface colonies, but it's not actually much bigger than the Brinktown I'm from.

The resemblance comes from its buildings: towers that reach

twenty stories, apartment buildings (full of mostly empty apartments, I'm sure), malls, and in the center, Lord Bleak's walled manse, which approaches the splendor of a palace. It seems a bit out of place in the middle of the other, more modern-looking buildings, but that probably isn't surprising to anyone. Bleak had it built himself, after knocking down the more modern dwelling that once stood there. So of course it's an eyesore.

Far above the city, or wannabe city, hangs a sky made from a layer of old display panels, which show a composite of the actual Larundan sky beyond, by way of sensors affixed to the balloon's exterior. Several of the panels have stopped functioning, and the sky is broken up by dark rectangles here and there.

But hey, I can't knock it too much. For a post-apocalyptic pirate balloon city, it looks pretty good.

Security seems pretty lax, in here. A couple guards are posted at the gates into the manse grounds, and I assume more could be called, but all in all the pirates seem to have an understanding that they don't attack or steal from each other. Plenty of Brinktowns to go around, I guess, not to mention that for the daring, the great corpse of galactic civilization has barely begun to be plundered.

"My lord," says the guard on the right as I approach, his forehead bunching up into lines. "What brings you back to Royal? I thought you'd be well on your way to Arbor by now. Weren't you heading there first, to prepare it for the ceremony?"

I blink at the guard. "Of course," I say in my best impression of Bleak's bass voice. Considering I've never practiced it before, it comes out better than expected, but I'm still not sure it's passable. When I continue, it gets a little better: "That's still the plan. But when we reached the slip coords, we realized we'd forgotten to bring my late wife's wedding dress. It's meant to be a surprise for my son's bride, so it wouldn't do to send back a message for her and Peter to take it with them, would it?"

"I suppose not, sir."

With a curt nod, I say, "Open the gates."

"Er—you want us to open the gates, sir? You won't be using the postern today?"

"That would be faster, wouldn't it? Unlock it for me. I left the key on my ship."

I'm treading on very uncertain ground, now—betting that Bleak would use old-style keys rather than codes or biometrics. When the guard pulls a necklace from inside of his shirt, I suppress a sigh of relief. I follow him to the right of the main gates, to a much smaller gate concealed behind some trees.

"My thanks," I say, and then I hurry across the expanse of grass toward the manse before he can ask me anything else.

It takes me a few seconds to realize that I'm headed for a part of the exterior that has no entrance into the house. As casually as I can manage, I turn right, hoping a door lies this way. I resist the urge to check whether the guard is staring after me in confusion, or worse, suspicion.

I need to move fast. Something tells me this isn't going to end well.

When I finally find a door, it isn't locked, and I head through—straight into a kitchen bustling with cooks and servants. Every one of them turns to me wearing expressions ranging from shock to fear.

"Carry on!" I yell. "Back to your tasks! This is a surprise inspection, and I see that everything is up to snuff. Good job, everyone. You're doing this household proud."

No one answers, and I stroll through, heading toward a door on the opposite end of the long room, praying it's not a broom closet or something.

It lets into a narrow hallway, which I start down.

"Lord Bleak?"

I turn to see a diminutive woman, middle-aged, peeking out from the kitchen entrance.

"Yes?"

"Are you all right? Something's wrong with your face."

"Really?" There's a window a few meters behind me, and I walk to it, peering at my faint reflection. My face appears to be a strange blend of Lord Bleak's face and my own. The clothes have started to turn color, too, darkening toward the Guardsman's black. "I'm fine," I say. "I've just been losing sleep, what with the…excitement."

"Yes," the servant says slowly. "It's quite exciting, my lord. It's truly a Romeo and Juliet wedding, between your son and that Sterling girl."

"Sterling girl," I say, my stomach sinking farther than it already was. "Yes. One for the ages."

The woman's approaching, now, trying to get a better look at me. I want to shout at her to go away, but instead, I concentrate on getting my disguise back in place. Luckily, the hallway's pretty dark, and hopefully it will hide the change.

"You're looking better already," the woman says, though there's a strange note in her voice. "Maybe it was a trick of the light. They say the Shiva Knights could change their faces, so it pays to be careful."

"So it does," I say, my heart hammering. "You're to be commended for your vigilance. Keep it up, and you'll go far."

The woman nods.

"Now, back to your duties."

She returns to the kitchen, glancing back at me once more before disappearing inside. With that, I turn and start jogging through hallway after hallway. This stupid plan is about to come crashing down on my head any second.

3

I sprint up the first staircase I find, but after that the hallways become more lavish. And more populated.

Pirates walk the purple-carpeted halls, past friezes and statues and vases. These pirates are much better dressed than Miller and his men, and some of them don't look like pirates at all. Some of them wear lab coats, and a few, expensive-looking business suits. Each person returns my nod, but to me, they all seem suspicious, now. Probably, word is traveling, and the possibility that I might actually be Lord Bleak is the only reason I haven't been stopped. I'd guess he would get pretty pissed off if someone accused him of being an impostor in his own home, and that's how I intend to react if it happens.

"Where is my son?" I ask the next pirate I see.

He shifts his eyes to the right, then says, "In his quarters, as far as I know, my lord. He's with his betrothed."

I *really* don't like the sound of that. "Thanks," I say before marching in the direction the pirate came from. He doesn't say anything, so I must be going the right way.

Another staircase, followed by another corridor, and I arrive at a set of heavy double doors that are ornate enough to belong to either Bleak or his son. I push through them and find Bleak's son, Peter Vance, sitting in an over-stuffed armchair in front of a roaring fireplace. Across from him, in an identical chair, sits my daughter.

"Father," Peter says, rising to his feet and clasping his hands in front of him. He's a skinny runt, blond, and soft-spoken. I've never met him before, but he seems to suffer from an eye contact problem. But maybe that's just when it comes to his father. "Why have you returned?"

"To make sure you haven't succeeded in making your fiancee hate you yet." It's not hard to tell that treating Vance like shit is going to be the best strategy for convincing him I'm really his father. I turn to Harmony. "Be honest, dear. Have you had your fill of him yet?"

She shakes her head. "Not at all. He's quite sweet, Lord Bleak."

"That's the problem. Sweet and *weak*. Like a woman. I'm sorry my loins produced such a pathetic excuse for a man."

"He would have done just fine, if he'd been born into a Brink-town," Harmony says, with a sly smile directed at Vance.

I laugh—a single, terse syllable. Vance looks like he might be about to cry. "True enough! Get out, Peter. I want a word with your betrothed."

"But father—"

"*Get out!*" I roar, and he scurries toward the doors, closing them behind him.

With that, I let my disguise drop, and Harmony actually squeaks. "Dad! How—?"

"Harmony, what the hell are you doing?"

"What do you mean?" she asks, suddenly the picture of innocence.

"What do you think I mean? I've heard all about the 'Sterling girl' marrying Lord Bleak's son, so stop playing dumb. *Sterling girl?*"

She nods. "It wasn't hard for Bleak to believe that I'm a favorite granddaughter of Daniel Sterling, considering I showed up in his ship. Bleak's been eating out of my hand ever since, and he wasn't very subtle about offering up his son, either. He sees it as a power move against the Five Families. Having a Sterling in the family legitimizes him. He's been advertising the wedding all over the Subverse, and he's having us fly to it in good old grandpa's ship, just to underscore the point."

I study her face in silence for several seconds, trying not to shake my head. Even as the most infamous Troubleshooter, I've always made a point to keep Harmony out of the public eye—it's far from common knowledge that I even have a daughter. Now, everyone in the Subverse will likely come to know her face, if they don't already. "I don't pretend to be a genius, but I have no clue what you're trying to accomplish, Harm. Is this part of your crusade to make your grandfather pay?"

Harmony laughs, and despite how baffled I am, it does me good to hear her looking and sounding well. It's a huge relief. "I think losing his ship gave Daniel Sterling more than enough to think about," she says. "I'm here to get to the bottom of the pirate attacks."

"By marrying Peter Vance?"

She shrugs. "Seems like the perfect way to me. I actually kind of like him, Dad, and anyway, I've learned a lot. Case in point: Bleak says he wasn't behind attacking the Brinktowns where children were abducted. Actually, he's been working to find those children, and he talks about putting them in good homes when he does."

Now, it's my turn to laugh. "Seems likely. Did he mention why he thinks the children were abducted in the first place?"

She shakes her head.

"So are you buying everything he's telling you, then?"

"Not necessarily. But I'm keeping an open mind. Listen, Dad, it's sweet that you came here—though I'm sure I wasn't the only reason. Either way, you need to go now. Bleak has an Essence, and he left him behind to watch over the manse. He checks in every day, and when he hears about 'Lord Bleak' wandering the house when he isn't supposed to be, he's sure to come looking for you. He'll know you're not Bleak in a heartbeat."

"*Fount.* Since when has Bleak had an Essence?"

"He's had one for years, apparently. He's just kept it quiet. I guess having one is more effective if no one knows about it."

"I'd say." An Essence is more than just a bodyguard. It's someone who's given up their physical body in exchange for having their upload to the Subverse paid for. That done, the Fount inside the purchased body is modified so that the buyer's consciousness can be copied over. Typically, an Essence is trained in various forms of combat. Who could be more motivated to protect you than yourself? It's the kind of thing that would have been illegal, if there were still laws.

"Harmony," I say, "it's a very bad idea to get tangled up with Bleak and his people. You may think you're playing him, but it's much more likely he's playing you." As I talk, my gaze drifts around the room. Armchairs. A metal stand with utensils for managing the fire. A table big enough for two to dine. Couches. Art.

"I'm staying, Dad. You came here for Faelyn Eliot, right? Well, Bleak says he did manage to recover her, and he told me where he's keeping her for the time being, until he can arrange to have her brought back to her parents."

"Where?"

"Somewhere called Xeo."

Xeo? What the hell is he planning to do there? But I don't let my surprise show. "Yeah, that's not a place you take someone you give a shit about," I say.

"Maybe. It doesn't matter. I'm not coming with you. I'm handling this on my own."

The hairs on the back of my neck stir, and I remember what the old Shiva said, about paying attention to what my body's trying to tell me—what the Fount is trying to tell me.

Then, I hear a doorknob turning behind me.

My first impulse is to run for the fireplace, maybe take cover behind an armchair. Could be I'll miss every shot, but if I can lure the Essence to me, I can surprise him with a fire poker through the abdomen.

But as the door swings open behind me, inspiration strikes, and I run straight at Harmony instead.

I wrap an arm tight around her throat, draw my blaster, and put the muzzle against her temple.

The Essence is a short, plain-looking man. He stares across the drawing room with eyes narrowed. "Clearly, you are not Lord Bleak," he says.

"Why do you say that?" I ask. "Am I not usually a total asshole?"

I begin walking Harmony toward the double doors —toward the Essence. "Move out of the way, or Peter Vance's fiancee dies," I growl.

The Essence complies, backing into the hallway beyond. For a moment, I'm worried Harmony will reveal that I'm her father. That wouldn't make this a very convincing hostage situation. Then, I realize that revealing me could mess up her story about being a Sterling, so she probably won't. She's smarter than that.

Outside the room, I see that the Essence didn't bother bringing any backup. Not surprising, considering he's essentially Bleak. The guy's always been a cocky bastard, from what I've heard.

"Stay right there," I say, backing away from him, "until we're gone."

The Essence says nothing, his eyes never leaving mine.

We reach an intersection of two corridors, and as I'm guiding Harmony around the corner, she twists her head sideways and lets herself go limp, sliding out of my grasp. I try to snatch her arm, but she's gone, running down a hallway perpendicular to the one we just came from.

Damn it. I think I probably eased up on my grip, for fear of hurting her. Now she's gone, and I have other problems. The Essence is running toward me, fishing a laser pistol from a hip holster. I get off a couple shots before he gets it out, but he veers left, and both bolts miss.

Then he's firing back, and I withdraw around the corner. I'm being forced in the wrong direction. I watch Harmony disappear around the corner at the end of the opposite hallway.

4

Bleak's Essence doesn't slow, his footfalls getting louder as he rushes the intersection. I decide I'm not likely to win a point-blank shootout, so I run, firing blindly over my shoulder.

My datasphere warns me of a shot about to pierce my heart from behind, and I dive into a forward roll. The neon-blue laser shot crackles through the air above me, and I come out of the roll, zagging right to avoid another.

Then I'm at the end of the hallway, turning the corner.

Pounding down its carpeted length, I try to look at this from the Essence's perspective. For all intents and purposes, it's Bleak chasing me through his own house. From what I know of Bleak, he's arrogant, and given I've made a fool of him, he probably wants to be the one to kill me.

That doesn't mean we won't run into more pirates as we tear through the house, of course. Either way, it would be best to deal with the Essence quickly.

Yanking a door open reveals an empty bunkroom—probably where Bleak's mercenaries sleep, or some of them, anyway. Door number two reveals a cramped room, not much bigger than a closet, where three pirates sit playing cards by lamplight. I manage to shoot one of them before the other two lay hands on laser pistols, and I slam the door shut to continue tearing down the hall. The Essence's footsteps pound closer.

I try the very next door and run inside, with the pair of pirates entering the corridor behind me. Slamming the door shut I barrel across what appears to be Bleak's great room.

Several options present themselves. I could make for one of the two living room-like clusters of furniture, arranged in front of cold fireplaces that face each other across the massive room. Or I could sprint for the other door, on the opposite end of the room, which probably leads back into the hall. Another option: try to tip over the massive dining table in the center to use for cover.

Then, I notice a fourth possibility: I could climb the scaffolding on the far side of the room, which partially obscures a floor-to-ceiling mural depicting Lord Bleak in combat. He wears a rictus of righteous anger and aims a laser pistol at a target out of the frame.

Figuring the furniture and table will burn under laserfire, and taking the other door will just allow them to outflank me, I charge toward the mural, ready to leap behind some furniture if I need to.

But by the time the door crashes open behind me, I'm already past the furniture. My datasphere warns me that someone's aiming at the small of my back, and I weave right. The shot crackles past, scoring Bleak's giant pant leg.

"Stop shooting!" cries the Essence, his voice slightly muffled. He's still in the hallway. "I'll handle this."

Seems my choice is paying off. Of course the Essence wouldn't want to damage the mural. He's just as conceited as Bleak, and when he sees the pirate lord, he sees his own face, not the one he actually wears.

I reach the ramp leading up to the first level of scaffolding and dash up it. My datasphere flashes black, forecasting laserfire a foot in front of me. I halt, and the Essence doesn't fire, adjusting his aim instead. As he does, I race ahead, toward the next ramp. He still doesn't fire.

Unable to focus on both avoiding his laserfire and shooting back, I focus on just staying alive. Soon, I'm on the third level, then I reach the fourth. With each level, the Essence's firing angle gets worse, and I gain higher and higher ground.

On the fifth level, I drop abruptly to the metal surface, drawing my blaster in the same motion. I hold it over the side to rain fire down on the pirates' heads.

One of the grunts topples over, and the other takes a bolt to his boot, sending him hopping. The Essence curses, then screams, "Return fire!"

The wounded pirate gets control of himself, levels his laser pistol at my location, and fires. The Essence does the same, and his aim is much better. I'm forced to flatten myself to the metal as laserfire crackles above and below, marring Bleak's chin and heating the metal I'm lying on. Sooner or later, it'll start melting, and I'll fall through, molten metal clinging to me. That won't be fun.

I decide not to wait for it to happen. Instead, I grip both sides of the metal platform, ignoring its searing heat, and I kick out against the wall with all my might. The entire structure teeters outward, then swings back to crash against the wall. I kick out again.

The scaffolding sails outward, and expressions of terror take hold on the pirates' faces. I get my feet under me enough to leap backward as it falls, toward a couch, and I even get a couple blaster shots off in midair, though neither of them hit.

My feet touch the couch cushions, but my momentum carries me over, and I crash into the coffee table in front of it. It snaps under my weight, and I end up on the floor amidst wooden shrapnel.

Gritting my teeth against the pain, I struggle to my feet between two levels of scaffolding. The Essence is standing at the same time, looking dazed. I shoot, and this time, I don't miss. His facial features burst apart.

I scramble over level after level to check for the other pirate, only to find him lying on his back, a bloody gash on his forehead, where the scaffolding must have gotten him. He looks pretty dead, but I don't bother checking.

Just as I'm about to leave the room, there's a *whoomph* behind me, and I turn to find flames climbing up an upholstered chair. The metal must have been hot enough to set it alight. A glance down at my uniform shows it's singed in parts. Fount, that was close.

The hallway's empty when I emerge from the great room, but not for long. Laserfire scores the carpet in front of my feet as I reach a staircase, and I spy a pirate leaning out of a doorway up ahead. "Stay right there!" he yells.

"Screw that," I mutter, and start hustling down the stairs. I just got a whiff of smoke—I'm pretty sure this place is about to burn down. I wonder what that means for Royal as a whole. They must have ways to put out fires before they compromise the entire colony.

More importantly, I wonder what it means for Harmony. I try to contact her, but she doesn't answer, which doesn't offer much comfort. So I get in touch with the *Ares*.

"Aphrodite here. What can I do for you, Captain?"

"Wire Miller the rest of the tokens, then tell, uh, Moe to take you out. I want to know if *Europa's Gift* leaves Royal. That's Daniel Sterling's ship. There should be a picture of it in the computer."

"I know what it looks like."

I narrow my eyes as I run along a corridor, checking over my shoulder for pursuers. "What? How?"

"Oh. I looked it up."

"Right." There's no good reason for her to have done that—she didn't know that was the ship Harmony took—but now isn't the time to investigate. "Pikeman out."

I reach a part of the manse I recognize from my initial ascent through it, and after that, navigation becomes a lot easier. On the other hand, the entire household is alive to my presence. My disguise is long gone, and pirates are shooting at me on sight. I return fire when I can, take cover when necessary, and flee the moment it becomes possible. I can't afford to get pinned down.

At last, I reach the dim, first-level corridor with the kitchen—only to find five pirates waiting outside it when I peer around the corner. Cursing, I backtrack. There has to be another way out.

Instead of an exit, I find another staircase leading down. For a few seconds, that makes no sense: I'm already at ground-level, aren't I? Then, I realize there must be an area between the "ground" and the bottom of the balloon.

Right away, the decor changes: from art-adorned hallways to an open-concept warren of metal walkways and ramps. As I descend, I start to glimpse the bottom of the vast open area, where row after row of great cabinets march from one end to the other.

Then laserfire crackles from above, and my datasphere goes black, warning that the next shot will hit me. I scramble out of the way, leaping to the next platform down—a ten-meter fall.

As much as I try to absorb the impact by buckling my legs as I land, it still sends shocks up through my ankles. Ignoring them, I continue downward.

When I reach the bottom level, I learn what the cabinets contain: the circuit boards and cables of server racks. What the hell? This can't be the Visby Subverse, can it? I've never been assigned to check on it, so I'm not sure where it's supposed to be located. But there's no way anyone would let pirates occupy the colony where it's housed.

But if not that, then what do the pirates need with all this equipment?

Whatever the answer to that riddle, the servers themselves provide excellent cover against those hunting me. I keep close to the racks on my right as I run, and the laserfire slacks off—clearly, they fear damaging the servers more than they fear letting me escape.

When I finally emerge at the far end, I spot a hatch a few meters to my left. I sprint toward it, finding it locked, and I shoot out the locking mechanism with my blaster. With that, I yank it open.

"Whoa," I mutter through my panting. This room holds everything you'd need to wage a small-scale war, complete with armored shipsuits for fighting in depressurized, oxygen-free environments.

Then, my gaze falls on them: bushels of plasma grenades arranged together on a shelf nearby.

I detach enough of them to line my belt, where they suction on, ready to be plucked off and used at a moment's notice. Then I arm five of the remaining grenades, quickly distributing them among their fellows. That done, I sprint across the armory for all I'm worth, toward a hatch on the other side. On the way, I grab a helmet from one of the armored suits, one that looks my size. Thankfully, my suit seals with it, and so do the gloves I snatch.

Behind me, pirates emerge through the hatch, and I fire my blaster back toward them as I reach the exit. This one isn't locked, and I pull it open, continuing to fire over my shoulder as I slip through. I push the hatch closed, then turn and run.

"Chief," I say as I run through the next room, legs pumping. My muscles are starting to burn from exertion. "Take the *Ares* underneath Royal and watch for me." For a split second, I'm distracted by the contents of this room, though I continue to dash across it toward the hatch on the other side. Shelves full of cages march around the perimeter, with any number of freakish-looking animals occupying them. A weird quadruped stands in one, twin antennae standing at attention as it hisses like a cat. Another holds a rabbit with bulging, green-tinged eyes. Another, a lopsided monkey with bulbous musculature.

"What do you mean, watch for you?" Aphrodite says, sounding confused. "What will you be doing?"

"Falling."

A prolonged, deafening roar sounds behind me as dozens of plasma grenades detonate in rapid succession. The armory walls looked pretty strong, but they're blown out all the same, bright blue light leaking out. Pieces of metal fly past me. One of them ends up puncturing my arm, a jagged dagger shape, and I clench my jaw.

Then, the room is tilting backward as Royal's main balloon starts to fold toward the puncture, the air rushing out. Shelves and cages slide toward the breach. I run faster, uphill now, dodging around a cackling hyena-looking thing and leaping toward the hatch in time to grab the frame before the chamber I'm in goes vertical.

With that, I'm hanging diagonally, clinging to the hatch frame, my feet dangling in the direction of the tear.

Thankfully, the pressure differential between inside and outside the balloon is such that it didn't simply pop. Still, I'm in serious trouble, and so is everyone else on Royal. If they're smart, they'll evacuate, though somehow I doubt there are enough ships or escape pods to take everyone. Even provided they make it to the crafts in time.

"Aphrodite?" I grunt.

"We're in the clouds now, though I don't know how we're going to see you, with what they do to the sensors."

"Go underneath the clouds."

"What?"

"Go underneath and wait for me to fall through. Open the airlock, tilt the ship, and catch me."

That brings a pause. "You really think you—Moe—can manage that?"

"No," I say. "Not really."

With that, I lose my grip and tumble toward the breach.

ARES

1

I wake in my bunk, hurting everywhere. Dice stands over me, staring down with his trademark impassivity, scarlet eye sensors glowing.

"Moe caught me?" I manage to wheeze.

"I am not acquainted with a Moe, fleshbag or otherwise. In fact, you've never introduced me to anyone, with the exception of your daughter."

"He's the new TOPO."

"In that case, yes, he caught you in the airlock. Otherwise, you would be a smear on Larunda's acidic surface."

Groaning, I push myself to a sitting position, though the all-over aching intensifies.

"It is not advised that you move."

"I'm fine. The Fount will do its job," I say as I stagger out the door, reflecting that Moe must have been trending downward when he caught me, to absorb the impact. If he hadn't, I likely wouldn't be breathing right now. I have to say, I'm impressed by his—my— flying. "Get in your closet."

"There's a brainprint for you," Aphrodite says as I settle into the command seat. "It's from Zelah Eliot. Will you take it in your cabin?"

I give her a look. She returns it with a blank expression, but I see past that. The OPO knows I'm in no shape to keep running back and forth between my cabin and the bridge.

"Where are we right now?" I ask.

"In geostationary orbit over Larunda, on the side opposite Royal. At last sight, the colony was sinking through the planet's sulphuric acid cloud cover."

I nod. Looks like I may have dealt quite a blow to any plans the pirates had for staging another uprising. Even though I know a lot of people must have died when Royal went down, for some reason it doesn't affect me like killing people up close has started to, recently. Because I didn't actually see them die, it feels less real, somehow. Of course, killing Bleak's Essence didn't particularly bother me either, but I think that's because the real Bleak has Harmony. "What about *Europa's Gift*?" I ask.

"That's part of the reason why we came to this side of the planet. Not just to hide from any pissed-off pirates, but also to maintain line-of-sight. We're tracking the trajectory of *Europa's Gift* right now, and if she enters slipspace, we'll know the coords."

I nod. "Good work."

"Will you take Mrs. Eliot's brainprint now?"

Shaking my head, I say, "No. I need to think." My hand feels heavy as I lift it to my forehead, massaging it. "I think I know where Harmony's going—the name of the place, anyway. But I don't know the destination coords, and without them, we can't follow. When I was impersonating Lord Bleak, a pirate asked why I wasn't at Arbor. Apparently, that's where Harmony is going to marry Bleak's son, Peter Vance."

That causes Belflower to raise her eyebrows, and Asterisk chuckles, though he doesn't look up from studying his digital nails. Two people exhibit much bigger reactions: Moe and Aphrodite.

"What the *hell?*" Moe says, and Aphrodite goes pale. Even

uploads will blanch when shocked—their avatars are programmed to reflect distress.

"All right," I say. "That's enough. Deactivate all crew except the OPO."

The WSO, TOPO, and Engineer all vanish, leaving only Aphrodite and me. I can tell she's trying to compose herself, but it's too late for that. "Why do you react so strongly whenever Harmony comes up?" I say. "And how did you know what *Europa's Gift* looks like?"

She stares at me, eyes wide, though not as wide as they were a few seconds ago. She opens her mouth as if to speak, then shuts it, her jaw set. "Because, Joe," she says at last. "It's me. Marissa."

Now, it's my turn to gape at her. On some level, I think I'd already figured this out, but it still floors me. The mother of my child. Aboard the *Ares*, all this time. "What...what are you doing here?"

"I'm here because I was sick with worry."

"Uploads don't get *sick*."

"You know what I mean. Harmony stopped taking my brain-prints, and even before that I could see the path she was going down."

"The same path as the guy who knocked you up?"

Marissa Sterling frowns. "I'm really disappointed in you, Joe. You haven't been there for her."

I sit up, which makes me wince, and I ease back into the seat. I settle for narrowing my eyes. "Seriously? *I* haven't been there? I'm not the one who ran away into the Subverse! I'm the one who's been working my ass off to send enough money back to Calabar to support her!"

"You know I had no choice in that."

"There's always a choice. You could have defied your father. Disowned him, if you had to."

"Are you kidding? He would have made my life a living hell. He *owns* that Brinktown, Joe, and you know it."

I'm shaking my head. "We could have figured something out. But whatever. I'm over it. *Very* over it." I pause, trying not to let my welling anger show on my face. "Why didn't you let me know you'd infiltrated my ship?"

She smiles, though I hadn't meant it to be a joke. "It wouldn't have been much of an infiltration if I'd told you, would it?" The smile fades when I don't return it. "Because, Joe. We both know you would have sent me right back to the Subverse. Come on. You know what I want. It's the opposite of what you want."

"You want her to upload to the Subverse. To be with you. The mother who abandoned her."

That makes her wince, and her eyes fall to the deck. "Not to mention, if I'd revealed myself, it would be all over the Subverse by now. I don't need Belflower versecasting my identity."

"Because you're still afraid of your father."

She doesn't answer.

"You're right, you know," I say. "I would have sent you back. I'd send you back right now, if I could."

"I know that," she says, her voice quiet. "But Joe, that's not all. I'm here to find out what's going on with Harmony, and to get her to upload if I can. But that's not all."

"What else?" I say.

When she speaks again, it's barely above a whisper: "I'm here to do the same for our son."

I frown, and it feels like my heart is sinking through my abdomen. "You'll need to run that by me again. Our *son?*"

"After I had Harmony…while my father was still arranging for my upload…you remember. We got together again. One last time, in the old warehouse loft."

Slowly, I shake my head. "No. You uploaded a few weeks after that. There wasn't time for you to have another baby."

"Dad only let people think I uploaded that soon. He took me off-planet to have the baby, *then* I uploaded. He sent the baby to live with the Fairfaxes."

I cover my mouth, staring into space. The image of Rodney Fairfax's war room taking shape in my mind's eye. The boy who stood next to Fairfax. Exactly the right age. And I know what was so familiar about him, now.

He had my ears. My jaw line. My eyes.

Raised by the Fairfaxes. Given to Rodney for a protege.

"What's his name?" I ask.

"Eric."

"Eric Fairfax?"

She shakes her head. "Sterling."

Still staring into space, I say, "Maybe that's why Fairfax didn't kill me. If Eric knows I'm his father, and he convinced Fairfax I'd be more useful to him alive than dead…" I shake my head. "I doubt Fairfax wants me to join him either way, after what I just did to Royal." A bitter chuckle escapes my lips.

"We have to follow Harmony, Joe," Marissa says. "We have to find this place, Arbor."

How am I supposed to do that? That's what I want to say. Go into the Subverse and waste a few days again, see if I can uncover the destination coords? There's no guarantee I'll find them, and I'm not about to get them from the Guard.

But that's not what's on my mind. Not really.

"I know what you're trying to do, going after the Eliot girl," Marissa says. "Maybe even you don't see it, but I do. You liked what you saw on Tunis. It woke up a desire you thought you'd buried. You're trying to protect the sort of family we were never able to create. But Joe, just because I'm in the Subverse doesn't mean you can't have that. You can fix things with Harmony. And maybe you can even get Eric back."

Eric. Eric Sterling. The son I just learned I had.

"Joe? Tell me you'll go after Harmony."

I study her face, searching for the right words. "I can't tell you that," I say at last.

"*Joe*—" she says, and I can tell she's about to get angry with me. So I shut her off.

"Deactivate OPO," I say. Then I stumble across the bridge and enter my cabin, ignoring Maneater. I sit on the bunk and put my head in my hands.

2

The moment I activate Zelah Eliot's brainprint, I can tell something's wrong.

"What happened?" I ask.

Her blond hair is in disarray, and her skin looks even paler than I remember. Her lower lip trembles, and she has this slightly hunched, defeated posture. Visually, brainprints are programmed to reflect the state of the subject's consciousness, and Zelah's certainly does.

"It's Arthur," she says. "He—he's done nothing to help you. He didn't use his contact in the admiralty, even though I begged and begged him. For years, he's been neglecting his responsibilities when it comes to the Guard—"

"No shit," I say.

Zelah shakes her head. "I always chalked that up to all the pressure. And the booze. But now that it's our daughter at stake, I can't sit by and watch him do nothing anymore. I had to tell you."

"The warning's a bit late, unfortunately," I say. "Thanks though."

With that, she bursts into sobbing.

"Hey," I say. "I'm fine. And I'm still searching for Faelyn. We're going to get her back, Zelah."

Nodding, she says, "I know. I know."

But there's something else. The way she flinches away from my gaze. Her general demeanor. The defeat and the desperation.

"Zelah."

She looks up at me, eyes wet.

"Has Arthur been hitting you?"

She doesn't answer, but she doesn't need to. It's in the way she flinches again. The way the sobs pick back up, with greater strength than before.

"You tell him I'm coming back with Faelyn," I say, my voice trembling with anger. "I'm bringing her back to the Grotto, and I'm going to look Arthur in the eye. If he hits you again, I'll know. And I'll kill him."

Zelah doesn't look up. She's still sobbing.

"Tell him, Zelah. You tell him. Promise me."

But she doesn't promise anything. Instead, she ends the conversation, and her brainprint vanishes from my cabin.

I rise to my feet, still hurting everywhere, but the pain is muted. Not just by the Fount's ongoing efforts to repair my body, either. It's muted by my rage.

I force myself to pace the bridge, back and forth, letting what Zelah just told me spin around and around in my head. No help from Eliot. No help from the Guard. No help from anyone other than the crew stuck on this ship on me, and the bot that hates me, and the dog that would probably rather eat me.

I'm alone, up against a network of criminals, who are awash with wealth. Cutthroats who abduct children to turn them into child soldiers, or who knows what else. I try not to think about the other possibilities.

"Activate crew," I say, and they appear. I'm still standing, few meters from the command seat. There's too much adrenaline pulsing through my veins for me to sit right now.

"We're getting them both back," I tell them, and then my gaze comes to rest on Aphrodite. On Marissa. "Faelyn *and* Harmony. But we're starting with Harmony. Is that clear?"

They all nod, but that isn't good enough.

"Is that clear?" I demand, and I'm answered with a chorus of "Aye, sir," and "Yes, Captain."

"That's better," I say. "We still have no idea what our destination coords are supposed to be. But if we head back to where Royal sank into the clouds, maybe we can apprehend a pirate who's still lingering near the scene. Maybe we can force him to tell the coords, if he knows them."

"I may have an alternative," Marissa says. "One that's certain to work."

I return her gaze, and I can sense her apprehension about whether I'm going to reveal her identity to the others. I have no plans to. Her cowardice is her own business. "I'm listening," I say.

"There's a spacescraper heading for the same slip coords where *Europa's Gift* entered slipspace."

I raise my eyebrows. Looks like "cowardice" may have been an unfair charge. "Are you suggesting we attempt to steal data from a spacescraper?"

Her gaze stays steady, and she doesn't respond. But I already have my answer.

"If we're caught, or if we destroy any of the data it carries, we'll be hunted for the rest of our short lives. Subverse residents travel on those things. Many of them are single-iteration humans. The consequences for tampering with spacescrapers are severe."

"But we're doing it," the chief says. "Right?"

"Right," I say, turning toward my digitized mirror image. "Set a course, Moe."

3

"Hands off your station," I tell Asterisk as he reaches for it. "You're not doing any shooting." I don't want to risk him damaging the spacescraper itself.

His lips tighten, and he leans back against the circular railing, arms crossed and face chains jiggling.

"TOPO, your job is to execute a series of flybys, fast enough that the 'scraper can't fix us with a steady beam. Stay ready to jag up or down, in case the AI tries to lead its shots."

"Got it."

"Got it, what?"

Moe glares at me.

"This is about saving Harmony," I tell him. "To have a chance of doing that, I'll require strict shipboard discipline."

"Got it, *sir*," he grinds out.

"Better. OPO—a spacescraper's laser turrets comprise its primary defense, and that's enough to scare off most adversaries. Any adversary that persists in posing a threat will have to contend with an arsenal of five Javelins. I need you to tag each one it fires."

"Aye."

I glance at Asterisk. "Ensign."

He raises an eyebrow. "Yes, Captain?"

"There *is* a chance I'll need your help to shoot down incoming missiles while I focus on the laser turrets. So pay attention to the engagement."

"Of course. Sir."

"Entering firing range on our first approach, Captain," Marissa says.

"Acknowledged," I say, then I drop into a sim to take control of the forward starboard laser turret. The ship's computer does its best to simulate the thrumming energy that should pass through the control handles as I fire on the enemy turret, but I swear I can tell the difference between this and the real thing. Soren used to make fun of me for saying that, but it's true.

Just as the *Ares* completes her pass and exits firing range, the turret I targeted explodes. "Flyby on the other side," I tell Moe, using the interlude to crack my knuckles.

"Aye," Moe says, and the resentment's gone from his voice, replaced with the grim tones of intense focus. He is me, after all.

Every spacescraper is on a tight timeline, and with the exception of evasive maneuvers at times like this, it will never deviate from its programmed course. Protocol tells the spacescraper to neutralize all attackers and continue on toward its destination. Losing spacescrapers is rare—few would dare attack them, and their defenses normally prove robust enough to protect them from would-be aggressors.

The fact they spend most of their time in slipspace also provides an effective cloak. To top it off, their destinations are kept a secret, and no spacescraper has a set, predictable route—the algorithm always switches those up.

Long story short, I can count on this 'scraper to keep flying toward the slip coords, till it either reaches them or blows up.

On the second pass, I manage to take out two turrets, and the automated vessel answers with a pair of Javelins.

"Loop around, now," I tell Moe.

"That'll take us within range of the stern turret," he says.

"Then make sure it doesn't hit us." But I don't want Moe's questionable flying skill to be the only thing standing between us and taking damage. I make a snap decision: "WSO, take control of the forward starboard turret and target that rear gun. Now."

"Yes, sir!" Asterisk says, sounding surprised.

I slide into the sim for our primary turret, on top of the *Ares*. From here, I'll have a firing angle on the incoming missiles no matter how they twist around us—unless they go under, of course. Then I'll have to extend the belly turret.

Moe knows enough to keep us traveling along a perfectly straight trajectory, which makes lining up my shot on the Javelins pretty easy. One goes down, and before I can shoot down the second, Asterisk succeeds in taking out the spacescraper's rear turret. "Good work, kid," I mutter as I neutralize the second Javelin.

Another ten minutes of flybys, dodging and shooting, and the spacescraper's weapons are all either spent or neutralized.

"Pull up next to it and keep pace," I tell Moe. "Align the *Ares'* outer airlock hatch with the space just above the 'scraper's nose."

"Yes, sir," he says.

I get up from the command seat and fetch the helmet and gloves from the supply locker.

When the outer hatch opens, it reveals the spacescraper just a few meters away. I leap, aiming for the space in front of the spacescraper. Immediately, its upper hull starts to flash past below me, and I scrabble at it for purchase, gloved hand bouncing off the rungs protruding from the metal surface. The second before the stern slides past, I grasp the last rung, and the jerk that follows feels like it almost rips my arm off. That's going to hurt later, Fount or no.

Grimacing, I pull myself along the hull, fighting against the increased Gs provided by the ship's forward momentum. At last, I reach the maintenance hatch and enter my Troubleshooter's credentials. The hatch surprises me by opening. Apparently, word of my insubordination hasn't been distributed across the entire automated fleet yet.

There's no airlock, and I drop inside with my helmet still sealed.

A few feet along the cramped corridor, a combat bot starts unfolding from a crevice in the bulkhead. Probably it plans to quiz me about my presence, and I'm not interested in finding out how that conversation ends. As it rises to its feet, I spam the blaster trigger, sending the bot staggering back. It's hard to miss in the tiny corridor, and after six shots the bot falls to the deck, motionless, chest and head sparking.

There's no bridge aboard spacescrapers. There aren't even branching corridors or chambers: just the one corridor, intended for maintenance, both digital and analog. The rest of the ship is devoted to motherboards, processors, and solid-state drives.

The main terminal is at the end of the corridor, near the bow, and I head toward it.

I've almost reached it when the old man appears in front of it, materializing from nothing, dressed in the same green robes as before.

I draw my blaster again and level it at his head.

"That's not going to do you much good," he says. "The bolt would go through me, and you'd damage this vessel. You'd have even bigger problems than you already do, then."

I keep the weapon where it is. "What *are* you?" I ask.

"A ghost, essentially. Not in the traditional sense, but it is effectively what I am. I died, and this is my afterlife, such as it is. All made possible through the Fount."

"If that's true, how'd you whack me with your staff on Gargantua?"

The knight sighs. "There were more than enough microorganisms on that station to lend me sufficient solidity to do that. I told you: the Fount has infiltrated all life in the galaxy. On planets and stations and ships—virtually anywhere humans can survive without a shipsuit—I can affect my environment using magnetic fields generated by the Fount circulating constantly through the air. I used that ability to fool you."

"Why'd you disappear from the *Ares* right when I needed you?"

"My physical abilities aren't consistent enough for combat. If I'd joined you on the *Ekhidnades*, you would have learned what I am, and that would have led to other questions, questions you aren't ready to have answered. Even if things didn't come to blows…Fairfax would have recognized me. He's the one who killed me, after all."

"I see," I say slowly. "So, you're here. You've revealed yourself. Have you decided I'm ready to know things, now?"

The old Shiva shakes his head. "Far from it. But I *had* to appear to you here. To stop you from making a grave error."

"I know what I'm doing."

"You do not. I didn't start training you because I thought you'd make a good knight. Even if you do manage to become a Shiva, in my opinion you'd be a terrible one. But it isn't up to me. I initiated your training because the Fount, in its infinite wisdom, has chosen you, Joe Pikeman."

"Chosen me for *what?*"

"To restore the galaxy. To return balance to the galactic order."

"Was that your job, before you died? You were supposed to restore the galaxy, whatever that means, and then you got killed?"

"I think you already know I can't tell you that. What I can tell you is that there's much more at stake than Faelyn's life, or yours. The galaxy itself is at stake. I can also tell you this: if you follow your daughter instead of going to Xeo immediately, where Faelyn Eliot is held, Faelyn will die. And so will you."

As I stare at him, my jaw starts to ache, and I force myself to unclench it. I want to tell him he's full of shit, but somehow, I don't think he is.

"Tell me Bleak's plan for when he gets to Xeo," I say, speaking slowly.

"He's planning to change the face of the galaxy, and not for the better. The path of the Fount leads to Xeo. If you walk it, I'll continue to train you. But if you refuse, then you'll doom us all. I will not walk that path with you."

At last, I lower my blaster, reholster it, and snap it into place. I think of Marissa—our conversation on the bridge, about family, and duty. About how we both just want to make the galaxy safe for our children, and barring that, to keep our children safe from the galaxy.

I open a channel with my Engineer. "Belflower?"

"Aye, sir?"

"I'm ready to start hacking the 'scraper's mainframe. I'm patching a visual feed through to you now. Standby to direct me."

"Yes, Captain."

With that, I walk through the old man, feeling nothing as I do so.

"What are you doing?" he asks.

"I'm going to Arbor," I answer. "And I'm getting my daughter the hell out of the mess she's in."

ARBOR

1

We emerge from slipspace into the Temperance System, home to Arbor. A few seconds later, I'm defiling the laundered barf bag with the contents of my stomach.

"What do you see, Chief?" I grunt through the nausea. "I want to know the second you spot Arbor."

After the excitement died down from destroying Royal and illegally boarding a spacescraper, I used the time in slipspace to learn everything my datasphere had to teach me about Arbor. It was—and still is—a giant, genetically engineered tree. Its DNA comes closest to an oak tree, but from its original sapling it grew many times bigger than any oak ever did.

Now, Arbor is self-contained. It has no "hull" except for its bark, heavily modified to survive space's irradiated vacuum. Its leaves were designed to survive it too, but they didn't. Not over the long centuries since humanity's flight into the Subverse. Arbor's mighty branches are completely bare.

The strange colony is one of humanity's many attempts to best nature—to use our tech to extend the limits of the galaxy's habitability. Most of those attempts were misguided, which the Fall showed.

The failure of Arbor didn't stem from its built-in life support system. According to the datasphere, it continues to function to this day, with the structure itself producing plenty of oxygen to be pumped through its hollow innards and consumed by the wildlife there, who breathe it out as CO_2.

No, Arbor's failure is its desolation. It orbits its star, alone, deprived of the interstellar supply lines that kept its tens of thousands of human occupants fed. There's a very good chance that Bleak, his pirates, and whatever other degenerates he's brought with him are currently Arbor's only human occupants. Them, and my daughter.

"I've identified what seems likely to be Arbor," Marissa says, "on the other end of the system. It's surrounded by seventeen ships, presumably belonging to pirates. There's a moon orbiting a gas dwarf much closer to us, and there are signs of activity there."

I take a moment to mull that over. There's no way we're going to be able to sneak the *Ares* past seventeen ships. "Tell me more about the moon."

"It has no atmosphere to speak of, but there's a transparent dome on the surface. The computer says it used to be a colony called Terminus. From what the computer can tell about the composition of the air inside the dome, it's breathable. Looks like someone kept the dome functional."

"The pirates, probably," I say. "My guess is they've been operating an outpost here. Probably why they felt safe choosing Arbor for the wedding." There are outposts like this all over the Andora Sector—places where the pirates will regroup after the destruction of Royal. That loss will set them back, but it's far from the end of piracy in this sector.

"A ship is parked outside," Marissa says.

"That will be them. I want it."

"The ship?"

I nod.

"Hold on," she says. "I have a visual on some figures going

back and forth between a building and the airlock. Looks like they're carrying supplies."

"How many people?"

"Looks like just five."

"Belflower, start probing that ship for cracks in its security. If you can own it, then we're taking it."

"Shouldn't be a problem," she says, bending to her work.

"Set us down directly behind that ship, TOPO, a few dozen meters back. Line up the *Ares'* nose with that airlock, and put her down as gently as you can. I don't want to tip them off to our presence if we can help it."

"Aye," Moe says, dropping us toward the moon at an angle that puts a horizon between us and the dome. When we're a few meters above the moon's pale surface, he starts to coast forward.

I'm impressed by his handling, not to mention proud, since if he can learn to fly this well then so can I. Despite his bitterness over getting press-ganged into my crew as an upload, Moe spent almost every minute of the two-week slipspace journey immersed in flight sims. And it shows.

"That ship is mine," Belflower says. "Her airlock's secure— they're not getting back inside without my say-so. Anything you'd like me to do with it, Captain?"

"Standby to lift it thirty meters, on my mark." Staring through a hull sensor at the dome, I know the next order I have to give, and what it's going to do to the people inside. It'll be an awful way to go. But they shouldn't have taken Harmony. "Asterisk, arm a Javelin."

"Yes, sir," the ensign says with gusto as the *Ares* drifts toward the surface. When she lands, puffs of white dust shoot into the air, but there's a lot less disturbance than I'd feared. As I watch through a hull sensor, the dust begin its stately return to the ground through the low gravity.

"Move that ship, Belflower."

"Yes, sir." The pirate ship rises to reveal the airlock beyond it

—dark metal recessed five meters or so. The dome's glass was no doubt designed to withstand meteor strikes, and therefore missiles. But not the airlock.

"Fire that Javelin, Ensign."

"Firing Javelin, sir," Asterisk says.

The missile sails forward, its shadow flitting across the moon's bone-covered surface. It blows the airlock inward, and though the vacuum soon quenches the fire on our side, the explosion is given full play through the dome's oxygenated interior. For a second. Then the fire blows backward, departing the dome, along with the oxygen. Spiderweb cracks radiate through the glass from the smoldering hole where the airlock was.

I'm already out of the command seat, snatching my helmet and barreling through the airlock I willed open a few seconds ago.

Outside, I sprint toward the breach—or rather, I bound toward it, as fast as I can, careful not to overcompensate for the low-G. Giving the pirates time to regroup isn't something I'm much interested in doing.

Two of their corpses await me a few meters outside the hole, blown there by the gale rushing out of the habitat. One of the bodies is still rolling.

Three of the pirates are still alive—I can see them through the gap, struggling to crawl back to the building they'd been ferrying supplies from. It looks like they know enough not to try standing: doing that would mean exposing their entire bodies to the force of the rushing air. Even so, they're clearly fighting for every inch.

Unfortunately for them, I'm not willing to risk there being a coms array inside that place that they can use to call for backup. I take up a position well back from the dome, where the wind slows to just above a breeze. I kneel there, carefully lining up my first shot.

It takes two blaster bolts to take out my first target, and three more for the second. I get the third on the first try.

Following that, I wait. Watching the pirates' bodies tumble

toward the airlock, until soon enough they're blown out one by one onto the moon, kicking up dust and coming to rest in awkward positions.

With a hole that big to exit through, it takes less than an hour for Terminus to expel all its air. I know because I spend the time pacing in front of it, waiting for the wind to die down. When it finally does, I head inside, toward the same building the pirates died crawling toward.

The entrance hatch sealed as soon as it detected the dome's integrity had been compromised. I'm able to operate the outside control panel without having to provide any credentials, and it informs me that the porch inside doubles as an airlock. I activate it, wait for the inner seal to slide into place, then head inside.

Past the inner seal, I find various boxes stacked near the entrance, and beyond them, a table bearing a transparent case designed to protect its contents from the vacuum of space.

The case itself is domed, as though mirroring the dome outside. Inside it sits a five-tier wedding cake.

"Fascinating," I mutter.

2

"Move aside," I grunt as I push the stainless steel cart from the airlock of the pirate ship, the cake wobbling on top. "Where's the cake artist? In the kitchens?" Cake artist is a term I looked up on the datasphere as I crossed the Temperance System.

The pirate standing outside the airlock eyes me closely, then the cake, then the ship beyond. I'm using the Fount trick again to make myself look like one of the pirates I left lying dead outside Terminus, and I'm better at it this time. Just as Moe practiced flying during our most recent slipspace trip, I practiced changing my face. The fact I really only have to focus on my face this time helps, too—I'm already wearing the dead man's clothes.

"Why do you need her?" he asks. "The cake's finished."

"Uh, yeah," I say. "About that." Rotating the cart around so he can see the other side, I add, "It took a bit of damage in transit."

"*Fount*," the pirate says. "You better hope Lord Bleak doesn't see that. Or hear about it, even."

"He won't."

"You don't have much time. The ceremony's about to begin.

"I'll be fine, so long as you get out of the way. There's still time to fix it."

"I'll take you to the kitchens."

"I know where the bloody kitchens are."

The pirate squints at me. "How? You ain't ever been here before."

"Anyone with a datasphere knows where the famous Arbor kitchens are!" I say, as if I can't believe how idiotic he is. "You'll only slow me down. Now get out of the way, or I'll pin this on you."

"Doubt that'll work," he says with a terse laugh. But he moves.

With that, I whistle, and Maneater bounds out of the airlock, muzzle in place.

"Whoa, whoa," the pirate says. "What's all this? Where'd the dog come from?"

"What, you haven't met, uh…Fido?"

"There was no dog on that ship when you left Royal, Squigs."

I guess Squigs must be my name. What a world. "All right, you got me. He came up to me on Terminus. No idea how he got there, or how he survived in that dome, but we're buds now. Don't tell Lord Bleak, okay?"

The pirate narrows his eyes. "No way a dog survived on Terminus. Dogs can't operate hatches, for one. It wouldn't be able to get at any food."

I suppress the urge to swallow. Clearly, I didn't think through my cover story nearly enough. "One must have been left open," I say.

"You sound funny, Squigs. Why do you sound funny? What's my name, Squigs? Tell me my name."

"Uh, y-your name?" I say, willing Maneater's muzzle to open. A *click* emanates from it, dampened by the bark walls of Arbor's landing bay. "Mincemeat, wasn't it?"

Maneater shakes the muzzle off and leaps, front paws landing on the pirate's chest. They go down, with the man's hand halfway to his laser pistol. As they hit the ground, Maneater's jaws descend, clench, and tear. The pirate tries to find purchase on the dog's neck, but he's having trouble.

Coming at the pair from the side, I sneak the laser pistol out of the pirate's holster, then I put it against his head and pull the trigger. As I do, Maneater snaps at my hand, and I pull back. "Hey! Bad dog." She looks up at me dolefully. "Come on." I toss the pistol onto the dead pirate, then I collect the muzzle. Pushing the cart toward the ramp leading up and out of the landing bay, I whistle to Maneater. She follows, and I clamp the muzzle back around her snout.

With a last glance at the pirate's mangled body, I continue pushing the cart, wincing a little. That wasn't the most pleasant way to die. But they have my daughter. To get her back, I'm willing to do a lot worse. "We just put ourselves on a strict deadline," I tell Maneater as I shove the cart through Arbor's twisting ways. "It's only a matter of time before someone finds that guy, and all hell breaks loose."

The tree smells like a faceful of earth. The datasphere wasn't lying about the ecosystem here: rats and mice scurry through the corridors and disappear through cracks, apparently unconcerned about my presence. Beetles and other bugs trundles through the roots, and worms dangle from the ceiling. One falls on the cake, and I pluck it off as gingerly as I can, though I'm not sure why I care.

Light comes from bioluminescent moss that adorns the walls. The corridors are mostly comprised of bark and twisted roots, as though the tree has grown inward instead of out. I come across a couple passageways where the floor is pure soil, but both times there's another way to take, and I breathe a sigh of relief. I doubt the cart would have made it across that.

I guess Bleak must want the ceremony as packed as he can make it, since I haven't encountered any pirates in the tunnels. Problem is, I have no idea where I'm going, and I need to move quickly if I'm going to stop my daughter from marrying a pirate lord's son. It's not just that he's Bleak's son, either—he's also a wimp. I can't decide which is worse.

Up, up, I push the cart, wondering if I've gone too high. The datasphere had no map of Arbor, but it spoke of the Main Trunk, where plenty of ceremonies had been held since the tree was first grown. Weddings, funerals, pagan moon rituals. Lots of pagan moon rituals.

That has to be where Bleak is marrying off his scrawny progeny to my daughter. That's where I have to go.

It takes me a while to realize that the ramp I'm pushing the cake up is getting steeper and steeper as it loops back on itself again and again. Arbor's equivalent of a staircase?

I pass three branching passageways, but I continue up the spiral, going on a hunch that it'll take me to the Trunk.

At last, the passage ends, and I'm right: I'm in the Main Trunk. But I'm also hundreds of meters above the wedding ceremony. This is a balcony, and I fight vertigo as I peer over the carved railing, down at the sea of people below. Organ music drifts upward to meet the curtain of vines hanging from the Trunk's ceiling.

Damn it. Maybe I can just shoot Peter Vance from up here?

Immediately, I scrap the idea. The way my aim has been since Harmony stole my laser pistol, there's a good chance I'll accidentally hit her instead.

Maneater barks, at the same time a voice says, "That isn't where the cake should be."

I whirl around to find Rodney Fairfax standing in the tunnel mouth, blue eyes shining brightly in the murk.

Beside him stands Eric Sterling. My son. His face is a mix of emotion: anger, hesitation. Maybe even sadness?

I plunge my hand into the damaged portion of the cake, then yank it out, fingers wrapped around my blaster's handle. Shaking it to dislodge some icing, I level it at Fairfax.

In retrospect, hiding the weapon inside the cake seems unnecessary, considering no one even checked me for a weapon anyway.

But here we are.

3

Mendelssohn's Wedding March drifts up from below, as old as the trees. As old as this tree, anyway—much older. Another relic of culture the galaxy loves to fawn over.

The ceremony has begun. My daughter is about to marry Peter Vance, unless I can manage to kill Fairfax and find my way down there in time.

"Drop the disguise, Pikeman," Fairfax says, striding across the balcony. "I already knew it was you, but the blaster clinched it."

I shoot at him point-blank, and the bolt leaves a blackened hole in his metal stomach. It barely slows him. He slaps the blaster out of my hand, and it lands in the cake pointing handle-out, as though waiting to be drawn.

My datasphere flashes black an instant before Fairfax shoves me one-handed, and I stagger back, arms windmilling till my back finds the railing. His hand darts forward to seize my throat, crushing it as he pummels me with his other hand.

Maneater lunges for Fairfax's hamstring, but her teeth seem to scrape off it, and the half-bot twists around to kick the dog savagely in the stomach. She comes at him again, and before I can stop him, Fairfax boots her in the head with a sickening crack. The

German Shepherd slumps to Arbor's floor, limp, and Fairfax stomps on her head, eliciting a crunch.

"Bastard!" I yell, making for the blaster. The bot-man whirls, fist flying, but I manage to deflect it, the blow glancing off my temple. The other fist comes round, and I sidestep, circling the cart, gripping it to try to tip the cake onto him. He evades it.

As the cake smashes against the ground, I push past my son and flee down the tunnel, abandoning the blaster. Eric doesn't try to stop me.

The tunnel vibrates as Fairfax gives chase, the sound of his heavy footfalls muffled by the bark.

As I run, knowing my enemy closes in behind me, my heart rate accelerates, and the adrenaline coursing through my veins seems to crank up the resolution of everything I'm seeing.

Time seems to slow. That's odd. Usually in battle, things would speed up. But that's not what's happening. Fear grips my chest, but as I focus on that fear, it's shrinking—I'm charting a winding path through it.

Beyond the fear lies…something else. Mentally, I reach for it, discovering I can interface with it.

Time slows even more, till it's a crawl. The dim tunnel seems to brighten. My hand rises before me in sync with my stride, and I realize with a slight jolt that I can *see* my heartbeat: my hand flashing red and returning to white, over and over.

My vision gets even crisper, till I can pick out short, thin hairs growing from the tree's roots. The fuzz of mold. Arbor is slowly becoming mold-infested.

Even muffled as they are, Fairfax's footfalls sound deafening, now. I can hear soil and sand and dust sifting out of a thousand crevices. The frightened squeak of fleeing mice.

Suddenly, it's within my power to increase my pace, and I do, running just fast enough to keep out of the man-bot's reach. I reach the first adjoining tunnel, and I throw myself around the corner. As soon as I judge I'm out of sight, I extend a hand toward the bark, planting my heel and using the bark to flip myself around. When Fairfax rounds the corner, I meet him with a combat boot to the groin.

He grunts, stumbling backward, and I wonder what sort of parts he has down there. Stepping forward, I go for a hook kick, but his hand snakes up to grab my foot, my datasphere turning black where it projects the danger. I twist instantly, breaking his grasp and hammering him in the face with the boot, propelling myself away.

Fairfax's head snaps back an inch or two, then he's advancing again, raining blows toward my face, chest, and groin. It's clear he's stepping things up a notch, but I'm keeping up, blocking or deflecting everything he throws at me. He tries to sweep my feet out from under me, and I jump, taking the opportunity to slam my foot into his throat. Something crunches—cartilage, circuitry, I don't know which—and he's thrown back against the bark again, but rebounds instantly.

When Fairfax rounded the corner, I saw that he's wearing the sword I first noticed on the *Ekhidnades*, along with the holstered blaster hanging from his other side. As we trade blows, I'm vigilant against the possibility he'll draw one of the weapons, but for now he seems to want to prove his might. Eric stands in the passage beyond, watching with his arms crossed, but neither of us pay him any heed, and he doesn't try to interfere. It crosses my mind to wonder whether Harmony is wedded yet, but there's nothing I can do about it if she is. This duel requires every ounce of concentration I have, every ounce of energy.

My datasphere warns of a jab to my throat. I watch Fairfax's arm prepare to deliver it.

But it doesn't come. Instead, he delivers a hook to my face, too fast for the datasphere to warn me in time. The blow breaks my nose, sending blood spurting toward the ground. My vision's sharpness wavers, and then comes Fairfax's boot to my gut.

I stumble back, clutching my stomach, and Fairfax steps

forward, backhanding me to the ground, much like he did in the theater back on Tunis.

Gazing up at him, I see him glance back at Eric, who gives a nod. Fairfax draws his sword, then, viper-quick. I start to roll away, but the sword flashes down, cutting through cloth, flesh, and organs.

The blade's tip thunks into the wood beneath me, and for a moment I'm pinned. Starbursts flash before my eyes. My ears ring. The entire world seems made of pain. Fairfax twitches the sword forward, toward my chin, and I scream as more of my flesh rips.

At last, he withdraws it, and every molecule of my body seems to settle into the bark below it.

Fairfax wipes the sword on my pirate's tunic, then sheaths it.

"Come," he says to Eric, spinning around, cape whirling.

Eric pauses at my feet and frowns down at me. Then he follows his mentor.

I watch them go through the shrinking tunnel my vision has become. When it dwindles to a pinprick, they disappear, and the world winks out completely.

4

I wake staring at the ceiling, with the same thought I have every morning: nothing means anything.

This apartment. No one bothered to decorate it—not the previous tenant, who skipped out on three months' rent, and certainly not me. I like to tell myself that he was a sim programmer too, and that with this dull place's help, he came to the same conclusions I have.

Dragging myself through the two-bedroom boredom factory, carrying out the same mundaneness as every other day of my gray existence. Shower, dress, stare out the window while eating toast I can't be bothered to butter. It's actual torture. The accepted definition of that word, "torture," is too narrow.

I pause with a crust halfway to my mouth. A glimmer of memory just entered my head: an image of lying on my back inside a giant tree, bleeding to death at the point of a sword. Did I dream that? The memory seems weirdly vivid.

Shaking myself, I snap out of the reverie. Part of me wants to tell someone about the dream, but I stopped being able to talk to anyone a couple years ago. It's a testament to the invisibility of my work that words can be drained of their content and yet still leave me with the ability to code. I'm not sure why it happened—I suspect I may have gone mad—but I know *how* it happened: Even in everyday speech, the sentences I put together fall apart under their own weight. To my hearing, anyway. Once spoken, I realize my words can be construed to mean any number of offensive, vulgar things. And I remain silent for even longer, next time.

I transmit finished work to my supervisor via datasphere parcel, and I acknowledge whatever scant praise she offers with a grunt. I'm done with speaking. It's not worth it.

I finish getting ready and leave my cramped apartment to trudge through halls hung with cheap, mass-produced art. You know the kind—the sort of pastoral watercolor you find on the back of postcards and playing cards.

Then I'm outside, passing blank-eyed zombies on the sidewalk. Terminus. The Impossible City, they call it—a title taken on by at least a thousand such cities scattered across this toilet bowl of a galaxy. Humanity is so proud of where its technology has brought us, as if putting a dome over some buildings make us gods. But we still all die in the end.

Terminus' residents—I won't dignify them with the word "citizen"—are sim junkies, all of them. Losing themselves in pretend narratives as soon as work lets out, desperate for their fix. Or, plenty of them don't even work. Plenty let themselves rot on the streets, refusing to leave the beautiful worlds their dataspheres show them till their last breath.

When I look at passersby in the streets, their eyes always flit away. The same happens if they chance to look at each other. Reality offends us, now, and meeting the eyes of another conscious being has become a terrifying ordeal. Better to punch in your time and go home to your fully realized fantasies, much more fulfilling than real life, designed to satisfy your deepest desire and most fleeting whim.

No one speaks to each other. Maybe they've arrived at the same conclusion about language as I have.

It occurs to me that I'm muttering to myself—dark snatches of internal monologue escaping my lips. It's drawing more glances than usual, as well as a few uncomfortable grimaces.

"So *sorry,*" I say to a woman who looks particularly aggrieved, and she increases her pace to be clear of me.

Then, as I continue through the city, bits of conversation do start to reach my ears. Talk of someone referred to as "the tyrant" and his dark deeds. I turn to see who's talking, but I see only the same furtive glances and averted gazes.

Tyrant? It must be something from one of their fantasies. Something like a tyrant in Terminus would be a break from the usual tedium. It would be interesting. Nothing truly interesting happens here.

A kitchenware store catches my eye, and I wander in, knowing I'll be late. Who cares? I take my work home anyway, and I always meet the impossible deadlines my supervisor sets. Completing a project is the only gratification life offers now, and so I fill up my life with work.

How does a place like this stay in business? Everyone already has cutlery. And dishes. Account for breakage and loss, and you still wouldn't have enough demand to keep a place like this in business. Not on Terminus, probably not in most places.

No, people buy from a place like this because outside the sims, they get their meaning from things. Dead objects that hold no inherent value for them, since they already have a fork to deposit food into their mouths and bowls from which to spoon whatever gruel they happen to be gorging themselves on. They see that Mary or Jim has this set or that brand name and then they rush to a place like this to fritter away their tokens.

A lot of the stores' wares are kept in glass cases, but the cheaper stuff is right out in the open. I pick up a steak knife, rubbing my fingers over its smooth plastic handle. Admiring how it gleams under the halogens, a gleam that would soon fade, no doubt, with repeated use.

"Sir?" an employee asks from over my shoulder. "Can I help you with anything?'

Without thinking, I turn and stick him with the utensil. His mouth forms a shocked O, and he even utters the syllable, which seems fitting. Scarlet blossoms from the fresh wound.

"You were standing too close to me," I tell him, yanking the blade out. He collapses to the sales floor.

Other than the dead salesperson, the store is empty, so I take my new knife out into the street. An alarm blares the moment I cross the threshold. I ignore it, but a passing teenager doesn't.

"Sir?" he asks. ""Do you know why the store's alarm is going off?"

I'm holding the blade by the tip so that its handle lies pressed against my forearm, to conceal it. Now, I flick it up, grab the handle in midair, and ram it through the boy's throat. He sputters, face quickly draining of color, clutching at his throat. When I withdraw the blade, I find the way he continues to stand there perverse. Whatever. I turn and continue down the sidewalk, no longer bothering to conceal the steak knife.

No one seems to notice it as I turn the corner onto the next street, where a tight-packed crowd waits to cross. Maybe they're blind to what has suddenly become a weapon. Blind to the possibility that something interesting is happening here. Here!

Stabbing, now. Stabbing. Everyone I encounter. Blood spurting. Screams, and a drawing back. Someone rushes at me, to try to stop me, and they get the blade, too. Everyone gets the blade. I'll treat myself to it, before the end, I think.

Someone grabs my arm from behind, and I twist away, spinning. I throw my fist into his face, causing him to stagger back. I realize that I'm good at this—that in my hands, the activity of killing is almost an art. Was I born with this talent? Where is it coming from? It's as though it's rising up from somewhere deep inside me. From my very blood.

Sirens blare to my right, and I turn to see police officers

climbing out of cruisers, combat bots among their ranks. "Drop the knife!" commands a human voice, but I won't. Instead, I bring it to my throat.

For some reason, the act brings a hail of bullets anyway, but I manage to drag the blade across my esophagus. Together, we collaborate on the project of my demise.

The pain is an explosion of sharp delight. It's torture, yes— my throat opened to the air, the rounds burrowing into my skin,passing in then out. But it's a *new* kind of torture. One that I can't help but relish. Finally, something has happened. Something real. *This* is meaningful.

But I wake again in my dismal apartment, staring at the ceiling, with the same thought I have every morning.

Nothing means anything.

5

I wake in Arbor's tunnel, with Dice bent over me, in the process of wrapping a thick bandage around my otherwise naked midsection. Maneater is standing near my head, licking my face.

"Holy shit, girl," I rasp. "You're alive?"

"Superficial analysis shows she suffered major head trauma, but appears to have already recovered much of her cognitive function," Dice says. "This seems to confirm the hypothesis that she's a genetically engineered being, and likely has a Fount of her own."

"Yeah, seems so," I croak, watching the bot's movements. "What are you doing?"

He looks at me, his blank face perfectly still, and he pauses before answering. "As much as I detest ministering to fleshbags, there's no one else around to do it."

"Get off me."

Dice rises to his feet and backs away, arms motionless at his sides.

"Go get my blaster," I tell him, sending him the route to the balcony overlooking the Main Trunk. Fairfax and Eric went the opposite way once they were finished with me, so the weapon should still be there, lying on the ground. The bot nods, then jogs off up the tunnel.

It takes a massive effort of will to raise my head enough to observe Dice's work with the bandage, and then to hold it there long enough to figure out what he was doing. Finally, I finish the wrapping by yanking it tight, then I affix the metal clips attached to the end of the fabric to the bandage underneath.

I force myself to breathe more deeply. Since waking, stabbing pain has kept me from drawing more than shallow breaths, but now I make myself breathe deeper, and faster, almost hyperventilating.

Gathering up the same iron will that's seen me through long, hard years of soldiering, I push to a sitting position, screaming as some of the "sutures" manufactured by the Fount inside me start to tear.

I don't stop. Getting a hand underneath me, I lever myself into the nearby wall, and I press through with my arm and my heel, slowly rising, feeling as though I'm doing squats with a weight that far exceeds my capacity.

At last, I'm standing, leaning against the bark. The overwhelming urge sweeps over me to place my forehead against the cool surface and weep, but I fight it off.

Then comes the first step. And the second. Each one sends pain radiating through my body from where Fairfax ran me through. Not to mention the throbbing mess that is my broken nose. I doubt that'll heal right, but who cares, I guess. I was never much to look at anyway.

Dice returns then, my blaster in hand. Good. He stands there for a moment, watching me progress slowly down the tunnel, and I can tell from the way he's standing that he doesn't approve of me refusing his help.

As I press on, he keeps pace behind me, with Maneater beside him, tongue lolling from the side of her mouth, head cocked slightly to the side as she gazes at me with what looks like concern.

In this way, we walk through Arbor's tunnels like a funeral procession.

It takes an eternity to reach the landing bay I entered Arbor through, and with every step I'm beset by the urgent command, rising from deep within, to lie down and succumb to unconsciousness. The only thing that keeps me going is the memory of the old man's words: that if I chose to go to Arbor instead of Xeo, Faelyn would die.

Well, I made my choice, and I've helped neither Harmony nor Faelyn. My daughter must be married to Peter Vance by now. I'm sure she never knew I was even here. She wouldn't have sat quietly by while Bleak and Fairfax left me for dead.

Can Faelyn really be dead? It seems too cruel an outcome for the universe to permit, but of course, I know the universe better than that. Then, I remember how unconcerned Arthur Eliot was with the prospect of his daughter's death, knowing that her consciousness was repeated thousands of times across the cosmos.

Whether she's dead or not, I have to find out for myself. I need to find her, whatever state she's in. If I don't, I know I'll never find rest.

After an eternity, I reach the *Ares'* airlock and stumble through, though I have no recollection of willing it to open, or even of entering the landing bay. Is the pirate ship we stole still here? I can't remember. I lean against the inner hatch, and when it opens I fall through onto the deck.

I think I blacked out, then. I'm not sure. At some point, I regain the presence of mind to look up, and I see the faces of my crew, gazing down at me with varying shades of concern and interest— or, in Asterisk's case, utter indifference. Dice stands to my left, wearing his usual expression.

"Get back in your closet," I yell, or try to. It comes out as a croak. But he goes.

To get myself off the deck and deposit myself in the command seat takes the greatest effort of will yet, but I manage it. That done, I lock eyes with the OPO. "Is the pirate ship still here?"

"Yes," Marissa says.

"And the pirates?"

"They left Arbor," she says, then pauses. "There's a brainprint here for you. From Daniel Sterling."

"It can wait." I shift my gaze to my Engineer. "Program the pirate ship to follow the *Ares*. We may need it."

"We could copy ourselves over to it," Marissa says. "It would give us more control."

I look at her—I'm not sure for how long. She holds my gaze, though it occurs to me that I've been staring into her eyes far too long for comfort.

"No…no," I say. "I don't want that."

"Where are we going?" Moe cuts in.

"Do we have the slip coords where the pirates exited the system?"

Marissa nods.

"And the computer will have the exit coords for Xeo. That's where we're going." The bridge has started to dim, though I've done nothing to affect the light levels.

"You have your orders," I say. And with that, consciousness slips away.

ARES

1

The first week of slipspace is characterized by strange nightmares and bouts of listlessness. Marissa insists on having the ship's medical software analyze brain scans taken by my Fount, and they show plenty of anomalous activity, which the computer seems to have no frame of reference for.

One thing seems clear: there was a definite break in consciousness after Fairfax impaled me. In other words, I died. The Fount can do many things, but it can't bring you back from death. At least, there are no documented cases of that ever happening.

Except, here I am.

Sometimes the nightmares resemble my dream—or vision, or whatever it was—of living on Terminus, which I remember in its entirety. Others depict Harmony dying before me, or Faelyn, or both at once. The only commonality is a pervasive sense of guilt underlying everything.

Now that I'm alive again, I recover fairly quickly, and after that first week I'm able to hobble around the ship, though not without considerable pain. Maneater keeps a careful eye on me, sometimes following me around. I no longer keep her tied up in the cabin. I figure sacrificing herself to save my life should earn her that much. At night, she sleeps on the deck near the foot of my bunk.

On the tenth day, I call Dice out of his closet with the crew turned off.

"Yes?" he says.

"Back in Arbor," I say. "You called me fleshbag."

"You've never told me not to."

"I shouldn't have to. You should show me that much respect, at least, even if you do take every other opportunity to remind me about the limits of biology."

"Is this stupid conversation really why you called me out of the Repair and Recharge module?"

I pause. "No. I called you out to thank you. Without you, I doubt I would have made it back to the *Ares*. Aphrodite told me you injected me with epinephrine before I woke."

"I wouldn't have done it if I wasn't programmed to."

"Yeah. How did you leave the ship, anyway? You're also programmed not to do that unless I order it."

"It's a function you apparently aren't aware of. If the Troubleshooter is in distress, the WSO has the authority to deploy his Cybernetic Partner."

"You're damn right I wasn't aware of it. If I'd known, it would have been disabled."

"Indeed. Your ignorance likely saved you. You might thank me for withholding the information from you, to protect you from yourself."

"Activate crew," I say, and all four of them appear at their stations, looking at me expectantly. "Delete protocol allowing the WSO to deploy the Cybernetic Partner under any circumstances."

"Are you certain you wish to delete vital safety protocol?" the ship asks.

"Yes. Confirm deletion."

"Protocol deleted."

Asterisk blinks. "You would have died if D1C hadn't left the ship."

"He only leaves on my say so. Ever." I turn back to Dice. "Get back in the closet."

As the bot heads toward his module without another word, I turn to Marissa. "Chief Aphrodite. How long after my death did the pirates leave the system?"

"Not long," she says.

"I have a theory why," Belflower cuts in.

I nod. "Go ahead."

"When you showed up, the pirates knew there was a good chance that people in the Subverse would learn their whereabouts soon. That must have prompted them to accelerate their plans."

"Wait—I thought people already knew their whereabouts. Didn't they tell anyone who'd listen about the wedding?"

"About the wedding, yes, but not where it was being held. Bleak wouldn't risk that—not when it could mean bringing the Guard down on their heads."

"Slim chance of that," I mutter. But her explanation makes sense.

"There's something else you should know," Marissa says. "The *Ekhidnades* didn't use the same exit coords as the pirates."

"I see. So we're not likely to find Fairfax with Bleak on Xeo."

"Not unless he let his ship leave without him."

"Doubtful." Fairfax's absence is good and bad. Good, because he won't be there to back up Bleak. And bad because I won't get the chance to exact some payback.

On another day, I activate just Marissa. I'm still mad as hell at her, but she deserves to know what I can tell her about Harmony. It isn't much, except that she's almost certainly bonded to Peter Vance, now.

"Joe…why didn't you want us all copied to the pirate ship?" she asks. "It makes tactical sense."

I study her deep brown eyes for a time. They're the only

feature she retained from how she's supposed to look—whether the "Aphrodite" avatar is one she adopted after uploading, or just the disguise she chose for her time on my ship, I don't know. Marissa is supposed to have whip-straight auburn hair that curls only at the ends. She's much slighter than Aphrodite, less curvy, but no less stunning.

"I don't care about the others," I say. "I just don't want you copied."

"Why not?"

"There's only one of you. There should only be one of you."

"Joe, I have hundreds of copies living throughout the galaxy."

"Yeah, but…" I take a breath. "You're the only one who wanted to be on my ship. The only one who seems to give a damn about what happens to us here in the real." I shift in the command seat, favoring my left side, where Fairfax ran me through. "Marissa, back in Arbor, when I, uh, died.…" Shaking my head, I press on: "Something really strange happened. I had a dream, I guess, except it was more than a dream. It was at least as real as a sim."

"Were you on Terminus?" she asks, her voice quiet.

"Yes," I say slowly, eyes narrowing. "I kept living the same day over and over again. I was completely crazy—I know that, because I've lost it before. But this was a lot worse. On the street, I kept hearing about someone called the tyrant. Then I started a killing spree. Each day, I used a different weapon, but each time I slaughtered as many innocent people as I could. Until, eventually, the authorities put me down." I swallow, trying to get rid of the lump in my throat, my eyes on the deck. "It probably sounds crazy, but I think *I* was the tyrant people were talking about."

When I look up, I find Marissa is crying. "It's my fault, Joe."

"What? How? What are you talking about?"

She draws a long, shuddering sigh, and casts her eyes across the bridge. "I became depressed after I uploaded to the Subverse," she says at last. "It didn't take long. A few weeks, and I fell into this black pit. My copies all throughout the galaxy were doing well. I guess they found things to occupy themselves. One of them fell in love with a wealthy man, in the second year, and her lover vowed to copy himself to every last Subverse where her copies lived. But I refused him here in Terminus, and I refused to let the algorithm synchronize me with the others, so that I could share their in-love state, their happiness. I didn't want it."

"Wait. You lived in this Subverse?"

She nods, and I'm about to demand why she didn't tell us the slipspace coords to get here, back when we needed them in the Visby System. But then I realize that's stupid. Living in a particular Subverse node doesn't mean you know how to reach its corresponding star system in the real.

"My other copies seemed to forget about you, about what we shared in Brinktown," Marissa goes on. "They seemed to forget about Harmony. That delighted my father, as much as *I* angered him. He would tell me I was only one copy of his daughter, and he even said at one point that maybe I was defective. I cried, but I knew he didn't mean it. He kept trying to get me to sync with the others, to be happy. I told him there was only one way I could be happy, and that was to be with you again."

Marissa's gaze returns to me, where I sit motionless in the command seat. It's hard to say what affects me more: that she remembered me, and missed me, or that all her other copies moved on so quickly.

It's not completely surprising that they'd forget about me and Harmony. The Subverse does that to plenty of families—splits them apart. Makes them forget about each other. After all, what's the incentive to spend time with each other, when you have eternity? You can always get around to it. And in the meantime, family members drift farther and farther apart, doing their own thing.

The whole concept of a family is seen as backward by a growing number of uploads. For biologicals, the whole point of a family was to get you ready for the world and try to keep you from being too screwed up. Most uploads are skeptical it ever actually managed that very well, but even if it did, why bother with it when you're immortal and everything's provided for you by the sim? When you can tweak anything you don't like about yourself—when you can just edit out your neuroses?

"It took years to convince him," Marissa continues. "But I did it. When I turned twenty-three, and he saw I was still as miserable as ever, he used his connections to get it done…his shadier connections. It was pretty illegal."

"Get what done?" I ask.

"The Subverse holds the consciousness of anyone who's ever used the Fount. We activated a copy of you, Joe. So that we could be together."

A large part of me wants to rage against the violation. But my eyes settle on the empty TOPO station, and I realize I'm no better. I activated a copy of myself too, knowing full well what torture it would be for Moe. He's a lot better about following orders, now, but it's not hard to tell he still despises me for what I did to him. I doubt I'll be able to command his loyalty for any longer than it takes to find Harmony.

"I'm guessing that didn't work out very well," I say.

"We were happy for a while. Sort of. It took a long time for your copy to forgive me for what I'd done, and the fact that no other copy of me had any interest in him angered him, a lot. He talked about sending you a brainprint, to tell the biological Joe what I'd done. But he decided not to, because of—"

"—because of Eric," I say. "You told him we had a son, and he knew that would drive me crazy. He knew that, if he sent me a brainprint, I'd get that information out of him."

Marissa's eyes are wide. "How do you know that?"

"Because I remember it happening. I think…I think I have his memories, now, Marissa. The memories of the uploaded version of me. I don't have full access to them, but I'm pretty sure they're up there."

A long silence follows. Then, Marissa says, "What else do you remember?"

I concentrate, in the same way the old knight taught me to concentrate. One by one, memories begin to leak into my mind. I have no idea why I can remember what happened to my Subverse copy, but I can, so I take over telling Marissa's story for her, speaking in fits and starts as I wait for more memories to fall into place.

"I learned to be happy, in the Subverse. With you. As long as I made everything about you...you were my anchor. But even that didn't last."

She nods, chin trembling.

"We were separated from our children. Harmony was still taking your brainprints, then, but she barely told you anything. I had no contact with her at all, and neither of us had any clue what had become of Eric."

I pause, leaning forward in the command seat slightly, glaring at the bulkhead as though trying to see through it to my missing memories.

"After a while, even our love lost its meaning," I say, and pause again, for longer. The memories are coming back, but processing them is another matter. "Love means it's the two of you against the world, against everything life throws at you...but there was nothing to *be* against. Yes, we could compete in games for points or tokens, but that was just sport. We could simulate a delicious meal, or a long, hot bath. But there was no dirt to wash off. We'd never starve, or get sick, or die. No one ever dies in the Subverse. That's what makes it wrong. Even the tastiest meal would get sickening if you ate it forever. The best book in the world only has meaning because it eventually ends—it resolves. The same goes for love. For life."

"But we were only together for a few years, Joe," she says. "I still don't understand how it wasn't enough for you."

"It was the knowledge that it would never end," I say, speaking for my copy. "Nothing would. It drained everything of meaning. And…" I lock eyes with her. "I lost it, didn't I?"

"Not all at once," she says, her eyes shining with tears. "I noticed it in little ways, at first. Things you'd say, which made no sense. How cynical you got, about absolutely everything. Then you became fixated with Vega9, who held the number one spot on the local leaderboard for token gainers. You started tracking his movements, and when I caught you doing it, you said you wanted to teach him what it meant to *really* win. To struggle against something, to persevere, like a human being and not a cow in a pen. You figured out how to delete the exits to his house. Afterward, the authorities told me you used a pair of nail clippers to get around the algorithm designed to prevent users from harming each other while in a safe zone. You tortured him till he went half-insane himself."

We both stare at the deck for a time. The fact a simulated universe would even need nail clippers…it's just another affectation that uploads use to blind themselves to the ultimate meaningless of their lives. An illusion.

Why include pain in the simulation at all? But I already know the answer, somehow. Maybe it comes from the other Joe living inside my head: pain keeps inhabitants from doing things they shouldn't. If they didn't have *something* to distinguish good from bad action, the Subverse would be devoid of any meaning at all.

"They had to put you in an underverse, Joe. If you'd had other copies, sane copies, you might have synced with them to get your sanity back. But you didn't. So they installed your consciousness in an underverse, and your mind constructed its own prison there."

"For a while now, the Fount has been connecting me to the Subverse randomly," I say. "So maybe, when Fairfax killed me, it connected me to my copy in the Temperance System. Merged us, so that my mind could live on while it put my body in nanodeath— long enough for Dice to find me."

Marissa lifts her shoulders slightly, then drops them. "That would explain your strange brain scans. Maybe your mind is trying to reorient itself."

I don't answer. I'm two Joe Pikemans, now—one of them insane, the other with a history of instability.

I wonder which one I am more.

2

When Daniel Sterling appears in my cabin, he takes a moment to cast his disdainful gaze around it, no doubt offended by the meager accommodations.

Sterling is well into his seventies, now. His product-stiff, iron-gray hair marches in lines toward the back of his head. His ex-wife had Marissa when he was in his early forties. She divorced him soon after he forced their daughter to upload, but she knew better than to spread that to anyone as the reason. Sterling runs the Calabar Brinktown, and he would have been willing and able to make his ex-wife's existence a living hell.

"Why are you here?" I say.

Sterling frowns. "Right now, my physical body is on Beimeni, with relatives."

"Oh, like real Sterlings, you mean?" I say, twisting the knife just for the hell of it. I know how sensitive he is about having less money than his relatives.

His mouth puckers as though he'd bitten into a lemon. "I've come to discuss a serious matter with you, Pikeman. A matter that concerns your daughter."

"Harmony? You've never shown interest in her before."

"It's the Bleak situation," he says. "Obviously. If you can get your daughter out, and get me my ship back, then the Sterlings are prepared to reward you handsomely. We can't have the entire Subverse thinking that we condone piracy in any way. We can't be party to giving Bleak this sort of legitimacy."

I cock my head to the left. "Is getting you your ship back actually a condition of the reward? Or is that something you decided to throw in yourself?"

I wouldn't have thought it possible for Sterling's expression to sour further.

"Didn't think so," I say. "Now that we've cut through the bullshit, let's talk numbers. You can't expect me to get motivated just by the sight of your ugly face." There's no need to mention that I'm already en route to Xeo, where I intend to get both Harmony and Faelyn back, if I can.

"We're prepared to offer you eight hundred thousand tokens, transferred directly into either your Subverse account or that of one of your associates, depending on the logistics of your current situation."

I know he means my standing with the Guard, and possibly with Bacchus Corp, both which will depend on how they choose to view my actions. It's kind of surprising that Sterling's being so tactful about my deteriorating reputation. He must really want this.

"I'll tell you what, Sterling," I say. "I'm in no mood for negotiating, so why don't you tell me the upper limit of what the real Sterlings have authorized you to offer me, right now. Hesitate or lie, and I'll delete you off my ship, with no deal made. I *will* know if you lie."

He swallows. "One and a half million tokens."

I smile, and say, "That's more like it."

3

We drop out of slipspace to find seventeen ships arrayed against us—a blockade around Xeo that groups together the moment we appear in-system.

"Stay frosty," I tell my crew, though in my transition-induced nausea I'm anything but. I shake myself, trying my best to snap out of it. "We can do this, but I need better than your best. All of you."

What follows certainly constitutes the best shooting of my career. Even Asterisk is in fine form, orchestrating the *Ares'* remaining laser turrets using macros Belflower helped him tailor for this specific situation. I take manual control of various laser turrets whenever I think I can make a difference. And Moe's flying exhibits moments that can only be called masterful. His sleepless nights spent practicing are really showing.

As for the stolen pirate ship, Belflower and Asterisk collaborated on macros that have turned it into a kamikaze dynamo—charging into the pirate fleet, disrupting their formations, and generally wreaking havoc.

None of it matters. The pirates' overwhelming firepower prevails, and they blow apart our pirate ship seven minutes after the engagement begins. Next, they destroy the *Ares*.

With that, the combat sim ends, and my crew and I are left staring at each other wearing expressions ranging from frustration to hopelessness.

"Again," I say, wincing at the prospect of enduring the transition sickness again. Technically, I could edit that out of the sim, but it wouldn't be a true representation of the conditions we'll face at our destination.

So we run the sim again, and we lose again. There's just no way we can fight past the pirates, with the numbers we know they have. No way we can get to Xeo to even begin the work of finding Harmony and Faelyn.

There's only one place on Xeo where they could have brought them: a scientific facility constructed long ago on the otherwise inhospitable ice planet. But that information won't do us much good if we can't actually reach the facility.

We appear to be screwed.

Then, Moe speaks up.

"I've been studying the slip we're inside of," he says. "And the way it interacts with Sledge, the destination system."

I lift my chin from my hand to study his face. "Go on."

"Well, the recommended exit coords are on the edge of the Sledge System, just like pretty much any other slip. But where most slips only graze the systems they pass through, sometimes creating exit coords that are tens of billions of miles from the star, this one runs *through* Sledge. It doesn't bisect it, but it does run through a nice chunk of it. And according to the information the computer has on Xeo's orbit, when we emerge, the planet's going to occupy space along where the slip intersects the system."

"So you're suggesting we exit between the pirates and Xeo," I say.

Moe nods.

"Exit coords are set outside star systems for a reason," I say. "Dropping back into regular space inside a system is risky. If we transition back inside of a moon, planet, asteroid—never an ideal situation."

"Is it as risky as trying to fight through those pirates?" Moe asks. "We've run the sim thirty-nine times, and we've lost thirty-nine times."

"He has a point," Belflower says. "But I see another problem. We can't communicate with the pirate ship we stole while we're in slipspace. Indeed, we can't even *see* the other ship while we're in slipspace."

"So it's going to emerge at the usual exit coords," I say. "And there's nothing we can do about that."

"Exactly."

"Then what about this. We exit at the regular coords, too. Then, all four of you transfer over to the pirate ship. You take it back into slipspace, and I'll do the same with the *Ares*. There's a good chance we won't be in the system long enough for the pirates to spot us. After that, we reemerge between their blockade and the planet."

Moe gives a terse chuckle. "How confident are you that you can fly this ship on your own?"

"Pretty confident. I can spend the rest of our time in slipspace running sims. And if we surprise the pirates like we hope to, I'd even give myself pretty good odds of making it down to Xeo alive."

"So is this really what we're going with?" Asterisk asks.

"Yeah," I say. "And I actually think it's a pretty good idea." I nod at Moe. "I'm glad I had it."

XEO

1

We drop out of slipspace, and a glance through a hull sensor shows our stolen pirate ship a couple hundred meters off our starboard side. I perform this check with my face buried in the mouth of the barf bag. Such is the magic of dataspheres.

It's a little bigger than the *Ares*, but not as well-armed. As near as I could tell during the trip from Terminus to Arbor, it's an ancient pleasure cruiser someone refitted at some point for combat. "Transfer everyone over to the pirate ship," I order Belflower. "If we're doing this, we need to do it now."

She nods, then keys in a command. With that, all four crewmembers disappear, and I'm left alone on the bridge of the *Ares*.

Before she left, Belflower slaved the slipspace functions to my datasphere, and I initiate the transition now. A rush of euphoria spreads through my body, more intense than ever before, followed by nausea worse than a few minutes ago. I've never done back-to-back transitions before…apparently, that compounds the effects.

A couple seconds later, the *Ares* transitions back into realspace. I slump in my command seat and the world goes dark.

"Captain? *Captain!*"

I blink, struggling to come back to consciousness. What's going on? Where am I?

"Captain Pikeman! Are you there?"

"M'here," I mumble, blinking at the 3D tactical display my datasphere's projecting onto the space between the empty crew consoles.

Where's the crew? Then, as I study the display, I remember.

The *Ares* is hurtling toward the planet Xeo. My throat tightens as I realize where the pirates' blockade is located: they're much nearer to the planet than we anticipated, and they're getting closer, screaming toward the *Ares* and accelerating.

Twelve ships are converging on the *Ares* and our stolen pirate ship nearby. Marissa's voice sounds in my ear: "We're already taking damage, sir. Please advise!"

I double check the visual display of the battlespace. The pirates haven't deployed any missiles, only laserfire. I'm not even sure they have access to missiles—the ship we stole from the pirates has none. They aren't cheap to manufacture, although if one finds its way to the black market the price tends to drop pretty fast as the fence scrambles to offload it.

"Keep up evasive maneuvers. Have Asterisk target the enemy ship that has the best firing angle on you, and accelerate toward Xeo."

"Belflower's concerned that we haven't seen any sign of the other five ships we know they have."

"I'm sure they'll be here soon, once they make it around the planet." I shift the *Ares'* attitude downward sharply, just barely missing a volley of laserfire that would have hit her primary turret. "The good news is, we'll enter Xeo's atmosphere pretty close to the facility. "

"Yes, sir."

I dodge another laser volley, then switch to controlling the ship's aft turret. As I'm lining up my next shot, Marissa contacts me again:

"Sir, are you seeing this?"

I drop out of the sim to check the battlespace. At first, I see nothing—until I glance at the area representing Xeo.

Five ships are rising from the surface to intercept us. They weren't on the opposite side of the planet after all. The pirates are planning to sandwich us.

2

"Prioritize the targets rising up through Xeo's atmosphere," I bark over the comlink. With that, I drop into the primary turret sim and start blasting the foremost of the five ships with laserfire.

None of this is going according to plan. Our slipspace maneuver was supposed to put enough distance between us and the blockade to allow us to get to the facility and hide the *Ares* without taking any damage. I was prepared to sacrifice the pirate ship if necessary, but now it's looking unlikely either ship will make it out of this intact.

"Concentrate your fire on this target," I say, painting the one I mean with my datasphere.

"We're taking heavy fire, sir," Marissa says.

"Continue evasive actions and just do it!"

I call up a preprogrammed macro to control the secondary turrets and then activate dorsal thrusters to dodge another volley of laserfire. With that, I jump into the primary turret sim and add the *Ares*' fire to my crew's.

Our target bursts apart. "Switch to the next," I bark, painting the one I want them to hit.

Both ships unleash a rain of neon-blue laser bolts, but as soon as our stolen ship finishes shooting, it explodes under enemy fire. "ALLY SHIP NEUTRALIZED," my datasphere informs me.

Our second target goes down, but there are still three ships in front of us, and twelve in close pursuit. And my crew just went down.

For a second, my hands go limp on the control handles, and I almost let them fall to my lap before tightening my forearms and continuing to fire.

I feel very alone, suddenly. Will I need to restore them from backup? When was the last time I even backed them up?

I'll probably need to bring them up to speed, something I have zero time for right now. Then, I curse, realizing all of Moe's training in the flight sims just got erased.

And Marissa…will she be the same? Or will the backup be just another copy?

I drop out of the sim to take control of the *Ares* herself, and when my vision switches to the ship's bridge, my crew are all standing at their stations.

That makes me cry out, partly in surprise, partly in relief. Moe and Asterisk give me sidelong looks before returning to their tasks.

"Why weren't you destroyed with the ship?" I say.

"I transmitted us over the moment before she went down," Belflower says.

"We don't have time to dwell on it," Marissa says. "We're entering Xeo's atmosphere." Even before she finishes her sentence, the *Ares* begins to shudder. I reach behind my head to pull the restraint webbing over myself, buckling it into the clasps along the seat. "We're closing with the enemy ships fast."

"Moe, I want you to try something."

"Captain?"

"Make it look like you're losing control in the turbulence. Introduce some random yawing and pitching."

"Aye."

Marissa's body is rigid at her console. "They're spreading out. Probably making sure we don't get through."

"They know they have us," I say. And that's what I want. I need them to be certain of it.

"Three missiles incoming," the OPO says.

So the pirates do have missiles. I drop into the direct control sim, the virtual cockpit materializing in front of me with its one-hundred-eighty degree view compiled from multiple hull sensors. Ignoring the urge to shield my eyes against the sun's glare off the snow-covered expanse below, I ratchet down the dimness instead.

Within seconds, my datasphere recommends an optimal course of action: activate retrothrusters to buy time to shoot down the incoming rockets, while directing a macro to use aft turrets in a point defense capacity against enemy ships approaching from the rear.

But it was following my datasphere's "optimal" course that got me killed back in Arbor.

I exit the sim. "TOPO, tighten up your flying and accelerate past the enemy missiles, full power."

Moe glances at me. "Are you sure that's—"

"Just do it."

The *Ares* leaps forward, and I watch the missiles' progress on the display. As they inch closer, for a moment it looks like I made a fatal error, and they're going to converge together on my ship.

Then we're through, and the missiles weave past each other through the air, two of them nearly colliding.

"Asterisk, treat two of the closest enemy ships to a Javelin each. And don't caution me about how close the range is. We don't have time."

"Yes, sir." And, a few seconds later: "Firing missiles now."

Not a moment too soon. The Javelins leap from their tubes, finding their targets after a brief flight. Both pirate ships blossom with flame, flinging shrapnel in every direction. The final pirate ship peels off.

"Excellent work," I say, and Asterisk looks surprised by the praise. "Moe, what course are you following to the facility?"

A pause. "The computer recommends a direct one, straight to the facility's landing bay."

"Ignore that. The pirates have too much advanced warning. We'll never make it past the landing bay alive."

"We?" Marissa asks.

I nod. "Me and Dice."

Belflower speaks up. "What's the alternative to entering through the landing bay?"

"Entering through the roof. TOPO, take us over the highest point of the facility. We're jumping."

3

It's excruciating, waiting for the right moment to jump.

The facility is a mole on an otherwise pale face, though my eyes are on the info my datasphere is flashing before my eyes: wind speed and direction, drop time, height differential between the top of the facility and the surface.

Wait too long or make our move too soon, and we'll end up in the snow.

"Now," I say at last, and me and Dice both leap from the *Ares'* airlock.

We hurtle toward the dark dot of the facility, the air whipping around us.

I've only had to do a couple aerial insertions during my time as a Troubleshooter, and this is the first time I've needed to coordinate with Dice.

The planet's surface sprawls below us like an ocean frozen mid-tide. According to my datasphere, it's rare for it to get this bright here, or this warm, not that it's what I'd call warm, exactly. But the sky, usually overcast, is clear.

"Chutes," I say, and we activate them at the same moment. They sprout from our backs, spreading out against the pale blue sky at a moment calculated so that we'll end up on top of the domed observatory that crowns the facility.

After that, it's all up to the wind as we drift toward our destination. As long as it doesn't change, we'll be good.

The journey through the air doesn't take long, because I didn't leave much time for drifting slowly downward. The less time we give the pirates to figure out what we're doing, the better. Right now, the *Ares* is making a run at the airlock, with the hope that the pirates didn't see us jump. As long as the ship behaves more or less as they expect, I'm hoping they won't look all that hard for two figures, minuscule against the frozen vista.

We chose the observatory because it's the only part of the facility not caked in snow and frost—I'm guessing the surface is heated, unless Bleak gave some poor bastard the job of scraping it off.

Our feet touch down on the top of the dome, then come our chutes, settling around us. Mine slides down the side right away, jerking me sideways. It turns out the dome's surface is more slippery than I expected, because I lose my footing and tumble.

Dice dives after me, grabbing my arm while a diamond-tipped spike unfolds from his forearm. He drives it into the dome, arresting our downward trajectory.

"Grab onto me," he says, and I climb up to grab onto his torso, trying to ignore the hundred foot drop to the facility roof below.

With that, he begins scaling the slick surface, making sure each spike is secure before hauling us up a couple more feet and driving in the other one. Both our chutes dangle below us, blowing in the wind, which doesn't make things easier.

All around us I can hear the sound of water dripping and ice cracking. When we're halfway up, a mini avalanche of ice falls from the bottom of the dome to the roof below. Of course we'd come on what may well be Xeo's warmest day of its solar cycle.

I keep expecting the pirate ships to spot us and start strafing us, but they don't, and finally we make it back to the top of the dome. Once we're secure, we cut away our chutes at last.

"Thanks," I say.

"Again," he says. "I'm programmed to prevent fleshbag death. Nothing more."

I nod, and then Marissa's voice sounds in my ears: "You were right, sir. The landing bay is heavily defended. Each time we try to approach, we're chased away by laserfire."

"Good," I say. "Keep it up. They think they've stopped us in our tracks. You're authorized to use Javelins to neutralize their defenses—see if you can get inside."

"Yes, sir."

Dice is looking at me. "Once we set off the breaching charges, they'll likely know we're here."

"Maybe," I say. "They're small—just enough to get us through. They won't make make much of a flash in this light." I'm being optimistic, I know, but I'm mostly disagreeing with Dice out of habit. Mentally, I'm prepared for the worst. "Set the charges."

Dice does, carefully unfolding a white charge from a compartment in his thigh. I brought a breacher's kit too, but I'd rather do as little maneuvering up here as possible. I'm clearly more susceptible to losing my footing and falling than Dice is.

Once the charge is set, we make our way to the other side of the dome, beyond the thick telescope that projects upward from it.

"Detonate."

The explosion sends vibrations through the dome, and more ice falls, crashing to the roof below a few seconds later. The blast seemed loud from this proximity, but there's a good chance that they didn't hear it inside, depending on what floors the pirates are occupying. We'll soon find out, anyway.

We end up wrapping the grappling hooks around the telescope before tossing the line down into the observatory.

I go first. "Cover my descent," I tell Dice. Then I grip the nylon rope and start to lower myself, hand over hand.

4

"Drop down," I tell Dice after I check the entrances, along with anywhere else in the observatory that could conceal a pirate. "It's clear."

There are no lights turned on here, but with the sunlight filtering through the frost-kissed glass, we have no trouble seeing.

By the time Dice touches down, I'm already at the exit, checking the staircase for hostiles. Here, I turn night vision on. The stairs seem empty, but they curve around the outside of the structure, and I can see at least one doorway to the left, which must lead to a room directly underneath the observatory. Plenty of places for the enemy to hide.

"We won't be able to advance as carefully as I'd like to," I tell Dice. "We've earned ourselves an advantage, and the only way to maximize it is to move quickly."

The grappling hook is smart enough to get itself loose, using tiny articulated parts. Once it manages to free itself, I will it to reel back to me, which it does, the line feeding through my belt until the hook hangs from my waist once more.

"Come on."

We trot down the spiraling steps, and I eye each door as we

pass it. But I need to trust the plan. There's no reason to think the pirates know we're up here.

At the bottom of the staircase, Marissa gets in touch. "Sir, we've managed to fight our way into the landing bay. And not too soon, either—we were taking heavy fire from the pirate ships outside. Things aren't much more comfortable in here, though. The pirates defending the facility are giving us hell, and it's all Asterisk can do to keep them at bay."

"Keep it up," I say. "It's only a matter of time till they realize I'm not aboard. Until then, you're buying us the time we need."

"Yes, sir."

Down is the only way to go, and so that's the direction we take, using stairways whenever we find them. The facility is massive, so unless we find an elevator, this could take a while.

As we pass through hallway, laboratory, lecture hall, and class-room, I keep having to go back and forth between regular and night vision, thanks to the skylights the builders installed whenever they got the chance. I guess it's fair enough—on a world like Xeo, you'd want to do everything you could to counteract the loneliness and desolation.

It's not that the skylights let in plenty of light. Maybe centuries ago they were kept clear, but now most of them are caked over with several feet of snow. Enough light trickles in, though, to mess with the night vision.

"What did your fleshbag species teach its children to do, here?" Dice asks as we pass through yet another classroom, winding our way through desks and chairs.

I glance at him. "This was a Bacchus Corp facility. They trained their employees, here."

"That doesn't answer the question. What did they teach them?"

I turn back toward the far door and continue toward it. "They taught them how to help humanity die."

After the classroom, we make our way through a long corridor, softening our footsteps as we reach an intersection. When I check around the corner this time, I see our first pirate—carrying a laser rifle across his chest, seemingly on patrol. He's facing us, and when he sees me his eyes go wide.

Both Dice and I step out into view, the bots' pistols snapping into place, making a total of three weapons trained on the pirate. Without hesitation, he drops the rifle and puts up his hands.

"I surrender!"

Dice shoots him twice, and he crumples to the ground.

I look at the bot. "Fount, Dice. What was that all about?"

"We are infiltrating this facility. Are we not?"

"Well, yeah."

"You did not kill the soldiers who surrendered back on the *Ekhidnades*, and it caused us problems. And so I have taken the liberty of neutralizing this hostile."

I raise my eyebrows. "All right, then."

The pirate's presence means one of two things: either we're nearing Bleak's operation, whatever it is, or the pirate lord is getting nervous enough to send grunts through the facility to make sure we didn't find another way in. I guess I'm hoping for the first one, though neither possibility seems particularly pleasant.

Next, we creep up to an intersection to find two pirates around the corner—their backs to us, patrolling in the other direction. Beyond them, I spy a door, and there's another door on our side: looks like a corner classroom with a way to enter from both intersecting hallways.

I subvocalize instructions to Dice using my datasphere. With that, I open the nearby door as quietly as I can, then I pad past a row of desks as. A visual feed from Dice hangs in the upper right corner of my vision.

I send Dice the signal, and he starts firing on the pirates from the corner. They turn around to return fire, and I throw open the classroom door behind them, popping out to shoot them in their backs before they can react. One goes down right away, but I miss my next shot, and the remaining pirate manages to turn and raise his rifle. Dice takes him out before he can pull the trigger.

"Let's go," I say, continuing down the corridor at a jog in search of a staircase or elevator. I switch to a two-way channel with Marissa. "Chief, what do you have for me?"

"They're finally turning down the pressure, Captain," she says. "For a while there it looked touch-and-go, but they've mostly fallen back. They left a few fighters behind to keep us honest, but I think they finally figured out you're not here."

The pirates we just killed may have something to do with that. "Acknowledged. Pikeman out." I meet Dice's gaze. "We'll have company soon."

5

Even in its wide open spaces, the facility is starting to make me claustrophobic. The way snow covers every window, the knowledge that it's stacked for feet, possibly meters on the roof overhead…

"Get a grip," I mutter, shaking my head.

It's growing darker, now, too. The skylights getting fewer. We continue to encounter pirates in groups of two and three, but we're always able to soak into them effectively, and with Dice's help I take them out handily. They haven't had my training, and they don't have the bot's cold efficiency, so we cut them to ribbons without much trouble.

Then I spot a group of four more pirates, chatting in the middle of an intersection, and I draw back, motioning for Dice to go the other way. No need to engage that many if we don't have to, and there's probably another way down.

I find myself pushing through a set of double doors into the biggest auditorium we've seen, with dozens of skylights breaking up the white ceiling. Sunbeams filter down here and there, illuminating random empty seats, and a sunbeam even touches the lectern, as though waiting for someone to get up and say something profound.

The chamber has an almost forsaken beauty, but we don't pause to admire it, jogging across the front instead. I peer up over the rows of seating, which march toward another double door at the back of the auditorium. Then, a flicker of movement catches my eye, and I yell, "Down!"

I dive for the lectern, and Dice takes some laserfire on the shoulder before returning some, suppressing two of the shooters. Popping up over the podium, I add my fire to his, and we buy ourselves a brief reprieve.

Something makes me glance to my left, and through rectangular, vertical windows I see a group of pirates rushing the double doors on that side. "Back!" We continue to lay down suppressive fire until we can make it to the front row of seats. Crouching in front of them offers scant cover, but it's something. Bent low, we run back the way we came, as fast as we can while hunched over like that and returning fire.

It's time to accept that whatever advantage we gained from sneaking in through the observatory is now gone. There is still one thing I can use, though: the fact that I care about this facility a lot less than they do.

As we flee through the auditorium doors, I snatch a plasma grenade from my waist and underhand it backward. The doors swing shut.

"Run faster," I say, and we do.

The boom comes just as we reach the same intersection as before, with the chatting pirates. They turn toward us, wearing expressions of shock and confusion, which doesn't do much for them as Dice and I mow them down.

We sprint over their downed forms. One of them is still conscious, reaching for his laser rifle, and I kick it away as we pass, aiming a blaster bolt at his head, but missing.

Just beyond the intersection, we find what seems to be a main stairwell, with a massive staircase that extends up and down for several floors.

Our feet flying over the stairs, I keep an eye below while Dice watches above. A door bangs open a few floors over us, followed by a stampede of feet racing down the stairs.

"Fount damn it."

Luckily, they don't manage to catch up enough to get the high ground on us. We reach the bottom of the staircase, and I peer through the vertical glass door at what looks to be a ground-level lobby, where snow broke through the ceiling at some point and now lies in drifts that cover most of the floor.

I throw open the door, and we charge across as best we can, though at times my legs sink past my knees.

It's not hard to see why the snow broke through at some point: the lobby's ceiling is entirely glass, or at least it was. Now much of it is shattered, sticking out in jagged pieces from a metal skeleton.

My datasphere informs me it's below freezing in here. After our skydiving, I opted to keep my helmet on as we infiltrated the facility, for some extra protection. Now, the sealed suit serves to regulate my body temperature, preventing the cold from affecting me. None of the pirates I've seen are wearing helmets, but I doubt that will slow them much.

The door bangs open behind us, and I vault over a snow dune, twisting over as I slide down the other side to fire over the peak. Dice does the same, leaning on a drift a few feet to my left and laying into the pirates with both laser pistols.

Laserfire makes the snow beneath us hiss and steam, obstructing our vision. I turn on thermal and continue firing. Soon, the pirates who've entered the lobby are down, and we're keeping the others pinned inside the stairwell.

"We can't stay here," I say. "Too much risk of getting flanked. We need to start making our way to the other side—you go first while I keep them busy."

Dice nods, turning to fall back over the snow while I continue laying down blaster fire. He settles onto a drift a few meters back, his eye sensors casting a red glow across the white. Then he returns the favor.

In this way, we leapfrog backward across the lobby. At one point, I have to crouch behind cover while I swap out my blaster's charge packs, but Dice has the situation well in hand as I do. With his twin laser pistols and his consistent ability to fire at two targets at once, he keeps the pirates at bay. Plus, they must be getting cold, now.

Finally, we make it to the end of the lobby, and the end of the drifts too. My first couple strides into the bare corridor, I skid, almost falling, but I manage to keep my balance. The snow caked onto the bottom of my boots is affecting my footing, and then the moisture nearly makes me trip again, but I manage to stay upright. We can't afford to slow down.

The lights are turned on in this part of the research facility, which seems like a bad sign. As though to confirm, laserfire comes from both sides as we sprint through the next intersection, and I dive into a roll while Dice throws both arms wide and gives some back. Then we're through, running toward the end of the corridor, where I spot the metal doors of what has to be an elevator.

"There," I pant. "That's our way down."

The elevator's at a three-way intersection. When I reach it, I slap the control panel and nothing happens. Then the pirates start shooting at us from behind, and we both take cover behind opposite corners.

"I can pull the doors open," Dice says across the hall—and across the hail of laserfire.

"The elevator car probably isn't there," I say. "And if it is, it probably isn't working."

"Do we have a better option?"

I glance at him. "Do it."

I cover him as best he can, but he takes a laser bolt to the shoulder as he works his fingers between the doors, and the wound starts sparking right away.

Arming another plasma grenade, I lob it down the hall toward the pirates, as hard as I can. It blows a few seconds later, sending tremors through the floor. It must have gotten pretty close to them, because the shooting stops for a while.

The doors screech open to reveal a cable dangling down the elevator shaft. No elevator car, though, just as I feared. Damn it.

"Cover me," I say, heading for the elevator. It seems futile—the pirates will shoot us down as we attempt to descend—but Dice is right. There's no better option. I holster my blaster, though I don't snap it in place.

After a few seconds of shimmying down the cable, I stop, gaping downward. The elevator car is right below us, stopped at the next floor.

If we can find a way in…even if we can't get it working, we may be able to exit through the doors onto the next floor and find another way down. "Dice, hold them off while I try to get this emergency hatch open."

Before I can descend more than a foot, the hatch opens by itself, and a pirate sticks a laser rifle into the shaft, pointing in my general direction.

Wrapping my left arm around the cable, I whip out my blaster with my right, shooting at him just before he manages to draw a bead on me. He ducks out of the way, and I keep my muzzle steady on the empty hatch, waiting for someone else to have a try.

I glance up to see Dice clinging to the cable, dealing with more pirates trying to shoot us from above.

We're pinned.

6

We fire back at the pirates with grim determination, knowing a single mistake could end us both.

Light filters into the shaft from the floor above and the elevator car below, through the emergency hatch. It gleams dully off the dark metal of the shaft's interior, giving it an ethereal quality—except when laserfire lances through the shaft, lighting it up with neon blue.

Dice has been reduced to shooting one-handed, though he shows no signs of exertion from holding himself aloft. He wouldn't, of course. That's one of the advantages they have over humans.

I try to keep an eye on the doors above as well, since Dice has a bigger area to cover. But swinging my arm up and down is taking its toll on my grip.

My legs and left arm are starting to tire, and I feel like I could lose my grip at any moment. I focus on lining up each shot to the exclusion of everything else, like the old knight taught me.

It turns out facing certain death tightens up your aim almost as well as a datasphere does. My concentration is total, and I shoot at anything that moves inside the elevator car below.

The pirates in there face challenges of their own. They clearly didn't expect to encounter this situation, and they've been holding each other up to the hatch. It must be unsettling to have your comrade die with your arms wrapped around his legs, knowing that it's your turn to climb up next.

The choke point below, combined with Dice's efficiency, serves to keep the pirates at bay for now. But we both know it can't last.

As I line up my next shot, I grunt from the exertion. Every time I move my blaster, it shifts my body ever so slightly, and my grip becomes that much more uncertain.

Soon, I find myself yelling as I fire on the pirates that pop up from the elevator to try to end me, or on the ones attempting to rush the doorway above.

I get one of the pirates above in the forehead, and he tumbles over, missing me by an inch and crashing to the car below, partially obscuring the hatch. If he'd hit me, I'm sure I would have gone down too.

More pirates crowd into the elevator car, and between them they manage to drag the downed pirate into the box, clearing the way.

Something needs to give, and now seems as good a time as any for drastic action. I fire five times through the hatch, to clear them away from there, then I holster the blaster as quickly as I can, pluck a plasma grenade from my belt, arm it, and drop it through the hatch. With that, I draw the blaster and take aim at the cable below me.

The first shot doesn't snap it, and I line up the second, knowing that if this fails, the explosion's going to cook me and Dice along with the pirates.

The cable snaps, sending the elevator plummeting. Several floors down, the grenade goes off, emitting bright blue flames that surge up the shaft, pushing a wave of heat that scorches my legs. I grit my teeth, grunting in pain.

"This is your chance," Dice calls down. "Throw up your grappling hook."

"What? Why?" Now that the elevator car is gone, it's as though the effort required to hold myself here has doubled. For some reason, knowing that falling now means certain death puts an even greater strain on my limbs. I manage to get my blaster up to shoot one of the two pirates crowding the doors above, and my blaster bolt tosses him back into the corridor.

"There's no time for discussion," Dice says.

I don't answer, and when he speaks again, he sounds resigned. "I'll secure the hook to myself, and then you jump. Cut yourself loose once you reach solid ground."

"By solid ground, you mean the twisted metal of the elevator I just blew up, right?"

"You have a better idea?" he asks me, for the second time today.

"No." I've been keeping an eye on the doors below, and now a pirate appears at them. I spam the blaster trigger to keep him at bay. "What will you do?"

"My duty. I'll remain here and hold them off for as long as I can."

I pause. "Okay, then. Thank you, Dice."

"It will be an honor and a pleasure to never behold your fleshy countenance again."

I will my grappling cable to switch to feed mode, and I toss up the hook to Dice. He catches it, opens a crevice on his thigh, and secures the hook there—one of the tongs fits snugly. "Go," he says.

"Okay. Bye, Dice."

I leap, letting off a few parting shots for the pirates clustering near the lower floor. Then, I'm hurtling through space, laserfire lighting up the shaft around me, crackling through air to melt the metal around me. None of the bolts hit.

Once I judge I'm a safe distance away, I will the line to start absorbing the fall, slowing my descent at a rate that won't jolt me and risk injury.

Soon, I'm descending at a pleasant clip, falling fairly quickly but not so fast that landing will shatter my ankle. I give silent thanks to Dice for holding on this long, and the thought that he probably won't make it causes a pang in my chest, which I didn't expect.

I've already switched to night vision, and before long the elevator comes into view below, just as damaged as I expected. Slowing my descent to a crawl, I pick my way through the wreckage, careful not to impale myself on any of the twisted spires of metal that reach up like wretched claws.

The elevator itself is full of dead pirates, whose bodies shift under my weight as I walk over them. When my boot finds solid floor, it's slick with something—probably blood.

Outside the elevator, the lights are off. I'm not sure whether that's a response to my presence, or merely meant to conserve power.

It doesn't matter. Detaching the grappling hook with a thought, I raise my blaster, then forge out into the green-tinged gloom.

7

I emerge from the wrecked elevator onto a raised platform overlooking a cavernous warehouse. On my right, a two-story staircase leads to the warehouse floor, across which stretches a sea of tilted, cylindrical tanks, all arranged in near rows, with meter-sized spaces between them. The tanks are messing with my night vision a little, and when I switch it off, I see that each one glows with a faint blue light.

No point in hesitating. I fly down the stairs, taking them two at a time with my blaster held at the ready in front of me. As I descend, I can't help but wonder what the hell this place is supposed to be. Could this be where they're keeping the children?

But when I reach the bottom of the staircase and approach the first tank, I find a fully grown adult floating in the blue-lit fluid inside. What the hell? I'll admit it: this is freaking me out.

It's a woman inside, totally naked, short black hair waving in the fluid. There's no breathing apparatus, so I figure she must be in nanodeath. But for how long?

Under each tank, a wide, metal grate is set into the floor. From the seam at the bottom of the cylinder, it looks like the tank opens there, leaving enough room to wheel in something to catch her when she slides out—a bed maybe, or a bot designed for the purpose.

A middle-aged man floats in the next tank, and an elderly woman in the one after that. Every single tank I pass is filled, and a few do contain children, though none that I recognize. Could these kids be from the Brinktowns the pirates raided, or did they come from somewhere else?

Then, it hits me: something I'd read once during one of my long slipspace voyages, about the era when people had first started uploading to the Subverse en masse. Bacchus Corp attempted to ease any fears their customers might have by advertising a guarantee that anyone who uploaded could always return to their physical body.

I don't know how many people took advantage of that guarantee. Possibly no one, judging by how unpopular living in the real had become. And no one even talks about it, now. When I read about the guarantee, I assumed that everyone had forgotten about it, and I doubted it was in effect anymore. My thinking was that if Bacchus had ever really stored all those trillions of bodies, then surely whatever facilities they'd kept them in were out of power, by now.

Yet here these bodies are, floating silent in tanks, just waiting for minds to inhabit them.

Creepy.

Could Bacchus really have kept trillions of humans all this time? Or had they kept only a small percentage, for their own purposes?

After a few minutes of walking, I come across a raised dais, in what seems like the very center of the warehouse, though it's hard to know for sure.

A staircase winds around the outside, leading to a platform encircled by a metal railing. When I mount the stairs, I find a terminal standing in the middle of the platform.

Using my datasphere, I'm able to access it with no trouble.

Either someone left themselves logged in, sure that no one unauthorized would ever make it down here, or someone else cracked the password and left the compromised account logged in.

Or maybe it had never had any security at all. Maybe Bacchus figured that if someone gained access to this room who shouldn't be here, the damage was already done.

Either way, I'm in. I glance toward the raised platform where I exited the elevator, and I find it empty. No sounds of anyone approaching from any other direction, either, though I glance around to be sure.

Then, I start screwing around with the interface. It doesn't take long to figure out I can order the list of tanks according to the most recent date anything was done to them. That done, I can select any number, and toggle over to a map, which shows me where in the warehouse the selected tanks reside.

Some near the perimeter have been opened recently, though according to the date those subjects were first interred—I can't think of a better word—it can't possibly have been any of the children the pirates kidnapped. In fact, everyone stored in this room was put inside their tanks centuries ago.

My heart rate is accelerating as I become more and more aware that the pirates must be closing in. But there's one more thing I want to check. With a bit more playing around, I discover that there are other subterranean warehouses like this one, in other parts of the facility. And it turns out I can search them.

I type "Marissa Sterling" and execute, but nothing turns up. Just "Marissa" doesn't get anything, either. Where did that bastard Daniel put her? Even these days, when you upload to the Subverse, it's still part of the deal that you turn over your physical body as well, for Bacchus' study and use. Yes, core members of the Five Families are exempt, but they're rich enough to pay for it. Daniel Sterling isn't that rich.

I type "Cal Pikeman," then just "Pikeman," but neither yields results. It was a long shot, but I wanted to check. Sometimes, I find myself thinking that maybe, instead of seeking the Crucible of Knighthood like he claimed, my father just used his Guardsman's salary to finance his flight into the Subverse. His flight from being my father.

That still might be true. But according to this terminal, his body isn't in this facility.

I try "Faelyn Eliot," and nothing comes up, though it occurs to me that may not mean much. If the pirates are storing the children they kidnapped in these tanks, they might have just given them code names, or not entered them into the database at all.

A hissing noise sounds from the warehouse floor, coming from a few meters away. Motion catches my eye, and I watch as one of the cylinders opens at the bottom, the transparent hatch rising into the air. The fluid used to preserve the body inside drains out into the grate below, and the body flops out, looking like it belongs to a boy just at the end of his adolescence.

He hits the grate with a wet smack, hard enough that I wonder whether he'll ever get up from it. His muscles won't have atrophied—the Fount sees to it that they're kept properly stimulated in nanodeath—but without something underneath the tank to catch him, that fall didn't look healthy. I try to decide whether I should go to him.

But then the boy stirs atop the grate, and staggers to his feet.

"You all right, kid?" I ask.

He doesn't answer, but the sound of my voice seems to draw his attention, and he stumbles to a halt halfway between the two rows of tanks facing each other. His gait is awkward, as though he can barely remember how to walk.

Then he turns toward me, blinking as though trying to focus his eyes. He meets my gaze, and then begins to stumble forward, faster than before, his limbs flailing crazily. My hand twitches toward my blaster.

"Stay where you are," I bark, but he doesn't. He starts up the stairs instead, toward me. Is there a chance he's heading toward the terminal? I back against the railing, so that I'll have time to see which direction he's headed in. "Kid?"

When he reaches the platform, it's clear he's of one mind. He heads straight for me, hands raised, grasping at air. The posture seems to throw him off balance, and he half-runs, half-stumbles toward me. Now that he's close, I can see how skinny he is, his ribs showing. That had to be what he looked like when they put him in the tank: people in nanodeath have no need to eat.

"Last warning," I say, backing up farther, but he gives no sign he even registers the comment. He closes the gap, hands reaching for my throat, and I lift a boot to shove him back. I guess I use too much force, because I send him flying backward, and when he falls, the back of his head cracks off the metal railing.

He slumps to the platform, completely motionless. "Shit."

Another tank hisses open, the lid rising and the liquid gushing out. The female occupant smacks against the grate, just like the kid did, but unlike him she doesn't stand.

Then a third tank frees its occupant, a well-muscled man of seven feet whose motor skills are apparently in better working order than the kid's. He strides toward the platform with minimal flailing.

More tanks are hissing open, all around me. Some of the occupants hit the grate and don't move, and some of them slither around without rising.

But most of them do gain their feet. And every one of them heads toward me.

8

The seven-foot man starts up the stairs, and when he reaches the dais, he heads for me, hands raised in a choking motion, just like the kid.

There's nothing for it. Taking careful aim, I put a blaster bolt in his head.

With that, I start moving around the circular railing, lining up shot after shot and felling the slick humans attempting to climb the stairs to get at me. For the most part, a single shot is enough to take out each one.

More and more tanks are hissing open to release their flailing occupants. Wet bodies begin to accumulate on the staircase, but the mindless drones don't let the pileup deter them. They clamber over the corpses of their fellows, heedless of the blaster fire raining down on them. Like bots ordered to sacrifice themselves assaulting an enemy position.

They make no sound other than grunts and groans of exertion, and their faces bear expressions that mix determination with hatred. What the hell happened to them? What's driving them to act like this? By themselves, they're totally ineffectual, but this warehouse must house thousands of those tanks. Eventually, I'll run out of juice for my blaster.

With that, my blaster's trigger clicks, and nothing happens. It's dry. I slap in another charge pack. Only two left after this one.

Soon, the bodies are piled high enough that the human automatons start tumbling off and onto the concrete below the dais. That takes care of them, for the most part. But others manage to make it to the top, and the corpse pile starts to spill over onto the platform itself.

I can only afford to focus on the staircase, now. A foot grabs me through the railing I've backed myself against, and I yell, jerking it free and stomping on the hand, feeling the crunch of finger bones under my heel. The owner withdraws the injured hand, only to stick the other one through. I move toward the terminal and shoot another naked form about to make it onto the platform.

Glancing back, I see a sea of people, packed together and surging toward the platform as one.

I need to take another approach. I shoot the woman about to crawl onto the platform, then I jog to the part of the railing closest to the tanks, eyeing the gap between them.

Probably, I can make the jump. As long as my wet-soled boots don't slip on the rail.

I hear someone tumble onto the dais as I lift myself to the middle rail. No time to hesitate. Steadying myself with my hands, I pull both feet under me and push off with all my might.

Almost, I don't make it. My body slams against the tank, and I begin to slide down its sloped surface, toward the waiting horde below.

But I find better purchase with my hands on the tank's metal top and pull myself up, my left arm still aching from gripping the elevator cable. The top of the tank is also slanted, and I nearly fall over the other side before stabilizing.

The drones' arms slap against the tank's glass, sending tremors through it, and though it's sturdy, I'm sure it's only a matter of time before they succeed in toppling it.

So I leap to the next tank, a meter away. Once I'm stabilized, I leap again.

The throng remains focused on me, their focal point shifting from tank to tank as I bound across their tops as quickly as I can gain my balance on each. Their grunting and moaning becomes louder, as though from frustration.

I leap across at least twenty tanks, with my pursuers milling around below. At the final tank, I look to the wall and see a closed hatch, with a control panel beside it. From here, I'm able to access it with my datasphere to check whether I'll be given access when I reach it.

I will.

But the bodies in front of it do pose a problem. There is a small space, but not big enough for me to land there and escape without the automatons getting at me.

So I take aim and start shooting those closest to the doors. My aim doesn't actually need to be that good. With this many targets, I just hold the blaster in their general direction and spam the trigger.

A space quickly clears in front of the hatch—clear of live drones, anyway. A number of dead ones are piled up there now, creating a low wall of bodies, but that will probably work to my advantage, as long as I don't lose my footing by landing on them.

My behavior doesn't seem to tip off the drones below me to my intentions. They continue to rock the tank I'm on, and abruptly, they succeed: something cracks off at the base of the tank, and now the only thing keeping it upright is the press of bodies all around it.

I leap, but the tank shifts as my feet push off it, and there isn't as much force behind the jump as there would have been. I land amidst the sea of drones, as though I'm attempting to crowd surf, like they do in novels and movies from before the Fall.

Except, the naked forms don't attempt to catch me. They let me fall to the floor, and the only thing that cushions my landing is the man I've knocked over. He reaches up at my face, and I push off him, stomping his head as I pass and bringing up my blaster to shoot another man at point-blank range.

I clock a drone in the jaw with the butt of my blaster and jab another one in the throat with my fingertips, sending him to his knees, gasping.

What feels like a hundred hands are clamoring to get a grip on my clothes, my limbs, but I won't stay still. I kick and punch and bite and pistol whip until I reach the line of bodies I downed before. Clambering over them, I slap the control panel with my palm.

The hatch slides open, and I rush through, turning to hit the control panel on this side. The portal hasn't even opened halfway, and now it slides shut again, before my pursuers can get a limb through and jam it.

Blaster trained on the closed hatch, I wait to see whether they'll open it and come through. But they don't. Either Bacchus intentionally denied them the authorization to open it or they just don't have the presence of mind to operate it. The first possibility sends a shiver through my spine as I contemplate what situations Bacchus might have wanted to safeguard against by denying them the ability to leave.

After a few seconds, I'm satisfied they're not coming through, and I turn to behold another warehouse that might as well be the same one: cylindrical tanks stretch as far as I can see.

9

The tanks here aren't lit up.

They flash by in the emerald gloom as I jog through the warehouse, and they're all empty. That lends credence to my idea that Bacchus probably didn't hold on to every one of the trillions of humans who've ever uploaded to the Subverse. Unless Bleak ordered them all removed and disposed of, maybe to conserve power.

Then, an island of blue light catches my eye off to the left, through the forest of tilted cylinders. It washes out my night vision, so I switch it off and proceed through the rows with caution while my eyes adjust.

When I reach it, my heart leaps into my throat. Every one of these tanks—probably a few hundred—holds a child.

I'm running faster, now, racing up and down the rows, peering into tank after tank. Looking for Faelyn.

I've searched maybe a fifth of them when I hear the hatch I entered through open at last, and the slap of bodies hitting the floor —probably pushed over by the drones fighting to get through behind them. Then comes the thunder of hundreds of footsteps as the naked mob spreads out through the warehouse, no doubt searching for me.

I check a couple more tanks before accepting that I need to go. Turning, I head back the way I was going originally—toward the other side of the warehouse, to check whether there's a hatch on that side too. As I pass the last lit tanks, I switch my night vision back on.

A drone spots me through the tanks and stumbles toward me, but I don't waste a blaster bolt on him. He's not fast enough to catch me, and shooting him will only draw the others. A couple others take notice as I sprint through the warehouse, but I make it to the hatch without incident.

Only to find it won't open. An "ACCESS REVOKED" message blinks in the upper region of my vision. Fount damn it.

Probably, Bleak is monitoring my progress through the facility and barred the hatch to trap me here. That makes me think he likely let the drones into this warehouse, too.

I open my breacher's kit and take out a door charge to slap it onto the hatch. Then I jog a few meters away, take cover behind a tank, and detonate it remotely.

When I emerge, the hatch is blown clean out of the frame, replaced by a haze of smoke. Of course, the blast drew the attention of every drone in the warehouse, and about a dozen of them are already clustered near the breached hatch. I shoot one and kick another out of the way, sending him stumbling into the next room as I run past. There's no longer any time to stop and consider my next move. The drones have been let loose, and they seem intent on chasing me until they die or I do.

I find myself in a long, low-ceiling room, bordered by rectangular windows on either side. There aren't any light fixtures in here, which tells me the windows are likely one-way mirrors, since the effect only works if the mirrored side is brightly lit while the other is dark.

From what I'm able to observe of the rooms on the other side as I dash past, they seem to confirm the notion: each one has just a table and two chairs, like an interrogation room. Every window looks in on two rooms, adjacent to but cut off from each other. That reminds me of the Prisoner's Dilemma, an old game theory scenario they used to teach in Assessment and Selection.

When I reach the other end of the long room, a glance behind me shows the opposite end is packed with the mindless drones, surging forward as one. Their grunting and groaning fills the room, seemingly louder than before, and they seem to be getting faster, too. Here's hoping they don't remember how to run.

The door into the next area isn't a hatch, but a steel door, and it's unlocked. Slamming it closed behind me, I continue on.

This room features four wrestling rings, with observation windows set high above. Aside from the door I just came through, there are three exits, though two are hatches which I assume lead to more warehouses full of tanks. The opposite exit is another steel door, and I sprint toward it.

I find the door unlocked. It lets out onto another square room, this one with a checkered floor. It takes me a moment to realize that the floor tells this chamber's purpose: it's a giant chess board. The squares are big enough to accommodate human-sized pieces, and again, observation windows overlook the arena from high above.

What did Bacchus do to people, here? Everyone knows they used the physical bodies uploads gave them for research into human behavior and psychology, the better to tailor the Subverse to human happiness. But actually seeing the sort of things the company subjected people to…it's unsettling.

I pass through a gym, again with the observation windows, and then a room with nothing but hundreds of recliners arranged in neat rows, probably to hold people as they're immersed in sims. Next, I come to what was once referred to as an Olympic-sized swimming pool, with raised, grated decks surrounding the long room in place of windows. The pool's filled with water that looks pretty clean. How long have Bleak's people been set up here? Have they been taking recreational swims between experimenting on children?

The ceilings in each of these last three rooms are covered in thick cables, held in place by metal brackets. The cables run in every direction before disappearing into walls. Probably, they're for transporting power to the various warehouses, and their presence suggests I'm in the center of the bizarre subterranean facility.

By the time I jog around the pool, the drones have started spilling into the pool area. Some of them head straight into the water, where they'll probably drown, since I don't see them having the motor skills needed for swimming. But most of them know enough to skirt the water to either side. Are they becoming smarter? They *were* able to figure out how to operate a doorknob, which I wouldn't have expected of them when they first started emerging from the tanks.

After the swimming pool, the next door opens to reveal a porch-sized room, with an opening to the left.

Looking up, I notice the wall in front of me doesn't actually touch the mirrored ceiling above. And when I head for the opening, I turn the corner to find a passage with several more openings.

Then, it hits me. I'm in a labyrinth. And I'll bet the entire ceiling is one-way glass.

As I fly around corners and down long passageways, I will my datasphere to track my orientation, so I'll be able to tell whether I'm making progress in a given direction instead of going around in circles. Even with that, it's challenging, and I run into plenty of dead ends.

I remember a trick I learned from an old book for escaping a maze: put your hand on one of the walls and follow it till you reach the exit. That would work, given infinite time. But as I backtrack from yet another dead end, I encounter the first drone and put a blaster bolt in his face, obliterating it. One way or another, my time here is limited.

Muscles tight with adrenaline, I continue the marathon the drones have driven me into. I'm taking turns without thinking, and the path I forge through the maze is haphazard.

Dead end after dead end frustrates my progress, and I eye the tops of the walls, wondering if I can make them with a running leap.

But then I turn a corner to find the next passage packed with drones, all flowing forward like a liquid made of humans.

I don't bother shooting into the mass of people—it would be pointless. I turn and run, praying they haven't trapped me.

I take a left, then a right, my datasphere providing encouragement by reporting that I've made significant progress across the room. If the exit is opposite the entrance, and this room is of a similar size to the others, then I should be close.

And then, suddenly, I'm at the exit—a hatch, which opens at my touch. A group of people catches my eye as I enter, but I spin around before I have time to register who they are, slapping the control panel to close the hatch.

A deep, sonorous voice speaks behind me: "So many innocents slaughtered," it says. "Are you auditioning to join us, Commander?"

I turn and behold Bleak, dressed in his Renaissance garb, standing next to Harmony and Peter Vance. Surrounding them are twenty armed pirates, all with laser weapons trained on me.

"Drop your weapon," Bleak says.

10

My blaster is still in my hand. I turn it sideways and spread my fingers.

"Not good enough," Bleak says. "Put it on the floor, nice and slow, if you please."

I do as he says, then rise again to my full height. That seems to satisfy him.

Bleak wears a deep-purple doublet checkered with white curlicues and what I can only describe as a skirt bearing the same color and design. A feathered purple hat that swoops behind his head, in an imitation of a pirate's hat—or maybe roadkill—tops the outfit. On his belt, a sword counterbalances a laser pistol, possibly in imitation of Fairfax.

My gaze meets Harmony's, and her eyes widen slightly, like she's trying to tell me something. Not wanting to draw suspicion, I break eye contact and look at her husband, whose arm is linked with hers. He winces slightly.

The room is broad, with a ceiling maybe twenty feet high, though the chamber's breadth makes it look low. Beyond the group of pirates, an observation window stretches across the far wall. It doesn't look like a one-way mirror. Whoever or whatever is on the other side of that glass, it apparently doesn't matter if it can look back. But I can't see its occupant, or occupants; just a ceiling. The floor lies somewhere below.

"Why didn't you lock the hatch?' I say.

"It's locked now," Bleak says. "If I'd locked it to prevent you entering, I'm sure you would have simply blown it open, and then we'd have a roomful of mindless savages in here with us."

"Where's Faelyn Eliot?"

Bleak smiles broadly, like I've made a joke, but he doesn't answer.

My gaze drifts to the wall perpendicular to the observation window. It's full of readouts and built-in instrument panels. Same with the wall across from it. There don't appear to be any exits, other than the one I entered through.

"Why aren't you saying anything?" I say.

"A moment of silence," Bleak says. "For all the innocent people you killed today."

"They tried to kill me first. I'm guessing you unleashed them on me."

"Their owners will never be able to return to their physical bodies, now. Not after what you've done to them."

I return his gaze and say nothing. After what I just went through, I'm not in the mood for Bleak's games, though somehow I doubt that'll prevent him from playing them. Not if his reputation is any indication.

"Not to worry," the pirate lord says. "It turns out it's much harder to transfer an uploaded consciousness back into a biological vessel than Bacchus Corp originally assumed. Uploading a consciousness is easy. *Downloading*, however…" Bleak shrugs. "After centuries in storage, a body loses many of its higher-order cognitive functions, including long-term memory. Yes, it can be given simple directives, helped along by aggression-promoting endorphins added to the preservative fluid prior to release. But that's all."

I glance at the observation window, mostly because no one else seems willing to. I'm sure Bleak wants me to ask a question, to prompt him to continue speaking, but I don't feel like it.

Eventually, he resumes his monologue. "The main problem with returning minds to physical bodies is that, from the moment we upload to the Subverse, our consciousness expands. And why shouldn't it? Even when given a digital body, an uploaded mind has only the limits that are programmed around it. Limits *are* necessary, of course, else we would lose our identities. But the limits can be peeled back. Believe me, Joe, when I tell you that in spite of your prejudices, life in the Subverse is much richer. Much fuller. We're capable of a lot more, there, and our intellects expand well beyond what our biology was ever capable of accommodating."

"I've been to the Subverse," I say. "I've lived there, too. It's not everything it's cracked up to be."

Bleak's eyes narrow. I know I sound crazy, but I don't care.

"Well." He clears his throat. "That's self-evidently untrue, but no matter. Quality of life inside the Subverse isn't important to my point. What I'm trying to tell you is that once a consciousness expands, the human body that evolution gave us is no longer capable of housing it. And that process doesn't take very long at all. Perhaps it would be possible for an upload to reenter his old body after only a week or two of Subverse residence, but not long after that it becomes impossible. Whether life is truly richer there or not, the people of the Subverse are, in fact, much more advanced than you or I. Some, incredibly so."

"Is that important to your point?" I ask.

"It is, actually," Bleak says, bearing his teeth in what might be called a smile. Clearly, he's delighted that I've begun to humor him.

Something crashes into the wall below the observation window, sending tremors through the room we're in and causing most of the pirates to start. Not Bleak, though. He smiles through it.

"What was that?" I ask.

Bleak's smile widens. "You came here to find a girl, did you not?"

I keep my eyes away from Harmony and say nothing.

"Father," Peter says.

"Shut up, Peter," Bleak says, and his son falls silent. "You have found the girl, Commander. She has enjoyed the singular privilege of participating in a historic first. Which brings me to our project, here in this facility. The project for which I've been hired, by none other than some of the most powerful men and women in the galaxy.

"We are tasked with nothing less than ushering in a new galactic age. You see, multiple members of the Five Families have decided they can no longer remain in the Subverse."

"Why not?" I say, and Bleak's toothy grin wavers at the interruption. "Didn't you just say life in the Subverse is richer?"

"Oh, it is. But there are certain factors you seem ignorant of. You see, despite that the most powerful Five Families members are as demigods in the Subverse, immortality starts to grate after a time. Especially when your efforts to graduate from demigod to full-on god are frustrated again and again."

"Frustrated by who?"

"Why, the Shiva Knights. Honestly, Commander, I thought even you would be more informed than this. Are you seriously telling me you're ignorant of even the knighthood's self-assigned quest?" He shakes his head. "Anyway. As I was saying. My clients' intellects have grown vast, far vaster than the average Subverse denizen. They wish to return to the physical world. To get out from under the thumb of the Shiva. But even if we could figure out how to give them back human forms, they're loathe to give up the unrivaled intellects they've acquired—or the power. And so, it is our part to work with them to engineer biological constructs large enough and complex enough to house their bulbous minds."

As Bleak talks, some things are starting to come together for me. Creatures like Maneater must have been organic 'prototypes'—the pirates' first attempt at engineering beings with enhanced abilities. That would explain her speed, strength, and intelligence.

The creature contained in the chamber beyond crashes against its prison wall again, so hard that a couple pirates lose their footing and fall to the floor.

Bleak's lips peel farther back. "What you hear behind us is the first viable result of our efforts, Commander. Please. Step forward and admire it."

Leaving my blaster lying on the floor is the last thing I'm interested in doing, but I don't have much of a choice. Feet like lead, I cross the room to the observation window and peer into the vast pit below.

At first, I can't make out where the beast begins and ends. Then, I see it: its massive, triangular head, surging restlessly across its own body. Its tail is lost beneath the great, scaled coils, and so is the floor. The creature fills the enormous pit, and I can understand why it's so upset. How claustrophobic it must feel.

Massive yellow orbs rotate in their sockets, their slit-like irises shifting till they seem to stare directly at me. A forked tongue darts out and disappears. Even through the glass, I can hear its hiss.

"Your goal, Commander. You've achieved it. You've found Faelyn Eliot at last."

11

My mind feels like shattered glass. Any plan I might have been formulating is lost beyond recovery.

At first, I want to disbelieve what Bleak says, but I know I'm not going to get away with that. I know the ring of truth when I hear it.

But if the beast at the bottom of that pit is Faelyn Eliot, then…I have no idea what to do with that information. The old knight said she would die if I chose to go to Arbor before coming here, and I guess in a sense, she did die. But this seems worse than death.

At any rate, getting her back to Tunis seems out of the question, now. I don't think she'll fit inside the *Ares*.

Absurdly, the thought makes me laugh, though I guess laughter is the best response. I'm pretty sure my other options include crying and going completely insane.

I continue chuckling, and I hear some of the pirates shifting their weight behind me.

Bleak seems undisturbed. Maybe he even expected this reaction. "It was necessary to recruit children for our program," he says. "Adults wouldn't do—not for the testing phase. Their minds aren't elastic enough. Even by adolescence, the human mind is too cemented for our purposes. Only a child's mind is malleable enough to be molded and stretched to fit an organism tailored to our clients' specifications. And we couldn't very well transfer our clients into our constructs without first testing their viability."

"So…you turned Faelyn into a god?" I say, my voice still tinged with mirth.

"Temporarily, yes. Soon enough, she'll be evicted and replaced by one of our clients. But for now, she resides inside a construct built to hold a god. Thankfully, she's too immature cognitively to take advantage of it. She's had no experience with having access to the cognitive resources at her disposal now, so instead of exploiting them, she spends her time confused, bewildered even. Not to mention enraged."

The snake rears, then, and slams its head against the glass barrier. Most of the pirates stumble backward, and a few let cries of fear escape their lips. I stand my ground, studying the snake impassively.

"Not to worry," Bleak says. "She can't escape from there. And soon, we will be ready for our client to take control of the construct. Her torment will be at an end."

"Why would your clients want to become giant snakes—like, with no arms or anything?"

"Oh, we'll be offering any desired upgrades as the project progresses. And not everyone will be a snake. But those are small details, almost irrelevant. The fact is that our clients will become the lords of humanity, with legions of biologicals to do their bidding. Who needs arms, when you have an army of servants to fulfill your every desire?"

I'm still standing at the viewing window, staring down at the tormented creature below. "Why her?" I find myself asking. "Why Faelyn Eliot?"

"I think you already know the answer."

He's right, of course. I do. "To send her father a message," I say. "Arthur Eliot showed signs of opposing you and your clients, though I'm guessing he'd been cooperating with you for decades before that. So you took his daughter. He knew that Faelyn's digital selves were at your clients' mercy, so he fell back in line, and fell deeper into drink. That about right?" I turn my head toward Bleak.

He nods. "The Guard might have posed a major problem for us. But other than that slight deviation, easily corrected, Eliot has been a valuable asset in keeping them at bay. Allowing the Guard's funding and resources to slowly dwindle."

"You've doomed us."

Bleak shrugs. "That depends on your definition of 'doomed.' The Guard were founded to protect the Subverse. But if humanity's elites are abandoning that place, what need of the Guard have they?"

"That isn't all the Guard does. They keep the galaxy stable. Or, they did."

"They did," Bleak says. "There will be a new order, now."

"I don't believe you that every member of the Five Families has signed up to buy one of your constructs," I say. "They can't all be corrupt."

"No," the pirate lord says. "Just the ones who'll rule the galaxy for eternity."

I've turned away from him again, to stare at the restless beast below. But Bleak continues: "I'm told you were offered the opportunity to take a place in the new galactic order. To be a person of consequence, and not a slave. You must be regretting your refusal of that offer, about now."

I turn my head toward him again, in time to see Harmony step forward, so that she's directly behind him.

"Harmony, no," I say the moment I comprehend what she's planning, but she's too fast for any of us, including the pirates surrounding Bleak.

She unsnaps his holster and plucks out the laser pistol. Before

Bleak can turn to confront her, she places the pistol's muzzle against the back of his kneecap.

Then she fires, blowing out the pirate lord's knee. He shrieks in pain, collapsing to the floor, clutching his leg.

12

"No one move," Harmony says, stepping over the pirate lord to level the weapon at his head. "Dad, get your gun."

I cross the room to where my blaster lies near the closed hatch and scoop it up. Bleak shows no signs of falling silent. On the contrary: his cries are getting even more shrill and desperate.

The pirates—the ones Bleak apparently hand-selected for his personal guard—mostly look baffled that Peter Vance's wife is behaving this way.

"Get with the program," I bark at them, and a few of them jump. "Toss your weapons on the ground and kick them toward me, every one of you. Or your boss gets a laser bolt to the brain." They hesitate, and I shout: "*Now!*"

Once the first pirate relinquishes his weapon, the rest follow suit. They just needed someone to follow. Like sheep.

The last one kicks his pistol over, and I look at Harmony. "They don't know you're my daughter?" I ask, squinting.

"Of course not."

"But Fairfax knew."

Harmony shrugs. "Guess their communication isn't great."

A pirate chooses that moment to sprint to a nearby control

panel. "Stop!" I yell, but he doesn't. I shoot him, but he presses something on the panel before slumping to the floor.

"What did he just do?" I say, glancing at Harm.

"How should I know?"

The snake crashes against the observation window again, its mammoth head filling the view before recoiling again.

"Peter," Bleak moans from the floor, where he continues to writhe. "Do something."

Bleak's son walks toward me, looking me in the eye. I can see he's trembling, but the steady eye contact throws me for a loop.

"What do you think you're doing?" I say.

He crouches, hand reaching toward one of the laser pistols, eyes still locked on mine.

My eyes are narrowed, but I let him take the weapon, more interested than anything else. If he points it at Harmony or me, I can shoot him before he even thinks of pulling the trigger.

He turns and approaches Harmony, pistol pointed at the floor. She moves aside for him, though she keeps her weapon trained on Bleak's head.

Peter Vance presses the weapon against the back of his father's uninjured knee. Then, he pulls the trigger, eliciting an agonized howl from Bleak that seems like it will never end.

The color's draining from Vance's face, but even so, he looks satisfied. He lowers the laser pistol to the floor and kicks it over to join the others.

"All right, then," I say, and clear my throat. "Bleak. Bleak!"

"What, you asshole!" He follows that with a string of darker expletives.

"We're leaving this place," I say once he's finished. "Call off your people."

"You are never, *never* leaving this place!" he shrieks. "*Ever!*"

The snake crashes against the glass, and the room shudders. Can the window really withstand that kind of assault?

I point my blaster at Bleak's head. "Call off your people, and tell me where I can find Faelyn's body."

"We don't have it, you filthy lowlife *bastard!*"

"What do you mean, you don't have it?"

"It's *gone*, Fount damn you. Disposed of. That was…one of the Allfather's commands. Eliot doesn't get his daughter back. Ever. Just like you'll never leave this place alive."

The snake slams itself against the observation window, and this time, there's an audible splintering sound.

Everyone in the room takes a step back from the window, eyes glued to it.

"Harmony," I say, my voice suddenly breathless. "Come away from there."

She shoots me a look, then gestures at Bleak with her weapon. "Kinda busy," she says.

"That's not—"

The snake head hits the glass again, and this time the glass shatters, sending fragments flying through the room in every direction. It hesitates, as though momentarily surprised at its own success. Then, it surges into the room, dripping blood as the remaining glass shards rip at its scales.

13

"Harmony!" I yell. The snake blocks her from view, and I'm terrified that it's crushing her right now beneath its girth.

It darts to the left, sinking meter-long fangs into a pirate who was attempting to flee toward the hatch. He's impaled in two places, which brings an end to his flight. The snake shakes him off, then engulfs him with its mouth, swallowing him whole.

I back toward the hatch, pointing the blaster at the beast and spamming the trigger, aiming for its eyes. Faelyn Eliot may well be inside there somewhere, but right now the serpent she inhabits poses a threat to my daughter—provided Harmony's still alive. Getting the thing's attention and drawing it away from here is probably the only chance to keep Harmony safe.

It ignores the blaster, its head darting across the room to devour another pirate, not bothering to chew this time. He disappears down the snake's gullet, and for a moment his screaming can be heard echoing up its length.

The floor is slick with blood, mostly the snake's blood, but the crushed and punctured pirates have no doubt made their contribution.

"Dad!"

It's Harmony, and I turn in the direction of her voice, fearing the worst. She cowers to my right, in the corner of the room, looking terrified but unharmed, as far as I can tell. Her husband cowers there with her, clutching her, looking at least as afraid as she does, probably more.

Her cry draws the snake's attention too, and it turns its massive head toward her, tensing to strike.

"*Hey!*" I bark. I stop spamming the blaster's trigger, draw a deep breath, and aim straight for its left eye slit. My focus is singular. I pull the trigger, and the bolt pierces the bulbous orb, sending blood and ichor spurting into the air.

The snake hisses, its sibilance filling the observation room, followed by a sound that's something like a croak crossed between an alien hatching from its egg.

It turns toward me. "Yes!" I yell. "Come and get some!"

My datasphere prompts me with the location of the hatch's control panel behind me, and I slap it without looking. For the time being, the way is clear of drones, at least according to the lack of warning black patches appearing across my field of vision.

I back through, yelling inarticulately and spamming the trigger with the blaster pointed at the snake's other eye. I miss every shot, but at least it's apparently getting the message.

The moment I set foot across the threshold, it lunges, and I stumble back just in time to avoid its fangs.

The wall around the hatch buckles toward me, and all I can see is the black hole down which the two pirates vanished. I fire the blaster down it, tensing, not sure what my next move should be. Are the hatch and wall reinforced? Does it matter? I have to assume the containment chamber that had once held the snake was reinforced, and it broke free of that.

The behemoth draws back, and I leap sideways as it throws itself against the hatch once more.

Again, I barely avoid becoming its next snack. The snake surges through the hatch, the metal blossoming around it. It collides with the labyrinth wall beyond, which suffers cracks up and down its length. The entire maze shudders, judging by the tumult rising from beyond.

I'm already running along the optimized path back to the doorway where I originally entered the labyrinth. The datasphere has optimized my course through it, cutting all the backtracking and circling around and presenting the way out as a green-tinged path on the floor before me.

But as the great serpent crashes through barrier after barrier, I realize this won't get me there fast enough. I start running into the tank people again, and though they concern me a lot less than they once did, they're slowing my progress too much.

I push through the first group of them I encounter as their fingers grasp at my suit for purchase, seeking flesh, and ripping and tearing with their nails when they find it.

I barely feel the scratches and tears they impart. The adrenaline pulses too powerfully through my veins. But I know they'll be the death of me, if this keeps up.

My blaster hand finds itself pressing the weapon up against one of the drone's chins, and I pull the trigger, blowing him up and back. Shooting two more drones point-blank clears my path, and just as I fight through, the snake crashes into the wall we're standing next to. The rest of the drones are crushed to death between the two labyrinth walls, and I have to snatch my foot out of the way to prevent it from going two-dimensional.

I stumble around the next turn and find myself standing at the start of a long corridor. A drone stumbles into it from a pathway to the left, but I shoot it, and it falls backward, clearing the runway I'm looking for.

Legs pumping, breath coming in ragged gasps, I sprint down the corridor. A tank person emerges at the very end, but I jump anyway, hands extended to grasp the top of the barrier.

My fingers find purchase, and my legs slam into the drone, pinning him against the wall. His hands wrap around my leg, and I kick his face with my other foot, which loosens his grasp. I pull myself up.

As I'm steadying myself atop the labyrinth wall, the snake breaks into the corridor I just ran along. It darts along its length, quicker than I would have thought possible, and before I can react it's smashing against the wall below me. I fall back onto the creature, tumbling over its head and onto its broad, scaled back, scrabbling for purchase.

There's nothing to grip. I flip off the beast instead, somersaulting against my will into the adjacent corner and landing on my shoulder.

Pain lances through my torso, emanating from the injury, but I grit my teeth against it and drag myself to my feet. I run to the end of this corridor and take a left, my datasphere's green path nowhere to be seen.

The snake has less leverage now to crash through in my direction, and I can hear it beating itself against the barrier separating it from me. That buys me time. When a drone comes into the hallway ahead, I grab him by his hair and toss him into the path behind me, where he hits the floor, sprawling. A snack for the snake, hopefully. Eat him, not me.

I hear the giant break through behind me, followed by its rustling progress toward me. The fact it's turning a corner must be slowing it down, though, since I have time to run, leap, and scrabble atop the next wall.

Then, the snake crashes into the wall I'm on again. This time, I have a leg hooked over the other side, and I manage to stay on top. As it recoils for another go, I let myself fall down the other side, turning right so that it'll have to go around more corners to get at me.

Soon, there won't be much left of the maze. It occurs to me that maybe I can backtrack and use the parts the snake destroyed to navigate, but I quickly scrap that idea. From what I saw of its length in the observation room, it won't run out of body before it completely encircles me, crushing or devouring me. I need to leave this place as soon as I can.

A tightly packed group of tank people appear around the corner up ahead, obstructing the only path I can take. They're in the way of a running leap, and the snake will get through behind me in a few seconds.

So I drop to one knee and point my blaster at them, spamming the trigger and sweeping it across, dropping them one after another.

Then the snake breaks through behind me, and I have to go. I make a run at the press of bodies, both dead and alive, and I attempt to use them as a height boost to get to the top of the next wall.

It doesn't work. My foot slips on some limply hanging limb, and I start falling backward.

Grasping desperately for something to prevent that, I find a wrist. When my fingers close around it, it grabs back, but the body it's attached to shifts with me, so that I continue to fall.

The snake is rushing toward us. My blaster hand finds the head of a drone who's still standing, and somehow I manage to use it to propel myself to the right, into the next passage.

The drone is still gripping my forearm, and I smash the blaster against her fingers until she releases me. Then, I continue on, hoping fervently that the snake will take the feast of people I just left behind for it.

I glance back—no such luck. The snake pushes through the body pile, crushing them beneath it and against both walls. They're slowing it somewhat, but not enough. Fount damn it.

Then, I see it: the green path! It intersects with this corridor, up ahead. I run for all my worth, skidding around the corner just as the snake catches up to me.

Its head slams against the wall a couple feet away, and I flee down the green path. Before I turn, I register how much blood coats its great triangular head. Its scales are wet with it, but it still shows no sign of slowing.

I take a left, then a right, then I have a long corridor to run down, the snake in close pursuit, rustling through the maze, always just a few meters behind.

And then, suddenly, I've reached the beginning. I'm back where I was.

Gripping the cold metal knob, I twist it, wrenching the door open and running through to the pool area beyond.

This is my fault, this situation. That's no mystery. I failed to protect Faelyn on Tunis, and I chose to go to Arbor over Xeo. If I'd come here first, I might have prevented her from becoming a giant snake.

One of my many failures. But given she *is* a giant snake, now, inside a biological vessel intended to soon house one of the beings apparently intent on dominating the galaxy…maybe it's a failure I can actually do something about.

I need to kill it. Her. Whatever pronoun is appropriate in this situation.

My negligence—mine—led to this situation. Not just losing Faelyn, but the risk of losing the entire galaxy.

I'm ready to accept that fact.

"Time to finally take responsibility for something," I mutter as I run to the right, around the pool and toward one of the grated observation decks.

14

I reach the bottom stair as the snake starts assailing the doorway and wall. The first thrust knocks the door almost out of its frame, though it's still holding on by a hinge. I start racing up the two flights of stairs that lead to the observation deck above.

The snake's snout pokes through with the second thrust, and it rears back for a third. By that time, I'm on the metal grate, trying to steady my breathing as I take aim at one of the brackets holding the central cable to the ceiling above.

A tumult of screeching metal and the snake is through, sending shrapnel to skitter across the floor and pool deck, some of it splashing into the water.

I've managed to blast away one bracket, and now I'm working on the next. It doesn't take long for the snake to spot me. It rushes forward, its great head hurtling through the air toward me.

I abandon my shooting, running across the metal grate at full speed. It shudders beneath my footfalls.

The snake's jaws clamp onto the deck, barely missing me. A fang punctures it clean through, and the snake jerks back, trying to pull away, but the caught tooth holds it there. It panics, then, body thrashing. A screeching, tearing sound, and it manages to pull the entire grate away from the wall. Luckily, I'm on the next section, which only bucks a little.

Part of the snake's body is in the water, now, and it sends waves splashing over the sides as it tries to free itself from the enormous grate protruding from its maw. I take the opportunity to finish shooting away the second bracket, then I start on the next.

Something snaps, and the grate flies across the room to crash against the far wall. The sound is deafening, but I manage not to flinch, through sheer force of will. My aim remains steady, and a fourth bracket comes away under my blaster fire. Then the snake refocuses on me.

I flee. The beast comes at me from below, this time, its head causing the deck to buck wildly. Suddenly, I'm airborne, flying toward the edge of this section.

Then I'm coming down on the edge, and the landing isn't graceful. I tumble forward to land face-first on the next section of grating, head smacking painfully against the corrugated metal.

Dazed, I manage to regain my feet, but when I try to look at the next bracket I find I'm seeing double.

I shake my head, but the snake is coming again, and I turn to flee.

It rears up, head hard against the cables above. Its intentions are clear: next, it's going to cut me off by coming in at me from ahead. Because of the ruined grates behind me, I can't retreat.

Gripping my blaster like the lifeline it is, I take aim at the eye I've already injured, then squeeze the trigger. The bolt hits squarely where the last one did, and the snake hisses, recoiling to crash against the opposite observation decks in a desperate bid to get away.

My eyes lock onto the next bracket, and suddenly my concentration is total, maybe because I know this is the last opportunity I'm likely to get. The fifth and sixth brackets pop off with one shot each, and then I'm firing at the cable itself, bolt after bolt to try to sever it in two.

The snake is recovering, and its hissing is louder than it's been. Clearly it's pissed, and it doesn't plan to miss again. It's lining up it's next strike, just like a Troubleshooter lining up his shot.

Then the beast is darting forward. I get off one more bolt, then I'm leaping for the grate that was knocked out of its brackets. The end nearest me is now too high for me to jump onto, but I manage to grasp its end with my left hand, clutching the blaster with my right.

As I hang there, the snake crashes into the wall behind me, and the cable sparks above us, holding on by a few tendrils.

Summoning what feels like the last of my energy, I raise my arm and fire at the cable one last time. The shot severs one of the tethers holding it in place, and the weight of the cable does the rest of the work. It tears away, and falls into the water.

With that, the snake shrieks—a piercing, otherworldly sound. It thrashes wildly, massive body spasming, muscles constricting. As it convulses, it pulls more and more of itself into the pool, until even its head is submerged.

Part of its body bucks toward the grate I'm clinging to, and I release, knowing the grate will carry the shock to my body if I don't.

I land poorly on the deck below, slipping on the slick surface and getting banged up in several places, though I manage to keep my head from smacking off the hard floor.

Across the room, more and more of the snake's length is pulsing through the breach it made as the electricity forces it to convulse and constrict. Then, its tail comes through, and I take my chance to escape without getting shocked or crushed against the wall.

Beyond, the labyrinth bears the signs of our passage. Great furrows have been gouged through, smeared with the blood of the snake as well as that of the tank people. Mine, too, probably, though I've had no time to take stock of my injuries.

Harmony is still with the pirates, so I hobble as fast as I can manage through the labyrinth, if it can still be called that. A glassy-eyed drone waits for me behind one of the battered walls, but he doesn't bother me. Maybe he's had enough for one day. I know I have.

"Fleshbag," someone calls from my right, and I turn, staring in disbelief.

"Dice. Holy shit."

He strides toward me, dark metal gleaming dully under the halogens. "Yes. An expression of surprise seems appropriate, given my escape from the pirates in the face of overwhelming odds."

"Incredible timing, too," I say. "I just finished dealing with a giant snake."

The bot tilts it head to one side. "A what? Have you lost your wits?"

Before I can answer, a rumbling comes from behind me, from the direction of the pool area. Fount. "Never mind," I say, frowning. "Turns out I didn't kill it. Come on. Follow me."

Together, the bot and I flee through the maze—an easier task than before, thanks to the new paths the snake trampled through it. My injuries don't help, but I try to ignore them as best I can.

"How did you get to the labyrinth without my seeing you?" I say. "Was there another entrance?"

Dice nods. "I came from a door in that direction." He jerks his thumb to indicate the way.

The snake seems slower than before. It apparently lacks the wits to retrace its path, and it batters new paths through, though with less vigor than before. It takes longer for it to break through.

"What is that?" Dice asks, glancing at me as we continue to run.

"I told you. A giant snake."

He faces forward again. I can tell he's still skeptical, but I'm sure it's hard to reconcile the idea that I've lost it with the sound of the behemoth chasing us.

"It's Faelyn," I say softly. "What's left of her."

"She's…inside the snake?"

"Yeah."

"Can we put her back where she was?"

"No. Faelyn's gone, Dice."

We reach the observation room, where most of the pirates have fled. Harmony is here, with Vance and Bleak, who they've dragged to a wall. Or maybe he was pushed there by the snake. Either way, they're all still alive.

"Get into that corner!" I yell at them, pointing at the same one Harmony had been in before. "Go!"

"I won't leave my father," Vance says, which seems like a change of pace from shooting out his one remaining kneecap.

"Harm, get in the corner!" I say. "Leave those idiots where they are."

But she helps her husband drag Bleak to the corner instead, and that will have to do.

"Down there," I say to Dice, pointing past the stalactites and stalagmites of shattered glass. "We'll make our last stand down there. Hopefully it will be enough."

A single tong projects from Dice's right forearm, on the opposite side of his arm from the laser pistol. It splits apart to become a grappling hook, which he secures between two broad glass shards.

That done, he leaps into the pit, and I follow him down, using his line to rappel down the wall. Above us, the broken glass rattles in its frame as the snakes surges nearer.

We reach the bottom, and the grappling line feeds fully out of Dice's arm, freeing him. I can hear the snake passing through the observation room as we sprint across the pit that once held it. Its birthplace, presumably, and hopefully also its place of dying.

We turn together to face the snake as it wends its way down toward us from the observation room, seeming to grin as its tongue flicks past its fangs.

It doesn't have much to grin about. I can hear the glass daggers ripping its flesh as it pushes past them. Blood runs in rivulets between its scales, falling to the floor in a curtain of red.

Dice and I open fire. "Aim for the eyes," I yell, before realizing he's already doing that.

We're jogging backwards, though Dice's aim remains steady enough that he might as well be standing still. My shots are finding their mark about half the time, which isn't bad, all things considered.

The snake's progress is slowing, and though it trends in our direction, both its eyes are now punctured, useless.

At last, it comes almost to a stop, but still inching slowly toward us.

It's dying—and not a moment too soon. We just reached the wall behind us.

"Wait," Dice says. "What if we transfer Faelyn's consciousness into me?"

I look at him. "Is that possible?"

He nods.

"What would happen to you?"

"Do you care?"

"No." I draw a breath to call out to Harmony, but I don't.

Dice does. "I can house a human consciousness," he shouts, voice amplified beyond what a human would be capable of. "There are precedents."

Harmony appears at the window, next to the snake, which is still oozing through the window but doesn't seem to pose much danger any longer. Her gaze runs along the snake's length, and she yells, "Come up, then. We don't have long."

The grappling line is trapped underneath the snake, so we end up climbing its scales, which isn't helped by the fact it's still pushing into the pit in its daze. Dice makes it look easy, and he's up well before I am. After a few minutes, Harmony tosses down a line she must have found somewhere, and I use it to clamber the rest of the way up.

Peter Vance crouches near his father, who appears to be uncon-scious—whether from pain, shock, or exhaustion, I don't know. Dice sits in an alcove in the wall to my left, connected to the terminal around him by several wires, and Harmony works at an interface nearby.

"I don't see us getting the snake back up here," I say.

"We don't need to," Harmony says. "It was engineered with implants inside its brain, so that it can receive a consciousness wirelessly. Shouldn't be hard to reverse the process."

"Won't Faelyn's consciousness be expanded, after getting transferred to the construct? I thought you couldn't transfer an expanded mind back."

"We wouldn't be able to—not back into her body, if we still had it. But D1C's hardware can accommodate her mind. It wasn't stretched that much. Most of the snake's consciousness was just noise, put there to prevent any risk of Faelyn from harnessing its full potential."

"How do you know how to do all this?"

She shrugs. "I watched Bleak's scientists while they worked. Listened to them. Wasn't hard to figure out."

Dice just sits there through all this, saying nothing.

"Thanks for doing this, Dice. It's…actually pretty incredible," I say.

He doesn't answer.

"And thank you for your service."

After another few minutes of fiddling with the controls, Harmony extracts what looks like a drive from the console. I have no idea what she's doing, but I trust she does. She punches in a few more commands, then turns, nodding. "We're ready."

"Dice?" I say.

"Do it."

Harmony enters a final command, and Dice gives a slight jolt. For a moment, he just sits there. Then, he rises shakily to his feet, staring down at his own hands.

But I can tell it isn't Dice any longer.

Faelyn Eliot falls to her knees, metal hands wrapped around her new body, emitting what sounds like sobbing.

I exchange glances with Harmony, and then she goes over to wrap her arms around Faelyn.

15

After Faelyn's transfer into Dice's body, Peter Vance ran from the room and returned ten minutes later with a medkit. I let him bandage up his father's knees as best he can.

Lucky for Bleak, the kneecap doesn't have any main arteries, otherwise he would have bled out by now. I should probably kill him myself, but hell. Maybe I'm going soft. He is Harmony's father-in-law, after all.

After Vance finishes ministering to the father whose kneecap he himself blew out, I make him lead us back up through the research facility, calling off his father's henchmen whenever we encounter them.

The pirates look surprised to be taking orders from Peter Vance, but they obey. I guess Bleak didn't find time to spread the word about what Vance did. Harmony being with us probably helps, too. A few of the pirates cast dark looks at Faelyn and I, no doubt remembering shootouts with me and Dice as we made our way through the facility.

As we walk, I bend toward Harmony and mutter, "Where did that laser pistol end up, that you lifted from me back on Calabar?"

"It's on *Europa's Gift.*"

"Do I get it back?"

"No."

Hmm. Just as well, I guess.

When we reach the landing bay at last, I find the *Ares* pretty banged up, but spaceworthy as far as I can tell. Diagnostics synced with my datasphere confirm that assessment. Good.

Among the other ships parked in the landing bay, I spot *Europa's Gift* settled near the doors.

Me, Faelyn, Harmony, and Vance now form a circle near my ship, with Harmony and her husband staring awkwardly at each other from opposite ends of it.

"Go back to your father, Peter," she says.

Vance blinks, his shoulders hunched. 'What will you do?" he asks softly, though I think he already senses the answer.

"I'm leaving."

"What? Without me?"

"That's right."

"But we're married," he says, whining now.

She nods. "And maybe we'll meet again someday. If you survive what your father's going to do to you."

Vance pales. "Let me come with you."

Harmony shakes her head. "You have things to face here. And I don't need a husband who flinches whenever I look at him. Look, we got married. That hasn't changed. And maybe, one day, you'll be up to it."

Peter flinches, then stares at her like a kicked puppy.

"Go," Harmony says firmly, and he turns to slink away, back into the facility.

That leaves just the three of us. Faelyn is twitchy but silent, and Harmony looks about to speak.

Before she can, I say, "There's someone aboard the *Ares* who'd like to speak to you, Harm." I've already sent the order to switch off Asterisk, Belflower, and Moe—no need to break it to her she has two fathers now, for the time being. Harmony will be coming with us now, anyway, so if Moe wants to see her I'm sure there'll be time later.

She gives me an odd look before turning toward the *Ares*. The airlock recognizes her as my daughter, opening for her, and she disappears inside.

"How are you doing?" I ask Faelyn, after a few minutes of silence.

"I'm scared, Joe," she says. The voice comes out as hers, not Dice's, though it bears the same reverberation as all bot voices. I'm not sure why she sounds like herself. I guess the software must compile whatever voice fits the consciousness inside the bot best, and the speakers project that.

But if you'd asked me before this, I would have told you that Dice's voice was just the one he came packaged with. I hadn't considered that he might have chosen that flat, disaffected sound.

"Of course you are," I say. Back on Tunis, Faelyn struck me as remarkably resilient, and she clearly is. But what she's gone through would be enough to break an adult. Forget puberty—her body didn't change gradually over years, it transformed radically, twice in the same week. "You've been through something no one should have to go through, let alone a girl your age."

She raises her metal hands. "I'm not a *girl* anymore. I'm something else."

"You're still Faelyn Eliot," I tell her. "You're still Faelyn."

She pauses. Then: "Back on Tunis, you said I shouldn't invite any bots to be in my play, because bots can't act. You said a bot just is what it is." Even synthesized, her voice trembles with emotion.

I study her blank face—the same face that had always fit Dice's detached persona so well. But why was Dice detached? What made him that way? The questions are rhetorical, of course. I'm sure I know the answers.

"I had no idea what I was talking about," I tell her.

Faelyn sits on the floor and cradles her metal head in her

hands. I continue standing, staring across the landing bay at nothing. Distractedly, I wonder whether P3P, the old family bot Harmony took with her when she left Calabar, is still inside *Europa's Gift*.

A few minutes later, Harmony emerges from the *Ares*, her jaw set.

"She tried to convince me to upload," she says, after I raise my eyebrows. "She's convinced the Subverse is the only place anyone can be safe and happy, anymore."

"What did you say?"

"I told her no."

"Of course. Well, I'm glad you see through what they're selling, with the Subverse. Now, let's go home."

She tilts her head. "Home? You don't mean Brinktown?"

"I do."

"I don't think so. Why would I want to go there?"

I'm about to respond, but I close my mouth again. There isn't really a good answer for that. Not any I'm aware of. "There's nowhere else to take you," I say at last.

"I wouldn't worry about that. You won't be *taking* me anywhere."

I draw a breath. "Harm. You can't keep doing this. I can't let you go off by yourself again."

"You can't stop me. Listen, Joe. I don't know what would have happened down there if you hadn't shown up. But I played a part in it, too. I helped you get the drop on Bleak." She shakes her head. "I was planning to escape in Sterling's ship in the next few days, to let you know what they were up to here."

"You were gonna escape through the blockade of pirate ships they had parked around the planet?"

She shrugs. "I would have figured it out. I always do."

"Where were you planning to go, after you left Xeo?"

"Out of the Brink. Coreward."

"How would you get past the sector barrier?" I ask slowly.

"Bleak had exit coords, and Peter knew it. I helped him access them without tipping his father off. Peter is good for some things, you know."

I rub my forehead, trying my best to process it all. The slip coords that link each sector are some of the most closely guarded secrets in the galaxy. I guess Bleak's clients must be just as powerful as he said they were. Still, the idea that a pirate has access to that kind of information…

"Harm…you don't know what you want right now. You think you do, but you don't. And that's understandable. You've had a messed up life, because I had a messed up life. But you have no idea what you'll find in the Mid-Systems. It could be anything. Or it might be nothing, and you'll starve. Food gets scarcer as you move toward the Core."

"I know that. And you're right—I don't know what I'll find. That's part of the adventure, isn't it?"

I shake my head. "That's a really naive way of looking at it."

"Joe, you've never really been a father to me. And you don't get to start now. Look, I'll give you the slip coords, if you want them. I'm sure Bleak isn't the only one working for the elites on projects like this one, and someone needs to stop them. I'm going to look for more information. But you can't follow me. Not yet. You have other things to face." Her gaze drifts to Faelyn. With that, she turns to walk across the landing bay, toward *Europa's Gift*.

"Harm," I call after her. She stops, turning her head.

"Did you…" I say, then clear my throat. "Did you consummate the marriage?"

She laughs bitterly. "And risk creating a baby to grow up in a situation as messed up as the one you left me in? Bleak thinks we did, but no."

She walks the rest of the way to her ship, and the airlock opens to admit her. I watch her disappear inside.

ARES

1

Marissa doesn't react well to the idea that Harmony is going off on her own again. I put off our discussion about it until we're in slipspace, by activating the other crewmembers and keeping them online till we make the transition.

Even then, I consider deactivating her along with them. But I know that will only make our eventual conversational even worse.

So after we reach slipspace, it's just me and Marissa on the bridge. Faelyn is in my cabin—I let her have it for the trip, and she went in there as soon as we boarded. She hasn't been out since. Eventually, she'll need to go into Dice's Repair and Recharge module, else she'll shut down. But folding herself into the cramped space isn't going to do much for her recovery.

"Do you think the others have started wondering why we spend so much time talking alone?" I say, before Marissa can speak.

"Yes," she says, her tone icy. "I think they suspect there's something going on between us. As in, romantically."

"What could be farther from the truth?" I say.

"Joe, how could you let Harmony leave? How could you subject her to that kind of danger?"

"I didn't subject her to anything. She makes her own choices, just like we did when we were sixteen. She'll be seventeen next month. I wasn't about to wrestle her onto the *Ares*, or try to force her to upload like you seem to want."

Marissa narrows her eyes. "I don't want to force her to do anything."

"You want her to upload. But you're making my point for me. I didn't want to force her either. That's why she's gone."

"You could have tried harder, Joe," Marissa says, though she's crying, now. Big, fat, digital tears. I'm starting to realize that I resent Marissa for uploading, even though her father forced *her*. "You could have said something."

"I'm not good with words," I say, then shut her off before laying back in the command seat and closing my eyes.

Just before we entered slipspace, a brainprint arrived from Dorothy Pikeman, but I'm not eager to crack it open to see what she has to say. I have plenty of time to speak to her, anyway. This leg of the journey is going to last three months, and the next will be nearly as long. It's a fairly direct route to Tunis, but we still have a lot of space to cover.

Almost six months. Plenty of time for the corrupt members of the Five Families attempting to break out of the Subverse to make more progress. I sent a message to Gauntlet alerting the Guard to the children held in stasis on Xeo, and I like to think they'll go to collect them. But even if they do, I'm sure it won't slow Fairfax and his people for long. They'll soon be back on track with their plans to enslave what's left of humanity.

Six months is also plenty of time for Harmony to get into trouble, with her father thousands of light years away. Much too far to help.

During the trip, I reactivate Marissa several more times, but each conversation is worse than the last. I find myself saying things to intentionally piss her off.

"That's my girl," I say when she mentions Harmony's refusal to entertain uploading to the Subverse. That gets a poisonous glare from Marissa, which I can understand. Convincing Harmony to upload would have been the only way for them to truly be together.

But Marissa doesn't get it. Harm is her father's daughter. She'll never upload.

I don't know why I keep reactivating Marissa to talk. Sometimes I let days go by, and once, on the second subspace leg of the journey, I let weeks pass. But I always bring her back onto the bridge eventually, to talk again. Maybe I do it just to guard my own sanity. Arguing with her is better than gibbering madly to myself.

One thing does come out of our conversations: Marissa lets slip that before leaving, Harmony asked her for a copy of every brainprint her mother ever sent her, straight from Marissa's "sent" folder. I spend several hours puzzling over why she'd make such a weird request, but I can't come up with anything. She'd have copies in her account of the conversations she had with those same brainprints, so why ask for her mother's?

Faelyn keeps me occupied, too. I do what I can to help her get used to life as a bot, and to kill time I play chess with her on a projected board. She beats me handily every time—it's like playing against a computer, and I wasn't very good to begin with.

I wonder what growing up will look like for her, now. Despite what I told her in the facility's landing bay on Xeo, she'll never become a woman. But will she still reach mental maturity, or will she forever be an eleven-year-old stuck in a bot's body? Bots aren't programmed to house a consciousness that's still developing, but maybe Faelyn's mind will take care of that on its own.

Mentally, she's still in chaos, but she seems to get better every day. She doesn't break down into synthesized sobbing quite so much, or suddenly become unresponsive, as she has three times since we left Xeo. The third time, she wouldn't react to any stimulus for two full days, even though she'd recharged just a few days before. That kept me awake, hunting desperately through my datasphere's storehouse of knowledge for a solution, until suddenly she came back to me. Ever since then, she's seemed better.

A couple weeks ago, she started spending time with Maneater, who instantly accepted her, to my surprise. They often cuddle on the bunk, and Faelyn is careful not to harm her with her newfound strength, even though I'm pretty sure the German Shepherd could withstand a lot.

It's still odd to look at my old partner's body and know that he isn't in there anymore—that an eleven-year-old girl has taken his place. I wouldn't have expected Dice to do what he did on Xeo. I wouldn't have guessed he had it in him.

But then, I've realized that even after a decade of serving together, I didn't really know Dice at all.

Near the end of the second trip through slipspace, I open Dorothy Pikeman's brainprint. We're alone on the bridge—I'm leaning against the railing that encircles Marissa's station.

Dorothy appears near Asterisk's, her silver hair disheveled, her mouth hanging open in dismay. "Joe, what in the galaxy is going on? Why haven't you opened this brainprint till now?"

"I've been, uh…avoiding the conversation."

Her eyes widen in anger. "Because you knew you wouldn't like what I had to say."

"That's about right, yeah."

"Joe, I've been kept completely in the dark by you. Ever since Harmony left, I've been all by myself here in Brinktown, wondering if she's even still alive. Then a ship came to pluck Daniel Sterling out of his mansion, without any explanation, which has everyone in a flurry. You said you would do something."

Suppressing a sigh, I say, "I did something."

"And? Is Harmony safe."

"I don't know."

"How can you not know?"

"She was safe when I saw her, a few months ago. But I haven't seen her since."

"You left her? Your own daughter. You abandoned her."

"I tried to convince her to come with me. But I failed."

"How can you be so calm? Joe, I can barely sleep. I spend every day pacing the apartment, waiting for a brainprint that never comes. I'm so alone here, and no one ever thinks of me. You never thought of me, not when you were out in the streets of Brinktown causing trouble for us, and not now."

"You're right," I say.

She pauses with her mouth open, then she closes it slowly. "What?"

"I agree with you."

Her eyes widen, but she doesn't answer.

"This is a big mess," I say, "and I played a big part in making it. Possibly, all of it's my fault. Seriously."

Dorothy blinks, then shakes her head, looking bewildered.

"All I can say right now, Aunt Dorothy, is thank you. My father left you with a lot, and then so did I. You were far from the perfect parent. But you didn't abandon me, and you didn't abandon Harm. You raised us up as best you could, for someone who never wanted kids in the first place. So thank you."

Dorothy's shoulders rise and fall as she takes a breath. "Thank you. For saying that."

I nod. "I'm gonna work on making things better, okay? Not saying I know the first thing about doing that, but I'm gonna try. I know saying that isn't much, but it's what I have to give you without bullshitting you. So I'm giving it."

"All right, Joe. All right."

TUNIS

1

Faelyn and I draw curious stares as we cross the Grotto in the dry heat. A lot of the damage from the pirate attack has been repaired in the months since. It seems peace has returned to Tunis. For now. I wonder how long it will last.

We near the red-brick monstrosity where the Eliots live, and I hear Faelyn start to sob quietly beside me. Out of happiness or fear, I'm not sure. It could be a mixture of both.

"Are you sure they'll take me back like this?" she asks, for the thousandth time since we left Xeo.

"Of course," I say. "They're your parents. They'll be happy to get you back in any form."

She doesn't look so sure.

"Hey," I say. "I'm leaving Maneater here with you. She'll be yours, from now on."

Faelyn's head whips toward me, and even in a bot's body, a young girl's excitement shines through. "Really? Thank you!"

"Don't mention it. Uh, maybe change her name, though. And try not to let her eat your parents." I've heard that once a dog has the taste of human flesh, there's no going back. So they'll probably have to keep the German Shepherd on a tight leash. Faelyn won't have any problem, of course, since she's made of metal now. And I'm sure she'll be responsible with controlling the dog around other people. As for Arthur, I for one won't care too much if he gets eaten.

We mount the front step, and I try the door without knocking. It's unlocked, so I pull it open and step inside, Faelyn right behind me.

"Eliot!" I yell. I stand facing Arthur Eliot's office door. Faelyn hangs back, staring at the floor.

A few moments of silence pass, and I wonder if he's even home. Then, the office door creaks open, and Eliot staggers out, clearly drunk.

"What?" he asks in that ugly way some people have when they're thoroughly intoxicated.

Originally, I'd planned to launch into a lengthy explanation of how Faelyn's consciousness ended up first inside a snake, and then inside my cybernetic partner's body. But Eliot's demeanor has robbed me of my will to do that. Instead, I try not to glare at him as I gesture toward Faelyn. "Your daughter. Returned to you."

A sneer twists Eliot's lips. "What kind of game is this?"

"I told you I would bring Faelyn back to you. And I have. Her physical body is lost, but her mind is now inside this bot."

"Wasn't that the whole point?" he asks. "To bring back her physical body? Her *mind* is copied a thousand times over, all across the galaxy."

I glance back at Faelyn, who has slumped even further. Then I take a step toward Eliot, hands curling into fists. "The *point* was to return your daughter to you, so that you can be together in this life. In *real* life, not some cheap copy of life, inside a magic trick performed by a computer."

"Arthur?" a voice calls from the stairs, and I look up to see Zelah Eliot's lithe form descending, a purple dress flaring around her legs. "What is it?"

"Mommy?" Faelyn says, and Zelah's eyes land on her, widening.

During this exchange, I'm using my datasphere to zoom in on Zelah's face, and I note the excess of makeup used there. Makeup to cover fresh bruises.

"You bastard," I say as I cross the foyer toward Arthur Eliot.

His face screws up in concentration as he puts up his fists to mount some manner of pathetic defense. My jab moves too fast for him to react, popping him between the eyes and putting him on the floor. That done, I pin him with my knees and begin smacking him with my fists, again and again. Blood spurts from his nose, his cheeks split, and his face is swelling already. Zelah is shrieking from the staircase, but Faelyn is completely silent, probably in shock.

"Stop this at once!" screams a voice from my left.

Then, a black-clad figure is knocking me off Eliot, and we're rolling together across the marble floor. I quickly gain the upper hand, pinning my assailant to the floor.

It's Sergeant Wile. I place a knee across his chest as he struggles to get up. "Stand down, Sergeant," I say, but he continues to fight. "*Stand down,* Sergeant," I bark, and this time he stays still.

I turn, then, heading back toward Eliot, who's still lying on his back, spitting up teeth and blood. I snap open my holster and remove the blaster, leveling it at his head.

"No!" Faelyn screams, and only the urgency in her voice stays my hand. She rushes forward and throws her metal body across her father, shielding him. A second later, Zelah arrives and adds her body.

"Don't," she says, looking up at me, her lip trembling. "Don't."

I stare at them both in disbelief. Then I lower the blaster.

"You don't have the right," she says, turning away, toward her husband. She lowers a hand to tenderly cup his bruised cheek.

That's an even bigger slap across the face. I stand over them, blaster in hand, seething. My teeth grind together, and my grip on the weapon is hard enough that I'm in danger of scoring their immaculate marble floor.

I could pull them off with ease and finish it. Maybe it would even be better for them, in the long run.

"You've been screwing the Guard for years, haven't you?" I yell at Arthur Eliot through his wife and cybernetic daughter. "Doing the bidding of the puppet masters behind this shitshow. Slowly killing what you created—the only organization that keeps the galaxy from descending into total anarchy." My breathing comes rapidly, now, my shoulders rising and falling, my back tense. "Then you started to show a little spine, so they took Faelyn, and you fell to pieces."

Eliot doesn't answer. I glance at the other Guardsman, where he stands near the bottom of the stairs, hands clenched into fists.

"Fount damn it," I spit. I march across the foyer and out the door.

Nothing about this feels right—leaving Faelyn and Zelah in the hands of the deranged thing Eliot has let himself become. But it's what they've apparently chosen, and I realize that ultimately, Zelah's correct: I don't have the right.

When I return to the *Ares*, I take Maneater outside and tie her to a post near the spacepad. Then, I kneel in front of her and ruffle her ears. "Goodbye, girl," I whisper. "Thanks for everything." She whines through the steel-cage muzzle, which I left on in case any unsuspecting Grotto residents happened upon her.

It's tough leaving her, but right, I think. Dogs don't belong in space. Definitely not on a ship as small as the *Ares*. "You held your own, though, girl." I kiss her on the top of the head, then I will the airlock to open and step inside.

When I do, there's a brainprint waiting from Daniel Sterling. I activate it right away.

"What?" I growl.

He raises his eyebrows. "Testy, aren't we?" He sneers, much like Eliot sneered a few minutes ago. "Where's my ship?"

"You'll never see your ship again. Where's my money?"

"What if I said the same to you?"

"Then the entire Subverse would hear about it, and the Sterling name would get even more mud on it."

The sneer widens. "Your tokens will be wired to your account."

"Thanks, Dad. I knew it was a good idea to get tangled up with a rich girl." Then I shut him off, for the contents of the conversation to make their way by spacescraper to whatever gaudy estate he's holed himself up in.

I drop into the command seat with my full weight and stare across the empty bridge.

I've always told myself that performing a Guardsman's duties meant protecting the people of this sector just as much as protecting Subverse infrastructure. But I'm beginning to think the Subverse isn't worth protecting, and the people of the Andora Sector don't want my help.

Well, that's unfair—I'm starting to calm down from the exchange inside the Eliots' foyer, and I can see that. The fact is, I've never had any idea how to actually help people. But somehow, in some screwed up way, I think I did the right thing by returning Faelyn to Tunis, even in cybernetic form. I may have even done a good thing, or at least something that will prove to be a net good.

And now that I have slip coords for entering the Mid-Systems...

"Activate crew."

Moe, Asterisk, Glory Belflower, and Marissa all appear at their respective stations.

Belflower gushes with enthusiasm. "Captain, your latest verse-cast is *blowing up.* Millions of people are glued to their datas-pheres, waiting to see where your story goes next. Your daughter leaves, after you went through all that trouble to save her? Faelyn Eliot turned into a snake, and then a bot, to be returned to her family in that form? It's *too* good. People are lapping it up."

I resist the urge to cover my face with my palm. For a moment,

I forgot that we were versecasting everything, now. "Wait. How do they know Harmony's my daughter?"

"Why, it was in the versecast I put out en route to Tunis," Belflower says, all innocence. "But I think it's time to change tacks," she says. "The 'lost-daughter' arc is played out, I think. But you've always had questions about your father's identity, right?"

My gaze snaps onto her face. "How do you know about *that?*"

Belflower waves her hand dismissively. "Please. You're the subject of an immense, crowd-sourced research project now. Every available detail of your life is being dug up by amateur biographers and held under the microscope. So, anyway. Here's what I have in mind: you're the classic troubled man, with lots of demons. You've done plenty of things you regret. And now you're on a quest, not just to save the galaxy, but to uncover the truth about what happened to your father. Did he really join the knighthood? Is he just a deadbeat like you consider yourself to be? Think of it, sir: a redemption story, combined with the quest to uncover your true origins. I'm going to make you the most famous versecaster in *history.*"

"Yeah. Fine," I say, trying to conceal how dazed I feel after the sound-bite-sized psychoanalysis Belflower just dropped on me. "Whatever." I turn to Moe. "I've transmitted exit coords to your console. Get me to them."

He stares at me for a long moment, and it crosses my mind to wonder how much longer he's going to be willing to follow my orders. He's been pretty pissed off ever since not getting the chance to see Harmony before she took off.

"Exit coords for this system?" he says at last.

"What? No. For this sector. Take the most efficient route through Andora. We're going to the Echo Sector. We don't have time for sightseeing, though we'll have to find somewhere to resupply along the way to Echo. I'm sure as hell not asking Eliot to do that." I pause, then add: "Harmony may need us, Moe."

His face sours, but he gets to work.

"We're going coreward?" Asterisk says, voice tinged with disbelief.

"That's right."

"Why? This isn't what I signed up for."

"None of this shit is what you signed up for. We're not a Guard ship anymore. We're effectively outlaws, now. Do what I say or I'll delete you. How about that?"

Asterisk turns. "You still haven't answered my question," he grumbles.

"You heard Belflower. We're saving the galaxy, or whatever. Just get me coreward."

Of course, saving the galaxy is so close to the end of my to-do list it might as well be missing. What has the galaxy ever done for me? There are two things I care about: making sure Harmony is safe and getting revenge on Fairfax—for kidnapping Faelyn and the rest of the children, for ruining their lives.

And for killing me. An eye for an eye, I say. Next, it's his turn.

ACKNOWLEDGMENTS

Thank you to my Alpha Team, who have been reading this book since its earliest stage and who've provided substantial feedback along the way, which helped me develop the story with my readers' desires foremost in mind. They are Rex Bain, Sheila Beitler, Mick Bird, Bruce Brandt, Iain Howard, Colin Oliver, Jason Pennock, Jeff Rudolph, and Ben Varela.

Thank you to my proofreading team, who helped eliminate scores of spelling and grammar issues. I take full responsibility for any mistakes that remain :) My proofreaders are Rex Bain, Bill Bartlett, Sheila Beitler, Bruce Brandt, and Jeff Rudolph.

A special thank you to my Patreon supporters at the Destroyer Captain, Supercarrier Captain, and Space Fleet Admiral levels. Your support helps me to package my books as professionally as possible while staying true to what my readers like best about my books. Thank you to Brent Lee Davis, Edward Goolsby, David Middleton, Lawrence Tate, and Michael Van De Hey (at the $25 Space Fleet Admiral level), Brian Loeung (at the $10 Supercarrier Captain level), and Andrew Mercer (at the $5 Destroyer Captain level).

Thank you also to Patreon supporters Rex Bain, Michael Bone,

Sid Echikson, Richard Gunn, Christian Kallias, John A Koenig III, Wynand Pretorius, Bill Scarborough, John Tava, Ben Varela, and Jerry Winiarski.

Thank you to Tom Edwards for creating such stunning cover art, as always.

Thank you to Steve Beaulieu for creating compelling cover typography and for formatting the interior.

Thank you to my family - Mom, Dad, and Danielle - your support means everything.

Thank you to Cecily, my heart.

Thank you to the people who read my stories, write reviews, and help spread the word. I couldn't do this without you.

ABOUT THE AUTHOR

Scott Bartlett was born in St. John's, Newfoundland – the easternmost province of Canada. During his decade-long journey to become a full-time author, he supported himself by working a number of different jobs: salmon hatchery technician, grocery clerk, youth care worker, ghostwriter, research assistant, pita maker, and freelance editor.

In 2014, he succeeded in becoming a full-time novelist, and he's been writing science fiction at light speed ever since.

Visit scottplots.com to download 3 free military sci-fi ebooks.